BEVERLY JENKINS

BEFORE THE DAWN

AVON BOOKS
An Imprint of HarperCollinsPublishers

This is a work of fiction. Names, characters, places, and incidents are products of the author's imagination or are used fictitiously and are not to be construed as real. Any resemblance to actual events, locales, organizations, or persons, living or dead, is entirely coincidental.

AVON BOOKS
An Imprint of HarperCollins*Publishers*
195 Broadway
New York, NY, 10007

Copyright © 2001 by Beverly Jenkins
ISBN: 0-380-81375-0
www.avonromance.com

First Avon Books paperback printing: October 2001

Avon Trademark Reg. U.S. Pat. Off. and in Other Countries, Marca Registrada, Hecho en U.S.A.
HarperCollins® is a trademark of HarperCollins Publishers Inc.

Printed in the U.S.A.

13

To Dorothy Jean Simpson:
9/8/32–1/11/00
She is missed.

Chapter 1

Ryder Damien's black eyes glowed with grim satisfaction as he read the wire informing him that his father, was dying. *So, the old man's finally getting his due*, he thought. *Hope Satan makes the pit nice and hot.*

Hardly the expected filial response, but Ryder hadn't seen his father in thirty years. He tossed the telegram onto his desk and walked over to the windows that looked out on the world from the second-floor office of the Damien Mining Company. According to the calendar, spring was coming, but you couldn't tell by all the snow on the mountains. The Colorado mountains never surrendered to warmer weather without a good fight, and this year proved to be no exception. Ryder hoped that by concentrating on something else, the news about his father would fade from his mind, but as much as he disliked admitting it, thoughts of Louis Montague wouldn't leave him alone. Why make contact now, after all these years? With all the suffering Ryder had

1

been forced to endure, surely Louis didn't believe he'd come running to his deathbed, mouthing absolutions?

Ryder turned from the window and went back to his desk.

Thirty-two-year-old Leah Barnett moved slowly through the nearly deserted tavern, collecting the last of the empty mugs and tankards. Her day at the Black Swan had begun at dawn, and now that night had fallen, she didn't know which felt wearier, her body or her feet. She looked over at the last of the regulars seated at one of the dark wood tables, and called out, "Tom, you should be getting on home now. Don't want the wife to have to come get you again."

Tom Pollard met Leah's frank dark eyes, then hung his head sheepishly. His wife, Bess, had paid a visit to the Swan four nights ago, and it hadn't been a pretty affair. Bess Pollard towered over her elderly husband by a good six inches, and she'd issued such a blistering lecture on demon rum and familial responsibility that every man in the place had gotten up and slunk home. Leah hadn't been pleased watching the night's profits go streaming out the doors, but witnessing the look of fear on Tom's face when his wife blew in like a November gale had almost been worth the loss. Leah had been telling him for months that he should be spending more time with his young bride and less time with his cronies playing dominoes and backgammon.

In response to Leah's warning, Tom shuffled to his feet and put on his coat, saying, "Caught a lot of ribbing about that. Don't want it to happen again." The slight sway in his old legs interfered with his attempts to fasten his coat buttons. "How's Monty doing?"

"Doctor says it won't be long," she responded sadly. Louis Montague, her mother's lifelong companion, lay upstairs in his bed, dying. "I'm going up to check on him as soon as I'm done here."

"Well, you want me to stay until you lock up?"

Leah smiled tiredly in reply. Tom had been coming to the Swan since she'd been tall enough to see over the tables, and she appreciated his concern, "No, Tom. I'll be fine. You go on. I'll see you tomorrow."

He nodded and headed out into the early-April night.

His exit left Leah alone, and she went back to cleaning up. Usually she savored the silence that settled over the place after locking up, but not tonight. Tonight her thoughts were heavy with Monty's fate.

Last April, the death of Leah's British-born mother, Reba, had broken Leah's heart. Now, Monty lay at death's door, too. Leah's world had always included the two of them, and she couldn't envision a future devoid of their presence and love.

The Black Swan had been passed down to her upon Reba's death, and Leah supposed she'd spend the rest of her life there, washing tankards and hauling in kegs. At the advanced old age of thirty-two she stood little chance of snagging a husband and having children, so she'd stopped hoping long ago. She'd also stopped wanting to see the world and its many wonders; women of her ilk weren't destined for such things. She'd been born in the Swan and would undoubtedly die in the Swan, just as her mother had.

The small drinking establishment, with its sturdy wooden tables and packed-earth floor, would provide her a frugal life at best. One of the few remaining coastline taverns that catered to Black British seamen, it turned enough profit to pay bills and buy necessities, but nothing more. Unlike her old friend Adele Sears, who'd married well and constantly ordered new gowns in order to rub shoulders with Boston's Black elite, Leah had to make due with gowns that had seen better days and shoes with pasteboard in them to cover the holes in the soles. Granted, because she had a way with numbers, Leah earned a few extra coins balancing the ledgers of some of the other businesses on the waterfront, but that went to pay the salaries of her two employees: a bartender and a waitress.

Done with the washing and sweeping, Leah checked the door's bolts, doused the tavern's lamps, and slowly headed upstairs to look in on Monty.

Leah had lived on the tavern's upper floor her whole life, and the space was as familiar as her own heartbeat. Reba and Monty had shared the big room in the back that overlooked the often moody Atlantic Ocean. Reba had drawn her last breath in that room. Monty seemed destined to do the same.

Leah entered the firelit room quietly. In the big walnut bed lay Louis Montague, apparently asleep. In the chair beside it sat his old friend, Cecil Lee. The short, brownskinned Lee, with his wire-rimmed spectacles, had always reminded Leah of a church mouse. The two men had come to Massachusetts together from Colorado almost thirty years ago.

Leah asked softly, "How's he doing?"

Cecil's brown eyes met hers. He shook his head sadly. "Not well. Two days—three at the most is all the doctor could say."

Leah walked over and touched his thin, stooped shoulders sympathetically. Cecil had been taking Monty's decline hard.

As Cecil removed his spectacles to wipe at the moisture on the lenses, Monty opened his eyes and snarled softly, "If the two of you don't put away those long faces, I'm going to go sooner than that!"

Both Leah and Cecil jumped with surprise. Leah looked down into Monty's tired but impish blue eyes and shook her head. Not even the impending jaws of death were strong enough to diminish his spirit. "We thought you were asleep," she scolded tenderly.

"Well, I'm not. There's much to do before I meet your mother on the other side."

Leah cocked her head. "Such as?"

"Securing your future. Tell her the plan, Cecil," he ordered brusquely.

Leah turned puzzled black eyes Cecil's way.

Cecil looked uncomfortable, but stated, "Louis has decided to make you heir to his estate."

"What estate?" Leah asked.

Monty answered, "The one your mother wouldn't let me leave her. It's a good thing I loved her because she was the stubbornest damned woman I ever met." Then he added sagely, "You're a lot like her."

A smiling Leah inclined her head. "Thank you, but again, what estate?"

Monty labored to a sitting position. Cecil moved to help him, but Monty waved him off. "I'm all right, old friend. I've still enough in me to see this through." Monty made himself as comfortable as he could on the wealth of pillows at his back, then paused for a moment to catch his breath.

Watching him struggle pained Leah. Six months ago, doctors had found a growth on his liver. The progression into the last stages of the terminal malady had been swift. He now bore very little resemblance to the tall, handsome man who'd walked into the Black Swan nearly thirty years ago and fallen in love with her mother at first sight. His *café au lait* skin was now lined and jaundiced with disease. As a result of all the medicines and tonics, the straight black hair that once framed his striking Creole features now grew only in sparse gray patches. He'd become so gaunt and frail during the past few weeks, it was hard to believe that this time last year he'd been a hale, muscular man of almost sixty years. Leah took some solace in the knowledge that her mother hadn't lived to see him this way; the sight would have broken her heart, just as it was doing to Leah's now.

Monty's papery voice broke the silence. "I should've married your mother. One of the greatest regrets of my life."

Leah chuckled softly. "The way you two fought?"

He grinned beneath the death mask. "I loved battling with her—made me feel so alive. More than I ever thought I could be." He went silent for a few moments as if going over the memories in his mind. He then whispered, "I miss her . . ." His sad blue eyes met Leah's, and he confessed, "I'm scared of dying, Leah. Didn't think I would be, but I am. Brought so much pain into the world, Satan probably has a pit just for me."

"I don't believe that," she pronounced. "You did real fine by Reba and me."

"But she wouldn't let me marry her. Kept waiting for Roman to come home from the sea."

Three months before Leah was born, Leah's father, an American seaman named Roman Collins, had been washed overboard during a tropical storm off the coast of Jamaica and presumed drowned. The ship's owners sent Reba a letter of condolence and the pay he'd accumulated, but she never gave up hope that someday he would return to her, his child, and the tavern they jointly owned and named. Yes, she'd loved Monty, but that hope, illogical though it might have seemed, made marrying him impossible.

"She promised him she'd wait until the day she died," Leah reminded gently.

"I know, but I wanted to do right by her. She shouldn't've had to bear the talk."

Her mother had endured much finger pointing and gossip because of her long relationship with Monty, but Leah knew that the high-and-mighty types like Adele's mother and her friends would have found fault with Reba, no matter what. Reba had no husband. She'd borne a fatherless child and managed a tavern. In their minds, certainly, there was no more godless woman on the face of the earth.

"She never minded the talk," Leah told him reassuringly. "She always said, 'If they're talking about me, I must be pretty important.' "

"Well, let me do right by you."

"Monty, you already have."

"What're you going to do once I'm gone?"

Leah shrugged. "Run the Swan. Make Cecil wash tables." Cecil smiled but didn't rise to her bait.

"Is that all you wish from life?" Monty asked.

"It isn't about what I wish," she replied matter-of-factly. "Life is about what must be."

"Suppose there could be more, what would you wish then?"

She thought a moment. "To have more than one gown. Travel. Maybe see what's on the other side of the Great Divide—walk the tropical islands my father wrote about in his letters."

"Suppose I could make that possible?" Monty said.

Leah's humor showed on her dark face. "How, by waving a magician's wand over me?"

"In a way."

Intrigued by the response, she cocked her head his way. While growing up, Leah had always thought Monty to be much more than the simple bootmaker he presented himself to be; simple bootmakers didn't recite Latin Classics, nor intelligently discuss any subject under the sun, as Monty was prone to do. In all the time she'd known him, though, Leah couldn't recall him ever offering any information on the life he'd led before coming to live in their small coastal town. She did remember being about twelve years old the one time she asked her mother if she knew anything about Monty's mysterious past. Reba had replied, "A man's past is his own, Leah, unless he's willing to share it."

Leah took that to mean she was to mind her own business, and as a result never brought the subject up again. That same curiosity resurfaced now.

Monty's voice brought her back. "You're awfully quiet, Leah."

She shook herself free of her musings. "Just thinking how I always imagined you were more than a bootmaker."

He nodded wearily. "At one time I was—" He looked up into her face, then said with pride, "You will always be the daughter I never had, Leah Barnett. Always."

He held out his clawlike hand. She enfolded it in her own, and said, "And you are very, very special to me too, Louis Montague. I don't need an estate to remember you by."

"I know, but let me do this for you. Cecil and I discussed the possibilities of my adopting you as my daughter, but that would take too much time. We decided you'd fare better as my widow."

Leah's eyes widened, and she chuckled. "Your widow? Monty, I can't marry you."

"Sure you can. It'll be a marriage in name only, but by the time anybody has questions, I'll be dead."

Leah was taken aback by his bluntness. "But—"

"And if you're worried about what folks around here might say, don't. After the money comes to you, you'll be your own mistress, and you can leave here and do whatever you wish. Go see those islands—go breathe the air near the Divide. Just let me go to the grave knowing I've done right by one woman in my life."

Leah looked to Cecil for advice, but his face remained unreadable. She turned back to Monty. The plea in his eyes pulled at her heart.

Leah knew she had no choice.

The next evening, Leah Jane Barnett put on her best clean gown and became the bride of the dying and bedridden Louis Montague.

With Cecil standing as witness, the sealing of the will and the wedding ceremony were performed by James Raddock, a prominent Massachusetts jurist. Leah had never met the elderly White man before, but Monty and Cecil assured her that they'd known him for many years, both as a valued customer and a trusted friend.

Once the legalities were done, Leah and Cecil walked the judge back downstairs to the Swan's door.

Cecil shook Raddock's hand, and said, "Have a safe trip home, Jim, and thank you."

"You're welcome."

Raddock then turned to Leah. His green eyes were kind. "Young woman, even though we've never met, I know how Monty felt about your mother, and how he feels about you. If after his passing you need any help, of any kind, have Cecil or someone you trust contact me. Monty's friendship has meant a great deal to me. The least I can do is offer you my services and my protection for as long as I am able."

Leah found his words comforting. "Thank you."

He nodded her way one last time, then exited into the night.

Cecil gave Leah a departing hug. "I'll see you in the morning."

Glad that she still had him in her life, she returned the embrace fiercely. "Good night."

Upstairs, Leah eased the covers over Monty as he lay in bed. Dictating his will and reciting the short vows required by the marriage ceremony had left him exhausted. "You should rest now. It's been a long day."

"Something I have to tell you first."

He looked paler and more wan than usual. His pallor concerned her. "Can't it keep until morning?"

He shook his head. "Morning may be too late."

The seriousness of his tone gave her pause. Straightening to her full height, she nodded. "Then tell me."

"I suppose this is what you'd call a deathbed confession."

Leah surveyed him, then said, "Go on."

"I left two sons behind in Colorado thirty years ago."

Shock froze her. He'd never mentioned having kin of any kind, least of all two sons.

"Seth should be thirty-six or -seven. Ryder two years younger."

Leah's eyes widened even further. That made her their *stepmother!* "Why didn't you tell me this before?"

"Because you'd have questioned the estate going to you and not to them, and I don't have the strength to debate. I'm a dying man, remember?"

The light of humor in his eyes glowed dimly, like that of a fading star. She smiled. "Surely you've seen them since then?"

"No."

Another shock. "Why not?"

He turned away, and for a few long moments he seemed to be searching for answers in the shadows filling the room. When he finally spoke, his voice sounded heavy with regret. "I didn't plan on time passing by so quickly. When I finally realized I wanted my sons in my life, twenty years had gone by. Before your mother died, she told me to make peace with them, but I was too guilty—too ashamed to try. I was afraid they hated me, if they even thought of me at all, but being at death's door makes me want to make things right."

His eyes were immensely sad. "Leah, I want them to know how sorry I am. Cecil wired Colorado a few weeks ago to let them know I was dying, but so far there's been no reply from either one."

Leah responded honestly, "You've been out of their lives a long time."

"I know."

Leah found it hard to believe Monty hadn't seen his sons

in thirty years; the Monty she knew had always shown great concern for the people in his life. "Have you been providing for them in the years you've been gone?"

"I left them the profits from a mine I owned. I assumed it was enough to give them a decent life."

"But you don't really know."

He shook his head. "No, I don't."

"You haven't inquired at all?"

He shook his head negatively.

"Monty, anything could've happened to them over the years."

"I know, Leah. I know," he said emotionally. "And now, it's too late."

Leah loved Monty like a father. Judging him harshly now wouldn't change the past, but she wished he'd contacted his sons earlier.

"I want you to go to Colorado and see them for me."

Her eyes widened.

"You said you wanted to see the Divide. Here's your chance."

Realizing she'd stepped into a trap, she shook her head at the deft way she'd been manipulated.

"Cecil's going to Colorado on my behalf with hopes that my boys can be found. Say you'll go with him."

Leah had an affectionate but amazed smile on her face. "Is there anything else you wish for me to do? Spin straw into gold? Dance on the head of a pin? How do you think your sons are going to react when I arrive on their doorstep and introduce myself as their new stepmother?"

He grinned. "I hope they're going to be so dazzled by your dark beauty they'll be perfect gentlemen."

"Oh, Lord," Leah declared, rolling her eyes. She dimmed the light by his bed. "We'll finish this discussion in the morning." She bent and placed a solemn kiss on his pale brow. "Pleasant dreams."

When she straightened, he took her hand. For a moment their eyes held, mirroring love, respect, and a sadness rooted in knowing his end was near. He squeezed her hand tightly, "You too."

Filled with emotion, Leah turned to leave.

"Leah?"

She looked back.

"Promise me you'll tell them I died a changed man. If they can find it in their hearts to forgive me, maybe Satan's pit won't feel so hot."

"I will," Leah promised.

For a few more moments they observed each other silently; no words were needed.

Finally, Monty whispered, "Good night, Leah."

"Night, Monty. I'll see you in the morning."

She quietly closed the door and went to seek her own bed.

The next morning, as she did every morning before venturing downstairs to open up, Leah tiptoed into Monty's room to check on him. The moment she walked in, she knew he was dead. His stillness made her heart sigh heavily. She knew if she started crying, she wouldn't be able to stop, so she forced back her tears and crossed the room to his bed, thankful he was no longer in pain.

They buried him the next day in the local cemetery. Leah, dressed in the same black dress and veil she'd worn the day she buried her mother, stood beside the grave, flanked by a few men from the Swan, the grief-stricken but stoic Cecil, and the reverend from the local church. As the reverend spoke the words, Leah let the tears stream unchecked down her cheeks. She'd miss Monty's kind and boisterous spirit for the rest of her life.

When the prayers were done and the others drifted away, she and Cecil were left alone. They stood silent, watching the gravediggers toss the last shovels of dirt onto the grave.

Cecil had purchased the plot next to Reba's for Monty's interment, and Leah thought that only fitting.

Once the gravediggers departed, Leah and Cecil stood in the cold April air silently sharing their grief. The wind blowing off the Atlantic whipped at her black skirts and ruffled the edges of her veil. She'd lived on the Massachusetts coastline all of her life; the stiff breezes were as familiar as her name so she paid it little mind. She focused instead on the twin headstones that were mute testaments to the two people who'd loved her best. The knowledge that neither Monty nor Reba would approve of her wallowing in self-pity made her wipe at her tears even as they continued to flow. She placed her black-gloved fingers against her lips, then laid a loving caress of farewell on each headstone. Pulling her shawl closer around her shoulders, she turned to the solemn Cecil, and softly said, "Let's get home."

He nodded in agreement, politely took her elbow, and slowly escorted her back to the buggy.

Leah had never traveled outside her native state of Massachusetts. The knowledge that she and Cecil were about to see places and people she'd only read about in the newspapers had her wondering if she were dreaming. But reality set in as soon as they reached the station and tried to board.

"Where do you think you two are going?" the conductor asked over the din of trains and people crowding the platform. He was a big, florid-faced man with a bulbous nose and bad teeth.

"To our car," Cecil told him.

"These cars here are private. Not for folks like you."

Leah could feel her temper rising. She knew what he mean by *folks like you*, and it didn't sit well.

"Move along before I send for the sheriff," the conductor ordered.

Cecil very calmly reached into his coat and withdrew a document. He handed it to the impatient-looking man.

"What's this?" the conductor asked.

"Read it, please," a tight-lipped Cecil responded.

As the conductor scanned the paper, his face reddened and a sneer curled his lip. He shoved the page back at Cecil and walked away.

Cecil smiled. "I guess we can board now."

"I guess we can," she agreed.

The document in question had been penned by Judge Raddock and it gave both Cecil and Leah permission to travel to Denver in his private railroad car. After the funeral ten days ago, Cecil had informed the old judge that they'd be traveling west to settle Monty's estate, and he'd very graciously offered them its use. He'd originally planned on sending it out empty to California later in the spring in order to provide passage back East for his daughter, son-in-law, and their new baby, but saw no reason why Leah and Cecil couldn't travel in it in the meantime. The railroad would send it on west once Leah and Cecil reached Denver. Evidently he and Cecil had foreseen such an encounter with the conductor because not only did the papers hold his bold, flowing signature but also bore the date and the official seal of his court as well.

Once she and Cecil finally found the car and boarded, Leah know she'd be forever grateful to the judge because he'd offered them a traveling experience usually denied the ordinary passenger. There was a sleeping area, a water closet, upholstered settees and chairs, and a large, beautifully appointed table at which to sit and enjoy their meals.

"This is lovely," Leah gushed as she looked around.

Cecil replied, "Indeed it is."

They were just settling in when the conductor came to the door. "Just want you folks to know that riding in here won't get you any special treatment. You'll take your meals in the gambling car with the rest of your kind."

Cecil and Leah had both nodded tersely. Seemingly pleased with himself, the man departed.

Now, as Leah sat on the cushioned window seat, watching the rich green spring of Illinois roll by, she put the offensive conductor out of her mind and recalled that less than two weeks ago, she'd been bemoaning the fact that life held such little promise for a woman like her, and now? Thanks to Monty's generosity, life held not only promise, but offered choices as well. Even though her race would continue to bind her socially, the abrupt change in her economic circumstances would offer her the chance to travel whenever and wherever she wished. She could go to California, or even China if she had a mind to. For the first time in her life every piece of clothing she had on was brand-new: from her underwear to her stockings to shoes. She had beautiful new cloaks, handbags, gloves. It was almost as if a magician had waved his wand over her life and turned her, a common tavern brat, into a woman of means. Leah looked back at Cecil seated on one of the settees, reading a newspaper. "Cecil? What's Colorado like?"

"Thirty years ago, it was one of the most wide-open places I'd ever seen. Mountains, valleys, pine trees, pumas."

"Pumas?"

"Yep, some folks call them mountain lions."

Leah wondered whether they'd encounter any. She'd certainly never seen one sauntering down the Massachusetts coast. "Have you ever had the sensation that your life is about to change?"

"Is that how you feel?" he asked.

"Yes. Ever since we left Boston, I've had a strange feeling of excitement inside. I suppose a woman of my years shouldn't be so giddy, but I can't seem to suppress it."

He looked over his newspaper at her and chuckled, "There's nothing wrong with what you're feeling. When Louis and I first came to Colorado, I felt the same way."

"Being on this train, wearing these new things—it's as if I've become a new woman."

"In a way, you have, and you have a whole new life ahead. Any regrets about leaving the Swan?"

She shook her head. "Frankly, I think leaving was for the best—too many memories, too many ghosts. After we buried Monty it seemed like everywhere I looked there they were. I'd hear Reba's laugh or see him coming down the stairs yelling for Tom and the other regulars to set up the backgammon board."

The memories rose fresh and strong. She knew that only time would heal the grief still filling her heart, but it would heal. "I think placing Tom's wife in charge of the Swan until I return was a good idea."

"I think so, too."

Leah was about to say something else when the train whistle bellowed. She turned her attention back to the tracks. They were pulling into a station.

Cecil got up, came over to the window and peered out. "Looks like we've finally made Chicago. We can get out and stretch our legs a bit if you'd like. We'll probably be laying over for an hour or so."

Leah thought that a grand idea. The early morning stop in Kalamazoo, Michigan, had been hours ago.

So, after the train halted, Leah grabbed her new fur-lined cloak and followed Cecil to the door. The portable steps needed to reach the ground had not been put in place by the porters. The area around the track was bustling with activity as passengers boarded, relatives waved, and porters strained under the weight of baggage. The air was filled with the sound of train whistles and the smell of smoke and cinders pouring out of the idling stacks.

"It's that conductor's doing, I'll bet," Cecil grumbled.

Leah hated to be judgmental, but the man's earlier nasty attitude led her to believe that the missing steps were one of those subtle, irritating slights that bigoted individuals often perpetrated as a way of keeping folks like her and Cecil in their place.

"We could always jump," Leah pointed out.

"You're not nine anymore, Leah."

She smiled. In her younger days, she and some of the boys in town would often jump from the bluffs into the ocean below. Her mother hadn't minded, but every time Cecil watched the feat, he'd sworn it subtracted years from his life.

Leah had no plans to stay perched on the edge of the car forever. "Cecil for heaven's sake, hop down, it's no more than a foot or so."

"You folks need some help?"

Leah looked up into the coal black eyes of the handsomest, most exotic brown-skinned man she'd ever seen. He was dressed no differently from the other gentlemen passengers but the black waterfall of hair flowing freely over the shoulders of his tailored, Chesterfield coat made him commandingly unique. Tall and muscular, he appeared to be of mixed ancestry. The hair was undoubtedly Indian, but the strong, proud features bore the stamp of African ancestry.

Realizing she'd been staring like a transfixed rube at a fair, she hastily settled her eyes elsewhere just as Cecil replied, "It appears as if we might. Our steps haven't been brought around."

"Well, how about we hand you down first, and then the lady?" Although the man had spoken to Cecil, his dark eyes were on Leah.

A bit flustered by his attention, Leah turned her gaze to

his companion, an older, gray-haired man dressed in a fine, dark suit and long gray coat. His ready smile seemed to steady her.

Sounding grateful, Cecil replied, "That would be appreciated."

Each man took hold of one of Cecil's elbows and eased him the short distance to the ground.

When it became Leah's turn, her pulses raced as the long-haired man stepped up, placed his large hands on her waist, and lifted her free of the platform. He brought her down slowly, so slowly their eyes mingled and the heat of their bodies touched. The aura in him was so overwhelming that a few moments passed before she realized she was standing on firm ground again. Gathering her senses, she stammered, "Th-thank you."

"You're welcome," he replied, his interest in her quite obvious.

More flustered than ever, she sought to calm herself by fussing with her big, feather-edged hat and straightening the hem of her matching blue traveling costume. It didn't work. She could still feel the warm pressure of his strong yet gentle hold on her waist.

"Do you have luggage you need to retrieve also?"

"No," she said, shaking her head "We're just going to stretch our legs, then travel on to Denver."

The older man interrupted by declaring in a pleased-sounding voice, "Why, that's where we're headed. You visiting?"

Finding it hard to pull away from the other man's powerful gaze, Leah replied, "Uh, no. Cecil and I are going there to settle my late husband's affairs. They both lived there a while back."

The elderly man said, "I'm sorry for your loss. When did he pass?"

"Almost two weeks ago," Leah responded.

Cecil took the initiative and stuck out his hand in greeting. "Name's Cecil Lee."

"Sam Waters," the old man said with a smile.

As the two men shook hands, Leah saw that Sam's companion seemed to be staring at Cecil in a curious yet ominous way.

Finally, the younger man asked, "You aren't the same Cecil Lee who once worked for Louis Montague, are you?"

Cecil hesitated for a brief second, then answered, "Yes, I am."

In response, everything about the man seemed to alter: his jaw hardened, his eyes glittered dangerously, and he drawled caustically, "So, Satan's Butler has returned."

Cecil stiffened in turn.

Leah stilled and stared at the man *Satan's Butler*? Who was he?

"Is he dead yet?"

Cecil's chin rose in anger. Leah noted that Sam Waters had grown visibly grim.

"Yes," Cecil finally managed to reply. "Louis Montague is dead. Who are you?"

The man didn't reply. Instead, he turned to Leah and beheld her with a such a wintry glare gooseflesh ran up the back of her neck. "And you are?" he asked coolly.

Leah didn't care for the mordant change in his manner nor his rude questioning of Cecil. "Leah Montague."

"Montague?" For a moment he seemed surprised by her reply. He studied her as if trying to discern the truth. "What are you, a long-lost daughter?" The deadly sarcasm in his voice reflected in his eyes.

Leah's dark chin rose in anger. "No, I'm his widow, and how dare you refer to Cecil as Satan's Butler."

"As your *bastard stepson*," he whispered vehemently, "I'll refer to him any damn way I please."

Leah's heart stopped.

Cecil's eyes went round. "Ryder?" he gasped. "Ryder Damien? Songbird's son?"

Confirming Cecil's deduction with a tight nod, the man called Ryder replied bitterly, "Yes, I'm Ryder. I'm surprised you remember my given name. My father certainly didn't."

"He remembered you," Cecil countered quietly. "He left you and your brother the Faith Mine."

"He left me nothing," he spat.

Cecil appeared shaken by this encounter. "But—"

"Why are you here?"

Cecil replied, "Louis wanted me to find his sons."

"Why? The thought of hell make him want to make amends?"

Leah stepped up. She'd decided she didn't like this man at all. "No, but he wanted you to know how sorry he was for running out the way he did."

"It's a little late for that. Besides, I don't want anything from him. Seth will though—he won't care. He has no shame."

His icy gaze settled on Leah once more, and it chilled her a January wind. She'd no idea what he might be thinking, but the anger hardening the chiseled planes of his brown face showed plainly. He asked then, "Did you know you were married to a man twice charged with murder?"

Leah's surprised eyes told all.

"No? Well, ask Mr. Lee. He does."

In the tense, thick silence that followed, his eyes continued to hold Leah's. For one brief second, she thought she saw regret there but couldn't be sure. A moment later, he nodded at Sam, and they both walked away. Leah's heart was pounding so loudly she couldn't speak. When she turned to Cecil, he was staring at their retreating backs as if he'd seen a ghost.

* * *

"You were pretty rough on her," Sam said to Ryder once they were out of ear shot.

"She deserved the truth."

"Not like that. A feather could've knocked her over."

Ryder didn't respond.

"Do you think she married him for his money?"

"What do you think?" Ryder replied bluntly. In his mind there could be no other reason for such a dark beauty to have married a man old enough to be her father. She wasn't even wearing the traditional widow's black.

"I think, I wish I had his money," Sam answered.

Ryder allowed himself a sarcastic smile and determinedly put his father's widow out of his mind. "Let's get our bags aboard and find something to eat. We have an hour until the train pulls out."

Leah walked over to the visibly shaken Cecil leaning against the car. "Are you all right?"

While Leah looked on with concern, he remained silent for a few moments longer, as if lost in thought. When he finally met her eyes, he quoted grimly, "And so it begins."

Leah, still in a state of shock herself, asked, "What did he mean by murder charges? That isn't true, is it?"

"I'm afraid it is."

"Cecil?"

He reached over and patted her hand. "Don't worry, Louis never murdered anyone."

"Then why did he say that?"

"Because at the time some folks in Denver believed he had."

He surveyed the surprise on her face, then slowly, seemingly wearily, got to his feet. "Come, let's go eat, and I'll explain."

Leah wanted an explanation now, but held on to her

questions—the biggest one being: What had she gotten herself into?

There wasn't a place near the station that would allow Blacks to enter and eat inside. However, one café did let them order at the back door and take their luncheon with them. Leah knew being angry about the discriminatory treatment meant nothing to anyone who was not of the race, so she offered a brittle smile of thank-you to the woman cashier.

The grassy field behind the small eating establishment held a few weathered benches upon which they could sit, and it was a beautiful day, so Leah sat down with Cecil. A few other Black passengers had sought refuge here, too, and were eating and talking in pairs and small family groups. Leah unwrapped the brown paper from her ham sandwich. The first bite confirmed the staleness of the bread, but there didn't appear to be any mold, and the meat tasted fresh. The lemonade they'd purchased held only the faintest hint of lemon, but it was cold and did a fine job of washing down the dry lunch.

"So, start from the beginning," she prompted Cecil.

Cecil looked up a bit wounded. "Don't I even get to eat?"

"No."

He gave her an indulgent smile and shook his head. "You know, you're getting more like your mother every day."

"Thank you."

Cecil knew Leah well enough to know she wasn't being deliberately disrespectful; she just wanted an explanation, an explanation Leah thought she rightly deserved in light of the startling encounter with Monty's younger son.

In the end, Cecil took a couple of bites from his sandwich, washed them down with some lemonade, then said, "Okay, but I have to start at the very beginning, or you may not understand how Louis turned into the man folks in Colorado called Satan Montague."

Leah still found that name hard to fathom but nodded for him to go ahead.

Cecil's tale began with Monty's childhood as the eldest son of Emile Montague, a French Louisiana planter and his blue-eyed octoroon mistress, a slave named Faith. Like many of the sons of such unions, Monty was sent to France for schooling in order to circumvent the segregation in the South. When his father died, Monty was manumitted, but the estate went to his two legitimate sons.

"He got nothing?" Leah asked.

"Nothing. Louis said he was mentioned in the will only once."

"In what way?"

"To my son, Louis Montague, I leave my best wishes and the hope that the education he has been provided will be enough."

"And that was it?"

Cecil nodded.

"Was he bitter about not inheriting?"

"Very much so. His mother had led him to believe he would be treated like the legitimate sons, but he wasn't."

"So what did he do?"

"Went west in the late forties and staked out a claim in the California gold fields. He was determined to make himself more wealthy than his père had ever been. It took him only two years." Leah's surprise must have shown on her face because he added, "There are legends about men who can sense gold. Louis turned out to be one of those legends. He could look at a stream and tell if there was gold in the sediment just by the face of the rocks around it. Most amazing gift I'd ever seen."

"Where'd you two meet?"

"In those same gold fields. Personally, I couldn't find gold if you led me to a lode," he added, chuckling, "but I could do numbers, so I kept records for the men who couldn't read or write. Louis and I became good friends, and when he left California I tagged along." Cecil paused for a moment, then said, "I was born dirt poor in Louisiana. I'd heard about the fancy, educated Creole men of New Orleans, but had never met one until Louis. He could speak French, Italian, Latin. He was the smartest man I'd ever met. I suppose I was flattered that he even tolerated my presence."

"Where'd you two go after California?"

"Headed east to Colorado, where he bought timber, land, and controlling interests in a number of mines. After that, he built the fanciest house around, then sent off to Louisiana for an even fancier Creole wife."

Leah looked on in disbelief. "Please don't tell me he was still married to her while he and my mother were together?"

"No. Bernice died about a year and a half after their son, Seth, was born. Many believed Monty killed her, although it was never proven."

"What?"

He nodded sadly.

Leah had to know. "Now, I heard you say he wasn't a murderer, but is that the truth?"

"Yes, it is. Louis was capable of many things in those days . . ." His voice trailed off as if he were remembering the past. ". . . Many things, but murdering his wife, no. When she became truly ill, the doctors he brought in from Denver thought she might've been poisoned, but they had no real way of knowing. She died a long, painful death."

"But why blame Monty?"

"Because everyone in town knew the arranged marriage wasn't a happy one. Bernice hated the mountains and everything connected with them, and voiced her displeasure as publicly and as often as she could."

"My goodness. How did Monty react?"

"Badly. He began spending less and less time at home

and more and more time acquiring profit. Maybe he used it as a substitute for the love Bernice refused to show him, I don't know, but I do know he drove his mine and timber workers like mules. He was as rich as Midas in those days."

Leah, more accustomed to the menial jobs and wages of the folks she knew at home, found Monty's wealth hard to believe. "But how could a member of the race accumulate such wealth?"

"By not declaring himself a member of the race. To the bankers and men he did business with, Louis Montage was a blue-eyed Frenchman from Louisiana, and I, his dark-skinned valet. If they suspected his true ancestry, it was never discussed within Louis's hearing. They didn't even seem to mind him opening up some of his land to Black homesteaders as long as his business deals continued to line their pockets with gold dust."

Leah was admittedly confused. How could a man some thought guilty of poisoning his wife be the same one who'd taught her to ice-skate and make crepes? "This is all very confusing, Cecil."

"I know."

"What happened to the baby, Seth, after his mother died? Did Monty raise him?"

Cecil shook his graying head grimly. "No. Louis gave his son's care over to his wife's sister, Helene. She'd initially accompanied Bernice from Louisiana to Colorado for the marriage and stayed on. Monty saw very little of Seth after that."

That saddened Leah, and she thought back upon the regrets Monty had confessed about his sons the night before he died. *Now, it's too late.*

"What about this Ryder? When was he born?"

"About two years after Bernice's death."

"He looks mulatto."

"He is. His mother was part-Black, part-Cheyenne."

He paused for a moment to ask, "Do you know the biblical story of King David, and how he was able to claim Bathsheba as his own?"

Leah remembered the story from her Sunday school lessons. "Yes, David deliberately sent Bathsheba's husband, Uriah, into battle, knowing he would be killed."

"Well, Ryder's mother was Louis's housekeeper. Back then, Louis had the arrogance and power to have anything he coveted, and he coveted her. Her husband worked in one of his mines. Louis sent him into a shaft everyone knew to be unsafe, and, just like David, the rival was eliminated. Louis never married her though."

Leah's whole body went cold. She recalled Monty's other words: *"I've cast so much evil in the world, Satan probably has a pit just for me."* An eerie chill crawled across her skin, and she rubbed at her arms, encased in the sleeves of her blue-wool dress. *Somebody walking over your grave,* her mother would have said in response to the feeling. Leah dearly hoped not. "So what happened to her?"

"She became his mistress, and then one night, a year or so after Ryder was born, she was found dead at the bottom of that same shaft."

Leah slowly brought her hands to her mouth.

Cecil's eyes were emotionless. "There was an inquest. Witnesses placed Louis at the scene and testified that the two were having an argument that night. Louis never denied that. He did deny killing her. When the sheriff couldn't produce a witness to the actual act the charges were dropped. Talk was he'd bribed his way out of them."

Leah felt overwhelmed. "Are we speaking of the same Louis Montague we just buried?"

"We are."

Cecil added seriously, "As he freely admitted, he was someone else in those days, Leah."

Their eyes met, and the cold truth staring back at Leah

sent another chill across her soul. "But he loved my mother."

"Passionately, desperately. She was the only thing life ever denied him. Although she loved him in her own way, she wouldn't marry him. Louis knew women all over the world, but he'd never met one quite like your mother."

So many conflicting emotions and questions filled Leah's head, she had no idea what to think or say. Finally, she asked, "What kind of reception will our arrival in Colorado fetch then?"

"If there are people still living there who were there when this all took place, not a good one I'm afraid. We left behind a lot of bitterness and much ill will."

She stared off into the distance for a moment as she tried to digest all she'd heard.

He continued in a soft voice. "We were responsible for many many terrible things, he and I: cheating our workers, evicting destitute families even though we knew they had no place else to go. We cut corners on safety and cost men their lives. Profit ruled our existence. Timber, livestock, gold, silver, copper. If it made money, Louis wanted it, and I helped him get it in any and every way I could."

"Why?"

"Because I relished the power I wielded in his name. Like Louis, I also have much to atone for when it comes time to meet St. Peter."

Leah paused to watch Ryder Damien and Sam entering the glade. Cecil did the same. Ryder, with his long unfettered hair and sweeping coat, walked as if he owned the earth. She had to admit he was glorious-looking.

"That's a very angry man," Cecil offered quietly.

"If he's convinced his father killed his mother, I'd say he has good reason to be."

A tight-lipped Cecil nodded agreement.

The two men took seats on a bench a few yards away. As

if sensing Leah's interest, Ryder glanced her way. Their gazes locked and held for a long moment. He then he turned his attention back to his sandwich and whatever Sam was saying.

Sam looked across the yard to where Leah Montague and Cecil Lee were sitting and asked his silent companion, "You see her over there?"

Ryder didn't have to ask who he was referring to. "I do."

"Mighty fine-looking woman."

The chewing Ryder didn't respond.

"Your brother's going to be after her like a puma on a hare."

"I'm sure he will."

"You're going to let him?" Sam asked.

"Nope."

Sam stared at Ryder as if he'd suddenly grown two heads. "She isn't going to give you the time of day after the way you just blasted her."

"Sure she will. Adventuress like her will do whatever's necessary to keep herself in new gowns. Shouldn't be too hard to get her attention."

"Suppose you're wrong?"

"I'm not," Ryder replied confidently, watching her covertly. The fashionable chignon left her beautiful dark face unencumbered. In the prim, high-necked, dark blue dress, she looked like a spinster schoolmarm instead of an old man's bauble.

Sam added wisely, "Seth's going to bust a gut if you two stake the same claim."

"That's why I'm going to do it."

"You sure this isn't about something else?"

Ryder looked Sam in the eye. "What else would it be?"

"She was married to your father. You can't put horns on a dead man, son."

"But I can put horns on my brother's ambitions. Louis has nothing to do with this."

"Long as you're sure," Sam commented.

"I'm sure, old man. I'm counting coup, nothing more."

"Well, she'll be a damn pretty addition to the Colorado countryside, whatever happens."

Ryder grudgingly agreed. In his grandfather's day, such midnight beauty would have commanded a bridal tribute of a thousand ponies. Her dark eyes had a feline slant, and the full mouth looked as lush as a field of blossoming columbines, but Ryder kept his full opinion to himself; she'd been married to Louis Montague.

Sam asked, "How long do you think she's going to stay in Colorado?"

Ryder pulled his eyes away from her. "Probably no longer than it'll take to read the will and get her hands on the estate."

Sam's voice held a hint of disappointment. "Too bad. Woman like that makes a man want to spend a lifetime waking up at her side."

Ryder shook his head at his old friend's musings. "You ought to be saving those pretty words for the widows waiting for you back home. And if you're not going to finish that last sandwich, hand it here. There's no telling when we'll get to eat again."

To Ryder's surprise, Sam handed him the sandwich without a fuss. Sam surprised him further by suddenly rising to his feet, and announcing, "I'm going over there."

A confused Ryder looked to the Montague widow and then back to his old friend. "Why?"

"Just want to talk with her a minute."

"Sam! Come back here! Sam!"

But Sam was already headed across the glade. Ryder cursed silently.

* * * *

When Leah saw Sam Waters heading in their direction, she asked Cecil, "What do you suppose he wants?" She wasn't in the mood for more insults, or any truths for that matter; she'd had enough drama for one day.

Cecil shrugged. "Don't know."

"Was he living in Denver when you and Monty were there?"

"Nope. First time I ever met him was today."

As Sam walked up and stopped before them, Leah nodded a greeting. In response, he politely removed his hat, then said, "Don't mean to bother you, Mrs. Montague, but I just came to say if you need any help while you're in Denver, let me know."

The offer seemed genuine, as did his smile, but Leah felt compelled to say, "I don't think your friend would like that, but thank you."

Sam waved a dismissive hand. "I'm not worried about him. All that different blood gets to fighting inside him sometimes and well—" He shrugged, as if that were explanation enough.

Leah didn't understand at all, but replied, "I see. Well, I wouldn't want to be the cause of a rift. Cecil and I are only going to be in Denver a short while."

"Well, the offer stands."

Cecil had a question. "Sam, how long have you known Ryder?"

"Ten, fifteen years."

"You two good friends?"

"I'd say so."

"Then do you know if it's true what he said about his father not leaving him anything?"

"Ryder wasn't left anything, far as I know."

Puzzled, Cecil shook his head. "Louis left them both the Faith Mine. I wonder what happened?"

Sam shrugged. "Can't help you on that one."

"Thanks."

"You're welcome, but like I said, call on me if you need help with anything else."

He tipped his hat to Leah. "Being seeing you, Mrs. Montague."

"Thanks, Mr. Waters."

He smiled, then left them to finish their lunch.

Chapter 2

The conductor gave Leah and Cecil a knowing smirk as they passed him on their way back to the car, but they ignored him. Moments later, the train sounded its whistle, shrilly announcing its imminent departure from the Chicago station.

Leah, now comfortable in the window seat, watched late-arriving passengers hurrying to board. Ryder Damien and Sam Waters were among them. Leah sighed. She knew they were on their way to Colorado, too, but had no idea they'd be on this particular train. Although she did like Mr. Waters, she planned on avoiding them. One encounter with the acrid Ryder Damien had been enough.

Cecil's tale had certainly given her plenty to ponder, the least being the dual sides of Louis Montague. If what Cecil said were true, she understood the bitter feelings Monty had evoked. Evicting families and cutting corners on safety in the name of profit were not the actions of a benevolent man.

Had she known him at that time, would she have called him Satan, too? Probably. The Monty of thirty years ago bore no resemblance to the one she'd known and loved.

As the train picked up speed and the open green land-scape began to stream by, her mind replayed her introduc-tion to Ryder Damien. What a handsome man. His compelling eyes could charm a woman out of everything she held dear, but mention of the Montague name had turned him to stone. As she'd told Cecil earlier, if he truly believed the rumors surrounding the death of his mother, his bitter reactions seemed well-founded. Would the other son, Seth, be as angry? Leah could only assume the worst. Monty had made a mess of things, and she had a strong feeling this might only be the tip of iceberg.

She looked over at Cecil. He'd been very quiet since their return to the car. She supposed seeing Ryder again had given him plenty to ponder, too. "Is there going to be more, Cecil?"

He glanced her way and offered a faint smile. "An honest question deserves an honest answer. I don't know."

Leah could feel impatience rising and didn't know if it was misplaced or not, considering the circumstances. "How could he not be concerned about the well-being of his own sons?"

Cecil shrugged. "That, too, is an honest question. Truthfully, the Louis of those days cared only about him-self. Yes, he had two sons but *he* was the one under in-dictment, *his* name and reputation were being dragged through the mud. In his mind, he'd made many of his ac-cusers back then extremely wealthy, and for them to ac-cuse him of murder not only once, but a second time? He thought they were ungrateful hypocrites. When he walked away he turned his back on the lot of them. His sons in-cluded."

Leah recalled Monty's anguish-filled confession the

night before he died, and the memory helped soften her feelings about him. "It was a decision he regretted in the end."

"I know. He and I talked about it quite a bit. He had many, many regrets. As do I."

She asked quietly. "What do you regret the most?"

He didn't hesitate. "That I never married—never had a family. Like Louis, once I finally realized the true value of life, it was too late."

Leah's heart went out to him. In a way his regret mirrored her own. Because of her age, she doubted she'd ever marry or have a family either. "You never courted?"

He shrugged. "There were a few ladies here and there, but I was too busy making money to spend the time."

"Well, if it's any consolation, Reba and I always considered you family, and I still do. Were it not for you, Miss Caldwell would never have let me back into her school."

He smiled fully then. "Ah, yes, Miss Caldwell's School for Young Women of Color. You were quite the hellion back then."

"The way they treated me, I should've burned the place to the ground."

He chuckled.

A knock sounded. A smiling Leah headed over to the door to see who it might be. She opened it to find the conductor and an obviously angry Sam Waters standing on the other side.

The conductor announced importantly, "We're riding Jim Crow from here to Denver, so he either rides in here with you or I put him off at the next stop."

Leah was taken aback by the man's declaration. He seemed very pleased with himself and his power. Leah didn't hesitate; in spite of the tension between their two camps, she wouldn't give the conductor the satisfaction of setting Sam Waters down on the side of the tracks in the middle of Lord knew where. "He's quite welcome here."

Leah could see the approval on Cecil's face. He obviously felt the same way. Neither of them wanted to aid the conductor in promoting Jim Crow's nefarious statutes. "Please come in, Mr. Waters."

Sam nodded his thanks and complied, but not before shooting the conductor a malevolent glare.

That left Leah standing eye to eye with the conductor. In an emotionless voice she told him, "Thank you. You may go."

The man's round face went red as a tomato. She doubted he'd ever been dismissed so pointedly by a woman of the race before. Leah didn't care. He didn't like them, and she truly didn't care for him or his high-handed posturing. He appeared as if he wanted to say something caustic in response, but because he'd seen the judge's document and knew she was traveling under his protection, his only recourse was to leave. So he did, but only after slamming the door for emphasis.

Sam Waters said, "Thanks, Mrs. Montague."

"You're welcome. We may have our disagreements, but I'd hope you'd do the same for us were the shoe on the other foot."

Sam turned and nodded a greeting Cecil's way. "Thanks."

Cecil waved off the thanks. "You're welcome."

Leah asked an obvious question. "Where's Mr. Damien?"

"Smoking car. He's going to ride out the trip there. Me, I'm too old to be up all night drinking and playing cards. The porter promised he'd bring me a cot to sleep on, if that's okay?"

Leah replied, "Certainly. We'll figure out where to put it when it arrives."

"Have a seat," Cecil said, gesturing to the settee and chairs.

"Thanks." Sam sat and gazed around at the car's plush red furnishings. "Mighty fine car you got here."

Leah smiled. "Yes it is. It belongs to Judge James Raddock. He was a friend of my late husband's."

Sam appeared impressed.

An awkward silence followed.

Cecil asked Sam, "Do you play cards?"

Sam's face lit up. "Sure do."

"Good, because this one's no challenge," he declared, indicating Leah.

Leah's fists went to her waist in a display of mock indignation. "Hey!"

The statement was true, however. Although Reba had been a terror at cards, the skill had not been passed down. The bespectacled Cecil grinned at her reaction, adding, "But don't play backgammon with her, she's a shark."

That was also true.

While the men began their game, Leah settled into the window seat with her own form of entertainment. Newspapers. She'd purchased a few outside the depot after their lunch in the glade and had been elated to find a lone vendor who'd sold Black papers as well. She took great joy in reading about the happenings and people in other parts of the country and the world. Now that she had the ability to travel to some of those places, her interest had risen even higher.

A two-week-old *Harper's Weekly* reported on the continued agitation for a standardized work day by an organization known as the Knights of Labour. Originally founded as a secret sect in 1869 so as to protect the identities of its organizers and members, the group made its public debut in 1879, throwing down the gauntlet on behalf of the workers of America. The Knights embraced laborers both skilled and non, and its ranks were open to all races. Although Leah knew a little bit about its goals previously, she was surprised to read that an estimated tenth of its seven hundred thousand members were Black. Equally surprising was the information that they'd conducted well over a thousand strikes in the past year against industrial giants such as Chicago's McCormick Harvesting Machine Company, and that many of the work stoppages had turned violent.

The issues surrounding the Knights were also given a thorough discussion in the two Black newspapers she'd purchased: a copy of the *Cleveland Gazette* dated February 20, and a March 20 issue of T. Thomas Fortune's *Freeman*, published in New York. Each paper threw enthusiastic editorial support behind the movement and cited the group's inclusion of Blacks as an historical turning point for the country.

As Leah scanned the rest of the papers for more on the movement, she hoped Denver had a newspaper so she could keep abreast of the Knights' progress.

Leah read for over an hour. When her eyes became bleary, she set the papers aside and stretched to relieve the stiffness in her arms and back. The card game was wrapping up. Sam and Cecil seemed to have hit it off. They spent the whole time laughing, winning each other's pennies, and arguing back and forth over which was the greatest Black regiment. Sam, a veteran of the famed Ninth Cavalry, naturally chose his old unit, while Cecil, a native of Louisiana, championed the Louisiana Native Guard.

Cecil gathered up the cards and proudly declared, "The Louisiana Native Guard fought for the French, the Spanish, and, during the War of 1812, helped Andrew Jackson become a national hero by aiding his defeat of the British on the plains of Chalmette in defense of New Orleans."

Sam scoffed. "Andrew Jackson? You'll get no thanks from the Cherokee for that. He stole their land, and I do mean *stole,* then made them walk the Trail of Tears to Oklahoma."

"Well that's ironic coming from a cavalry soldier. You're no savior to the Indian either."

Their tones made Leah think maybe they weren't getting along so well after all, but Sam smiled and shrugged. "You got me there, but I wasn't like a lot of our troops. Some hated the Indians as much as folks like Custer and Jackson. They didn't care that the government was destroying a whole people and using us to do it."

Leah had never thought about the government's campaign against the Indians in quite those terms before, but decided Sam was right. Ironically, Washington had pitted one downtrodden race against another.

Once the cards were all gathered up and the debts squared, Cecil backed away from the table and stood. "Well, I'm going to head to the smoking car and stretch my legs a bit. Care to join me, Sam?"

"Sure. I can see how Ryder's doing."

Cecil went still.

Intuitively, Sam said, "Don't worry. He's probably still too angry at the conductor for threatening to put him off the train to remember he's mad at you, too."

Leah asked, "Are you sure?" She didn't want Cecil subjected to any more venom.

The old cavalry soldier looked her in the eyes, and said, "Mrs. Montague, I've known Ryder a long time. Deep down inside, he's a good man."

Leah wanted to believe him, but Damien's wintry visage remained a vivid memory.

Cecil seemed satisfied, however, so asked her, "Will you be all right here alone?"

She nodded. "Sure. If something happens, I'll send a porter for you."

"Fair enough," Cecil replied. "We'll see you in a while then. No more than an hour or two."

After their departure, Leah sat down at the table and played solitaire. When she tired of that, she went back to the window seat, stretched out and read some more items in the newspapers. She'd just started in on an article about the antics of the forty-ninth Congress when a knock sounded at the door.

"Come in," she called, guessing it might be the porters with Sam's cot.

It was Ryder Damien.

Soundlessly, she set the paper aside and sat up. She watched his eyes scan her slowly from her head to her black-stockinged feet. Her shoes were on the floor below her. The faint mockery in his eyes made Leah want to hide her feet beneath her blue-wool dress.

"Do you always run around without your shoes?" he asked.

She didn't like the veiled censure in his tone, so, just to be contrary, she replied, "Yes."

It irritated Ryder to find her even more beautiful than he remembered. Over the course of the afternoon, he'd tried to convince himself that he'd only imagined the ripe lure in her mouth, exaggerated the sultry feline cut of her eyes and the exquisite richness of her midnight skin. Her black-diamond beauty whispered to him so strongly, the hair on the back of his neck stood up, and he unconsciously touched the small medicine bag he wore beneath his clothing for spiritual protection.

Because the room had gone too silent, and the air had become too thick, Leah felt the need to say something, anything. "If you're looking for Sam, he and Cecil went to the smoking car."

"What kind of woman marries a man old enough to be her father?"

The bluntness of his attack threw her, but only for a moment. "One who loves him very much."

"Him or his money." It was a statement not a question.

She looked him up and down. "Are you always this rude?"

"Some call it rudeness. I call it truth."

"I doubt you'd know truth if it slapped you in the face."

Ryder raised an imperial eyebrow. He'd not expected return fire. "So, the lovely widow has claws—tiny ones, but claws nonetheless. You're braver than I thought."

"I'm more everything than you thought, Mr. Damien. So, again, what do you want?"

Ryder grudgingly admitted to finding her combativeness impressive. Her raised chin and flashing dark eyes let him know she wasn't easily intimidated, but he supposed a woman of her ilk needed to be tough to survive. "I brought Sam's gear."

Leah noticed the valises at his feet for the first time. "Set them there by the door."

He complied, then said, "Thanks for taking him in."

Leah nodded frostily. "Mr. Waters is more than welcome."

"How about me? Am I welcome, too?"

Leah surveyed his too-handsome countenance. She'd willingly bet that when he chose to do so he could make a woman melt like ice on a hot day. "Yes, you are, but you'll have to leave your animosity at the door."

"It's well-founded."

She didn't begrudge him his anger; he'd borne the pain, she hadn't, but she refused to be savaged in Monty's stead. "I don't doubt that, but it serves no purpose here."

There was no doubt in Ryder's mind that she'd married Louis Montague to get his money. For all her prim speech and clothing, her sensual aura was strong. Any initial misgivings Louis might have had about succumbing to her charms had undoubtedly faded the moment he took her in his arms. She was as alluring as a dark-skinned siren at midnight; that mouth alone could have commanded a fortune. Her slim lines seemed to emphasize the generous flare of her hips and the lovely swell of her bosom. He knew very few men who'd walk away from such a tempting piece, and Louis Montague had never walked away from a beautiful woman in his life.

Leah wondered what he might be thinking but decided it didn't matter. "Is there anything else?"

"Yes."

He closed the door behind him.

Her jaw tightened.

He crossed his arms. "Tell me about yourself."

"Why? You've already decided who I am."

"And who might that be?"

"A simple, predatory adventuress."

He shrugged the magnificent shoulders. "Adventuress, yes. Simple, no. From what I know of Louis, he wouldn't have left his money to a simple woman."

"On that we agree."

By the Spirits, she was beautiful, Ryder thought to himself. His half brother, Seth, would undoubtedly try to bed her as soon as the formal introductions were over, stepmother or not.

Leah had no intentions of telling him her life story. A man that arrogant wouldn't believe the truth anyway. She also guessed if he knew she'd married Monty on his deathbed, he'd move heaven and earth to keep the estate out her hands in spite of Judge Raddock. "So, do you need to stay here with us until we reach Denver or not?"

"No."

Leah thought that a blessing.

"You look relieved," he replied bluntly.

Her reply was equally as blunt. "I am. I don't want to spend the rest of the journey verbally defending myself."

"You seem to be holding your own."

"Compliments now?"

"More truth."

They silently evaluated each other.

Leah wanted him gone. "Is there anything else?"

"No, not at the moment."

"Then, as I said, Mr. Waters is in the smoking car."

Ryder inclined his head, turned and exited.

Leah growled at the closed door.

That evening, Leah shared dinner with Cecil and Sam. She had a grand time listening and laughing at their stories. Nobody mentioned Ryder Damien, and that made it grander.

Leah, Sam, and Cecil spent the balance of the trip playing cards, backgammon, and enjoying each other's company. Leah was especially glad to have Sam along because his friendliness toward Cecil seemed to have helped ease Cecil's pain over losing Monty. Ryder Damien stayed away from their little group, and that suited Leah just fine.

When the train finally reached Denver, the travel-weary Leah looked forward to walking around on terra firma. Denver turned out to be a surprisingly robust town. She'd expected it to be quiet and small, instead it was as busy as any big city back East. The depot was noisy with people, vendors hawking their wares, and the sounds of train whistles and engines. As she stood on the windy platform waiting for Cecil to retrieve their trunks, the cold gray day made her shiver inside her thick black cloak. After the monotonous sameness of the plains, she thought the mountains would be an exhilarating sight, but they were as gray as the day. The rugged peaks resembled dour, almost disapproving faces.

Sam, trunks in hand, came over to say good-bye. "Be seeing you around, Mrs. Montague. Thanks for the help."

"Anytime, Sam."

"Remember what I said about calling on me if you need anything."

"I'll remember. Thanks for the company."

"My pleasure. I already said good-bye to Cecil. He'll be along directly. Do you want me to wait here with you until he gets back?"

Leah was pleased by his generosity. "No, that won't be necessary. I should be okay. Besides, Mr. Damien's waiting for you. I don't want him any angrier at me than he is already."

Sam looked over at the tight-lipped Ryder standing and waiting just a few feet away. "He'll come around. You'll see."

Leah didn't want him to come around; she didn't want anything from Monty's bitter youngest son.

Sam departed with a wave.

While the hustle and bustle of the depot swirled around her, Leah patiently waited for Cecil's return.

"Excuse me, miss?"

Leah turned in response to the male voice and found herself staring into the watery brown eyes of a sad-faced, skinny little White man in an ill-fitting brown suit. Beside him stood the conductor. The pleased look on the conductor's face should have warned her.

"You Mrs. Leah Montague?"

Leah answered warily. "Yes."

"Got a summons for you."

A confused Leah took the document from his out-stretched hand. She opened the seal and her heart stopped. She was being sued!

The server said then, "Be at the Denver courthouse at nine tomorrow."

"But what is this about?" she demanded.

The little man shrugged. "They just pay me to deliver. You'll find out tomorrow, I reckon."

The conductor looked so pleased with himself Leah wanted to punch him. "Thank you," she told the process server frostily, then turned her back.

Once they were gone, her eyes frantically searched the platform for Cecil. She saw him a ways off accompanied by a porter pushing their trunks on a cart and hastened to meet them.

Cecil must've seen the distress in her face because he asked, "Leah, what's wrong?"

She handed him the summons. He scanned it and then raised his widened spectacle-aided eyes back to her. "Where'd you get this?"

"Process server. He must've been waiting for the train because the conductor brought him over to me. What is this about, Cecil?"

"I've no idea, but someone is challenging your right to inherit the estate."

He looked as stunned as Leah. Cecil took a moment to reach into his pocket and extract a tip for the still-waiting porter. The man nodded and departed.

"Could it be his other son, or some long lost relative?"

Cecil seemed at a loss for further words.

Leah had a bad feeling about this, a very bad feeling. "I don't like this."

"Neither do I. Once we secure a room, we'll see what we can learn."

The elderly Black driver of the hack they hired ferried them and their luggage into the city. Once again she was struck by how well built Denver appeared to be. The street they were traveling down was choked with vehicles of every kind. Because of the slow pace she had an opportunity to view all the glass-windowed stores, the fancy hotels, the sturdy plank walks, and the fashionably dressed people of all races going about their day. The city even had a street-car system.

As their journey continued, the traffic thinned and the area became less impressive. The big buildings and glass windows gave way to an area of saloons, small clapboard houses, and stores that appeared to serve a different segment of the population.

"This is our side of town," the driver confirmed. "You folks got a preference for where you want to stay?"

"Where would you suggest?" Cecil asked. "I haven't lived here in thirty years."

"Right here," the driver declared as he brought his ancient mule and buggy to a halt. They were in front of a large ominous-looking place that stood like a sentinel amongst the smaller houses nearby. The weathered two-story Victorian house with its faded green paint, gables, and cornices reminded her of the mountains—grim, imposing, bleak.

The driver said, "This here is the best Denver has to offer. Lady named Miss Helene owns it. She looks down her nose at most folks, but she runs a decent place."

Cecil seemed to have turned to stone.

Concerned, Leah asked, "For heaven's sake, what's the matter?"

Cecil didn't reply. He instead asked the driver, "What's her full name?"

"Helene Sejours. Been here a long time I'm told. Fancy Creole woman."

Cecil looked to Leah, and said, "This is the house Louis built for his wife, Bernice. I never imagined it would be still standing."

Leah's eyes swept the foreboding-looking place once again. That same odd chill she'd felt before crept over her skin.

Cecil explained further. "Helene Sejours is the sister of Bernice."

Leah could just imagine how the woman might react to having Monty's new wife under her roof. "Maybe we should stay somewhere else, Cecil."

"We'll stay here," Cecil replied as if he'd made some type of decision.

Leah didn't like the idea. "Cecil, I don't think—"

He cut her off. "It'll be fine."

Leah didn't believe it for a minute but followed him out of the carriage and up the walk to the door.

Their knock was answered by a suspicious-eyed, light-skinned woman, who appeared to be in her mid-fifties. She wore the black dress and white apron of a servant. Her silver-streaked brown hair was pulled back into a severe bun. "May I help you?"

"We're in need of a room," Cecil answered.

The woman looked them up and down. Her eyes settled on Cecil's face, and she asked, "Aren't you Cecil Lee?"

Cecil didn't deny it. "Yes."

"Do you remember me?" she asked coolly.

Cecil shook his head. "No, I'm sorry I don't."

Her reply was frosty. "I'm Mable France. I'll get Miss Helene. Wait here."

Leah wondered why the woman thought Cecil should remember her. This was not going to be a pleasant stay. The specter of tomorrow's court summons played on the edges of her mind, but she refused to think about it now.

Mable France returned accompanied by a woman

whose true features were hidden beneath a thick dusting of white face powder. It was impossible to tell her age, but if she were using the powder to highlight her youth, she'd failed. She was taller than most women. Her green gown looked as weathered and old as the house. "So, you've returned," she said to Cecil.

Cecil replied emotionlessly, "I'm here to settle Louis's affairs, nothing more. The driver said you have rooms to let."

"I do."

She then turned her eyes to Leah. "Who's this?"

"Louis's widow, Leah."

The woman couldn't hide her surprise. She looked Leah up and down as critically as Mrs. France had done. "What is she, all of twenty-five?"

Leah told her coldly, "No, I'm thirty-two."

"So old? What was Louis, sixty? You must've been quite a comfort to him in his final days."

Leah's chin rose angrily, but she didn't respond.

Cecil asked crisply, "Do you have rooms or not, Helene?"

"Oh, I have rooms. Poverty dictates that I open my sister's home to anyone with the coin to pay."

The blue eyes staring at Leah were frosty. "Seven dollars a week. Six more if you want meals."

"That's fair," Cecil allowed.

"Mrs. France will show you up."

After giving Leah one last look of dislike, Helene Sejours turned and disappeared back into the house.

"This way," Mrs. France told them.

The interior of the house was dimly lit and literally choked with furniture. Fat, overstuffed, fringed chairs and settees competed for space with fringed lamps, short ornate tables, and large footstools. The burgundy-velvet furniture and the matching fringed drapes had probably been fine and costly once, but were now shiny and faded by time.

Leah and Cecil followed Mrs. France up a short staircase to the house's second floor. She opened one of the doors, then turned to Leah. "This one's yours. Mr. Lee's down the hall."

Leah stepped into the small room and looked around. Its two windows offered an unhindered view of the trees and bleak gray mountains off in the distance. The brisk air rivaled outdoors.

Mrs. France offered, "I'll bring up some wood for the grate. This room's rarely used."

"That would be appreciated," Leah responded, trying not to shiver visibly.

The bed appeared comfortable enough and was covered by a heavy navy quilt. The bureau and a small dressing table with a vanity mirror were the only other pieces of furniture.

"Are there any other tenants here?" Leah asked.

"No. Facilities are down the hall. I don't carry water, so if you want a bath, heat it yourself."

Leah wondered if the place's lack of tenants could be traced to Mrs. France's unfriendly attitude. She also wondered if they were being treated this way because Cecil didn't recall ever meeting her before, or if the housekeeper was always this brusque.

While Mrs. France showed Cecil to his room, the driver carried in Leah's trunks and set them by the door. He couldn't manage it all in one trip, so it took two. After he did the same for Cecil's things, Cecil paid the man, and he departed with a smile.

"Dinner's in an hour," Mrs. France announced. That said, she headed back down the hall to the stairs.

Leah shared a silent look with Cecil, who shook his head, and said, "The sooner we get away from here, the happier I'll be."

"I feel the same way. So do I really have to go to court tomorrow?"

"Yes. We need to find out what this is about."

"Do you think Mrs. Sejours might know?"

"*Miss* Sejours. Helene never married." He shrugged. "I'll ask her, but there's no guarantee she'll tell me the truth."

"You don't trust her?"

"No."

"Then why are we staying here?" Leah asked, struggling to keep her voice low so they wouldn't be overheard.

"Because this house and everything in it was left to Ryder and his grandmother. Why Helene is living here instead is beyond me, but I plan to find out."

That gave Leah pause. "First the mine interests that Ryder said he never received and now this house?"

"Exactly. Can you think of a better place to get at the truth?"

"Given a few minutes' time, I probably could, but I'll follow your lead."

He smiled. "Good. Once we get this lawsuit question out of the way, time here should be easier."

Leah hoped he was right.

Dinner was a tense affair. Although Helene had seemingly nothing to say to Cecil, she kept viewing Leah as if she were an exhibit at a fair. At one point Helene remarked, "I never imagined Louis would marry a woman younger than *both* his sons."

Leah sensed the barracuda beneath all that white powder. "To be truthful, I was surprised to find out he had sons. I only recently learned of Monty's family here."

"Is that an English accent I hear?"

"A small one. My mother was British."

"And your father?"

"American."

"And did your parents approve of this marriage?"

Leah answered without hesitation. "My father died when

I was young, and Mother passed away last year, but yes, she would've approved." Leah knew she was right. Monty's attempts to secure her future might have been unorthodox, but Leah sensed Reba was applauding his ingenuity from her spot up in heaven.

Helene's blue eyes were bright and sharp as a hawk. "How long will you be with us?"

"Once our business is completed, Cecil and I'll be in a better position to know."

They were interrupted by the appearance of Mrs. France. "Mister Seth is here, ma'am."

Helene's face brightened. "Ah, send him in and bring him a plate so he can join us." As Mrs. France went off, Helene said to Leah, "Aren't you fortunate, you're going to meet Louis's son."

When Seth walked into the room, he looked so much like Monty, Leah felt gooseflesh run up her arms. Helene said something else, but Leah heard nothing; she was too busy staring at the wavy black hair, the pale golden skin, and the familiar hawklike features. He was as urbane in his appearance as she imagined a high-toned Creole would be, and the thin moustache seemed to enhance his handsomeness. The frock coat he handed to Mrs. France appeared to be very costly, as did the brown suit he wore beneath. He had dark hazel eyes instead of Monty's midnight blue, but the shape and sparkle were the same.

Leah gathered herself and looked over at Cecil seated on the other side of the table. He, too, looked stunned.

Helene called affectionately, "Darling, there's someone here I believe you should meet."

Leah noted that in his own golden way, Seth Montague was as handsome as his brother.

As he neared the table, his aunt said, "Seth, meet your father's last wife, Leah Montague. Leah, my nephew Seth Montague."

If his aunt's surprising introduction caught him off guard, he hid it well. He bowed his head respectfully in Leah's direction, and said, "I'm sorry for your loss."

After enduring his brother's rudeness, Leah was touched by his sentiment. "Thank you."

Helene waved a hand toward Cecil. "And this is your father's business partner, Cecil Lee."

Cecil stood, "Good evening, Seth. You were very young the last time I saw you."

Seth grasped Cecil's hand in a solid greeting. "No more than seven or eight if I remember. Sorry we couldn't have met again under better circumstances."

"So do I." Cecil replied, still staring at the son who so resembled his late father.

"Did he pass peacefully?" Seth asked of Leah as he took a seat at the table.

She nodded gently. "Yes, in his sleep."

"That's good to know. I've been in Carson City for the past few weeks. I didn't know you'd wired until I returned home today. I'd hoped to meet your train and help get you settled in, but I was too late."

Leah said, "We appreciate the thought."

Helene drawled, "Well, now that we've all gotten reacquainted, shall we finish our meal?"

Leah didn't care for the woman's sarcastic tone, but picked up her fork and resumed eating.

As the meal wound to a close, Cecil took a sip of water from his heavy glass goblet, then set it back down and said, "Leah was served with a summons when we arrived today. Either of you have any idea what it might be about?"

Both Seth and Helene stiffened noticeably. Leah watched them share a look, then Seth asked, "The summons didn't say?"

"No," Leah responded. "I'm to appear at the courthouse tomorrow morning at nine. I'm assuming it has something to do with Monty because he's the only tie I have here."

Seth shrugged, "Then that could be anything. Louis didn't leave behind many friends."

Cecil asked, "So, you've no idea?"

"I'm afraid not. Aunt Helene?"

"No, but as my nephew said, if it does have to do with Louis, it could be anything. He was not well liked, by anyone."

"Yourself included?" Leah asked.

Helene took a moment to scan Leah's face. "You're not the mouse I assumed you to be, are you?"

"No, I'm not."

"Good for you. Well the answer is yes, myself included. Louis killed my sister. I will hate him for the rest of my life." Evidently finished with her dinner, Helene stood. "I'm sure Seth can answer any other questions you two might have. Excuse me."

And she left the room.

Seth broke the silence that followed. "You'll have to forgive my aunt. She holds my father responsible for everything bad in her life."

Leah replied, "No apology necessary. Her pain is her own. Who are we to judge?"

"Thanks," he said.

Cecil stood. "Well, I hate being ambushed, so I'm going out to see if I can learn anything about this summons. Seth, it's nice to see you again. Leah, we'll speak when I return."

She nodded.

Cecil's departure left her alone with Seth. "Please," she told him, "if you have an appointment, you should go ahead. I'm fine here."

"Trying to get rid of me?"

Leah smiled. "No, I just—"

"When I'm ready to go, I'll let you know."

"Okay." Leah noted how comfortable she felt in his presence.

"Now, tell me about yourself."

"Well, I'm from a small village on the Massachusetts coast."

"A seafaring woman."

Leah's smile peeked out again. "Not really. I went to England once. My father did all the sailing. According to my mother, he'd been as far as China and Egypt. He died before my birth."

"Sorry to hear that."

"Thank you. What about you? Have you ever sailed anywhere?"

"France once when I was twelve. Been all over the West though."

"I hope to see some of the world after Cecil and I are done here."

"I hope that wish comes true."

After meeting Ryder, Leah hadn't expected Seth to be so easygoing or so nice. His hazel-eyed handsomeness made Leah wonder if there was a Mrs. Seth Montague.

"I met your brother on the train," she confessed.

Seth showed only faint interest. "Did you. Wasn't on his best behavior, I'll bet."

"You'd win," Leah admitted. Ryder hadn't been very respectful, and she could still feel the chill from his penetrating dark eyes.

"The only good thing I can say about Ryder is that he's my *half* brother. Did Louis tell you about him?"

"No." Leah didn't reveal the fact that she'd not known about either son until the night before Monty died. She didn't know if the revelation would bruise Seth's feelings.

"Well, there's no reason for you not to know about the

skeletons in the Montague closet. After my mother's death, my father had an unfortunate liaison with a half-breed, an African-Cheyenne woman. Ryder was the result. It's been rather, shall we say, awkward living in the same town with him."

With those words, the golden Seth became brass in Leah's eyes. Because the sea had taken her own father's life before he could return and marry her mother, Leah had grown up hearing the same contemptuous sneering from the busybodies in her town about her own illegitimate birth.

Seth then added, "You'd be wise to avoid Ryder. He's trouble. Always has been."

Leah stated the obvious, "The two of you don't get along, I take it."

"No."

His curt tone made Leah believe the brothers were at odds over more than just Ryder's out-of-wedlock birth but Seth changed the subject. "That's the oddest thing, that summons."

"I agree. I'm also puzzled as to how someone would know Cecil and I were traveling here. I don't believe he wired anyone other than you and your brother."

Seth replied, "That's no mystery. The telegraph operators aren't exactly sphinxes. They could've told anyone about those wires."

Leah supposed he could be right. "Well, I certainly would like to know what it's concerning. I don't like being ambushed either."

"Maybe Mr. Lee will find out something."

"I hope so."

Leah found herself genuinely liking Seth and told him so. "You're much more pleasant to be around than your brother."

"*Half* brother."

"Sorry, half brother."

"I'll take that as a compliment though."

"And well you should."

"Unlike Ryder and my aunt, I live in the present, not the past."

Leah saw a sharpness firm his jaw for a second, as if he were seeing something in his mind. A second later the brightness returned to his eyes. "If you think it's proper, I'd like to escort you around while you're here. Denver has quite a bit to offer."

"I'd like that." Even though Leah was supposed to be here as Monty's widow, she saw nothing wrong in spending time with Seth. He seemed nice enough, and she had promised Monty to plead his case with his sons.

He nodded. "Good. I'll stop in after the hearing tomorrow. I hope everything goes well."

He stood and Leah followed suit, saying, "I do too."

He pushed in his chair. "It's been a pleasure meeting you, Mrs. Montague."

"Please, call me Leah."

"Well, it's been a pleasure, Leah."

"A pleasure meeting you also."

He was close enough for her to feel the heat of his body. Even though his intolerant words about his brother's birth hadn't reflected well, they hadn't diminished his attractiveness.

"Have a pleasant evening, Leah."

"You do the same."

He departed and Leah was left alone.

By ten that evening Cecil had not returned, and Leah began to worry.

She sought out Helene Sejours and found her going over accounts at the table in the dining room. At Leah's entrance she glanced up. Her blue eyes were filled with irritation. "Yes?"

"I'm starting to worry about Cecil. He's been gone for some time."

Helene went back to her ledgers. "Frankly, I wouldn't put it past him to have run off and disappeared again. Remember, the last time he took off, it took him thirty years to return."

Leah doubted that possibility and felt frustration rise in the face of the woman's manner. "I apologize for disturbing you."

She headed to the door only to be stopped by Helen's voice. "Stay please. No need to run off in a huff. Sit so we can chat."

Leah turned back. "To what end?"

Helene responded with a brittle smile. "You are a brave young woman, aren't you? Giving me tit for tat. Louis always did like his women saucy."

Leah didn't know whether to leave or stay. She also had trouble gleaning Helene's true nature; one moment she was sarcastic and caustic, the next offering up compliments. Leah admittedly felt off-balance.

Helene gestured Leah to one of the upholstered chairs. Leah held the ice-blue eyes for a moment and in them she read power, ambition, and the knowledge that Helene would be a formidable enemy, should she choose that role. However, Leah had grown up with the most formidable woman she'd ever faced: her mother, Reba. And if Reba taught her one thing it was this: Never run. Stand and fight.

Buoyed by those thoughts, Leah sat.

"So," Helene said, "how long were you and Louis married?"

Leah had no intentions of telling her the truth. It wasn't any of her business. "Not long enough."

Helene let the vague reply roll off her back. "Clever too. How quaint, but I suppose you'd have to be to have gotten Louis to the altar. It is a legal marriage, isn't it?"

Inwardly, Leah chuckled bitterly at the veiled slap. "Do people generally wilt beneath your sharp tongue?"

"Generally yes. You're different, however."

"Yes I am and yes, the marriage was legal." Leah stood. She'd had enough.

Helene looked up at her. "Well, we've taken enough measure of each other for one night, don't you think?"

"I do."

"Then get some rest. You'll probably need it in the morning."

Again, Leah didn't know how to take Helene's words.

"And I wouldn't worry about Cecil. If he returns, he will. If he doesn't?" She shrugged her thin shoulders in the worn green dress as if it didn't matter. "Frankly, I'd worry more about your own well-being. Louis's women seem to meet unfortunate ends. Let's hope you're not next."

The tone of Helene's voice and the blankness in her eyes gave Leah a chill. "Good night, Miss Sejours."

"Good night, dear."

Later, as Leah climbed into bed, she found it hard to rid herself of the effects of Helen's parting words. Were they meant to be a threat? Surely coming here wouldn't get her killed. She reminded herself that two women involved with Monty had met untimely deaths here under mysterious circumstances. Leah had no doubts Helene had planted that seed deliberately, just to make her worry. She'd done a good job. Now, not only did Leah have the court summons and Cecil's whereabouts to worry about, concerns about her own safety had been added to the pot. Leah couldn't wait to leave Denver.

Leah awakened the next morning, bleary-eyed and stiff. She'd had a restless night and hadn't slept much at all. Dragging herself over to the basin she'd filled last night, she splashed water on her face and rinsed her teeth. Slowly dressing, she wondered if Cecil had returned during the night. She hoped so.

Downstairs, the house was silent. Sunbeams streamed playfully into the rooms. The house held the same quiet the Swan always had at this time of day, and it made her think of home. The only thing missing was the tantalizing smell of fresh coffee. Having spent her life around seamen, Leah had developed a fondness for the brew and become accustomed to having a cup or two to fuel her morning. It was especially needed this morning. In a few hours she'd be at the courthouse to answer the summons, and she needed bracing.

When Leah walked into the kitchen, Mrs. France was seated at the table. The housekeeper glanced up from her coffee and oatmeal with a glare.

Leah offered up a hasty apology. "I didn't mean to impose. I'm accustomed to rising early, and—"

"Is there something you want, Mrs. Montague?"

So much for apologies, Leah thought testily. "Coffee. If there isn't any, I can brew it myself."

The housekeeper's steady stare made Leah feel as if she'd been magically transported back in time to her school days and was once again standing before the headmistress of Miss Caldwell's School for Young Women of Color for committing yet another infraction. "If this is your private time, I can come back later."

The woman's demeanor didn't change. "Coffee's over there on the stove. Miss Helene doesn't usually come down until ten."

"Ten?" Leah echoed loudly. Realizing how rude she sounded, she shut her mouth and went over to the coffeepot. Leah had never slept that late in her life. First of all, her mother wouldn't't've tolerated such laziness, and secondly, there'd always been chores to do or school to attend.

As Leah poured herself a cup of coffee, she wondered if small talk would make the woman unbend a bit. "Did you know Mr. Montague?"

"Yes. My husband and two brothers were killed in one of his mines thirty-two years ago."

Leah sloshed hot coffee all over her skirt. It was not the answer she'd been expecting. Hastily setting the cup on the counter, she grabbed a nearby dish towel to dry herself. Still reeling, she also saw that she'd made a mess of the kitchen floor. Not knowing what else to say, she asked, "Where's your mop?"

Mrs. France pointed toward the kitchen's door. "Out on the porch."

The cold air felt good on Leah's face. She took in a few bracing breaths to steady herself, then went back inside to take care of the spills.

A few quick swipes of the mop's rag head returned the wood floor to its previously pristine state.

Upon viewing Leah's handiwork, Mrs. France cracked, "You handle that mop like you've actually seen one before."

Leah stiffened. "Why wouldn't I have?"

"Fancy women like you usually have hired help for that."

Leah's chuckle held no humor. "I've been mopping floors since I was eight. There's nothing fancy about me."

Mrs. France looked skeptical, but Leah saw no reason to try to change the woman's mind. "I'll put this mop back."

After returning the mop to the porch, Leah stepped back inside and poured herself another cup of coffee. Under Mrs. France's suspicious eyes, she left the kitchen without another word.

Upstairs, Leah changed out of her wet skirt. She stood in front of the windows and sipped her coffee. She thought back on her encounter with Mrs. France. *Fancy woman.* Leah shook her head and wondered if the housekeeper had meant *fancy* as in rich, or *fancy* as in kept? Although neither description fit Leah, she could just imagine what she'd be called once it became known she'd married Monty less than a day before he died. What a mess. Leah could still hear the bitterness in the housekeeper's voice. It was fairly obvious the woman held Monty responsible for the tragic demise of her husband and son. How many others were holding on to grudges from the past? Leah had many more questions than she had answers.

A knock on her door broke her attention. When she called, "Come in," Cecil entered. She was certainly glad to see him. "Good morning. What time did you return?"

"Late. You were asleep, I could hear you snoring."

Leah's hands went to her hip in mock indignation. "I do not snore."

"Whatever you say," he responded with a smile.

"So, what did you learn?"

He shook his head grimly. "Nothing. The people I could've gone to for information are either dead or have moved on. A few of Louis's former business partners are still around, but when I approached them they claimed not to know me and turned me away from their doors."

Leah didn't like the sound of that. "So we go into the courtroom blind?"

"I'm afraid so."

Leah didn't like the sound of that either. "Okay, well, I need to dress. I'll be down directly."

After his departure, Leah wanted to fuss at him again for leaving things here to fester for thirty years, but knew it wouldn't do any good. The past couldn't be changed. She was embroiled in a conundrum not of her making, and there was nothing to do but try and unravel it head-on.

Leah dressed herself in black. As a widow it was what society expected. Since she had no idea whom or what she might be facing, she hoped her attire would remind them that she'd just buried a husband and should be dealt with accordingly. Of course Leah knew that those rules didn't necessarily apply to a woman of color, but it didn't hurt to hope.

Dressed in a plain but well-made black gown, Leah looked at herself in the mirror. The woman reflected back looked less tired than Leah remembered, probably because she wasn't up at dawn hauling kegs or scrubbing floors and tabletops at midnight. After working herself to the bone for the past twenty years, Leah admittedly enjoyed this simple life of leisure Monty's generosity had provided. She hoped she wouldn't have to fight to keep it.

Downstairs, she was surprised by the sight of Seth talking quietly with Cecil. Both men looked up at her as she descended the stairs. Cecil nodded, and Seth inclined his head. He had on a nice brown suit and a snow-white shirt that appeared fresh from the laundress. Leah wondered what he was doing there.

"Good morning, Leah," Seth said.

"Good morning to you, too, Seth. Are you here to see your aunt?"

"No, I thought I'd go to the courthouse with you and Mr. Lee. Hoped it might help."

Leah smiled. "Why thank you. What do you think, Cecil?"

"Don't see how it could hurt."

Leah didn't either. Before this was settled she might need all the support she could find.

She then looked to Cecil, and asked, "Are we ready?"

He nodded.

Seth gestured toward the door. "My carriage is right outside. Shall we?"

Leah brought her veil down over her face and allowed

herself to be escorted out. As Seth handed her up into the expensive-looking rig, Leah glanced back at the house. In an upstairs window she could see Helene Sejours looking down on their departure with such a predatory smile on her white-powdered face it raised the hair on the back of Leah's neck.

Chapter 3

~~~ഗഗ~~~

Leah sat in the backseat of Seth's fancy carriage wondering where the morning's sunbeams had gone. The once-bright sky had now turned ominous and dark as if rain were on the horizon. Leah hoped it would hold off. She was already anxious enough—arriving at the hearing soaked and bedraggled would not help matters.

They soon reached their destination. Guided by Seth's hand, Leah stepped down onto the plank walk in front of the courthouse. She fought to ignore the butterflies in her stomach, but couldn't. Her hand, enveloped in Seth's, shook with nervousness. He must have felt her shake because he looked down into her tight face, and said kindly, "Hopefully it will be over soon. Keep your chin up."

Leah smiled as best she could.

Inside they were shown into a dimly lit judge's chamber and told to take seats and wait. Moments later, seven well-dressed White men filed in, silent as a jury. Leah wondered who they were and why there were in attendance, but none of them uttered a word nor acknowledged Leah's party. Their silent presence increased Leah's anxiety.

She leaned over and asked Cecil softly, "Do you know any of them?"

"Two. Neither were friends."

Leah closed her eyes in reaction.

All other questions were set aside as the judge entered the room. His name was Andrew Moss. He was a big man. His flaring white moustache coupled with the large build made him resemble a walrus. Everyone stood at the request of the bailiff, and when the judge sat, they all retook their seats.

The judge looked up and said, "Would the representatives of the Montague estate please stand."

Cecil and Leah rose to their feet.

The judge appeared surprised. Leah wondered if he'd dismiss the case solely based on his response to their color. She knew he could. In many areas of the country, members of the race were unable to have their day in court due to the legal shackles of Jim Crow. Testifying against Whites was forbidden as was being able to sue. Because of the times, this judge had every right to void the estate altogether if he wished on the grounds that she, as a Black woman had no rights to inherit. If he did, she'd have very little recourse. *Monty, what have you gotten me into?*

He scrutinized Cecil first, then the veiled Leah. "Where's your counsel?"

Cecil said, "We haven't had time to engage anyone, your honor. We just learned of the suit yesterday."

"I see." The judge scanned the documents before him. "It says here that this judgment was rendered more than thirty years ago, but that the estate was only attached three weeks ago because Mr. Montague couldn't be found."

Cecil raised an eyebrow. "I was unaware of the judgment, sir."

"Are you Louis Montague?"

"No. Mr. Montague passed away recently. I'm Cecil Lee, his former business agent, and this is his widow, Mrs. Leah Montague."

The judge's attention shifted to the veiled Leah. "Sorry for your loss, ma'am."

"Thank you, your honor."

"Well, Mr. Lee, those gentlemen over there represent folks who say you and your boss left them high and dry thirty years ago. Say you left unpaid bills, swindled them in a fraudulent stock scheme, and slunk out of Colorado in the middle of night so you wouldn't have to pay the piper."

Cecil stiffened. "Not true. We prided ourselves on settling our debts, sir. Any losses these gentlemen may have incurred were also incurred by my employer, and we didn't sneak away in the middle of the night."

From behind them one of the men interrupted in an impatient voice. "Your honor, this is all irrelevant. The judgment has already been rendered in a Colorado court of law. The estate should be made to pay."

Leah forced herself to breathe slowly.

The judge then asked Cecil, "Did Mr. Montague leave a will, Mr. Lee?"

Cecil nodded. "He did, Your Honor. Mrs. Montague is the sole heir."

"Did you bring the papers with you?"

"No, sir. They're in a bank vault back East."

The judge took a moment to peruse more of the documents before him. "According to what the plaintiffs have discovered the estate's worth about seventy-five thousand dollars in land and cash. That sound correct to you?"

"Yes sir, it does."

"Well, the judgment owed is ninety-thousand. How do you propose to pay the other fifteen thousand, ma'am?"

Leah's world began to spin. Not only had she just forfeited seventy-five thousand dollars, she now owed fifteen thousand dollars more! She had no proposal; she couldn't even think. "I'd like to have a few days to talk with Mr. Lee about my options, if I may."

One of the men drawled amusedly, "Pay up or go to jail, those are your options honey."

Chuckling could be heard. Leah's jaw tightened.

The judge snapped. "You will show respect, sir."

Once the silence resettled, he said to Leah, "Unfortunately, the gentleman is correct. The estate is hereby taken from the heirs by the court as partial payment for these debts. If you can't make good on the rest, you'll be sentenced to the territorial prison for women. You have until noon, day after tomorrow. Court dismissed."

Had Leah been the fainting type, she would have slumped to the floor right there. Instead she kept her head high as she gathered up her cloak and bag. She was escorted to the door by a somber Cecil and Seth.

On the ride back to Helene's, Leah cursed the fates that had brought her all the way to Colorado just to send her to jail. All she'd wanted was a life free of drudgery and filled with a little joy. Had she been wrong to want something so inconsequential?

"They're not going to put you in jail, Leah," Cecil told her reassuringly as he looked back at her in the seat.

Leah had no such illusions. "Does Monty have more money?"

"Not that I know of."

"Can your personal finances cover the difference?"

He shook his head solemnly.

"Then I am going to prison."

Seth had been driving silently, but now said, "The judge

said that settlement was thirty years old. I can't believe the court still intends to collect."

Leah couldn't believe it either.

Upon entering Helene's house, Leah felt as brittle as a piece of glass. The thought of incarceration loomed like a gathering storm. She could see nothing but dark clouds and terror ahead.

Helene took one look at Leah's face, and said, "I take it the hearing didn't go well."

Seth answered for her. "The judge threatened Leah with prison."

"Whatever for?"

Cecil replied bitterly, "A thirty-year-old settlement I knew nothing about."

"Why don't we go into the parlor?" Helene told them all.

Leah wanted to go straight to her room but followed the others into the parlor and took a seat on one of the over-stuffed burgundy chairs.

Helene leaned forward and said, "Now, tell me everything."

Seth gave her the details. When he finished, Helene looked over at Leah and shook her head sympathetically. "Now that's a shame, and the women's prison is such an awful place."

Leah's chin rose. Helene's false smile and triumphant eyes weren't improving her mood.

Helene then added, "Now that I think back, I do remember a judgment against Louis. It was right after the two of you disappeared, Cecil."

"Why didn't you say something about this yesterday?" he demanded.

"I told you. I just now remembered. Messy affair, too, if my memory serves correct."

Leah wanted to shake the woman.

"Then tell us now," Cecil replied evenly.

"Let's see, there were miners in Central City who were never paid. Timber cutters in Boulder, suppliers from Virginia City to St. Louis. Then there were those mining stocks you and Louis advised everyone to buy. Turned out to be worthless. Many people were quite angry when they learned you two had slunk off in the middle of the night like thieves."

Leah thought that for a woman who hadn't remembered anything yesterday, Helen sure had a whole trunkful of memories today, now that it was too late.

Cecil shook his head in contradiction. "Louis and I both lost money on that stock deal, and you know as well as I that we didn't slink away in the middle of the night. And we did not leave unpaid bills behind."

"That isn't the story your workers and business partners told the court. Three months after your disappearance some of your White associates brought suit against Louis for all those unpaid bills. Since he wasn't here to defend himself, and no one knew his whereabouts, he was convicted of swindling. Hundreds of people added their names to the list of injured parties."

Leah's eyes widened. This conundrum was becoming more and more convoluted.

Helene looked to Leah and cooed, "By now, the judgment must be higher than Pikes Peak."

Seth answered. "It is, and Louis's estate doesn't hold enough to pay it off."

"Isn't that too bad," Helene replied, voice dripping with insincerity. "I'm certain that Louis is somewhere anguishing over the mess he's left you, my dear."

Cecil cast Helene a cold look. "Well, we have a day and a half to try to right this. I'm going back into town to talk to the judge. Maybe he'll listen to reason."

Seth stood. "I'm headed back. I'll give you a lift."

Seth then turned to Leah. "Try not to worry, Leah. Mr. Lee and I, we'll figure it out."

Leah gave him a weak smile.

Cecil added, "Seth's right, don't worry."

She knew that she would worry, but told Cecil, "I won't. I know you'll fix this."

Helene chimed in, "Of course he will. He's Satan's Butler. In his prime he could fix anything."

Cecil ignored her. "I'll see you later, Leah."

Seth promised Leah, "I'll see you later as well," then followed Cecil to the door.

Since Leah had nothing further to say to the sly-eyed Helene, she left her sitting in the parlor alone.

That afternoon, after a silent lunch in her room, Leah began to pace. Since returning from court, she'd tried to come up with a solution, a way out, but no matter where her mind turned, prison stood. Where in the world would she get fifteen thousand dollars, and in two days no less? She could sell the Swan, but even if she could find a buyer in a day and a half, the proceeds wouldn't come close to covering the balance due. She contemplated selling all of her new clothes, but doubted that would be enough either, even if she could find someone to sell them to. The Swan and the clothes were all she owned; she had no jewelry or other valuables she could convert to cash. In her past, such items had been beyond her grasp. Soon, freedom could be beyond her grasp as well.

Seated in his office at the Damien Mining Company, Ryder read over the figures from his upstate copper holdings and found them troubling. Mineral veins in Colorado were petering out. Having to strip the tiny bits of metal from the base rock was becoming more and more expensive, thereby making the digs less and less profitable. He'd been thinking about selling his shares for weeks. Looking at these reports sealed the matter. Ryder was still reading when Sam came in, as usual without knocking, and challengingly slapped a newspaper down on his desk.

"Have you seen this trash?" he demanded.

Ryder picked up the paper. It was the one of the city's dailies.

"It's this afternoon's edition," Sam snarled disgustedly.

Ryder scanned an announcement of an upcoming recital in Denver, and another on the two-headed calf born a week ago to a milk cow owned by a farm couple up in Boulder. "What am I supposed to be looking at?"

Sam jabbed his gnarled brown finger at an item at the bottom of the page. "This!"

Ryder began to read:

In court today, the widow of former mining king Louis Montague was hit with a ninety-thousand-dollar judgment against her late husband's estate. Thirty years ago, many of Montague's associates were left holding the bag when he and his business partner, Cecil Lee, snuck out of Denver in the middle of the night. It's been said that Louis Montague was a swindler, a thief, and possibly a murderer. Mrs. Montague, a colored woman, has been ordered to pay the judgment or serve time in the woman's prison.

The article went on to relate the scandals surrounding the deaths of Monty's first wife, Bernice, and Ryder's mother but Ryder didn't read the rest.

Setting the paper aside, he looked up into Sam's angry face. "Why are you so upset?"

"That little lady doesn't have anything to do with this."

"She's his widow."

"What if she doesn't have enough money?"

Ryder shrugged.

"Are you going to stand by and let her be thrown into prison with a bunch of prostitutes and murderesses?"

"They aren't going to throw her into prison. Those claims are thirty years old."

"Do you think the judge cared about how old those bills are? A Black woman? They'll put her in prison, and you know it."

Ryder had to admit, Sam had a point. Granted, there were two levels of justice being meted out in the country nowadays, but money had a justice all its own. Many of the men who'd done business with Louis were still alive and were as predatory in their business practices now as they'd reportedly been back then. He had no idea how much Louis had left his widow, but if the estate held any value, Louis's old enemies would feast on her like wolves.

Unsettled by those thoughts, Ryder tossed the newspaper back down on the desk. "So what do you want me to do?"

"Something."

Ryder searched Sam's lined face. "Why? She's done nothing but give me the back of her hand since we met."

"And she had no reason?"

Ryder chose not to answer that. "Since when did you become a knight in shining armor? You've known her less than a week."

"But I've known you longer. She's been on your mind, whether you want to admit it or not. I also know that any woman who'll stand up to you is worth her weight in Colorado gold. You need a wife, and I think she'll do."

Ryder's dark eyes widened with amazement. "A wife? What have you been drinking? I'm not marrying anyone, especially not that proper-talking firecracker. Didn't I tell you she was an adventuress?"

Sam waited.

The silent standoff lasted for a few moments longer, then Ryder sighed resignedly. "All right. I'll see what I can do. Not because of her, but because you'll nag me until next Christmas if I don't."

Sam smiled.

"And don't smile yet," Ryder warned. "If I do have to intervene, I do it my way. I don't want to hear a peep out of you about my methods."

Sam turned an imaginary key in his lips. "Not a peep."

They both knew he was lying. Asking Sam to keep his opinions to himself was akin to asking the seasons not to change.

Ryder shook his head good-humoredly. "Go home. I've work to do."

Sam smiled and left.

As Ryder watched the door close, he acknowledged that Sam was the only person he allowed to see his true self. After his mother's death, his Cheyenne grandmother, called Little Tears, raised him. She taught him life, the history of the Cheyenne, and how to survive the bittersweet, day-to-day existence forced upon the tribes by the ignorance and greed of those in power. She died the day after he left to attend school in Minnesota. It was almost as if her purpose for living ceased upon his departure. Miss Eloise, one of the local residents, had wired him to inform him of her passing. Had it not been for her, Ryder doubted he would have even known. No one else in the area gave a tinker's damn about him or his redskin kin.

He met Sam a month after arriving in Minnesota. At the time, the old man had been a cook at the boardinghouse where Ryder rented a room. The job suited Sam well after his years of cooking for the men and the mules of the highly decorated Ninth Cavalry. Initially, Ryder met Sam's attempts at friendship with suspicion; soldiers, even retired ones, were symbols of death, bitterness, and betrayal to a man with Native blood, especially in light of Ryder's personal connection to the massacre of the Cheyenne and Arapaho at Sand Creek. He wanted nothing to do with Sam, and bluntly told him so.

But Ryder's attitude changed the day Sam came across Ryder being beaten by some local town toughs. There'd been six of them. Ryder could've handled three, maybe even four, but his inability to handle all six cowards alone could be measured by his bloodied, swollen face and the way they were kicking him as he lay nearly unconscious in the dirt.

To this day, Sam refused to tell Ryder how he extricated him from that hate-fed encounter, but Ryder knew he would have been kicked to death were it not for the old pony soldier. They became solid friends after that; Ryder listened to Sam's stories about his life, and Sam listened to his. When the time came for Ryder to leave school, he asked Sam to return with him to Colorado and help him make his fortune and Sam agreed; they'd been together ever since.

However, Ryder found Sam's championing of the Widow Montague surprising. Sam rarely butted into Ryder's private life, and never before had he ever mentioned any woman and the word marriage in the same sentence. Ryder shook his head. He could just imagine himself married to Leah Montague. They'd spend every waking moment arguing. He had no plans to hitch his fate to such an ornery female. If and when he decided to marry, he'd pick a woman with a lot less sass and a lot more deference. That didn't mean he wouldn't welcome Leah into his bed though. Sam was right, she had been on his mind. He found her dark beauty as desirable as an untapped source of gold, but claiming that gold would take a patience Ryder never had to exercise before when pursuing a woman. Usually he beckoned, they smiled and came willingly. He sensed the Widow Montague would be as combative as a wild mare, but taming and claiming her would undoubtedly be worth the loss of a finger or two, not to mention how it would affect Seth.

His eyes strayed back to the paper. If the report about the lien on the Montague estate were true, prison could indeed be her fate. Ryder assumed Cecil Lee was out working his legendary magic in an attempt to get her a reprieve, but Ryder knew the Butler would find times had changed in the thirty years since Louis's day; the cutthroat rules of business and finance were the same but the players had changed. Syndicates and foreign investment were now running things, and they had more gold than Zeus and more lawyers than an indicted politician. The political climate had changed also. With the death of Reconstruction, men of color were less tolerated and more likely to be given short shrift in everything. Without Louis's influence and wealth behind him, Cecil stood little chance of gaining access to anyone powerful enough to aid the widow's case. Maybe Sam was right, maybe he should intervene. But what would he gain? She'd probably not appreciate his help, and therein lay the challenge. Just like the wild mare he'd mused upon earlier, she'd fight his lariat all the way, but, given time and the proper handling, he saw no reason why she couldn't be gentled. After all, the Cheyenne had always been excellent horsemen.

Later that afternoon Mrs. France came up to Leah's room to inform her that she had a visitor waiting in the parlor.

A wary Leah asked, "Is it a creditor, or someone with a summons?"

"No."

Leah felt relief flood her. "Who is it then?"

"Mr. Damien."

"Ryder Damien?"

"Yes, ma'am."

For the life of her, Leah couldn't come up with a reason why he'd want to see her. Unless he'd heard about her dilemma and had come to gloat, she told herself. Noting that Mrs. France looked a bit impatient, Leah finally said, "Tell him I'll be down momentarily."

Mrs. France departed.

Leah took a deep breath. Ryder Damien was the last person she wanted to see today. She had enough on her mind.

When she walked into the parlor, Ryder was again caught by her beauty. Her dark skin was as pure and as clear as a jewel. The fashionably piled hair made him imagine how it might look after a night of lovemaking. As always his eyes slid admiringly over the tempting figure. The long-sleeved black dress sported a narrow band of black lace at the wrists and around the high-necked collar. She presented a prim widow's innocence he knew she didn't possess, and that made her even more desirable.

"You wished to see me?" she said from the doorway.

"I do. Word has it you're having financial difficulties."

Leah didn't deny it. "Yes, I am. Have you come to gloat?"

"No."

"Did Seth send you?"

"The only place my brother wishes to send me is to hell."

"Isn't that where we are?" she asked in response.

He raised an eyebrow. "Sarcasm?"

"Truth."

He watched her walk fully into the room and take up a stance at the windows, her back to him.

"You are more everything than I thought," he admitted.

She turned to view him over her shoulder. "Do you always offer such backhanded compliments?"

"Only when necessary."

Leah sensed the male in him subtly seeking out the woman in her, and it made her look away from his penetrating eyes. "What did you want?"

"Sam thought maybe I could help in some way."

"Do you have fifteen thousand dollars you can spare?" she asked boldly.

"Yes."

Leah looked back at him once again.

He shrugged those magnificent shoulders. "Obviously, I have more of my father in me than I care to admit. Making money seems to come easily."

Leah scanned him silently. Could he really extricate her from this awful situation? If so, what would he ask in exchange? She already knew the answer, but needed to hear him say it. "And in return?"

"That you be on my arm. Grace my table. The rest you know."

Leah fled from his unreadable eyes. His mixed ancestry had produced a man as beautiful and as formidable as a pagan god; women probably knelt at his altar often. "I'd like to wait until Cecil and Seth return before I make a decision. They may have found a solution."

Ryder hadn't expected her to agree readily, and she hadn't disappointed. "I have no quarrel with that."

For the first time Leah could see that he, too, bore a strong resemblance to his father. The chin and the shape of his mouth mirrored Monty's exactly. As a result, pleasant memories of Monty rose unbidden. "He was a good man, your father."

"He left behind two dead women and abandoned two small sons. I see nothing good in that."

Leah was stung by his response, and her chin rose defiantly. "At the end he was sorry for abandoning you. He'd wanted to close the breach but was afraid he'd be rebuffed—afraid you and Seth hated him."

"An astute man, that Louis."

Leah wondered how much of Ryder's bitterness was rooted in anger and how much pain. She sensed a great deal of both. "Do you truly hate him? Truly?"

"I hate what he did to my mother, and to me."

"Is that why you don't carry his name?"

"I don't carry his name because he never married my mother."

Leah felt the chill in his words. "But you don't really believe he murdered her, do you?"

"And if my answer is yes?"

"I'd say you were wrong."

"Then we disagree."

Ryder supposed it made her feel better to believe in her version of Louis Montague, but Ryder had lived with the truth all his life. "A woman like you should know that men are capable of anything."

Leah stiffened. *"A woman like me?"*

Ryder heard the temper in her voice. "We are who we are."

"And, as I told you before, you wouldn't know the truth if it slapped you in the face."

"You didn't marry Louis Montague for his money?"

The question was filled with such confident disbelief it only reinforced what she'd deduced earlier; even if she told him the truth, he wouldn't believe it, so why bother?

Leah's voice dripped with sarcasm. "I'd be lying if I said, 'hope to see you again,' so I'll simply say, good day."

He stepped forward to block her passage. She didn't feel threatened; she was too busy being aware of his body's heat mingling with her own and the faint spicy tones of his cologne.

"You play the offended widow well."

"And you the bitter, estranged son."

He inclined his head. "You joust well, also."

"Another compliment?"

"An observation. I don't like women who run and hide."

"I'll be sure to pass that along to anyone who might be interested."

"Your claws are showing."

Leah had grown up in a seafaring town; she'd met men from all over the world but never one as commanding or provoking as Ryder Damien.

In spite of the tension in the room, Ryder didn't want her to leave, even as he wondered how many other men she'd known in her past. "Is my brother treating you well?"

"Unlike you, Seth's been a gentleman."

"It's one of the things he's best at. Shall I emulate him?"

Leah searched the sculpted face framed by the falling black hair. "To what end?"

"My own."

In response to his low-toned words, something she had never felt before snaked up past her bad mood, making her respond to his silent, potent call. "Women surrender to you easily, don't they?"

"I've never had a problem in that area."

"It shows."

"I like you."

Leah held his gaze. "But, I *don't* like you."

"You prefer my brother?"

"Why should that matter?"

"He and I have fought over everything our entire lives."

"So, if I took an interest in him?"

"Then I'd do everything in my power to turn that interest my way."

At first she thought he was merely being sarcastic, but seconds later realized he was quite serious. He exuded a power that put a haziness in her blood. A woman as inexperienced as she had no idea what type of defense to deploy against such an overwhelming man, yet she was contemplating being his for a price.

Ryder wanted to ease her into his arms so he could determine once and for all if her mouth tasted as lush as it appeared. The charged air between them was filled with the thunder of their volatile interactions and the lightning of their unacknowledged, mutual attraction. In time, the situation would explode with the force of a summer storm, but he had the patience to wait.

They were both so attuned to one another, neither of them noticed Seth's presence in the room until they heard him demand, "Leah, what's he doing here?"

Ryder replied, "Offering the lady a way out of Louis's trap." Only then did he turn his cold eyes on his brother. They faced each other like the adversaries they were.

Seth shot back smoothly, "What can you offer?"

Ryder posed a question of his own. "Then you have the money she needs?"

Seth's face reddened.

Ryder's smile was icy. "I thought not."

Ryder directed his attention back to Leah. "I'll be by tomorrow morning for your decision."

Leah nodded almost imperceptibly.

Seth seemed unwilling to concede defeat. "Leah, you aren't seriously considering an offer from him?"

She asked him frankly, "Shall I go to prison instead?" and waited for his response.

He didn't have one it seemed. Although Leah enjoyed being in Seth's company, she had to look beyond emotional reactions and deal with reality. Ryder had a solution.

Seth held his brother's eyes, and said, "Mr. Lee will never let her agree."

At that moment, Cecil entered the room, "What won't I agree to?"

Leah's chin rose. "Mr. Damien and I have been discussing a way of out my predicament."

"Entailing what?"

"That's between Mr. Damien and me, Cecil," Leah told him quietly.

Cecil studied her for a long silent moment, then turned to Ryder. "You *are* your father's son if you take advantage of her this way."

Ryder seemed unmoved.

"Will you at least offer her marriage?"

Silence.

Seth uttered a soft curse.

Leah started shaking inside. "Gentlemen, I need some air. Pardon me please."

Picking up her black skirts, she hastened from the parlor.

Outside it was raining. The covered porch deflected most of the moisture, but she could still feel the damp spray on her face. Could she really let herself be purchased like a common doxy? Knowing the alternative to be a filthy, dangerous, prison, Leah's answer continued to be a firm yes. She understood Cecil's concern; he took his role as surrogate parent seriously, and being someone's mistress certainly didn't sit well with her or her upbringing, but *she* was the one staring incarceration square in the face. Her ship was sinking fast, and Ryder Damien had tossed her a lifeline. She'd be a fool not to grasp it. Luckily she knew few people here because once word got around she'd have no reputation, but reputation meant nothing to an inmate of the state prison either.

She heard someone step out onto the porch behind her. The person's presence was so strong she didn't need to turn to verify that it was Ryder.

"I'm heading home."

Leah nodded, but didn't turn to face him or speak.

"And so you'll know: I've never raised my hand to a woman, nor forced one into my bed. I don't plan to change with you."

Her eyes closed in response. "Thank you," she managed to whisper.

Could she really be that good an actress, Ryder asked himself. A less cynical man would be moved by the sense of distress that lay beneath her quiet armor and offer her comfort and reassurance, but Ryder was convinced it was nothing more than an act on her part; a damned good one, but an act all the same. They both knew she was no lamb being led to the slaughter. "Should your answer be yes, there'll be papers to sign at the courthouse."

"I'll be prepared."

"Then I'll see you tomorrow."

Leah didn't respond; she didn't know what to say.

A moment later he was hurrying through the rain to his black carriage, tied up at the post. She watched him until he drove out of sight. Only then did she ask herself, *What have I done?*

When she went back inside, both Seth and Cecil were still in the parlor. Helene had joined them and was splashing liquor into short ornate glasses. From the animated expression on her face one would think she was celebrating.

Upon seeing Leah enter the parlor, she called, "Ah, here she is. A drink, my dear?"

"No, thank you. Cecil, may I speak with you please?"

Leah could see by the accusatory glint in Seth's eyes that he was still angry, but she had no plans to offer solace. Right now she had too many problems of her own to spare the time to deal with him.

She and Cecil went up to her room. Inside behind the closed door they discussed her decision.

"But Leah, this is a small town. What about your reputation?"

"I'll have none either way. Right now, being a kept woman sounds a ton of a lot better than being a prisoner of the state. I don't have a choice, Cecil. None."

"You're right of course, but—" His spectacled eyes brimmed with renewed concern.

"I know. No woman wants to be reduced to this, but it's prison, Cecil. Prison."

Leah loved Monty dearly, but she wouldn't go to jail for him, not for something she had no hand in. "So, were you able to talk to the judge?"

"No, he refused to see me."

"Can we appeal in another court?"

"I thought of that, but we'd need a lawyer, and according to the bailiff none of the local lawyers take our cases."

"So the estate's gone."

Cecil nodded sadly. "Yep. Everything Louis has worked for since leaving here thirty years ago will go to these so-called creditors."

"But it isn't prison," she pointed out softly. Leah had resigned herself to the inevitable. By this time tomorrow, she'd be a woman bought and paid for. Even though she'd be trading one form of incarceration for another, it wouldn't be prison. If she kept reminding herself of that fact, she'd be able to look herself in the mirror every morning and not see shame.

She turned her attention back to Cecil and said genuinely. "Thanks for trying."

He nodded, tight-lipped. "I feel as though I've let you down."

"You shouldn't. You did your best. You didn't know about the suit, and neither did Monty."

"But to do this—with Ryder—"

"As I said, I've no choice."

His lips tightened solemnly.

Much to Leah's relief, he changed the subject. "Do you want to go into Denver for dinner? There's a few more people I'd like to speak with about this."

She shook her head. "No. I think I'll just have a tray in here. I'll see you in the morning."

He gave her a small smile then left her.

The next morning, Leah arose early. To her surprise she'd slept peacefully and awakened refreshed and ready. Her optimistic spirit clashed with the knowledge that today would not be a happy one. She wondered if she'd gone around the bend last night while she slept because she didn't feel doomed or distressed. Instead she felt a strong will to survive, and as Reba'd always told her, *a girl doesn't need much more than that!*

Leah dressed carefully, however, by the time she finished her hair and picked up the gold hoops for her ears all the calm she'd awakened with had disappeared. She was as nervous as a cow in a slaughterhouse. It took her shaking hands two tries to put the ornaments in her ears. Telling herself she needed to remain calm didn't seem to matter. In less than an hour she'd be entering a phase of her life that would change her forever. And she was absolutely terrified.

Downstairs, Leah declined the breakfast Mrs. France had spread out on the table and opted for a cup of coffee instead. Cecil was dressed and seated at the table, but didn't appear really interested in eating. He was toying with his eggs, his mind seemingly elsewhere.

"Cecil, I'm not going to be able to get through this if you mope."

He glanced up and smiled wanly. "I'm sorry, Leah. It's just that none of this has gone according to plan. We were supposed to come here, find the boys, and leave. Now?"

"It seems the fates had other plans, but," Leah said brightly, "I'm not going to prison, and that in itself is a blessing."

"So, you're going to tell him yes?"

"Yes."

She held his sad eyes and tried to reassure him. "Don't worry. He and I are like oil and water. Maybe once he realizes we don't mix, he'll change his mind, and you and I can get on with our lives."

Ryder arrived less than an hour later. Mrs. France escorted him into the parlor where Leah stood waiting.

"Good morning," he said.

Leah managed a fairly solid, "Good morning," in response.

He was no less handsome. The dark brown planes of his face were framed by the black hair pulled back in a single braid. The impeccably tailored suit and the soft blue shirt showed him to be a man of style and taste. He seemed to fill the room.

"Have you made your decision?" he asked.

"Yes. I—accept your offer."

Ryder felt pleased but noted that she looked young, uncomfortable, and scared. That didn't sit well, mainly because she had nothing to be afraid of. He was healthy, wealthy, and clean. What more could a woman like her want? "Then we should go over to the courthouse and get the papers signed."

He gestured her to the door. They found an anxious-looking Cecil waiting in the hall.

"Well?" he asked, his eyes moving questioningly between the two of them.

Leah spoke up. "I've accepted—we're on our way to the courthouse."

Cecil looked up at Ryder. "This isn't right."

"Would you rather she went to prison?"

Cecil held Ryder's eyes for a long moment, then, sighing defeatedly, turned away.

Burying her emotions, Leah grabbed up her cloak and let herself be escorted outside to where his carriage stood waiting.

The ride into town was a silent one. Leah supposed small talk was in order but found herself unable to focus on the mundane; she was too aware of him. What would life with him be like? Where would she live? Would she be allowed to come and go? So many questions, but having never been kept by a man before, she had no answers.

At the courthouse he helped her down. The heat of his flesh easily penetrated the thin fabric of her black gloves. She tried to ignore it, but the warmth lingered even after he released her hand.

The execution of the documents took only a few minutes. He signed his name in all the places the clerk indicated, then handed over a bank draft for fifteen thousand dollars. Once everything was stamped and dated, she was debt-free. All of the creditors had been taken care of and she owed no one, except Ryder Damien.

Back in the carriage, Ryder picked up the reins. It had begun drizzling while they were inside, and she looked as joyless as the gray day. "We'll go by Helene's so you can gather your things."

"And then where?"

"To my place, at least for now."

Leah's chin rose. Well, she had one of her questions answered. She'd be residing with him. "That's fine."

In spite of Leah's misgivings about her future with him, she was still grateful for his intervention and assistance. "Thank you for your help with all this. Fifteen thousand dollars is a great deal of money."

Still holding the reins, he said, "Yes, it is, but in my grandfather's day, it wouldn't have been gold."

Leah didn't understand. "What do you mean?"

"The price for a woman like you would have cost a brave like me hundreds of ponies . . ."

Leah watched his eyes lower to her mouth, and her heart began to pound. He raised his gaze to hers and she began to tremble.

"And afterward, I'd have taken you up into the mountains and made love to you until the seasons changed . . ."

Shards of heat pierced Leah. She couldn't breathe, couldn't speak.

He chuckled quite softly. "Never thought I'd see the day you were speechless."

And she remained that way as he slapped down the reins and headed them out of town.

With his heated words still echoing within, Leah looked out at the passing landscape from her seat in the carriage, but saw nothing. The force of his presence blotted out everything: the sky, the trees, the looming mountains. She didn't hear the birdsongs or the sounds of the carriage wheels on the unpaved road. Ryder Damien filled her mind, blood, and being. *"And afterward, I'd have taken you up into the mountains and made love to you until the seasons changed . . ."*

She hugged herself against the sensual chill.

"Cold?" he asked, looking away from the reins for a moment.

She shook her head. "No. Just a chill, I'm fine."

"There's usually a blanket stowed beneath your seat. Pull it out if you need to."

"Thanks." She turned her eyes back to the passing countryside.

Ryder's jaw tightened. How long would this go on? She

was acting like a defeated queen being ferried to exile. The male in him certainly hadn't spent fifteen thousand dollars for this, but the man in him began to wonder if maybe his assumptions about her had been wrong. What if she were just a decent young woman as Sam insisted and not a well-traveled adventuress? Because he didn't want to entertain that possibility, Ryder put the thoughts aside. He was not wrong.

At Helene's Leah packed her trunks silently while a sad-faced Cecil looked on. The stay had been so short that gathering her things didn't take much time.

Cecil asked, "Do you think I'll be able to visit you at least?"

Leah shrugged her shoulders as she refolded a blouse and placed it on top of the other folded items in the small trunk. "I can ask."

Cecil shook his head grimly, "I feel absolutely terrible about this."

"Don't," she answered. "There's nothing either of us could've done, so—"

She closed the trunk and snapped the lock.

He had so much despair in his eyes, she went over and gave him a long hug. "I'm going to be okay," she whispered through the tears in her throat. "You'll see."

He hugged her back with a fierceness equal to the love he felt. "Go to Sam if you need to contact me. I'll stay in Denver for a while and make sure everything goes okay with you."

"I'd like that."

They parted then, with Cecil saying, "You go on down, I'll bring your trunks."

At the bottom of the stairs stood a smug-faced Helene, and she asked Leah, "Are you all set, dear?"

"Yes, Cecil's getting the trunks."

Leah didn't see Ryder and wondered where he'd gone.

As if reading her mind, Helene said, "He's outside. We don't get along. I remind him of his past, and he reminds me of mine."

Helene then added, "I was so looking forward to seeing Louis humbled, but you were a fine substitute."

Leah stiffened.

"I'm just being truthful. Louis left me and Seth here to rot, but watching you has been a sweet revenge. You've had to sell yourself to the highest bidder, and I hope Louis is somewhere screaming in pain knowing his pretty Black bride is going to be ridden by his half-breed son."

"That's enough."

The deadly warning in Ryder's voice silenced her. Leah hadn't heard him enter; she'd been too focused on Helene's cruel words.

Helene mockingly inclined her head, then, smiling, left the room.

Ryder asked Leah, "Are you ready?"

Seeing Cecil arrive with the last of the trunks, she replied, "I—yes."

The two men faced each other for a silent moment, then Cecil said to Ryder, "I'll help you carry these out."

Leah followed.

As they drove away, Cecil watched from the porch. Leah held his eyes until they were out of sight. For the first time in her thirty-two years Leah Jane Barnett Montague had no one to rely upon but herself. Swallowing her emotions once more, she set her eyes on the road ahead.

After a long few moments of silence, she asked, "Has Helene always been such a viper?"

"Yes. She wielded a lot of power around here when I was young, but when the Faith Mine failed, so did her influence.

Poverty's forced her to take in boarders in order to make ends meet. Fancy Creole that she is, it's killing her."

"Monty told me he left that mine to you and Seth."

"It went to Seth only."

"But that isn't—"

"How about we talk about something else?"

Leah quieted, then added, "We're going to have this discussion eventually."

He looked her way. "I know, but it won't be now."

Leah had no recourse but to accept his statement.

They were driving away from town via a road less than a plate wide that seemed to be climbing toward the mountains. The wide-open landscape was sparsely populated, showing only the occasional wood cabin and crudely built structures with tar-paper roofs. The carriage rounded a bend and on the side of the road stood a small, neatly kept cabin surrounded on every side by brightly blooming spring flowers. The riot of colors was a beautiful sight on such a tumultuous day. "Who lives there?" Leah asked.

"Lady named Miss Eloise. In the old days she was a laundress, now she tends her flowers and paints."

Leah noted how his voice softened when describing the woman. "Is she a friend?"

"Yes."

"Well, her gardens are beautiful."

"I'm sure you'll get to meet her."

Leah thought she'd like that.

For the next hour and a half the ride took them through areas of tall, towering pines and meadows green with grass. Hawks and eagles circled above their heads while smaller birds challenged them shrilly. The sun came up, and for the first time, Leah saw the beauty of the land. Everything looked lush, healthy. The wildflowers seemed richer, the grasses fuller. She now understood why Cecil had talked so much about Colorado's beauty. Basking in the sunlight, the land and mountains were transformed majestically.

They arrived at the border of his land a short time later. He drove them up a long winding cinder drive lined with big pines that stood like sentinels welcoming home a king. Then up ahead, the house came into view. The flat, low-slung roof sat atop a sprawling structure made of boulders, wood, and glass. It appeared to be two floors high, and the ground around the house's perimeter had been paved with smooth flat stones. The stones gave the place a welcoming effect and added style to its overall appearance. There were well-constructed pens and sheds off to the right. Near them stood a large fenced-in corral.

Knowing that this was his home set off another round of uncertainties. What would be her role here? Where and who would she be in a year's time?

The sound of him removing her trunks from the carriage's boot brought her back to reality. She was just about to ask how long he'd live here when the door was flung open, and there stood Sam. He fussed, "It's about time you got back here. I—"

The sight of Leah in the carriage seemed to render him speechless. Leah spoke first. "Hello, Sam."

"Miss Leah?"

"Yep, it's me. How are you?"

He was staring at her like he'd never seen her before. "I'm fine. What're you doing here?"

Leah looked over her shoulder at Ryder. Would he explain or force her to do it?

Ryder answered. "She's here as a guest for a few days, Sam."

Leah hoped Sam couldn't see how much difficulty she was having smiling.

He could. "Well, come on in then," he said brightly.

He walked over and guided her down from the carriage. The smile Leah gave him was genuine. "Thanks."

He nodded, then led her inside.

Chapter 4

The interior of the house was as grand as the man who owned it. She'd never seen a house made of such magnificent stones and wood before. The ceilings seemed to be sky-high, and the wooden beams that ran freely across it were thick and gleaming. The room that she followed Sam into felt warm from the heat of the huge fire in the massive fireplace. The grate was constructed of large stacked boulders and polished rocks that narrowed into a chimney that rose up the wall to the roof.

The black-velvet furniture was surprising, but fit the wide-open interior perfectly. She wondered if he'd picked it out himself. There were well-polished end tables and glass-faced sideboards holding delicate china and expensive-looking glassware. On each side of the fireplace was a pair of elk heads adorned with large full racks. They also seemed a perfect fit. The hand-hooked rugs on the floor held the muted but vivid colors and patterns associated with the Native tribes. What caught her eye more than anything, however, were the floor-to-ceiling windows that made up one whole wall. She couldn't imagine how much it must have cost him to have so much glass shipped here.

She didn't realize she'd been staring around until she looked up and met Ryder's eyes. "I'm sorry. I know better than to stare so rudely, but this a very grand place."

"Do you like it?" Sam asked.

"I do," Leah replied truthfully.

Sam gave Ryder a triumphant look, then asked her, "Have you eaten?"

Ryder asked Leah, "Are you hungry?"

"Maybe just something light. A sandwich?"

Sam nodded with a twinkle in his eyes.

Ryder said, "Come. I'll show you your room."

Leaving her cloak and muff with Sam, Leah followed Ryder around to the back of the house to a large open room. There were rugs spread out on the floor, and, like the other rooms she'd passed, this one also had a huge fireplace. Centering the room stood a big bed covered by a beautiful Indian-designed quilt. The bed and a stately armoire with a carved face were the only furnishings.

"I'll get Sam to see about more furniture."

"That isn't necessary. This is fine."

In fact, it was more than she'd expected, really. She hadn't imagined she'd have a room of her own. The tall wide windows looked out over rolling acres of forest.

"For now, you can place all your things in my room."

"I don't mind living out of my trunks for a while."

"I do."

Again, Leah wondered where this would lead. "If you want me in your room, you should say so."

"I want you in my room, but I can wait."

Heat swept over Leah, a familiar, breath-stealing heat.

He told her, "Store what you can in the armoire, if you wish. Sam will take the rest to my room."

That said, he left, and Leah let out her pent-up breath.

Leah was unpacking her gowns and suits and hanging them in the large armoire when Sam came in with her sandwich and a frosty glass of lemonade on a tray.

"How're you coming with your unpacking?" he asked, placing her plate on top of the fireplace's empty mantel.

"This armoire can almost hold all my gowns. He wants me to have the rest taken to his room. Once I have furniture, I'll move everything back."

Leah heard herself babbling, but couldn't help it. She had no idea how much Sam knew about her circumstances, but she didn't have it within her to explain it to him, at least not presently. What must he think of her if he did know the details?

His next words did much to reassure her. "You're among friends here, Miss Leah. I certainly don't condone Ryder's methods, but you couldn't go to prison."

So, he was aware of the bargain she'd made. Leah's lips tightened with emotion. "I know."

"I'll let you finish up. I'll be in the kitchen starting dinner if you need anything."

"Thanks."

He smiled and exited.

Leah ate her lunch seated on one of the wide window seats. With only the silence and her own thoughts for company, she began to relax for the first time since leaving the courthouse. It came to her that she needed to place her fears behind her and face the truth. This situation could be as bad or as pleasant as she made it. Now, if someone had told her that she would be bought and paid for, and have her innocence taken by a man she barely knew, she'd have checked to see if their drink had been spiked, yet here she sat on the verge of just that. He thought her an adventuress, but how would he react when he learned the truth? Would he be ashamed of himself for slandering her so? Leah didn't know the answers, but gleaned a measure of satisfaction knowing he'd eventually have to eat crow.

Done eating, Leah gathered up her lunch dishes and left the room to find Sam. In reality she supposed she should be looking for Ryder, but knew time with him would come soon enough.

Down the hallway an open door showed her a formally furnished dining room, complete with an elaborate chandelier and expensive-looking table and chairs. Leah knew being nosy wasn't polite, but curiosity drew her to tiptoe in farther. The interior's size and elegance rivaled anything she'd seen back East. The beautiful curtains were as snowy as the covering on the long table, with its carved legs. She wondered how often he entertained and who his friends might be. She also tried to imagine herself seated at one end of the table while he sat opposite her at the head. Would people whisper about her being his live-in whore? Leah hastily turned her mind away. Leaving the silent room, she continued her walk to the kitchen.

Another open door showed her what appeared to be his office. The walls were paneled with dark wood upon which shelves upon shelves of books rested. She hadn't had time to wonder about his education, but if all the books were any indication, he'd had a fine one.

A door down the hallway that circled back to the front of the house led to a room that held only one item: the grandest piano she had ever seen. She wondered if it were merely a showpiece or if someone in the household actually played. The beautiful gleaming instrument bore only a faint resemblance to the old out-of-tune piano sitting back home at the Swan. Leah left the room and made a mental note to ask Sam about it.

The kitchen turned out to be on the end of the house opposite her room. As she entered, Sam looked up and grinned.

"You found me, I see." He was plucking a fat chicken.

"Yes I did," she said, helping herself to a seat atop a tall stool by the door and looking around. Like the rest of the house, the kitchen was well-appointed and large. The stove and other fixtures looked fairly new, and there were enough cupboards positioned on the walls to make a cook think she'd died and gone to heaven. "I like your kitchen."

"Only the best," he pointed out, scanning his domain. "Did you take a peek at the rest of the house?"

Leah chuckled. "And here I was telling myself being nosy wasn't polite."

"Nothing nosy about wanting to know the lay of the land. I'll have Ryder give you a real tour when he gets back."

"Where's he now?"

"Out looking for signs of the elk king." Sam turned the chicken over and began plucking the back.

"The elk king?"

"Yep, biggest elk around these parts. Antlers like tree branches, stands almost tall as a man. Ryder's been after him a long time. Only problem, and Ryder won't admit this—elk's smarter than he is. Only way he's going to bring that elk down is if he convinces the King to turn the gun on himself."

Leah chuckled.

"It's the truth," Sam swore. "Every year he chases that elk, and every year it gets away."

Sam looked up, and said, "It's good to hear you laugh."

Leah lowered her eyes.

"Long as you're here, everything will be all right."

Leah didn't know if she believed him, but she did believe in his sincerity. "So, when will he return?"

"Probably not until dinner. Said he wants you to dress."

Leah's chin rose.

"Don't like taking orders, do you?" Sam asked.

Leah met his eyes. "No."

"Neither do I. You'll be good for him."

She didn't want to be anything for him. "We'll see."

"Chicken okay with you?"

She nodded.

"Squash?"

Leah found his efforts to please touching. "Yes, Sam. Whatever you feed me will be fine."

"You sure? Don't want to fix something you don't like."

She grinned and shook her head. "I'll be pleased by whatever it is as long as its not rhubarb. I'm allergic."

"Now see, you needed to tell me that. I don't like rhubarb either, but if I'd made a pie or something it would've gone to waste."

She shook her head again and slid down off the stool. "I'm going to take a walk. What time is dinner?"

"Five sharp. Don't get yourself lost."

"I won't, and when I get back, I'll dress for dinner."

Sam smiled his approval.

She was almost out the door when she remembered. She turned back to ask, "Sam, does anyone really play that beautiful piano I saw?"

He nodded. "Yep. Ryder does."

A surprised Leah left him to his pots and pans.

Outside the air was warm and the sky bright. Leah stopped for a moment to bask in the heat of the sun on her face. She hadn't felt the sun so intensely since last summer's slide into fall. How warm did it get here? she wondered. Were the seasons as sharply defined as they'd been back home? She had no answers, however, so she began to walk. Sam's advice and common sense dictated she stay within sight of the house until she learned her way around, so she held to that.

Her wandering steps took her down near the pens. In them were pigs and chickens, a thick-coated ram and two playful black-and-white goat kids. She watched their antics for a moment, taking time out to scan the peaceful pastoral surroundings. If one could set the ocean somewhere nearby, the spot would be perfect.

Leah headed off once more; this time on a quest to see just how far she could walk and not lose sight of the house. By the time she had her answer she'd walked a good thirty minutes and was standing on a tree-covered bluff looking down at the house below. Because of her hiking and climbing, the hem of her skirt was caked with dirt and mud, she'd lost the little spool heel on one of her fancy city shoes, her hair was a mess, but she felt wonderful. The air was clear as a bell and scented with the smells of earth and pine. She couldn't remember how long it had been since she'd explored a stand of woods. Had she been thirteen years of age or fourteen? Her memory was fuzzy, but she did remember being forbidden to join her gaggle of male companions on adventure treks after she'd gotten her first cycle. Reba explained that Leah could no longer jump off cliffs or search the woods for arrowheads or race around now that she was a young lady. At the time, Leah was convinced Cecil had had a hand in her being reined in. Only as she got older did she realize it had been done for own good.

Now, she was a female full grown and she planned on exploring forests, kicking up piles of dead leaves, and catching her hair on branches anytime she chose. She liked it up here. Surrounded by nothing but the sky and the trees, she felt insulated from the tribulations plaguing her life.

This was a perfect place for silence and reflection. She pledged then and there to come back to this spot as often as she could.

The positioning of the sun in the sky told her it was time to head for the house. Dinner would be served shortly, and she still had a half an hour's walk back. It was a bit awkward trying to walk on a shoe with no heel, but it helped that the path was downhill. At least she thought it helped until she hit a slick patch of moss and found herself on her backside sliding down the slippery incline at a fairly good clip. The ride took her down and around, over rocks and roots. Watching everything around her go flying by so quickly was thrilling, exhilarating, scary. She found herself screaming with joyful terror until she reached level ground again and came to a thudding stop. Still laughing hysterically, Leah threw back her head and froze. Towering above her sat Ryder Damien mounted atop the biggest horse she'd ever seen. He did not look pleased.

With as much dignity as a mud-covered woman could command, Leah slowly got to her feet. Her attempts to brush her skirt free of the twigs and forest litter made little difference to her overall bedraggled appearance, but it gave her something to do beside look up into his stony face. "Hello," she said.

"You scared the hell out of me. I thought you were in trouble."

A guilty Leah lowered her eyes. He must think her mad. "I—my apologies. I slipped, and next I knew I was on a carnival ride."

She could see him scanning her mud-covered shoes, bird-nest hair, and dirt-smudged face.

He asked, "Is that why you were screaming?"

"Yes, it was the surprise I think."

Ryder shook his head. Had he inadvertently bought himself a hellion? "What're you doing out here in the first place?"

"I was taking a walk."

"Some walk," he quipped. He took a moment to survey her grimy appearance again. "If I wasn't sure Sam would tan my hide for being late for dinner, I'd make you walk back because you're far too dirty to ride up here with me."

"Then I'll walk."

"Not in those shoes you can't."

Leah looked down at her feet, then back up at him. He reached down his hand. The tight-lipped Leah took hold of it and let herself be placed behind him on the horse. As much as she wanted to stand and argue with him, it wouldn't accomplish anything, and she didn't wish to be late for dinner either.

She was surprised to feel nothing beneath her but a soft blanket. "Where's the saddle?"

"Cheyenne don't need saddles to control their horses," he pointed out succinctly. "Hold on so you don't fall off."

Leah would much rather have nestled up to a thorny rosebush, but wrapping her arms around his waist, she did as she was told.

"Closer," he said.

Behind him Leah snarled silently. She hiked her skirts up her thighs a bit, then moved until she was flush against his back. Once she was settled, he turned the horse's head and they proceeded forward.

Because of the woody terrain the horse couldn't really travel any faster than Leah could have on foot. That distressed her because it meant it would be a while before she could turn Ryder loose. Her skin burned everywhere their bodies touched: her arms, her breasts, the insides of her upper thighs. A less hardy woman would have already swooned.

Ryder admittedly liked the feel of her weight against

him. Even as dirty and mussed as she was, he found pleasure in her holding him. In reality he should be lecturing her on her antics back there. One, she had no business prowling around alone, and two, she could have broken her leg or her fool neck sliding down those rocks like a ten-year-old boy. He'd been only a few yards away when he heard her screams pierce the forest's silence, and he knew instantaneously that it was she. Filled with panic, he'd turned his stallion and picked his way through the trees as quickly as they could go. He'd been standing in the clearing trying to get a fix on her position when she landed at his feet like she'd been shot out of a cannon. Her sudden appearance had frozen him with his mouth open, and then to realize it was indeed she under all that mud and slime, it took all he had not to laugh out loud.

He took a moment to look back at her, all but hidden behind him. "You play in the mud often?"

Leah met his eyes and saw the humor there. "Only when I have the opportunity."

"You're not going to be a conventional mistress, I'm thinking."

"Is that what I'm to be?"

"Yes, unless you know a better term."

She did but none were very flattering however, so she said, "Mistress is fine, I suppose. I take it I'm not your first."

"No, but then neither am I yours."

Leah tightened.

"Oh, stop acting so offended. I'm not your first, and you know it."

Leah told him, "Just pay attention to what you're doing before you run the horse into a tree."

Ryder turned back again. "What are you so mad about?"

"Nothing. I'm very happy being called a whore."

"No one called—"

"You may as well have," she responded frostily. "You've

been looking down your kingly nose at me since the moment we met. I'm not some cheap dockside whore willing to be bedded for a few coins." Leah didn't realize how angry she'd become until she told him. "Stop this horse."

Ryder complied. Before he could turn around to see what she was about, she slid from the horse's back and began to storm away; or at least she tried to. The uneven heel gave her a comical up-and-down gait that he had to keep from chuckling at.

Leah knew it would probably take her a month to get back to the house walking this way, but she didn't care. She uttered an unladylike curse. Damn him!

"You know, it's going to take you a while to get home in those shoes."

"Go away."

"Look, you're going to make us both late for dinner."

Leah didn't break stride.

"Why don't you tell me about yourself, and then I'll know the truth."

"And give you more ammunition to shoot me down? We've already had this conversation on the train, remember? You'd formed your opinion back then." She stopped and looked up at him. "You know nothing about me," she whispered fiercely. "Nothing."

The emotion she displayed touched him. "You're right. And if you say you didn't marry Louis for his money, I believe you."

Leah shook her head, "This isn't about what you believe. For the past few days you believed I was a whore. Surely you haven't changed your mind that quickly."

His lips thinned. He didn't like hearing himself described so accurately. Could he have been wrong about her, or was she just that good of an actress? "I'm sorry I offended you."

Leah kept walking.

Still riding slowly beside her he said, "You're determined to be stubborn."

"I'm determined I don't like you, is all."

"Are you always so fiery?"

"Only with ill-mannered men named Ryder Damien."

He looked up to the heavens for guidance. She was certainly giving him his comeuppance. The only person allowed to flay him this way was Sam, and now her. In truth, be she virgin or whore, he didn't care as long as she agreed to be his. He sensed that he'd genuinely hurt her feelings, though, but was at a loss as to how to fix it. It wasn't something he admitted easily. "I rarely apologize for something I've done, but I'm making an attempt now . . ."

The quiet strength in his voice melted away some of her anger even as her mind fought against it. Unable to stop herself, she turned to face him. His dark eyes were open and sincere.

Ryder extended his hand. A silent Leah looked at it a moment, then grabbed hold, and he pulled her back atop the horse's back. They both knew the issue hadn't been resolved and that there would be more confrontations just like this one, but for now they shared an unspoken determination to let it be.

Sam was waiting outside the back door when they rode up. Leah didn't want him to see the crossness in her face but he would have had to be blind not to.

Sam's face was concerned, "I see you two met up."

Leah slid down off the horse without waiting for assistance. "Yes, we did."

Sam's eyes went wide as he took in the full effect of her appearance." What happened to you?"

Ryder drawled, "Playing in the mud."

"I was not," she shot back.

Sam was still staring at her as if she'd just been transformed into a frog, so Leah asked, "Where can I heat some water, I need to wash up before dinner."

"I'll say you do," Sam said in amazed tones. "Look at your hair."

"Sam," Leah said warningly. "The water please."

"Sure, sure," he replied. "But you're not going inside in those muddy shoes. Take them off."

Leah cut him a look. Bobbing up and down on her uneven heels, she made her way over to the hitching post. Using it for balance, she removed the broken shoe and flung it to the heavens. After doing the same with its muddy mate, she stormed into the house in her stockinged feet.

There was silence as the two men stared after her. Sam looked up at Ryder, and offered sagely, "She's going to be a handful."

Ryder's eyes glowed with excitement and challenge. "Yes, she is."

In her room, Leah paced while she waited for word on her water. Ryder's smug words kept coming back to taunt her. She was almost looking forward to being in his bed just so she could watch him squirm when he realized she was a virgin and had to apologize.

A knock on the door drew her attention. "Come in."

Sam took one look at the temper on her face, and scolded, "You save that glare for him, missy. I'm the one who made you chocolate cake for dessert."

Leah couldn't keep her smile from peeking out. "I'm sorry. You're not the one I should be snapping at."

"Made you mad, did he?"

"Like a bunch of riled hornets."

Sam smiled. "Come on with me, and I'll show you where you can wash."

Leah grabbed up a robe and followed him out.

He led her down the hall and opened the door to a most amazing bathing room.

She assumed all the pipes and spigots meant there was indoor plumbing, which was by no means common in the homes of the folks she knew back home. There was a shower also, and just when she got over the shock of that, she saw the large red-and-gold tub holding court on the far wall.

Exotic didn't come close as a description. Leah walked closer, drawn by the odd power it seemed to exude.

"Ryder won it off a French count in a card game in San Francisco. Had to have it shipped home."

Leah couldn't resist running a light hand over the gold fleur-de-lis curling up from the edge of each corner. "Does he ever use it?"

"Rarely."

"May I sometimes?"

"I don't see why not."

Leah looked around again at all the plumbing work. "Who did all this?"

"He did. He's an engineer, you know."

Leah was surprised. "No, I didn't."

"Yep. Got his college degree from a mining and engineering school in Minnesota. It's where I met him."

Leah noted that Sam spoke of him with the pride and affection usually reserved for family. "You're very proud of him, aren't you?"

He nodded. "I am. He's made his own way, and had a big enough heart to invite me to come along. I never regretted saying yes."

Leah let the words sink in. Was he trying to tell her she hadn't made a bad decision by agreeing to Ryder's offer? Leah had no real way of knowing. What she did know was that she was beginning to itch from all the dirt and grime, and the sooner she washed, the better. After getting Sam to explain how the spigots worked, she shooed him out, threw the small brass bolt on the door, and stripped off her nasty clothes.

She opted for a shower as there wasn't time for the tub. Leah turned on the spigots. It took her a moment to get the temperature adjusted, but once she did, she let the hot stream melt away the day. After a few more moments of bliss she washed up hastily because she had no idea how long the hot water would last. She assumed the boiler Sam told her about heated only a finite amount of water, and she didn't want Ryder grousing because she'd exhausted the supply.

Back in her room, Leah scanned the gowns in the armoire. Should she be conservative or dazzling? Since he'd already pegged her as a scarlet woman, she decided she might as well look like one and chose dazzling. She and Cecil had gotten into an argument over this gown in the dressmaker's shop back in Boston. Leah had agreed with him on the dress's beauty but *twenty-seven dollars*? The price was far too extravagant for her taste. He'd purchased it anyway.

Leah wished for a mirror so she could really see how she looked because the gown made her feel so unlike herself. She felt sophisticated and worldly in the bare-shouldered creation, not like a small-town girl playing mistress, which was the reality. The low-cut décolletage was far more daring than she was accustomed to, but she'd seen dresses in the Boston shops that were far more scandalous, ones that made her own seem prim. As long as she didn't bend forward too far, she had no fear of exposing herself, but having never worn a dress like this before, she could only cross her fingers and pray everything would stay put.

With the aid of her hand mirror, she put a bit of rouge on

her cheeks and a dab of paint on her lips. She'd braided her hair French style and twisted the ends into a coil that rested on the base of her neck. Giving it one last pat, she slipped into her fancy pumps, picked up a black-silk shawl for her shoulders, and set out to face the evening.

She saw Ryder coming up the hall. He was dressed in a well-tailored black suit and white shirt, and his hair was loose. She thought no man had a right to be so magnificently made.

He looked at her in the black dress, barely able to wonder if she was still mad. He'd thought her beautiful before, but he had no words to describe her loveliness now. If this were a children's tale, he'd be the prince and she his princess. The gown, her hair, the subtle paint on her mouth all conspired to leave him a bit breathless. He wanted to make her the evening's appetizer, main course, and dessert. He said, "I came to meet you. I didn't know if you knew where to go."

"Thank you," Leah replied. "I didn't know where to go."

"We're eating on the porch. This way."

He soundlessly extended his elbow. Leah met his eyes for a moment, then placed her hand on his arm.

The porch turned out to be a large glassed-in room that flared off the back of the house. The tall ceiling-to-floor windows gave yet another spectacular view of the countryside. She imagined it offered a stunning look at the setting sun. The high beamed ceilings and black-and-gray stones were evident here also. The heads of two bears stared down from the wall above the mantel of the fireplace. The fierce eyes and ferocious teeth seemed to view her warningly.

Sam was there waiting for them, and he'd set up a small table and two chairs near the windows. On the table lay a white tablecloth, silverware, china, and silver-topped serving platters. "You look very lovely, Miss Leah."

"Thank you, Sam. You set a lovely table," Leah replied genuinely.

"My pleasure. I'll be back later with your chocolate cake."

They were then left alone, and an awkwardness rose up in Leah that was so strong she had to walk over to the window and pretend to be looking out at the countryside. When she hazarded a glance over her shoulder he was standing across the room, watching her silently. She didn't want to become embroiled in another confrontation. She turned back, wishing she could read his mind.

"Think we can eat without jumping down each other's throats?" he asked her quietly.

For some reason she didn't find it surprising that he could read *her* mind. "I'd like to try."

However, she had other things on her mind too: such as his true intent. She turned and asked, "What are you really about, Ryder Damien? Was this whole bargain just a way to get back at your father?"

"If I told you no, would that matter?"

"Maybe," she confessed truthfully. She immediately wanted to snatch the word back. He'd undoubtedly use her answer as confirmation that she was indeed the kind of woman he'd accused her of being: a woman trolling for protectors. "That isn't what I meant."

"What did you mean?"

"That a man should want a woman for herself, not for what or whom she represents."

"So if I wanted you for myself, you wouldn't mind the deal we struck?"

That question caught her off guard, as did the heat that slowly spread across her senses. "I've only known you a few days, and honestly, what I've known I haven't much liked."

He gave her a rare grin. "You're hell on a man's pride."

She shrugged. "One of my charms, I suppose."

"Then stay charming and don't ever apologize for speaking the truth. It's good for me, I'm told."

He then gestured toward the table. "Shall we?"

Leah nodded and walked over. As he politely helped her with her chair, his nearness slid over her, making her think about how this night might end.

Standing behind her, Ryder could smell the faint notes of her perfume. The urge to fill his senses with the tantalizing scents tempted him, but he forced himself to back away.

They spent a few silent moments unfolding the linen napkins and placing them across their laps. Leah felt as if she were dining with a king in his palace and was as uncertain as a virgin concubine. Daring a look his way, she thought the glossy black hair falling onto his shoulders meshed perfectly with the strong line of his jaw, the proud nose and chin, and the raven black eyes. The cuffs of the pure white shirt led her eyes to his large hands with their short-clipped nails. When she looked up, his eyes were waiting.

Ryder wondered how long he'd be able to restrain himself. He had every intention of treating her with the respect she kept insisting he show, but knew it might make for a long and somewhat frustrating evening. "Pass me your plate, please."

Leah did.

Beneath the covered dishes atop the table they found slices of roast chicken, potatoes, and squash. She watched him spoon a portion of each offering onto her plate. He handed it back, then filled his own.

As he picked up his fork, she said, "We must say grace."

He searched her eyes for a moment, then set the implement down. Nodding acquiescence, he lowered his head.

The resulting silence prevailed for so long, Ryder raised his eyes once again, only to find hers waiting.

"This is your home," she pointed out quietly. "You should do the blessing."

At first, he thought she might be kidding, but when her calm didn't change, he realized she was quite serious. Caught off guard he frantically searched his mind for a suitable verse, then suddenly out of a place long buried, the words rose and he spoke them with a soft reverence.

> *"Oh Great Spirit whose voice I hear in the winds,*
> *And whose breath gives life to all the world, hear me.*
> *I am small and weak.*
> *I need your strength and wisdom."*

In the silence that followed the last word, he looked up, and a very moved Leah said, "That was inspiring."

Ryder found himself beset by both embarrassment and resentment; he hadn't prayed in years. The fact that this woman had been able to draw up a part of himself he'd turned his back on, made him unconsciously finger the medicine bag hidden beneath his clothing. "It's one of my grandmother's prayers."

Seeing his gesture, Leah wondered what hung from the string of rawhide circling his brown throat. "Is she still alive?"

"No."

The mask that closed down over his features made Leah sense there might be pain tied to his grandmother's memory, so she didn't press for more details. She turned her attention to her plate instead. "Everything looks so wonderful."

Grateful she'd changed the subject, because he didn't like speaking of Little Tears, Ryder replied easily, "Sam cooked for the Ninth. He's pretty good around a stove."

"I knew he was with the Ninth, but he never said he'd

been the cook. He did say you two met in Minnesota but not how long ago."

"We've been friends over ten years. Met him when I was going to school in Minnesota."

"He's a nice man."

"Trust him with my life."

He observed her for a moment, then asked, "Is there anyone you'd trust your life to?"

Leah didn't need to think about the answer. "Cecil's the closest thing I have to family. So it would have to be him."

From the look on his face she assumed he didn't consider her choice a good one, but Leah didn't care. The many times Leah found herself in trouble at Miss Caldwell's School, it was Cecil who caught the train and came up to try and reason with the school's board of trustees. Had it not been for his diplomatic skills, she was certain she would have been tossed out and asked never to return. She wondered how Cecil was faring.

Talking of Cecil seemed to remind both Leah and Ryder of the barriers between them. As a result, an awkward silence resettled, so they concentrated on their meals. After a while, however, the air in the room became so thick and overwhelming, Leah tried for small talk. "The windows must give a spectacular view when the sun sets."

Ryder was glad they were speaking again. "It does. Folks called me loco for putting in all this glass, but I grew up in a tar shack with no windows."

Leah paused and scanned his face. "Sounds like a hard life."

"It was, but it's in the past. I prefer to look forward."

"Except when it concerns your father."

He looked up from his plate, and drawled, "That's a good way to start another argument."

Leah winced. "My apologies. You didn't deserve such a flippant remark."

"Even if it's true?"

She didn't respond to that.

Ryder answered for her. "It's true. I do blame him for that hard life."

Leah dearly wished he'd known the Monty she'd known. Had father and son been reconciled before Monty's death, she was certain they would have benefited from the results. "He died a painful death."

"There's little sympathy here, so let's talk of other things."

Leah's chin rose. "Such as?"

He shrugged. "Where'd you go to school?"

"Miss Caldwell's Private School for Young Women of Color."

"Sounds fancy."

She forked up a bit of squash. "It was, and as a result I spent more time in Miss Caldwell's office than I did in the classroom."

He chuckled. "Why?"

"I was, as Miss Caldwell once pronounced, a walking, talking, make-trouble machine. I was held up as an example as to what a cultured, young Colored woman was *not* supposed to be."

His eyes lit up. "So, you are a hellion."

"Only when necessary. But as time there went by, I called on necessity more and more."

He decided he enjoyed her crisp New England speech. "Didn't the teachers like you?"

"They liked me fine. It was the other girls I kept bumping heads with."

"Why?"

As Leah thought back, the pain of those years resurfaced as fresh and as raw as if it were yesterday. "I was different," she said softly. "I had no legitimate father—I was poor, and my mother owned a tavern."

Ryder stared at her over his raised water goblet. "Your mother owned a *tavern?*"

"Yes. In spite of what you may think, it was quite a respectable place. It was called the Black Swan. I grew up there."

He was still staring.

Leah told him plainly, "So, we're a lot alike you and I. Both bastards."

He spit out his water.

Leah smiled at the reaction. "See what I mean about causing trouble? I know decent women aren't supposed to utter such a word, but it's who I am. Besides, I was called that most of my life."

Ryder realized she was truly an extraordinary woman. "It didn't bother you to be slurred that way?"

"Of course. Why do you think I spent so much time in Miss Caldwell's office? After a while they stopped slurring me to my face, especially the ones I gave bloody noses to, and started a more subtle campaign. They poured the chamber pots in my bed, stuck my shoes to the floor with hot tar. Someone even sneaked into my room in the middle of the night and cut off my hair. I caused such mayhem after that, I was sent home for the remainder of the term."

He looked at all that fine thick hair and tried to imagine it cut short as a child's. "Where was this place?"

"Upstate Massachusetts."

"And this was a ladies' school?"

"That's what it said on the door."

He shook his head. "How long did you attend?"

"Three years."

"And you were what age?"

"Twelve."

"Your mother must've been a very thrifty woman to be able to pay for such a school."

"She didn't. Monty did."

Once again he found himself rendered speechless. He ran his eyes over her uncommonly beautiful face. "My father waited a long time for you then."

Whether the dig was intentional or not, Leah wanted to slap him soundly. Instead she asked coolly, "So, are we even now? One nasty remark from me and one from you?"

He raised a kingly eyebrow. "Are you saying he didn't wait around for you to grow up?"

"You're intimating that he was a cradle robber, and he was not."

"Explain it to me then. Maybe if you told me the whole truth, I wouldn't jump to these conclusions."

But Leah couldn't tell him the truth, at least not about marrying his father on his deathbed. Who knew what he might do? "There's nothing to tell."

Ryder didn't believe her for a moment. Beneath her testiness, she looked downright uncomfortable, making him all the more determined to find out what she was hiding. "How long were the two of you married?"

Leah gave him the same pat answer she'd given Helene. "Not long enough."

It wasn't really an answer, and they both knew it. She could see the tightness in his jaw. Their time together this evening was well on its way to becoming confrontational. Again.

Leah eased back her chair. "Maybe I should simply go back to my room. We're like oil and water, you and I."

"More like a match and a stick of dynamite."

He held her eyes, and the dry humor reflected in them made Leah's smile peek out. "That probably is a better analogy."

Ryder found her smile warming. "Let's make a pact?"

"What type of pact?"

"To set the past aside for now and enjoy the rest of our evening."

Leah realized that it was a simple request really. She saw no reason not to agree, so she stuck out her hand. When he grasped it, the contact sang across her body like a softened current of lightning. Her first instinct was to draw away, but he held on to her gently.

Her heart beating fast, Leah watched him slowly turn her hand over and peer at her palm. Years of scrubbing floors with harsh lye soap had taken their toll. She'd never have the smooth soft hands of a gentlewoman, unless red chapped skin somehow became fashionable.

Ryder found the scars and calluses both surprising and disturbing. It was the hand of a woman who'd worked hard, maybe her whole life.

Still holding her hand, he looked into her eyes, and asked, "Scrubbing?"

Leah nodded. She wanted to draw back so he wouldn't see her cracked nails or the work-toughened skin.

"They're healing, it appears."

She stammered, "I—probably because I haven't had to scrub . . ." Her voice trailed off.

His eyes found hers again. "Who are you really, Leah?"

The room seemed infinitely warmer to Leah. She knew without a doubt that this was not a man she could lie to much longer. There was something in his eyes that demanded truth, and her ability to stand firm was slowly beginning to crumble. "I am who I say I am. Leah Barnett Montague."

"And you're not just some actress Cecil Lee hired to play the part to get at Louis's estate?"

"No, I knew your father most of my life. I loved him, he loved me."

Leah had answered him truthfully. He continued to scan her hand though, and the resulting sensations made it hard for her to think.

He slowly worried his thumb over the calluses ridging

her palm. The touch was as gentle as Leah imagined a caress would be.

"I'll get you some aloe," he offered. "It should help them heal."

Even though she had no idea what aloe might be, she nodded nervously, then asked, "May I have my hand back now?"

He observed her for a few seconds more, then released her.

Leah's heart was beating so fast she had to close her eyes and take a deep breath in order to regain her calm. Ryder Damien, with his long hair, dark eyes and Rocky Mountain physique was far too vivid a man for a simple coastal girl like herself.

There was a definite tension in the room now. Unlike the earlier moments, this wasn't rooted in anger or misunderstanding but in the age-old attraction between a man and a woman. The current arcing back and forth was thick enough to touch. Leah wanted to pick up her skirts and run. She felt as skittish as a fish near a baited hook.

Ryder sat back in his chair and tried to figure her out. On one hand she looked as sensual as a sultan's concubine, but on the other hand she was acting as if she'd never been touched before. He could still feel the trembling in her hand when he held it just now. It had been like stroking a virgin, but Leah Montague wasn't a virgin; widows couldn't be virgins. Could they? What was she hiding? He felt as if the answer to the puzzle lay right under his nose. Maybe he was simply too close to see it, he theorized, but given enough time he was certain he could unearth the truth.

Sam walked in and asked with a grin, "How was the meal, Miss Leah?"

Leah was *so* glad to see him. "Everything was fine, Sam, just fine."

He came over and picked up their cleaned plates, "You want that chocolate cake now? Got some ice cream, too."

"I'd love some."

Sam looked pleased. "Let me get rid of these plates, and I'll be right back."

The cake and ice cream were good. "This is heavenly," Leah gushed softly as she ate from the wedge of the heavily frosted cake.

Ryder thought the happiness on her face far sweeter than any dessert. He found himself wondering if her kisses would be sweet as well. Even though Ryder had no true recollection of what his father looked like, he suddenly found himself imagining her in the arms of an old man, kissing him, being caressed by him, making love to him. He pushed his cake away.

Leah looked up from her plate just in time to see the sour look on his face. "Is something wrong?" she asked.

He bored her with eyes so foreboding, she unconsciously drew back.

Ryder lied. "No."

Leah knew he wasn't being truthful; the dark clouds gathered over his face were rooted in something. She thought back over the last few moments in an attempt to determine if she'd said anything that might have brought on the abrupt change of mood, but came up with nothing.

Ryder sensed she didn't believe him. He looked at her velvety black skin, those expressive feline eyes, and that sirenlike mouth, and knew that the man he hated most in the world had had her first.

Unable to get past that reality, Ryder set down his fork. Tight-lipped, he pushed back from the table and stood. "I'm sorry. I just remembered a report I was supposed to finish tonight. I'll see you tomorrow."

Leah sat there speechless. Confusion warred with hurt

and anger. Had he done this purposely? Had he made her get all dressed up just to treat her this way? In the end, she told herself it didn't matter. Her chilly response acted as armor. "Then by all means, go and finish your report."

"Feel free to finish your cake." "

Leah stood. "No thanks. I've lost my appetite."

For a moment, as their eyes held, she thought she saw regret reflected in his, but that didn't matter either. His leaving did, and the sooner the better.

He inclined his head in a silent good-bye.

When he left her alone, Leah let out a sigh of regret. She didn't know any other way to describe her feelings; she'd actually enjoyed parts of the evening, but something had set him off, and she'd be willing to bet it had to do with Monty. His memory seemed destined to surface and cause conflicts no matter how hard they both tried to pretend otherwise.

Hearing someone entering the room behind her, she turned and saw Sam. He had what looked to be regret in his eyes. "He's gone I see."

Leah set aside her emotion. "Yes. I'm going to my room. He said he'd see me tomorrow."

"Then will you stay and finish your cake with me?"

The plea in his eyes touched her, melting away her anger. "Of course."

While Leah finished her cake, Sam kept up a steady flow of conversation. She found his stories about his years with the Ninth fascinating enough to make her forget all about the maddening Ryder Damien.

"Yep," Sam was saying, "spent a whole lot of years up there in Montana. Terrible winters, just terrible. After one blizzard, found one of the mules standing up frozen solid in his stall. We ate him of course," he added grinning.

"But of course," Leah replied with a smile.

Yes, she liked Sam Waters. He had an easy way of look

ing at life that seemed to contrast sharply with Ryder's dark
view.

"You know," Sam pointed out, "even though the Tenth
gets a lot of recognition, the Ninth had its share of adven-
tures and decorations too."

"Where were they stationed?"

"Oh, Montana, Kansas, Texas, Oklahoma. We rebuilt
Fort Davis down in Texas, you know."

Amused, Leah replied, "No, I didn't."

"Well, we did. We chased bandits, Kickapoos, Apaches.
Guarded lumber trains and wagon trains. Put up telegraph
wires, cleared roads. You name it we did it. Served under
Major Albert P. Morrow."

"You sound mighty proud of the time you were a soldier."

"Mighty proud. Only place in this country where a Black
man is allowed to be a man. Of course, like the Tenth, we
got cast-off supplies and broken-down horses, but we had
no control over that. Instead we concentrated on being the
best unit in the West. And we were. The Tenth'll probably
argue, but hey, we were the best."

When he was done boasting, he looked her way, and
asked, "What did you two fight about?"

Leah knew he was referring to Ryder. "Nothing actually.
One moment we were eating cake and the next he had thunderclouds all over his face. I got all dressed up for nothing it
seems."

"Well, he can be a touch slow at times, but—" He paused
dramatically.

Leah looked over. "But what?"

"He's never brought a woman up to Sunrise before."

"Sunrise?"

"That's what this ranch's called."

The implications of that floored her for a moment.
"Never?"

"Never. That's why I looked so surprised to find you getting out of the buggy."

Leah couldn't help herself. She had to ask a second time. "Never?"

"Ever."

She had no idea what to do with such a startling piece of information.

"Pretty surprised, are you?"

"Very surprised, Sam."

"Means you're special."

"It means he paid fifteen thousand dollars for me. I don't wish to be special. Besides, he and I will never resolve the issue of his father."

"Give him time. Like I said, he's a touch slow sometimes, but he usually makes up for it once he's got everything figured out."

"Has he told you how long I'm going to be here?"

Sam shook his head. "You might want to ask him."

"I suppose, but it won't be this evening. I've had enough of him for one day."

"He can be prickly, but he has a good heart. Just needs a good woman."

Leah looked at him and snorted. "Now I know it's time for me to go to my room. A good woman?"

Leah couldn't help herself—she laughed. "Sam, are you matchmaking?"

He placed his hand over his heart. "Never let it be said that I've ever lied to a beautiful woman. Yes, ma'am, I am. You see, I'm gettin' old, and Ryder's going to need someone to look after him once I'm gone."

"Hire a nurse."

"Not when you'll do so much better."

"If I was his woman, he'd need an undertaker, not a nurse."

Sam howled with glee. "Yes, ma'am, you'll do just fine."

An outdone Leah grinned and finished off the last bites of her cake. She could just imagine herself married to the Dark Lord of the Mountains. They'd spend the entire time hurling lightning bolts at one another; scaring the children, and frightening the wildlife.

Leah did like Sam though.

Hours later, alone in his bedroom, Ryder stood before the large windows staring out at the night. The only light and sound came from the wood burning in the fireplace. Leah was on his mind. Why couldn't she have been a woman he'd met by happenstance? Why did she have to be his father's woman?

When Ryder heard Sam come in, he didn't turn around. "She okay?"

"Yes," Sam said tightly.

"I sense disapproval in your tone, old man."

"You didn't do right by her tonight."

"I know," Ryder replied quietly. It was a large admission from a man who rarely faced his shortcomings.

"Why are you treating her so badly?"

"Because I want her and can't have her."

"Why not?"

"Would you want a woman who'd lain with your enemy first?"

"Depends on the woman. Take her for who she is now, not who she might've been."

Ryder turned back to the night. "Easier said than done."

"I agree, but for a woman like that . . ." Sam's voice trailed off as if the statement spoke for itself.

"Even for a woman like that."

There was silence then.

Sam broke it a few moments later. "Well, I'm going on to bed. She's too nice to be treated like trash, Ryder."

Ryder didn't respond.

"See you in the morning," Sam told him.

"Good night, old man."

Once he was alone again, Ryder thought back on Sam's words. *Take her for who she is now, not who she might've been.* If only it were that simple. On one hand he wanted to toss aside his past and pursue her fully, but on the other hand, to do so would be to betray himself. Life had been so orderly before her arrival. Now, all Ryder could think about was a black-diamond beauty named Leah Barnett Montague and that she'd slept with his father.

Chapter 5

That next morning Leah awakened to the smell of coffee. As she lay in bed, looking up at the faint traces of dawn on the ceiling, she thought about last night. Was this her destiny, to be tossed about like a small ship on his moody seas? One moment he'd been tenderly caressing her hand, and the next cold as ice. It was not an auspicious beginning.

Leah got out of bed. After washing and dressing, she went to greet the day.

"Morning, Sam," she called as she entered the kitchen. "Coffee smells wonder—" Her words faded at the sight of the shirtless Ryder coming in the back door. He was carrying a load of kindling and the hard brown muscles of his arms and chest were dewed and shiny. Leah forced her eyes away from his chiseled physique.

"Good morning," he said emotionlessly. He set the wood in the box by the stove. There was a blue-checked flannel

123

shirt hanging on the peg on the back door. He took the shirt down and put it on. "Sam's out getting eggs."

Not certain how they were supposed to interact after the way they'd parted last evening, Leah asked, "Where does Sam keep the cups for coffee?"

He opened a cupboard near his head and handed her a painted teacup.

Leah looked skeptically at the dainty little thing. "Do you have anything larger?"

He reached back into the cupboard and extracted a much larger one, one any coffee lover would be proud to fill. "Large enough?"

"Yes."

Avoiding his eyes, she took it from his hand, then filled it from the pot warming on the stove. The curls of smoke rose up fragrant and familiar. She blew on it a moment and then took a tentative first sip. It was terrible! "Who made this?" she asked before she could call the words back.

He raised an eyebrow. "I did."

"Is there another pot? I'd like to make my own."

Ryder had never met so frank a woman. "I make decent coffee."

"For whom, your horses?"

He stared. In fact, he was still staring when Sam walked in. Sam took in the stormy look on Ryder's face and the determination on Leah's, and asked Ryder, "What did I miss?"

Ryder said coolly. "She was just telling me how bad my coffee is."

In response, Sam grinned, then cackled, "I knew she was smart the day we met her. Mornin', Miss Leah."

"Morning, Sam. Do you have another coffeepot?"

"Sure do. Ryder, get the little lady that other pot in that sideboard behind you."

Leah could see how displeased Ryder looked but she

wasn't going to start her days drinking swill, not even for fifteen thousand dollars.

Sam began cracking eggs into a bowl. "I've been telling him for years about that stuff he calls coffee. Ain't another person alive can drink it. Hogs don't even like it, and you know they'll eat steel wool."

Leah's snort of laughter slipped out.

Ryder said frostily, "Call me when the food's ready."

"Sure will," Sam promised.

Ryder left.

In his office, Ryder waited for Sam to finish preparing breakfast by staring moodily out of the windows. The sun was coming up, and the fog that always held sway at this time of day covered the landscape with its softness. He'd planned on starting the day by having breakfast and checking the stock market figures in the two newspapers delivered to his office in Denver yesterday, not by having his coffee-making abilities maligned. His fifteen-thousand-dollar bank draft had purchased her opinions too, he supposed, opinions as frank as she was beautiful.

Beautiful women were supposed to be docile, even-tempered things—not complex riddles. They certainly weren't supposed to criticize his coffee.

When Leah appeared in the doorway with a steaming cup of coffee in her hand, he turned her way. He was thinking that no adventuress had the right to look so fetching yet so prim and proper. She was wearing a high-necked white blouse and full navy blue skirt.

"Will you taste this?" Leah asked, holding out the cup. His skeptical face made her add, "I just want to know if it's strong enough for your liking?"

Wary, he took the offered cup from her hand. "You planning on taking over the coffee-making duties?"

"Maybe."

He observed her for a moment, then took a short sip. "Not bad." In reality, it was quite good.

"Back at the Swan, I made the morning coffee," she explained. "The men always asked for more, so I suppose they found it decent."

Ryder had no trouble telling the difference between his pot and hers—hers had flavor. The lure in her made his sour mood fade like the fog. "If you promise to make coffee like this each morning, I promise never to make coffee again."

The light of humor in his eyes made Leah smile shyly in spite of herself. "You have a deal."

"May I keep this one?"

"Yes."

He set the cup on the windowsill. "I thought back East women like you drank tea."

"I do, but not first thing in the morning. I need something more substantial to start my day."

The interest she saw in his dark eyes made her wary, so to cover her uncertainty she turned to scan the titles on some of the neatly aligned books filling the dark wood shelves. Most had to do with mining, engineering, and geology. "I don't think I've ever seen so many books in one person's home."

"I'm glad there's something about me that impresses you."

Leah glanced over her shoulder at him and felt her senses touched by the deep tones of his voice and by whatever else it was that made her susceptible to him. She didn't know how to respond. The unresolved issues that had caused yesterday's disastrous dinner still clung to her. "There are probably many things about you I'd be impressed by—if circumstances were different."

"You mean if there were no bargain between us."

She nodded, refusing to meet his eyes.

"If there were no bargain, would you stay?"

Leah met his eyes. Although she didn't know very much about him, she sensed the honesty in his question. "I don't know. You're handsome, intelligent, but—I don't know you well enough to say, yes, I'd be your lover if there was no bargain."

He appreciated her honesty. "Shall I court you like a gentleman then?"

She began to shake inside.

He slowly walked over to where she stood. The intensity in his eyes was plain enough to touch. Although the power in him wafted around her like thick sweet smoke, she still had to know. "Why'd you leave me the way you did last evening?"

Ryder heard the ghost of hurt in her voice. He knew his abrupt departure had upset her; he hadn't known she'd been hurt by it. "Hurting you wasn't my intent."

She looked away. He wasn't supposed to know her feelings had been bruised.

He reached out and gently turned her face so he could see into her dark eyes. "My demons got the best of me. I'm sorry."

"If you don't let go of the past, it will consume you."

"I know, but it's easy to say, hard to do."

Leah watched his eyes linger over her mouth and her heart started to pound.

She raised her gaze back to his, and the parts of herself that had never experienced a man's desire began to tremble. When he lowered his mouth to hers, she didn't protest; she let the warmth of his lips whisper over hers like a soft breeze. He repeated it, and then as the kiss deepened he brought her body closer, letting his solid nearness fill her, tempt her, dazzle her.

After a few long moments, he pulled away. Her eyes were closed. When they opened they were hazy with the first buds of passion.

Smiling down gently, Ryder worried his brown thumb over her slightly parted lips, savoring their softness. "You have a gorgeous mouth . . ."

Unable to resist, he kissed her again; this time deeper, his hands moving slowly over her blouse-covered back as he held her against him. He husked out against her ear, "I'd rather seduce you, than court you . . ."

Leah swore she was at the center of a lightning storm. His kisses now moving over her jaw and the soft trembling skin beneath her chin sent sparks all over the room. He thought her experienced in this, but each touch of his lips was new; so new her virgin's body began to respond with its own will, overriding her mind's efforts to remain in control. She wanted his kiss, wanted to know all the things he could teach her even if there was no commitment for the future.

Shocked by that revelation, Leah wanted to pull back so she could think, catch her breath, but the woman inside wouldn't move. He brushed warm lips against her ear, asking hotly, "Shall I court you . . . or seduce you?"

Leah melted right then and there. Her legs were like pudding, her mind no better.

"Shall I take you to the theater like a gentleman . . . or teach you how to ride a Cheyenne warrior . . ."

Leah groaned. While his kisses continued to ripen her lips, his hands were very slowly learning the curves and shape of her body. Under his coaxing palms her nipples were rising, hardening. The novel sensations arched her back, and a dewy warmth began to spread between her thighs.

On the edges of his consciousness, Ryder could hear Sam calling them for breakfast from the kitchen, but found this meal far more tantalizing. The feel of her rising to his touch and the rich, lush taste of her lips were demanding he close the door and make love to her right here, however he knew Sam would come barging in fussing if he didn't respond promptly, so he reluctantly pulled away from her lips, and yelled back, "Be there in a minute."

Leah hadn't heard Sam's call; she'd heard nothing but the call of her own heated senses. What a wanton, explosive moment. Is this what her future would be like, too, more of these powerful episodes that left her breathless and pulsing? She hadn't known a woman's body could be so consumed.

Ryder looked down at her. "I seem to have found another way to impress you."

Leah couldn't deny that truth. She was tingling and blooming everywhere. "Are all Cheyenne braves as modest as you?" she asked with a quiet sassiness.

He bent down and kissed her soundly in response. When he let her go, he looked down into her passion-lit eyes and asked, "What do you think?"

"I think we'd better go eat before Sam comes in here with his switch."

Beguiled by the spell in her, he used a finger to slowly and possessively trace her kiss-swollen mouth. "You have to answer my question first."

Leah found it hard to think. "What question?"

Unable to resist Ryder touched his lips softly to hers once again. "Do you wish to be courted or seduced?" he whispered.

Through the haze and fog, Leah fought to form speech. "Both . . ." the woman inside herself answered.

Ryder's manhood tightened. He'd guessed there was heat simmering beneath her prim exterior, and now he knew he'd been correct. "Then you shall have your wish . . . Let's go eat."

As Leah sat across from him at the small table on the glassed-in porch, she was admittedly still pulsing from his kisses. Her lips felt swollen, and her blood was racing. Who knew he'd be able to affect her this way? She felt desired, wanted, but, did he want her for herself? She still didn't know.

Turning her mind to the more calming prospect of breakfast, Leah looked at all the choices on the table and wondered if Sam cooked this banquet every morning. There were grits, eggs, and sourdough toast; stewed apples, panfried potatoes, bacon, and sausage. To her further surprise, Ryder helped himself to all of it.

"What's the matter?" he asked, as he worked a bit of butter into his grits.

"Are you going to eat all of that?"

He seemed confused by the question. "Yes."

Leah shook herself free. "I'm sorry. It's just—I've never seen anyone eat so much, is all."

He raised one dark eyebrow. "Say the grace."

Hiding her smile, Leah searched her mind for a moment, then said, *"May God give us his blessing, and may all the ends of the earth stand in awe of him."*

And so, they began their first breakfast together.

Leah had never had breakfast with a man before. There was a certain intimacy in the atmosphere she supposed couples shared all the time, but it was as new to her as the passionate interlude in his study. She also supposed married couples passed the time talking of the upcoming day, plans for dinner, and current events, but what did a man and his paramour discuss? Since she had no answer, she began on her plate.

As Ryder savored his eggs, he also savored the remembered feel of her in his arms and the taste of her lips. The vivid memory made his manhood rise hard as a length of wood. He cut into his potatoes with a promise to sample more of her as soon as it could be arranged.

Every time Leah met his eyes across the table the heat in them seared her softly. Her nipples rose shamelessly, and the pulsing between her thighs renewed its echoing beat.

Her responses couldn't be proper, but she felt certain he preferred them that way. Ryder Damien was a descendant of Black and Cheyenne warriors, and he'd promised to teach her to ride.

Shocking herself with that vivid thought, Leah picked up her coffee in an effort to compose herself; his kisses seemed to have addled her brain. She'd been bought and paid for; she wasn't supposed to be enjoying this, was she, or did that matter anymore? It certainly hadn't back in his study.

"I'm going to have to go into Denver, after we're done with breakfast. Do you mind staying here with Sam?"

"Not at all. He and I are becoming fast friends."

"Good. I'll ask him to give you a tour of the countryside, if he's not too busy."

"I'd like that."

"Did you like my kisses?"

The question caught her off guard. She looked over at him and remembered all he'd made her feel. It was too late to lie now. She nodded. "Yes."

"I liked yours, too." And what aroused him most had been the innocence he'd tasted in her lips. Even though he knew she wasn't a virgin, her kisses had been at first tentative, unsure, almost as if she'd never shared passion before. It came to him that maybe she hadn't been introduced fully to the game of love, and the possibility of teaching her all he knew made him want to say to hell with going to town and carry her up to his bed. "I probably won't be back until late. Will you wait up and have dinner with me . . . ? I promise I won't leave you . . . and I'll be on my best behavior."

The implications of that washed over Leah like a wave. She had difficulty keeping her breathing even. Her eyes strayed to his mouth. Would the evening end with her in his bed? The thought gave her the shakes in more ways than one. "Yes, I'll wait up for you."

Her affirmative answer was rewarded with one of his rare

smiles. He pushed back his now empty plate and wiped his mouth on his linen napkin. "I need to go, then, so I can get back."

Leah had trouble reconciling herself to the idea of being desired by such a man. Because of her age and poverty-stricken circumstances, she'd buried her hopes of ever knowing a lover's caress long ago.

Leah began to tremble again as he came around to where she sat. He reached out a hand. She grasped it and rose to her feet.

Ryder took a moment to stare down into her ebony eyes. "Let me have a kiss. It's all we have time for right now."

Leah's knees melted, and as he lifted her chin and gave her a fiery, lingering kiss, the rest of her melted as well.

He touched her dark cheek as a fleeting caress good-bye, then quietly exited, leaving her hazy, dazed, and yearning for more.

As it turned out, Sam didn't have time for a formal tour. "I have to go over to Miss Eloise's today—I chop her wood on Thursdays. You're welcome to come along if you like."

So Leah did.

It was a beautiful day, the sun was shining, the temperature so warm Leah didn't need her cloak. While Sam guided the buckboard over the uneven open land, he pointed out landmarks, gave her the names of blooming wildflowers and circling hawks. They saw foxes and rabbits, deer and butterflies. It was a visual treat, but Leah still thought the place needed an ocean.

"Who is this Miss Eloise, Sam?"

"Lady about my age. Old friend of Ryder's. Says she knew his father, too. Been here a while."

Leah recalled going past Miss Eloise's house with Ryder. "I have a feeling I'll like her."

"Don't see why not. Everybody else does."

"Even Helene Sejours?"

He cracked. "Well, not everybody," he added as they pulled up in front of a small cottage surrounded by fields of blooming flowers. Sam set the brake. "Miss Eloise used to be a laundress back in the gold rush days. Now she just paints and tends her flowers."

As Leah stepped down from the backboard her attention was grabbed by a woman in faded trousers, shirt, and an old hat digging in the flowers on the side of the house. She looked up, and a smile lit her face. "Morning, Sam."

He waved as he hitched the team to the post outside her whitewashed fence. "Morning, Eloise. Meet Leah Montague."

By now the brown-skinned woman was coming down the narrow path that served as a walk through all the flowers. "Glad to meet you. Leah? You're Louis's widow, aren't you?"

Leah nodded a bit uncertainly. Although Sam had vouched for the woman's sweet nature, Leah didn't know what memories she had of Monty. Had Miss Eloise been one of the people he'd been unkind to also?

The woman regarded her for a moment. "Heard you were in town. I'm sorry for your loss," she told Leah, seemingly genuinely. "A lot of folks won't miss him, but I will."

Leah decided she liked Miss Eloise. "Thank you. Your flowers are beautiful."

"They're what keeps me going, them and my paints."

She pulled off her soil-stained gloves. "Would you like a tour?"

Leah nodded. "Yes, I would."

"Then come on with me. I'll show off my gardens while Sam does the wood."

Sam gave them a wave of his hand and went around to the back of the house.

Miss Eloise took Leah on a wandering walk through the

extensive beds. There were flowers, newly planted spring vegetables, and in the field of flowers behind the house stood a beautifully sculpted statue of a laughing little girl holding out a pan. It was the most unique birdbath Leah'd ever seen and so lifelike it took her breath away. "Where on earth did you get this?" she asked Miss Eloise.

Every detail appeared to have been lovingly rendered: from the sparkle in her eyes, and the wind-ruffled hem of her dress, to the tiny buttons on her little high-topped shoes. Even the short curls of her hair looked soft and touchable.

"Made her myself," Eloise replied proudly. "Her name's April."

Leah couldn't hide her surprise. "You made this?"

"Yep."

"Did you use one of the local children as the model?"

Eloise shook her graying head. "No. She came out of my mind."

The love and care that had gone into the rendering was quite apparent. "Well, she's adorable."

Eloise nodded. "I call her the daughter I never had." Eloise touched April's head affectionately. "And she'll never grow up and leave me."

Leah smiled.

Eloise said, "I was heating water for tea. It's probably hot by now. Why don't you come on in?"

Inside over tea, Leah looked around the small neat cabin. It was furnished simply and devoid of the stifling, overstuffed furniture choking Helene's house. Instead of fringes and velvet there were framed paintings everywhere. Many were landscapes, others were portraits. All showed as much mastery as the statue of little Alice. "Sam told me you did paintings, but I'd no idea you were so prolific or so talented."

"Are you trying to give me a swelled head, young woman?"

Leah smiled over her cup. "No, ma'am. Just speaking the truth."

"Well, I'd be honored if you'd let me paint you."

"I'd like that."

They spent a companionable hour talking about everything and nothing. Leah wasn't surprised to learn Miss Eloise had come to Colorado as a slave from Texas in 1845. Nearly everyone Leah knew had been a captive at some point in their life.

"I was seventeen," Eloise explained. "It was me, the master, and a milk cow. Walked most of the way. Master died three days after we got here."

"So what did you do?"

"Called myself a free woman and opened up a laundry. Did real well, too."

She then turned her frank brown eyes on Leah. "How're you and Ryder getting along?"

Since Leah didn't know how much Miss Eloise knew, she didn't know how to answer.

Miss Eloise sought to assure her, "I'm not trying to be nosy, well, I guess I am, but everybody's buzzing about what happened with the estate and all. You made a good choice, I think. No woman in her right mind would choose prison, given another way out, and Ryder's a good man. I've known him most of his life."

"We're getting along as well as might be expected, I suppose."

"Well, he can be an enigma sometimes. Sorta like his father. Every female within fifty miles of here was in love with Louis. Myself included." Eloise looked to Leah. "I'm not talking out of turn here, am I?"

Leah shook her head. "No." Leah didn't feel offended in the least. In fact, she was a bit flattered that Eloise felt comfortable enough to reveal herself this way.

Eloise looked off into the distance as if recalling memories, and her voice softened. "He wouldn't have me of course. I was just a common washerwoman. He wanted someone better, like that fancy Creole Bernice he shipped in for his wife."

"Was she really as unhappy here as I've heard?" Leah asked.

"More. She spent the first few weeks terrified that she'd be scalped by Utes or Cheyenne, even though most of the tribes had been hunted down and put on reservations. Those poor folks," she added sadly. "Have Ryder tell you about those days, sometime."

Leah nodded. "Did Monty know how you felt about him?"

"Oh, sure, but it didn't make him no never mind though. What would a washer woman know about sitting at the head of his table?"

Leah thought she sounded a bit bitter, but Eloise was soon smiling again. "Can I get you more cookies?" the woman asked.

"No, ma'am. If I eat any more I won't fit on the buckboard." The molasses cookies had been outstanding and reminded Leah of the ones Reba often had waiting for her when she came home from school.

Eloise poured herself another cup of water from the kettle. "Heard you were staying at Helene's. How she treat you?"

Leah wondered if she could tell her the truth, and then decided she could. "Frankly? Not well."

Eloise shook her head in disgust. "Never did like her. Never will. She and that sister of hers came here from New Orleans and you'd've thought they were visiting royalty. Spent the whole time looking down their noses at the rest of us like we were sluice water."

Leah was glad to hear she wasn't alone in her feelings about Helene.

Eloise added, "I have to say, Helene did do well by Seth while he was growing up, but she's a rattler."

Sam stuck his head in the door. It was time to head back. Miss Eloise looked disappointed. "So soon?"

Sam nodded. "Yep, got to get back."

She then asked Leah, "Will you come and visit again now that you know where I am?"

"First chance I get. You promised to paint me, remember?"

"And I shall. Tell Ryder I said hello."

Leah promised she would, then she and Sam drove off with a wave.

Once they were on the road again, Leah told Sam, "You were right. She's a very nice lady."

"That she is. Does most of the doctoring for our folks around here because the hospital in Denver won't take us."

"Is she a trained physician?"

"Naw, but she knows more about healing and herbs than anybody else around. Ryder said she learned a lot about plants from his grandma. I guess Miss Eloise was one of the few people who treated Ryder with any respect."

"What do you mean?"

"Everybody else around here called him *Squaw Boy* while he was growing up."

"Squaw Boy?" Leah was appalled.

"Yep, but now Squaw Boy is one of the richest men in Colorado. Pretty ironic if you think about it."

Leah agreed. Having also grown up being slurred because of the circumstances surrounding her birth, she'd spent a lot of time fighting. How had Ryder handled it? Making yourself wealthy enough to thumb your nose at your former tormentors sounded to her like very apt revenge indeed. Did folk respect him now or still call him Squaw Boy? she wondered.

Back at Sunrise, Leah helped Sam pare vegetables for

dinner, then spent the afternoon trying to occupy her mind
with something other than thoughts of Ryder and sharing
his bed. She first tried reading one of Denver's local papers
but couldn't concentrate because thoughts of kisses and being held against his broad chest kept interfering with the
words. She then went to his study, hoping a book might
hold her interest better, but since the choices were limited to
geology, engineering, and mining, she found no respite
there.

In the end she went outside and sat on a wooden bench
that had been positioned to face the distant mountains. Out
in the quiet she let her mind have its head. She replayed
everything that had happened to her in the few days since
she'd arrived and realized how life-changing the experience
had been. In the process she'd gone from being Monty's
widow, to his son's paramour. Of course that questionable
title wouldn't be official until the deal was consummated
but Leah didn't think that would be too far off. She'd chosen scandal over jail and still felt as if she'd made the only
logical decision. Leah didn't care about all the gossip that
was sure to be nipping at her heels; she'd been gossiped
about since the day she was born. She did care about going
through with her end of the bargain, however, and in reality
she was scared to death. Her knowledge of what a man and
a woman did behind closed doors was limited to the few
peeks she'd gotten at the bawdy books surreptiously passed
around back at Miss Caldwell's school, but she doubted
spinsters were supposed to act like those fictional, wanton
heroines. Although Monty and her mother had had an ongo-
ing relationship most of Leah's life, they'd been very discreet in their dealings in her presence. Leah'd never seen
Monty give Reba more than a friendly swat on the behind or
a quick kiss on the cheek in all the years she'd known him.

She assumed Ryder knew what to do, however, and
therein lay another dilemma. How would he react when he

found out she was a virgin? She didn't see him being pleased; he thought her a widow and would undoubtedly accuse of her of intentionally deceiving him. He'd be right of course, but would he hear her out and applaud his father's ingenuity? Leah hoped everything would go well, but because there were so many variables, she knew disaster could strike in an instant.

Leah couldn't deny her nervousness as she dressed in a beautiful navy silk gown and left her room to see if Sam needed help. She knew she wasn't dressed to do anything more than set the table. As efficient as Sam seemed to be, he probably didn't need any assistance at all, but she needed something or someone to occupy her mind. All she could think about was her evening with Ryder and that after tonight she'd be a woman in every sense of the word.

Upon entering the kitchen, she asked, "Sam what time is—"

Ryder turned and froze with the glass of lemonade to his lips. For a moment he stood speechless as he fed his eyes on her loveliness. How can a woman be more beautiful with each passing moment? he mused inwardly as he took in the sight of her in the navy blue silk dress. Once again he felt as if he were in a children's tale and was being graced by a princess. The midnight blue gown seemed to sparkle against her dark skin. The sleeves were little more than bands across her upper arms, offering the eyes an unhindered view of the lovely slopes of her shoulders and her neck below her upswept hair. The straight-line bodice rode fashionably low and flowed seamlessly into the tempting bands of her sleeves. Around her neck she wore a simple sapphire locket that rested on the smooth plane above her breasts. It was a spot he wished to place his kisses against.

A nervous Leah hadn't expected to find him there. Watching his eyes taking her in so slowly let her know he approved of her attire and filled her with an odd mixture of uncertainty and womanly power. "I didn't know you'd returned."

"Got back only moments ago. You look very beautiful."

"Thank you."

"Sam's out hitching up the team."

"Is he leaving?"

"Yes, he's going courting."

Leah couldn't hide her surprise. "Courting?"

He nodded. "If I'm not mistaken, it's Mable France tonight."

Leah's eyes widened even further. "Mable France? The woman who works for Helene Sejours?"

"Yep. With his pension and all, the old pony soldier's quite a catch. Widows have been trying to put a saddle on him for years."

"But—Mable France? I didn't even know she could smile."

"Little to smile about working for Helene."

Leah supposed he was right.

He drank down the last of his lemonade, then set the empty glass in the metal dishpan. "Away from Helene, Mable's quite nice."

Leah still found it a bit hard to believe, but knew that if anybody could bring out a person's warmer side, Sam could.

Sam entered as if cued, dressed in his dark suit, starched shirt, and string tie. His gray hair was brushed and combed, and Leah smelled just the faintest scent of cologne.

"How do I look, Miss Leah?"

"Very handsome, Sam."

"You're looking mighty good yourself, if I might add."

"Yes, she is," Ryder seconded, his eyes glowing over the picture she made.

Leah turned away to hide her responding smile.

Sam said, "Well, I gotta get going. Mable won't like me

being late." He looked between the two of them. "I was going to ask if you two were going to be all right, but that's a dumb question. Don't wait up."

Ryder had eyes only for Leah. "We won't."

Sam's departure left them alone.

Just looking at Ryder made Leah remember this morning's kisses and her own vibrant response to them. She assumed tonight would be much the same, only more. Lord knew she wanted to brazen this out, but didn't think herself able. The memories of being in his arms were more than enough to set her blood racing. But second thoughts arose about what she guessed would come *after* the meal. She wondered what would happen if she told him she'd changed her mind. *Prison would happen*, the little voice in her mind responded. *Prison.*

Ryder thought he saw worry cross her face, but it was gone so swiftly he wondered if he'd imagined it. What could she be concerned about? "Something bothering you?"

"No," she lied. Hoping to change the subject, she asked, "I thought you weren't going to be back until much later."

He shrugged. "Did what I had to do and canceled the rest. Had a more . . . pressing engagement."

Leah knew he was talking about their dinner. "I wouldn't have minded waiting," she answered truthfully, softly.

"But I would have . . ."

His words seemed to charge the air in the kitchen and Leah as well. Her lips parted, and the now familiar drumming began to echo faintly between her thighs. She turned her back lest he see how much she'd been affected.

When she heard him cross the floor and come up behind her, her eyes closed in response to her sharp reactions. The light touch of his finger slowly mapping first one bare shoulder and then the other made her softly suck in a breath. She held on to it as the finger traced up and then down her trembling neck. He placed a kiss there. She quietly ignited. He flicked his tongue over the dark crown of her left shoulder. She dissolved. He repeated the tribute on the right shoulder. She moaned softly. He reached around and gently turned her face to his, then kissed her so exquisitely she lost all sense of time and place. When their lips parted she couldn't have told him her name.

He whispered. "I'm going to wash up. Will you meet me on the porch in, say, twenty minutes?"

Since she couldn't speak, she nodded.

He smiled and left her alone.

When he joined Leah on the porch, she was standing at the windows with her back to him. She turned at his entrance. Sensual shivers of anticipation traveled over her, and her first instinct was to flash back around in order to escape what she saw in his eyes, but she didn't. Instead she let herself be touched and stroked by his gaze, let him get his fill. As she'd admitted to herself earlier, it was too late to retreat now.

"I hope I wasn't too long," Ryder told her quietly. He wanted to caress her with more than his eyes. His hands itched because he knew that her skin was as silken as it appeared.

"No," she answered, wondering if her breathing would ever return to a normal rhythm.

"Are you ready to eat?"

Dusk was falling, and the shadows in the dining room added to the mood. "Yes."

He gestured her to the table, helping Leah with her chair, and just like last night, the heat of his nearness surrounded her senses. There was a current in the air, a current that made her vividly remember him saying: *Then I'd take you up into the mountains and make love to you until the seasons changed.*

Standing behind her, Ryder had to force himself to back

away. The urge to whisper his lips across the bare back of her shoulders roared as strong as it had last night. Once again, he wanted to make her the first course, second course, and dessert. Instead he said, "Sam left dinner for us. I'll get it."

Leah waited. She brought her hands to her cheeks in an effort to calm herself. Her palms were damp, her heart racing.

He returned a short time later pushing a tray laden with covered serving dishes. Silver and china had been set out on the table by Sam earlier. Leah realized that even though last night's dinner had been intimate, this time it would be even more so.

He took his seat across from her, and in order to keep herself from being singed by his dark gaze, Leah unfolded her napkin and placed it in her lap.

"You seem nervous," he said as he poured himself a glass of wine.

She didn't lie. "I am a bit."

"Then we'll go slowly so you can relax."

Leah doubted her ability to relax; inwardly she was as nervous as an overboard sailor floundering in shark-infested seas.

"Do you want wine?"

She shook her head. "No, thank you. I'm not much of a spirits drinker." Leah had never acquired a taste for alcohol.

He set the bottle back on the table, then raised his glass to her in toast. "To beauty . . ."

The floundering Leah turned away. Maybe if she'd had a beau at some point in her life she'd know how to handle this, but she hadn't; men rarely wanted to bring the bastard daughter of a tavern owner home to meet their mama. When she looked up again his eyes were waiting.

"Your turn to say grace," he told her.

Under the influence of his distracting presence she didn't

think she could come up with a verse, but somehow managed to do so. *"Ye are blessed of the Lord which made heaven and earth."* She raised her gaze to his. "How was that?"

"Just fine."

His voice, quiet as the room, swept over Leah like a faint caress. Her eyes strayed to his mouth. She found herself wanting to feel his lips against her own in spite of where it might lead.

"When a woman stares at a man's mouth that way, it makes him want to stare back . . ."

The heat of embarrassment rushed across her cheeks. "My apologies."

"None needed. It shows you're still interested."

Even more heat filled her face. "I thought you were going to be on your best behavior?"

"I am."

It was like flirting with a tiger. In a minute or two she knew he planned to eat her up, but she was so fascinated by his tempting presence she didn't care.

"Pass me your plate. The sooner we eat, the sooner we can enjoy each other."

The desire in his eyes rocked her with such sweet force, she swayed in her chair for a fraction of a second and her hand went to the locket above her breasts. Who knew there were men like this in the world? She certainly hadn't.

He set her plate beside his and removed the tops from the evening's offerings. There were tiny boiled potatoes, string beans, slices of ham dripping with maple syrup, warm yeast rolls oozing butter and short, glass bowls of sweet, spiced peaches.

"What would you like?" Ryder asked, knowing his own answer to the question had nothing to do with food.

"A bit of everything, I think."

He nodded and placed the food on her plate. When he was done he handed it back, then filled his own.

Ryder watched her eat a bit of the vegetables and ham, but when she forked up a portion of the spiced peaches to sample, he found himself wanting to taste the spicy sweetness on her lips. He shifted slightly in his chair to accommodate his hardening desire. "Are the peaches good?"

"Very good," she replied, unconsciously sliding the tip of her tongue over her lip.

The innocent but provocative gesture made Ryder think he might explode. He inhaled a deep breath and forced himself to concentrate on his potatoes. It was hard, though, because so was he. "Sam said you met Miss Eloise today."

Leah nodded. "I did. She wants to paint me."

"That's quite an honor. She doesn't do that for everyone."

Leah thought back on the visit and remembered Miss Eloise telling her to ask Ryder about the tribes. Leah didn't think now to be the right time, but she did have a question. "Do you consider yourself a man of the race, or an Indian?"

He glanced at her. "I was raised Cheyenne, but I've always considered myself both. Each part has strength and honor. I wouldn't disrespect my ancestors by favoring one over the other."

That made sense to Leah. "Did the Cheyenne once own this land?"

"No, this all belonged to the Arapaho. We lived on the plains near the Colorado-Kansas border."

The Arapaho were not a tribe Leah was familiar with. Back East the papers seemed to concentrate on the more well known tribes like the Cheyenne and the Sioux. She hoped to learn more about the nation's native peoples during her time here with him.

After they finished the main course, he left the table and threw a few more logs on the fire in the big stone grate. Its flaming light shimmered around the darkening room. When he removed his suit coat and placed it over the back of the small, black-velvet love seat in front of the fire, and then undid the top buttons on his shirt, a thousand butterflies took wing in Leah's stomach.

He looked her way, and said, "Think I'll have my peaches over here by the fire. Join me?"

Leah didn't know if her shaking legs would support her but she stood, picked up his bowl of peaches and what remained in her own, and carried them both over to the fire. He took his bowl and fork from her hand.

"Thanks."

A very nervous Leah sat down with her own bowl of dessert. He sat beside her, his long legs stretched out comfortably in front of the flames. She felt as shy as the virgin she knew herself to be and found it hard to meet his gaze. To give her something else to concentrate on beside the warmth of his nearness, she dipped her little finger into the juice in her bowl and tasted it.

Watching her, Ryder had to take in another deep breath. Did she know her effect on a man? he wondered. He assumed she did. Being around her would keep a man in a perpetual state of arousal.

"You seem to be enjoying those peaches."

"I am," she admitted as she used her fork to polish off the last two pieces of fruit in her bowl. "I don't think I've ever had any this good. Did Sam put these up, or did he buy them from someone?"

Ryder shook his head. "No. He does them himself. He usually does enough to last all winter. I think he said this was the last jar."

Her disappointment showed plainly on her face.

He chuckled. "I promise there will be more later in the year. Do you want some of these? I can share."

She shook her head. "No."

"Are you sure?"

Leah did want another bite or two—she'd had a sweet tooth for as long as she could remember—but she didn't want him to think her a pig. "No. You go ahead."

He peered around to look into her eyes. "You don't have to act like a perfect lady with me. If you want some, say so."

She lowered her head to hide her embarrassed smile. "I would like another bite."

He forked up a piece of fruit. "Here."

She reached for the fork, but he drew it back. Confused, she paused.

"Open your mouth . . ." he said quietly.

She had no trouble reading the desire in his eyes. Another series of tremors rippled through her softly. Angling closer, she drew the fruit from the fork, savoring the taste of the peaches and his heated stare as she slowly chewed and swallowed. When she was ready, he silently fed her another piece. She swallowed and trembled all in one motion. Eyes glowing, he slowly lifted out the last sliced peach, but this time, instead of feeding it to her he teased the juicy edge back and forth across her lips until they parted. He then leaned in and kissed her hungrily, thoroughly, treating himself to the sweetness left there by the spicy juice. When the kiss ended, Leah came back to herself dazed, her head resting on the sofa back.

He then dipped his finger back into the juice and drew a line across the tops of her breast. Leah's eyes closed, and her nostrils flared. She gasped as his lips began to trace the sweet trail his finger created. His lips were hot, her skin trembled, and she moaned in rising response. He raised his head and looked into her eyes. He put more juice on his finger and again mapped her lips. When her lips parted he helped himself to her flavored mouth, a dessert far more tantalizing than any other before.

"I know we made a bargain, but we're lovers tonight . . . nothing more . . ."

Leah's eyes closed. *Lovers.* What would he do when he found out she'd never done this before? The worries went away because she was too busy reacting to the line of juice he was now drawing across the hollow of her throat. He kissed the spot in tender tribute, his tongue potently flicking to taste the skin; she'd never view peaches in the same way again.

As Ryder savored the scents and tastes of her throat, his hands began to wander and explore. The male in him wanted her nude and sighing beneath him right now, but the lover in him wanted to prolong this heated, erotic play for a lifetime. "Stand up for me . . ." he whispered.

The haze veiling Leah's senses made her move like an automaton. Rising to her feet, she did as he asked and stood pulsing, her lips parted.

"By the Spirits you're beautiful," he husked out as he drew a finger across her lips. "Will you take off your dress . . . ?"

The honey-filled invitation set off a flare inside Leah that burned so brightly she had to close her eyes. No man had ever asked such a thing of her before, yet while his eyes held her prisoner, her hands went around to the back of her gown and undid the small set of hooks and eyes at the base of her spine. The fabric loosened, giving the watcher a brief glimpse of the fancy black corset she wore beneath. Holding the undone dress to her chest, Leah slid free of one sleeve and then the other.

Ryder smiled sensually. He found her seemingly innocent air highly arousing. The reticence in her movements were an arousing contrast to the passion lidding her eyes. At that moment, Ryder didn't care how many men she'd had before, or who they might have been. All that mattered was that she be his tonight and his alone.

He reached out and gently eased her hand away from her dress. The navy silk swished quietly to the floor, leaving her standing before him in her black corset and dark stockings.

Consciously or not, the corset had been designed to please a man's eyes. It was cut high enough for him to enjoy the rich fullness of her thighs and hips and low enough to burn his gaze over the sweet swells of her ebony breasts. The thin dark stockings encasing her beautiful firm legs were held up by small black garters delicately bordered with a midnight blue lace that mirrored her dress. Filled almost with awe, he etched a finger over the gossamer flesh rising above the corset. "*Seda* . . ." he whispered thickly. Silk. Her skin was like silk; an exotic, marcasite colored silk.

Leah had no idea what the word meant, but the worshipping intonation filled her with shuddering response.

He pulled her down onto his lap, and Leah could feel his hardness beneath her hips. His big hand cupped her face gently, then slowly circled a cajoling finger over the parted curves of her passion-ripe mouth. Easing her to him, he touched his lips to hers in a series of short, soft kisses that set her ablaze. His lips were gentle yet masterful and filled with an expertise even a novice like Leah could sense. This was not some fumbling youth, but a man knowledgeable in the pleasuring of a woman.

When their lips parted, Leah could feel the rush of her blood, the beat of her heart and the blossoming of her body. His hand came next, trailing down her bare throat and over the raised tops of her breasts, making her moan. He did it again, slower this time, lingering over the edges of the corset where it met her skin, then bending to kiss the hollow above the locket around her neck. As he kissed his way back up to her mouth his hand strayed boldy over her corset-encased breasts.

Without a word, he raised up and moved to untie the corset's black-sateen ribbon. As he worked, his hot fingers brushed against the flesh of her breasts. All thoughts, all fears of her virginity and his reaction were lost in the sensations, the feel of her corset being lazily undone.

Ryder took his time. He wanted to unveil her slowly, brazenly. The sounds of her sighs and the sight of her desire-filled face made his manhood throb. Beneath the show of primness lay an untapped heat, a heat he planned to ignite until she screamed his name.

To that end he pushed aside the halves of the now open corset and placed a kiss between her breasts. Leah thought she would burst into flame. Any thought she might've had about confessing her virginity died in the blazing feel of the palm he brushed across her breast. The nipple hardened like a dark jewel, and Leah wondered if she'd ever draw another breath.

"How do you think you'll taste with peach juice . . ." he whispered hotly against her lips.

Leah's world careened.

"Shall we see . . . ?"

While she rippled in the wake of his sensual winds he circled a juice dampened finger around the tight dark aureole of her breast, then bent his head to taste the nipple. Her soft strangled cry broke the silence. He prepared the other breast; dallying, lingering, watching her arch to his bliss-filled ministrations while his manhood rose vibrantly beneath her warm hips.

He raised his head. Leah could feel the dampness of his play on the tightened buds of her breasts. How much passion could one woman hold? She was throbbing and pulsing everywhere.

Ryder wanted to take her right in front of the fire, but he wanted to lay her across his bed even more. "Let's go somewhere more comfortable."

Rising to his feet with her still in his arms, he carried her through the dark house and up the wide-open worked stairs to his rooms.

The fire inside gave the room a den-like aura. It was her first look at his inner sanctum but she noticed little but the big brass bed he was now placing her upon, that and the desire flowing in her blood. He boldy reached down and undid the side ties on her drawers and slid them from her. Her stockings and garters soon followed.

Seated beside her on his big, quilt-covered bed, Ryder wondered if she knew what a bewitching picture she presented. Against the flame-lit darkness, dressed in nothing but her gaping corset, she was as enticing as a pasha's favorite. The hard buds of her breasts drew his hands to tease them. His palms wandered over her dark skin touching, stroking and exploring while his eyes glowed at the sight of her body rising for more.

Leah once again wondered how much desire one woman could hold, but as his finger lazily circled her navel the question soared away. She soared also when his touch slipped between her thighs. Tenderly, slowly he awakened the deep secrets hidden there with such intimacy a strange new yearning took hold, and a strangled moan escaped her lips. He teased her, plied her, enticed her to widen the way even farther, and she did so, shamelessly, wantonly. The results of his play made her twist and moan and moments later, shatter. The shuddering force of her completion tore a hoarse cry from her soul, and her being was flung across the darkness like shooting stars.

Ryder watched her ride out her pleasure. He didn't want to stop touching her but needed to remove his clothes so they could continue. As she lay panting and pulsing, he wondered when she'd made love last, because it hadn't taken him very long to bring her to fulfillment. As he undid the buttons on his trousers and took them off he realized it didn't matter; only her passionate responsiveness had any bearing here.

When he rejoined her on the bed, Leah, still recovering, crooned responsively to the fevered kisses now playing over her skin. His hands worshiped, his teeth nibbled, his body covered hers, and she felt something hard and hot working blissfully against the opening of her shuddering core. Then came pain. She stiffened and cried out.

An incredulous Ryder looked down at her. Every fiber of his being was on the verge of exploding but he held, barely, while he tried to make some sense of something that made no sense. When he moved to withdraw from her, she grasped his waist and tried to keep him close. "Please, it's all right."

Ryder could see the sheen of painful tears in her eyes. "You're a virgin?"

"Yes but—"

His eyes widened.

"Ryder, I can explain—" Leah didn't want this night to end bitterly, not after all they'd shared. "I know I should've told you before, but—"

"But what, you have an aversion to the truth?"

He withdrew from her, bringing her body relief from the fiery hurt but also leaving her with an odd feeling of emptiness.

"Did you hope to force me into supporting a child?"

"No," she whispered vehemently.

"So, my father never had you, did he?"

She shook her head, then said, "No. Monty and—I—"

"Were you really married?"

"Yes, we were but—"

"Dammit!"

Ryder got off the bed and grabbed his trousers. He pulled them on. A virgin! How was that possible? What kind of explanation could she offer? He decided he didn't want to know. He'd made a vow to stay clear of anything and everything connected with his father, and he'd broken that vow, for her. Now, he stood looking down at the ripest, hottest little piece he'd ever known, but had no idea who she was or what she was.

Leah scanned the thunderclouds gathered in his face and

stated coolly, "I suppose you don't care to hear what I have to say."

It was a statement, not a question.

Ryder's jaw tightened. He'd forgotten how brave she could be. "No, I don't. In the morning, I'll take you back to Helene's."

Leah's eyes widened. "But—"

"Don't worry. Your debt's paid."

She felt as if she'd been slapped. Getting off the bed, Leah didn't care that she had on nothing but her corset, thereby making her appear as brazen as the whore he'd assumed her to be. She was sorry for not confessing earlier, but if he didn't care to hear or to believe the truth, she couldn't force him to do so.

Without bothering to gather the clothing he'd removed so splendidly, she left him in the quiet of his firelit room.

Ryder wanted to throw something. What in the hell was she doing being a virgin? No man in his right man would have married her and not have consummated the union. So had she really been Louis's wife? She swore she had been, but who knew what to believe? Just thinking about how supple and full she'd felt under him a moment ago made his manhood throb, adding to the storm inside. How dare she pass herself off as someone she was not? The deception led him to the next question. Why? Why would she not tell him? Had she truly been trying to trap him into something? Had she and Lee come at the behest of some unknown business enemy in order to achieve some goal? He didn't know, and doubted he'd get the truth if he asked her.

Leah lay on her bed in the dark. The disaster she'd anticipated had come to pass. One moment they'd been making love and the next—She pulled the quilts up over her and burrowed low. Her debt had been paid, he'd said. The price of freedom had been her innocence. Although she was relieved to no longer be tied to him in that way, tonight's passion had resulted in far more troubling ties. He'd made her body sing; she now knew what men and women did behind closed doors, but it wouldn't happen with Ryder again for reasons that had nothing to do with pleasure. The past had gotten in the way again. Even though Leah knew that decent women weren't supposed to admit something like this, here in the dark she could: he'd left her with a yearning that only he could heal, and she didn't know what to do about it or how to make it stop.

The next morning Leah rose before dawn and showered away the remnants of last night. Gone were the traces of the fevered kisses Ryder had placed against her jaw and throat. Down the drain went the heady touches he'd left on her skin, the caresses he'd placed on her breasts. She washed away the tingling memories of scandalously applied spiced peaches and the intimate bliss he'd awakened between her thighs.

When she stepped out of the stall he was standing there. The rise in her temper kept her from being stunned by his presence. It also kept her from wanting to hide her wet nudity from his eyes. *Let him look,* she said boldy to herself. After all, he'd paid fifteen thousand dollars for the privilege, and he already believed she was a whore.

Dripping wet, Leah coolly took the towel from his hand and began to dry herself. "Good morning. Have I not prepared to leave early enough? I didn't think you'd begrudge me a shower. I was pretty sticky after all that juice."

Ryder's eyes glowed with his own rise in temper. And his manhood glowed with the sight of her damp nakedness. Vivid and erotic memories of last night rose in his mind but he pushed them away. "You're awfully brazen this morning for a woman who was a virgin last night."

Leah placed her foot on the seat of a short metal chair so she could dry her leg. "Isn't this what you paid for?"

Ryder looked at her ripe hips as she bent over to towel

herself and could do nothing about the desire that flashed
through his blood. "Brazen and sassy."

"I told you I was more everything than you thought when
we met. It's how we virgin whores are."

Leah knew that if she held on to her anger, he wouldn't
be able to hurt the parts of herself that had been left so vulnerable by their parting last night. She stood there nude as
Bathsheba before David. "Is there a reason you're here?"

Ryder ran his eyes over the dark jewels of her breasts,
the long marcasite legs and the hair curling over the junc-
ture of her thighs. What he wanted he couldn't have—ever
again. "I came to tell you that Sam'll be taking you back."

"That's fine."

Ryder knew he should turn and leave now, but everything about her made him want to sweep her damp beauty
up into his arms, take her back to his bed, and slowly finish
what they didn't finish fully last night. However he
squelched the need by reminding himself that he didn't
know who or what she was.

Leah could plainly see the desire hiding behind his
stormy eyes. Yes, it called to her, but, like him, she pushed
it away. "Is there anything else?"

"Yes, this." He held out a stack of folded bills. "I know
you haven't any at the moment."

Leah scanned his eyes, wondering just how much more
he planned to offend her, but she took the offering because
she knew she'd need it. Pride rarely fed a person as needy as
she knew she was going to be. "You're very generous."

That said, she wrapped the large drying sheet around her
nudity and left him standing there.

In the silence that followed her exit, a stunned and angry
Ryder wondered when and how he'd lost the upper hand.

After dressing in a burgundy traveling costume and a
matching feathered hat, Leah took a solitary breakfast in
her room, then met Sam at the front door. Her trunks were

packed and ready to go. She took one last wistful look around the house. It was indeed beautiful. She doubted she'd ever see it again.

As if he'd read her mind, Sam said quietly, "You'll be back, don't worry."

Leah didn't reply.

Chapter 6

Sam was loading Leah's trunks into the wagon when they spotted a carriage thundering up the drive. Seth was behind the reins.

"Wonder what he wants?" Sam voiced curiously.

Before Leah could speculate, Seth pulled back on the brake and jumped down. His golden face was lined with anxiety, his horses lathered from the fast pace. "Leah, Cecil's ill. Eloise says you'd better come fast."

A shiver passed over Leah. "How ill?"

"Very. He may not last the day."

Stunned, Leah looked to Sam, who replied without hesitation, "Go on with Seth. His buggy can get you there faster. I'll bring your trunks."

"What's happened?"

Everyone paused. Ryder. He was standing in the doorway.

Leah told him, "Cecil's taken ill. Miss Eloise wants me to come right away. She sent Seth."

157

Ryder held his brother's eyes for a long time, then declared, "I'll take her."

After all that had happened, Leah didn't want him involved. "That isn't necessary. Seth can—"

"I'll take you." His voice broached no argument. He turned to his brother. "Tell Eloise we're on our way."

The two siblings faced each other like opposing forces on a battlefield until a stormy-faced Seth finally said, "As you wish, brother." Stalking over to his black carriage, he whipped his horses around and headed back up the drive.

Leah wanted to shout at Ryder for interfering, but her need to see Cecil overrode all else.

Ryder turned to Leah. "I need to ride out to my office— Eloise's place is on the way. I'll drop you off, then go on to town. Give me five minutes to change clothes."

She wanted to give him a leaky boat and send him shark hunting, but held her tongue. They could argue later. "You have four," she told him pointedly.

He went back into the house.

While she and Sam waited for Ryder's return, Sam tried to make small talk, but once it became apparent Leah wasn't in the mood he gave up. After more long moments of silence though, he finally told her, "You may as well tell me your side because he's going to tell me his whether I want to hear it or not."

Leah shrugged. "Nothing to tell. It seems my virginity angered him."

Sam stared at her with wide eyes.

Leah responded with a thin smile. "Bet you're sorry you asked."

Sam nodded. "You're right about that, and pardon me for being nosy, but did he explain why he's mad about that?"

"He didn't have to. I know why. He'd prefer I be someone else."

Sam seemed to think on that for a moment, then offered, "Well, like I said, he can be slow at times."

"Fish are smarter."

He chuckled at first, then his manner became serious. "Do you really want to go back to Helene's to stay?"

"No." Leah had quite enough of her sharp-tongued hostess.

"Well, Miss Eloise has a small cabin in back of her place that she lets out every now and then. Maybe you can stay there, providing all goes well with Cecil."

"Providing," she echoed. She'd already lost everyone else in her world. She hoped he wouldn't be taken from her, too. Thoughts of her ailing friend made her impatient for Ryder's return. "Where is he?" she asked Sam.

As if cued, Ryder and his carriage came barreling around the side of the house. She could see he'd changed into a soft hide shirt with rawhide ties down the front. He halted the two-horse team near where she stood with Sam, and asked, "Ready?"

Leah wasn't ready to go anywhere with him, but for Cecil she'd endure even his presence. "Yes."

With Sam's assistance, she climbed in. A blink of an eye later, she and Ryder were under way.

Leah knew the journey to Miss Eloise's would take over an hour and in that time she hoped they wouldn't argue; however, she wanted to know exactly why he'd insisted on driving her. "Why are you doing this?"

"We have unfinished business."

Leah looked his way. "You said my debt was paid."

"It is, but you owe me the truth."

"You didn't want to hear the truth, remember?"

Ryder's jaw tightened. She was right, of course, he hadn't, at least not then; he'd been too angry, too shocked. In reality, he wasn't really prepared to hear it now, but she'd been a virgin last night, and, dammit, he wanted an explanation. "You could be carrying my child, you know."

That chilling reality swept over Leah with all its ramifications, but she pushed it away. "And I could *not* be."

Ryder had to hand it to her, she was tough. "Was my father unable to perform his marital duties, is that why you were untouched?"

Leah surveyed him for a moment, her temper rising, but she kept herself under control. "Last night, you put me out of your bed and this morning, out of your house. I don't owe you anything, least of all answers."

Ryder heard her anger and the underlying hurt in her voice. He didn't want to be affected by it, but he was. Rather than give credence to the fact that her feelings were slowly beginning to penetrate the well-established barriers he'd set up around his own emotions, he concentrated on driving. Neither of them said another word for the rest of the trip.

As soon as Ryder halted the carriage in front of Miss Eloise's house, Leah hopped down and ran up the walk to the door. She knocked loudly.

As Seth opened the door, Ryder rode away. "I see you made it," Seth said.

"Yes, where is he?"

Eloise appeared. "Oh thank goodness. Cecil's in here."

Without giving Ryder or anyone else a second thought, Leah hurried to follow Eloise.

Cecil was lying on a small cot in a back room. His body looked so still that for a moment Leah thought she'd arrived too late, but the pain-wracked moan that slipped from his lips let her know he was still holding on. It gave her hope.

She walked over to the cot. "Cecil?"

His eyes slowly slid open, but they appeared so unfocused it was hard to determine whether he knew she was there or not. A heartbeat later the lids closed once more. Moved, Leah took a seat on the edge of the thin mattress and softly stroked his brow. He was sweating profusely but his skin felt ice cold. "What's wrong with him?"

Eloise shook her head sadly. "I wish I knew. According to Seth, Helene said he began vomiting this morning and was complaining of fuzzy vision, his throat burning, and that everything looked greenish yellow."

Leah stared confused. "Greenish yellow. Was it something he ate, do you think?"

Eloise shrugged. "Maybe, but he can't seem to speak, so I don't know."

"He can't speak?"

"Seems that way. When he first got here he tried, but it was as if his face had stiffened up and he was having trouble moving his mouth."

Leah looked up with alarm. "Like a paralysis of some sort?"

Eloise nodded affirmatively. "And he's getting worse. He's only been here a few hours, but he's had numerous convulsions and vomiting. I can't give him anything if I don't know what's ailing him."

Leah understood. She could see how concerned Eloise appeared, and it mirrored her own reaction. Leah didn't want him to die. If he was going to pass, she wanted to at least let him know beforehand how much he'd meant to her and how much she loved him. He let out another series of anguished cries that literally broke her heart. "Can't you do anything for him? What about the doctors in Denver?"

"They won't treat us. Closest one who will is in Boulder."

Leah continued to mop Cecil's brow. "His breathing's very shallow."

"I know and it's getting slower. I wish I knew where and what he'd eaten."

While he continued to moan and toss, Leah reached

down and tightly held his lifeless hand. "Did Helene know or say anything else?"

"Only that he left her house last night to meet someone. She doesn't know who. When he returned he mentioned being a bit nauseous but thought it would pass, so he went on to bed."

Leah looked down at Cecil and called softly, "Cecil, what did you eat last night?"

He responded with more guttural moans that seemed rooted in pain.

"Cecil," she called again, this time a bit louder.

Silence.

Eloise said, "I'm going to take a chance and give him something to clean out his body—see if that helps."

Leah nodded and began to pray.

For the rest of the daylight hours, Eloise went in and out of the sickroom with cups of herbs and medicinals. Leah assisted as much as she could, boiling water, washing soiled linens, and mixing Eloise's carefully measured elixirs. For a while during the late afternoon, they thought he might be rallying: his skin felt less feverish, and he seemed more lucid, but evidently didn't possess the strength or the mental clarity to recall his whereabouts before he'd taken ill because he never spoke a word. When he slipped back into unconsciousness Eloise put a consoling arm around Leah's shoulders and gave her a soft squeeze of encouragement. "Don't give up hope—he may pull out of this yet."

A numb Leah nodded. If he didn't, she'd have no one. Everyone she'd loved would've been buried, all within the last year.

Eloise said, "Why don't you get you some tea, then go out and sit with Alice? I find she helps me at times like these."

Leah didn't want to leave Cecil's bedside.

"Go," Eloise commanded softly. "We may be at this all night, and you'll need your wits about you."

Leah agreed and reluctantly took the woman's advice.

Outside the sickroom sat a worried-looking Sam and Seth. Sam had arrived a bit after she and Ryder, and she was glad he'd remained. She was also grateful to see that although the men were from warring camps, they seemed to have momentarily set aside their differences in order to offer their help and support. Leah was hardly surprised that Ryder had taken off without so much as asking after Cecil.

"How's he doing?" Sam asked.

Leah shook her head sadly, "We thought he was coming around, but now—"

Seth asked, "Does he have family back East, anyone you might want me to wire and notify?"

"No. He has no one but me." *And I have no one but him.* "Eloise suggested I get some tea and try and relax. She thought talking to Alice might help. Anyone care to join me?"

Sam stood, saying, "No, I need to get on home, but I'll be back first thing in the morning."

Leah didn't want him to go. Sam Waters was well on the way to becoming a good friend, and she could dearly use one during this time of trial, but knew he had to return to Sunrise. She also knew him to be a man of his word; if he said he'd be back first thing tomorrow, he would be.

Seth looked to Sam. "I'll stay with her, Sam," then he added, "that is, if my brother doesn't mind."

Memories of Ryder pierced Leah's heart. She pushed them away. "Ryder's not a consideration."

She saw the curiosity in Seth's eyes but chose not to address it now. They'd have plenty of time to talk later. "Sam, thanks for bringing my things."

Her trunks were stacked up by the parlor door.

"My pleasure. I'll be back in the morning."

After giving Seth a short nod, Sam departed.

There was an awkwardness in the air once she and Seth were alone. Leah knew he'd been very upset about the deal she'd made with Ryder, and now probably had a fairly low opinion of her moral makeup as well.

Seth broke the silence. "How about that tea, though at this point I'd personally prefer something a little stronger."

To her surprise he opened a sideboard and extracted a cut-glass decanter.

"Scotch," he explained as he splashed a small portion into a shot glass. "Any for you?"

Leah shook her head.

He set the decanter back. "Let's go."

Outside, dusk had painted purple-and-orange swatches across the sky. After being inside most of the day, the cool air felt good on Leah's face. She and Seth walked through the field of flowers to the back of the house and over to the stone bench positioned only a few feet away from Eloise's beautiful stone daughter, Alice. Leah once again found herself overwhelmed by the beauty and detail. Looking at Alice's laughing face, Leah asked, "Do you know when she made this?"

Seth took a small sip of his scotch, then said, "I must've been eight or so. She's very lifelike isn't she?"

"Yes, she is."

"When we were young, Ryder was afraid of her."

Leah held his gaze over her tea. "Of Alice, why?"

"He thought she was real. Thought Eloise had turned her into a statute for being naughty."

"Why on earth would he think such a thing?"

Seth took another swallow. "Because it's what I told him."

Leah thought he might smile and view the episode as a

simple sibling prank, but the cold eyes told her otherwise. "You wanted to frighten him."

Seth nodded. "I hated him. Eloise would make arrangements for us to be here with her every summer. I guess she thought we needed to know each other, but every summer I tried to make the time as miserable for him as I could." He quieted as if recalling those times. "Not too proud of myself now though."

The confession made Leah feel better about him.

"Oh don't get me wrong, he paid me back in spades. In fact, once he retaliated while I was sleeping. Smeared rancid bear grease all over my face and in my hair. It took Eloise all day to get the grease off, and a week for me to stop attracting flies."

Leah chuckled.

"It's good to see you smile again."

"Haven't had much to smile about," Leah admitted.

"So what happened? Couldn't help but see Sam loading your trunks in the wagon this morning back at Sunrise," he added quietly.

Leah searched his light brown eyes. She knew he was referring to the bargain she'd made with his brother. "He's forgiven my debt, then asked that I leave, so I have." She had no intention of telling him more than that.

Seth drained the last of the liquid in the glass. "Can't say I'm disappointed. You're a beautiful woman, Leah. I'd rather see you on my arm than his."

She didn't reply.

"Do you think Cecil's going to pull through?" he asked.

Leah was glad he'd changed the subject, but found this one no less troubling. "I don't know. I pray he will."

"You consider him family?"

She nodded. "Yes, I do. Always have. Whenever I got in trouble Cecil always helped fish me out. Even stood up to my mother on a few occasions." The sadness Leah had been fighting all day welled up and threatened to swamp her, but she forced it away. There would be plenty of time for joy, or sorrow, soon enough. "I should get back. Eloise may need me."

He escorted her back inside.

Having spent the day at his office, Ryder returned to Eloise's around midnight. He wasn't pleased to find his brother sitting in her parlor, nursing a scotch. "What're you doing here?" he asked bluntly as he took off his wet slicker and hat. It had been pouring rain most of the night.

"I could ask you the same thing," Seth drawled. "Leah said you put her out."

Ryder hung his wet gear on the peg behind the door. "It doesn't concern you."

"I think it might."

"Go home, Seth."

"And miss this golden opportunity to make myself look good in her eyes? Never."

"Go home, Seth. Now."

"Or what?"

They faced each other silently until Seth said, "She laughed when I told her about you being afraid of Alice when we were young. When was the last time she laughed for you, brother?"

Ryder's jaw tightened. "Out, or I'll throw you out."

Seth set down his glass then walked over to the pegs and took down his coat. "You'll never shed your heathen beginnings. A man's dying, yet you want to fight."

"If the threat will get you out of here, I'll wear the name heathen."

Seth smiled coldly. "Well, continue playing that role, and she'll be mine before you know it."

The room went silent as they assessed each other once more.

Seth asked lightly, "Does she know you're called Squaw Boy?"

White-hot anger flared up inside Ryder, but he didn't let it show. He refused to give Seth the satisfaction. "Good night, Seth."

A smug Seth tipped his hat and stepped out into the night.

Cecil died in the wee hours of the morning. Leah was asleep in a chair near his bed when Eloise roused her and related the sad news. Leah didn't attempt to stem her tears. "Are you certain?"

Eloise nodded.

A solemn Leah sat down on the edge of his cot. She scanned the familiar brown face, now quiet with death. He'd been a friend, a champion, and an important part of her life. His final hours had been agonizing; but he was resting now, free of pain for an eternity. Tears blurred her eyes as she leaned down and gave his brow a final kiss good-bye. "Sleep old friend," she whispered from her heart. "Sleep."

Eloise came over and squeezed her shoulder sympathetically. "My pastor can do the burial if you'd like."

"I'd appreciate that. Thanks." Leah wiped at her tears.

Eloise told her kindly, "You go and handle your grief. I'll take care of things in here."

Leah nodded. She gave Cecil one last parting glance, then left the room.

Upon seeing Ryder seated alone in the dimly lit parlor, Leah struggled to pull herself together. "Where's Seth?"

"Gone home."

"He go of his own volition or at your insistence?"

"The latter. He wanted to stay, but he's too much of a

gentleman to cause a ruckus in a house with a dying man, so he left."

"You, of course, have no such reservations."

"No."

"Well, Cecil's dead."

Ryder couldn't explain it, but her pain seemed to cause him pain. Admittedly, he didn't trust her or care one way or another about Cecil Lee's death, but nonetheless he found himself moved by her very visible grief.

"Why are you here?" she asked.

"Thought you might need someone."

Even as his words touched her, Leah wiped at her eyes with the heels of her hands. She was determined not to let him add to her heartache. "And you think that someone might be you?"

"You have no one else."

In that moment, she sensed him enter her soul. He was a man capable of taking everything that made her woman and making her his, but she doubted he'd give her that much of himself in return. She told him softly, "Ryder, please go. I already ache enough."

The plea in her voice and the new tears spilling down her cheeks brought him to her side instead. Giving her no time to protest, he gently folded her in his arms, eased her head against his chest, and held her close. "You need this," he whispered, "and I can give it . . . Go ahead, let go . . ."

So she did. Leah slid her arms around his waist and silently sobbed until her body shook. Losing Cecil hurt, deeply. He'd been the last of her family, the last person who'd raised her, looked out for her, loved her. And now, he, too, was gone.

Every sob of her heart tore off a piece of Ryder's own. He didn't care for this. Her sadness filled him, humbled him. It made him ache for the woman she was inside. If he could raise Cecil Lee from the dead, he would if only to stop her pain. But he couldn't, so he held her and let her cry.

When the crisis eased, he picked her up and silently carried her over to Eloise's well-worn, flowered love seat. He sat with her in his lap. No words were spoken or needed.

Leah came back to reality with her head against his heart and his arm sheltering her tenderly. He extracted a clean handkerchief from the pocket in his shirt, and she blew her nose. Sniffling, she dearly wished they could be this way all the time, for the rest of time, but knew it wouldn't be. Unsure how this short interlude might be turned against her later, she avoided his eyes as she soundlessly left his lap. Standing with her back to him, she stammered, "Th-thank you."

"You're welcome."

Ryder sensed the barrier going up between them again. The moment was over. The disappointment he felt was also hard to explain. "Is Eloise going to help you with the burial?"

"Yes. We haven't talked cost or anything though."

"I'll handle that end."

Leah wanted to turn and look into his eyes but forced herself not to. Why was he acting so concerned? This morning he couldn't get her out of his sight quickly enough yet a moment ago he'd held her as if she were as precious as gold. Was he purposely trying to break her heart? Lacking the strength or the will to argue further, she simply said, once again, "Thank you. I'll repay you."

Ryder didn't ask how or when; repayment wasn't his concern. He was concerned about her however. In spite of the unfinished matters that lay between them, he preferred her feisty and fighting. This soft, vulnerable side of her made him want to provide her shelter and protection. He'd never experienced such feelings with any other woman before, and the realization was disturbing. "Is there anything else you need for the burial?"

"I'm not certain. When I talk with the pastor, I'll see."

Ryder stood then. "Let me know."

"I will."

Because he viewed her so silently for what seemed like so long, Leah thought he might have more to say. He didn't. Instead he walked over to the door and took down his slicker. He put it on, then his hat. Turning to face her one last time, he exited, leaving her to her grief.

Cecil was buried the next day. Eloise's pastor, a young Methodist minister named James Garrison, read the words. Leah paid for everything out of the money she'd been given by Ryder the day she left Sunrise. Standing over the grave with Leah were Eloise, Sam, and Seth. Ryder didn't attend.

The ride back from the cemetery in Seth's carriage was a silent one. Behind her black veil Leah's eyes were red and swollen from grief. She hadn't been in Colorado a week, yet it felt like a lifetime.

Seth looked her way and said, "Do you know what you're going to do?"

"Besides going back East, no."

There was silence for a moment. He then asked, "When are you leaving?"

"Soon as I can."

"Wish you'd stay."

Leah shook her head. "There's nothing here for me, Seth."

And there wasn't. This ill-fated trip had cost her her innocence and taken Cecil from her life. She had nothing left to give.

"You're wrong about there not being anything here. I'm here, Leah."

Leah didn't want to discuss that. "I need to go by your aunt's and retrieve Cecil's things."

Seth scanned her face for a moment. "Leah, I—"

She placed a quieting hand on his arm. "Please, not now, okay?"

He held her eyes for a moment, then nodded his acquiescence. "We're not too far from Aunt Helene's. Do you want to do it now, or wait a few days?"

"No, let's do it now."

In reality, Leah wanted to handle the matter now; she didn't want ever to have to darken Helene's doorway again.

When they reached the house, Mrs. France opened the door. She looked at Leah, and said genuinely, "Sorry for your loss, Mrs. Montague."

"Thank you. I've come to get his things."

"Of course." As Mrs. France stepped back to let them enter, Helene walked into view.

"Afternoon, Aunt Helene," Seth said quietly.

She returned her nephew's greeting with a smile. The thick white face powder made her look ghostly. "How was the funeral service?"

"Fine," Seth responded. "Leah wants to get Cecil's things."

"Help yourself."

Leah started toward the stairs, but stopped when Helene called out softly, "You know, Leah, my sister died much the same way as Cecil. Pain, facial paralysis, seeing everything greenish yellow. In the end her organs collapsed, and her heart stopped. The doctors thought it was something she ate, too, but I knew better."

Leah looked back over her shoulder. "What are you saying?"

"That my sister was poisoned. At the time I swore it was Louis, but he's dead, so what evil have you reawakened by coming back and resurrecting his memory?"

"Aunt Helene!" Seth snapped.

Helene bowed her head to her nephew mockingly. "Just the musings of an old woman, nothing more."

Seth told Leah, "Come, let's get done so we can go."

He ushered her up the steps, but as Leah looked back she saw Helene watching her with emotionless blue eyes.

Because they hadn't been in Denver very long, Cecil, like Leah, hadn't had time to unpack most of his things. As a result, there was very little to gather up. Leah placed his shaving kit and a few odd items of clothing into a carpetbag and Seth began taking the trunks out to his carriage. Leah went over to the small writing table and opened its lone drawer, to make sure they hadn't left anything behind. A telegraph message lay inside. Picking it up, she read:

ARE PRAIRIE DOGS ON THE JUDICIAL BENCH IN COL-
ORADO. NO LEGAL PRECEDENT FOR THIRTY-YEAR JUDG-
MENT. NONE. WILL CONSULT COLLEAGUES. RADDOCK.

When Seth came back in, a shaken Leah handed him the note. "Read this."

Seth did. His surprise mirrored Leah's. "Does this mean you may get the estate back?"

"I've no idea." Cecil must have wired the old judge. It was just like him not to give up, she thought bittersweetly. He probably hadn't mentioned it because he'd been waiting for further comments from Raddock. Leah forced her breathing to slow down so she could think. She had to wire the judge first thing. She needed to know what this was about, and he needed to be informed of Cecil's passing. "Can you take me to the telegraph office?"

"Sure can."

"Now?"

"Help me get the rest of this out to the buggy, and we'll be on our way."

Ten minutes later, they were headed for Denver.

Unlike the tents, shanties and crude shacks put up by the miners during the gold rush years of 1858 and 1859, Denver of 1886 was as built up and as bustling as any big city back East. There were competing newspapers, opera houses, fine hotels that served oysters and champagne; churches, a library, a bookstore, and the US Mint. Gone were the raucous days of the past when gamblers at the Denver House kept the six gaming tables going twenty-four hours a day in order to fleece the miners out of their gold. Back then, bartenders had to arm themselves to keep the drunk and disorderly from shooting at them for sport. Guns and vigilantes were no longer the only law, and the town fathers no longer prone to betting and losing whole blocks of the city on the turn of a card, as their predecessors had done. The Denver Seth rode Leah into represented a city on the verge of greatness, a shining symbol of the new west.

When she and Seth entered the telegraph office, Leah wrote out the message and handed it to the disinterested-looking young clerk, who asked, "Do you want to wait for an answer?"

She turned questioningly to Seth. She didn't wish to monopolize his day, especially if he had other appointments.

Seth replied to the clerk, "How long might it be?"

He shrugged. "Two, maybe three hours."

"Well, here's my address." Seth handed over a calling card. "We'll check back here in a couple of hours or so after lunch. If it arrives after that, send someone around to deliver it."

Seth then reached into his pocket of his well-tailored brown suit and gave the clerk a few coins. "For the delivery and for your trouble."

The clerk looked at the shiny coins. He now appeared more amenable to doing his job. "Thanks, and don't worry, I'll take care of everything."

Seth nodded and escorted Leah out.

* * *

Ryder had had enough of the mystery surrounding Leah Montague. The tall red-haired man seated on the other side of Ryder's desk was Pinkerton Agent George Taggart.

Taggart was taking notes. "What did you say the name of the tavern was again?"

"The Black Swan."

"But you don't know the name of the city?"

"No."

The man scanned his scribblings once more. "Okay, Mr. Damien. I believe you've given me enough information on her to get started. If I find out she's wanted by the law or something serious like that, I'll wire you immediately. If not, you can expect a report soon as I'm done."

"Thank you."

"My pleasure." The man stood and smiled. "Never worked for a half-breed before."

Ryder burned him with an icy stare.

The Pinkerton visibly gulped. "Sorry. I-I'll be in touch."

"Make sure you do," Ryder warned. "Pick up the advance on your expenses from my clerk outside. Good day, Mr. Taggart."

Taggart's face was as red as his hair, his exit hasty.

In the silent aftermath, Ryder mused over what he'd just set into motion. He was certain she'd throw a fit were she to learn he was having her investigated, but it was something he should have done the day they met. He could still remember how beautiful she'd looked standing on the platform of that fancy railroad car and how surprised he'd been seeing her there. Little did he know she'd become the one thing he couldn't allow himself to have.

Ryder stood up and walked over to the windows. Now that she'd buried Cecil Lee, he assumed she would be heading back East as soon as the arrangements could be made, but he didn't care if the report came in after she was gone. He needed to know.

He looked down on the busy street below. Had Louis sent her here as a cruel joke, his final flourish in the tragic opera that was his life?

How could she have been a virgin? That question continued to plague him, haunt him. And what if she were carrying his child? Although his penetration of her hadn't lasted long, it didn't take long for a man's seed to establish itself. Overwhelmed, he ran his fingers through his long black hair and decided to put off thinking about that portion of the equation for now. If she were with child, he'd address the matter when the time came. Right now he needed to find out who she was and what she was. Especially after last night. Holding her while she cried opened up spaces within himself he didn't even know he had, spaces that seemed to echo with emptiness once he turned her loose. As if that weren't enough, he'd dreamt of her last night and awakened this morning hard and thick with lust; he'd had hot, sultry, erotic dreams whose memories made his manhood stir even now.

Pushing her out of his mind, he vowed to keep his distance from her until the Pinkerton filed his report. There would be no more holding her or arguing with her or wanting her in his bed. Dreams or no dreams, he needed the truth.

Ryder checked his watch. He didn't usually leave the office until early evening, but today he needed air. Feeling like a caged puma, he grabbed his coat and hat. Maybe getting something to eat would help steady his mood.

As he headed down the crowded walk, Ryder remembered a time when these same streets held nothing but miners, Indians, and gamblers. Back then you only needed three fingers to count the homes or businesses with glass windows or wooden floors. Now there wasn't a shop or a business that didn't have glass, and people were everywhere. The place was so built up old-timers were complaining about not being able to find their way around, and gold was the reason. After the first gold strike, thousands of Easterners descended upon the area—five hundred a day at the height of the rush, bringing with them grass-killing wagons, tree-killing axes, and their versions of civilization and decency. They turned what had been home for the Arapaho, Utes, and Cheyenne into something his ancestors would no longer recognize. Manifest Destiny, is what his professors up in Minnesota had called the conquering of the land and its Native peoples; the American pioneers felt the Creator had given them dominion over everything; it was their destiny to rule, and anything or anyone ignorant enough to get in their way would be mowed down like locusts swarming over the plains.

The Arapaho had found that out, as had the Cheyenne, their Sioux cousins, and every other tribe who'd been living on the continent for countless generations before the Spaniards first sailed ashore. The West was now being civilized. Gone were the buffalo and the herds of elk. The traditional songs sung by his grandmother could no longer be heard. The male descendants of Chiefs Black Elk and Roman Nose would never count coup, or wear the black-feathered headdress of the Cheyenne Dog Soldiers. Everything they'd valued, cherished, and loved had disappeared like puffs of smoke, just as the legendary Cheyenne prophet Sweet Medicine had predicted, but no one had listened.

Ryder shook off the bitter memories of the past. They wouldn't help his mood. He instead focused his attention on walking to the diner.

Since it was extremely difficult for Blacks to get a seat or be served in the city's White diners and restaurants, Seth took Leah to lunch at a place in the city's Black district. The small, wood-framed house was painted a sunny yellow and had a sign above the porch which read: DINAH'S DINER.

As Seth handed Leah down from the carriage, she asked him, "Is the owner's name really Dinah?"

"No, it's Florence, but she thought Dinah sounded better."

Leah smiled as she pulled back her black veil to free her face.

Seth asked, "Are you sure you're up to this? I can take you back to Eloise's."

"No, this is fine. I'll be by myself soon enough." And she would be. "Right now, company's what I need."

"Then I'll be on my best behavior."

Leah stopped. Another man had said that to her; a dark-eyed man with braided hair, a man she'd been trying not to think of.

Seth peered down into her face. "Are you all right?"

Leah shook herself free. "I'm sorry. I lost myself for a moment there. Let's go in."

He nodded and they started up the walk.

The place wasn't very crowded. There were ten small tables spread around the medium-sized room, each sporting a dark blue tablecloth. Enjoying Dinah's luncheon fare were a group of suited businessmen, a family with two adorable little girls, a couple of solitary miners, and at a table in the back four young women, all in competing hats, sat laughing and giggling over their meal.

"How about over there by the window?" Seth asked.

Leah could see the sunshine falling across the table he'd indicated and approved of the choice. "That looks fine."

Under the curious eyes of some of the other diners, Leah preceded Seth to their table. He helped her with her chair, then took his own seat.

Leah picked up her menu. The funeral had not left her

with much of an appetite, but she knew she needed to eat something. "What would you suggest?"

"The beef stew's awfully good."

"Then that's what I'll have. And a glass of lemonade."

Seth gave their order to one of the white-aproned, male waiters. The young man thanked them and headed to the kitchen.

Leah could smell bread baking and chicken frying. The fragrant aromas made her think the cook might be pretty good. Having run her own establishment, Leah was impressed by the efficiency of the waiters moving in and out of the tables, delivering trays laden with eye-pleasing dishes. She was just about to ask Seth how long Dinah's had been in business when Ryder walked in.

Their eyes met across the room. She thought about last night and the solace he given. He'd shown her a decency that had been touching; a decency she'd needed. On the heels of that came remembrances of other times. Every fiery moment she'd ever shared with him flashed across her mind. Every kiss, every caress . . .

Grabbing hold of herself, she looked back to Seth. He must have seen something in her expression because he turned toward the door to investigate. When he saw his half brother he groused, "What the hell's he doing here?"

Leah didn't know, but watched silently as he took a seat on the far side of the room.

"He didn't bother you last night after I left, did he?"

"No," she replied quietly. She didn't think Seth needed to know what had occurred. No one needed to know, but it was a moment she would treasure in spite of her and Ryder's differences.

Ryder had been momentarily stunned to see Leah in the diner. What the hell was she doing here, and with his gentleman brother no less? He knew they'd buried Cecil Lee this morning, but he'd made a vow to stay away from her, and he couldn't very well do that if he tripped over her every time he turned around. He needed to speak with her, though, if only for a moment. Last night, he'd offered to pay the funeral costs, and he was a man of his word. Pushing back his chair, he crossed the diner.

When he reached her side, her black attire and the grief in her swollen, red eyes opened up another of the spaces he'd mused upon earlier. "I'd like to talk with you."

Leah looked up. He was standing too close. All she could think about was last night. "I paid for the funeral, out of the money you—I had."

Their eyes held, mingled, searched. He said quietly, "I thought we'd agreed—"

"It's okay. Please. Seth and I are about to have lunch. Can we talk about this some other time?"

Ryder's jaw tightened. "I suppose."

Seth said coolly, "Then leave us."

"I'm not talking to you, Seth."

"You're not talking to her either. Or are you deaf?"

Seth stood.

By now, people all over the diner were staring—discreetly, but staring just the same.

Ryder drawled coolly, "The lady has been impressed by you, Seth. Don't spoil the illusion by showing her your true self."

Leah could feel her temper rising. "Stop this!" she hissed.

Both men stared down.

"Cecil was put in the ground less than two hours ago," Leah reminded them, her tone curt. "I came here to set aside my grief, not to be fought over by two morons fighting like gulls over a piece of dead fish!"

Both men looked properly chastised.

Leah lowered her voice. "Now, Ryder, you are going to go back to your table. I will speak with you later. Seth and I are going to have our lunch."

Ryder's jaw grew tighter in response to the light of triumph glowing in Seth's gaze.

Leah saw it, too. She snapped, "And Seth, if you gloat, I swear I'll leave here right now and *walk* back to Eloise's if I have to."

Ryder's eyes glowed with satisfaction.

Leah glared up at him, asking, "Are you still here?"

The light died. "Enjoy your lunch," Ryder said frostily. He turned and walked out of the diner.

By the time the waiter brought their meal, Leah, ignoring the wary stares of the other patrons, had just about regained her calm. Seth, still smarting from her short tongue-lashing, hadn't said a word.

Once they began on their stew however, he asked, "Are you still angry?"

"No." She wasn't.

"Then let me apologize for my behavior. Ryder makes me loco."

"I could see that. Apology accepted."

"If you want to know the truth, I haven't been blistered like that since the summer Ryder and I drank all of Eloise's dandelion wine."

Leah looked up from her plate. "When was this?"

"I think I was twelve. Ryder must've just turned ten. We were so drunk, we thought we could fly and jumped out of a tree. I broke my right leg, he broke his left."

"So the two of you did have some good times, then?"

"If you want to call being sick as dogs for a full day afterward good times, I suppose we did. After Eloise set our legs and we stopped puking, she whipped us up one side and down the other. Last serious whipping she ever gave us if I'm not mistaken."

He looked over at Leah, adding, "Haven't thought about that for a long time."

She wondered if he were pleased by the memory. "You two should bury the past."

Seth took a large swallow of his lemonade, then put the glass down. "Tell him that."

Leah shook her head. Did they not know how precious family could be? Evidently not. Leah thought it best she change the subject. "Tell me about yourself, Seth."

"Well, I'm thirty-eight, unmarried—" he stated looking directly into Leah's eyes.

She didn't blink. "And?" she prompted.

"I'm presently working with a group of men trying to start a Black town. We've sent flyers back East, and so far the results have been encouraging."

"Where will the town be?"

"South of here. If we can get the money to buy up the rest of the land, we could open for business tomorrow."

"That sounds exciting. How close are you to your goal?"

"Another two thousand or so should do it. Hard for folks like us to get our hands on that kind of capital though."

Leah nodded understandingly. "Well, I wish you luck."

"Thanks."

They finished lunch and drove back to the telegraph office. The clerk smiled when they entered. "Your reply's here."

He handed Leah the response, and she read:

SO SORRY TO HEAR ABOUT CECIL. STILL LOOKING INTO JUDGMENT. PLEASE STAY IN DENVER. WILL WIRE ADVICE SOON. SORRY FOR YOUR LOSS. RADDOCK.

But she didn't want to stay. She assumed he wanted her to remain in Denver because contacting her on the long train ride back East would be next to impossible. A deflated Leah sighed. She had no desire to stay here at all, but she would.

"The judge wants me to stay here," she said, handing the message to Seth to read.

He replied, "I'd be lying if I said I was disappointed."

Leah took the compliment but said nothing in response.

"Who knows," Seth added, "maybe after everything's all said and done, I can convince you to stay here permanently."

Leah had no trouble reading between the lines; Seth found her attractive. Admittedly, Leah found the golden-skinned Creole and his thin moustache attractive as well, but she didn't see the two of them advancing any further in their relationship, at least not in the near future. She wouldn't be ready for any commitments or promises until the events swirling around her life were settled and laid to rest.

The young clerk sat watching them as if they were in a theater show.

Leah ignored him, and said to Seth, "How about we let the future take care of itself for now and just enjoy each other's company?"

"I've no problem with that. Do you want to wire the judge anything else?"

She shook her head.

"Then let's get you back to Eloise's."

When they returned to Eloise's, Leah told her about the telegram from Judge Raddock. "He seems to think the court ruling can be reversed."

"That's promising news," Eloise replied. She was seated in her small parlor. Having just returned from driving her pastor back to his home, she was still dressed in the black dress she'd worn to the funeral.

"I suppose, but he wants me to stay here while he looks into it. Sam says you have a cabin out back you sometimes let?"

"I do."

"No offense, Seth, but I don't wish to stay with your aunt a moment longer."

He smiled. "I understand."

Eloise asked brightly, "Does that mean you want to move into my cabin?"

"Yes, if I could."

"I think that's a great idea. Me and Alice would love the company."

Leah smiled.

Eloise hoisted herself off the flowered love seat, and said, "Well, let's go take a look at it then."

The cabin had one room. There was a fireplace, a bed, a table and chair, and little else. It was clean however. There were leather shades over the paneless windows and a hooked rag rug on the plank floor.

As Leah set her handbag on the bed and removed her veil, Eloise said, "It's not a palace."

"But it will do nicely," Leah replied, looking around. "How much do you want a week?"

"If you help out around here, I won't charge you a thing. The place'll be here whether I get any money for it or not."

"But Eloise—"

"Don't insult me, child. Right now you need a haven, and this is it."

Leah wanted to haggle over the issue a bit longer, but the sparkle of warning in Eloise's eyes made her keep her mouth closed.

Eloise smiled knowingly and nodded at Leah's wisdom. "Now. Seth, all her trunks are still in the parlor where Sam left them yesterday. Once you bring those, there's a dresser in my back room we can move in here."

Leah didn't know what she'd done to have such an angel come to her rescue, but she dearly appreciated the woman's many kindnesses.

Once Seth had moved in the trunks and the dresser, it was early evening. He stood with her in her sparsely furnished new place, and said, "I need to be getting back to town, Leah."

"Thank you for all your help," she told him genuinely. He'd stood by her at the funeral and for most of the day. He'd been an angel of sorts as well.

"You're more than welcome. In reality I'm hoping it'll get me some points."

She grinned. "It has."

"Then I leave here a happy man."

Their eyes held for a long moment. She felt the pull of his maleness but noted it lacked the power and intensity of his brother's. Banishing thoughts of Ryder, Leah walked with Seth out to the road, where his carriage waited.

He got in. Looking down at her, he said, "I know you're grieving and you have a lot on your mind right now, but friends of mine are having a dinner Saturday night, and I'd be honored if you'd let me escort you."

Saturday was a few days away. Leah didn't know how she'd feel by then, but decided she'd go, if only so she wouldn't sit in the cabin and brood. "I'd like that, Seth."

"Careful now," he cautioned with a smile, "you're giving me hope."

She laughed. "What time Saturday?"

They spent a few more moments discussing the details of their outing. When they were done, Seth said, "Get some rest."

"I will."

He slapped down the reins and she waved good-bye.

Leah walked up to the house and went inside. Eloise had on her hat.

"Are you going out?" Leah asked.

"Yes. Old Lady Crumwell needs more salve for her arthritis. Promised her I'd bring it this evening. Will you be all right alone?"

"Sure."

"Well there's chicken and dumplings in the icebox if you get hungry. Me and Ol' Tom'll be back late."

"Who's Ol' Tom?"

"My mule."

"I see."

Miss Eloise smiled. "You sure you don't want someone with you?"

"No, I'll be fine. Truly."

"All right then. You can have full run of the house. Take a bath if you like. Ryder fixed me up one of his fancy bathing rooms, and there's plenty hot water in the boiler."

Leah thought that a grand suggestion.

"There's only one place you're not allowed, and that's the room down at the end of that hallway there. It's where I keep the paintings and sculptures I'm working on. I don't like them seen until they're finished."

Leah had no problems respecting Eloise's privacy. "Don't worry."

Eloise's voice turned serious. "Things didn't work out with you and Ryder, I take it." It was a statement not a question.

"No, they didn't," Leah admitted.

"Well, I won't pry, your spirit's been bruised enough I sense."

Leah was grateful for the woman's understanding.

Miss Eloise said encouragingly, "You'll survive. We women always do. Get some rest. I'll see you in the morning."

"Thanks, Eloise."

Slowly nursing a drink, a brooding Ryder Damien sat on his fancy, black Victorian sofa, his well-polished boots resting comfortably atop an equally fancy coffee table. When Sam came in, Ryder looked up at him and raised his glass in silent salute.

The gray-haired Sam took one look at Ryder's feet, and barked crossly, "If you don't get those boots off my table . . ."

Ryder smiled. "Your table? As I remember, I signed the bank draft."

"Did you go all the way to San Francisco to get it? Do you dust it and polish it so it'll stay nice?"

Because Ryder knew he couldn't answer yes to either of the questions, he put his feet down. "Happy?"

"Very. What're you so riled about?"

"Saw Mrs. Montague, this afternoon."

"After the funeral?" Sam asked.

"Yes, she was in town with my gentleman brother." After a few moments of silence, Ryder added, "Tried to talk to her—"

"But she told you to go waltz with a bear."

Ryder smiled. "Something like that."

"Well, what did you expect?"

"Just what I got, I suppose."

"Give you guff?" Sam asked.

Ryder thought back. She challenged him in a way no woman had ever done before. "Lots of it."

Sam's voice intruded upon his thoughts. "She says you were mad and asked her to leave Sunrise because you want her to be someone she's not."

"I was mad because she was a virgin and didn't tell me."

"*I* told you she didn't belong in a cathouse, but did you listen?"

"No, Sam, I didn't."

"Well you should've." Sam then added, "But if she was a virgin—does that mean she wasn't married to your pa?"

Ryder shrugged. "See the problem I'm having? Who knows what the truth is?" Ryder drained his drink. "Maybe I'll just let Seth have her."

"Pigs'll fly first."

Ryder raised his glass in yet another salute. No, he'd

never surrender anything to Seth, certainly not the black
jewel Leah Montague, even though that was a direct contradiction to the vow he'd made this morning.

"Well," Sam said, "I'm going over to see Mable. You?"

"Going to sit here a minute or two more, then work on
some reports."

"Okay then. I'll see you later, and keep those boots on
the floor."

Amused, Ryder nodded.

Sam's exit left him alone. As the quiet resettled, Ryder
set down his empty glass and stretched his tired arms and
shoulders. He had a stack of papers on the desk in his study
a foot high and he wasn't looking forward to them. After
being tossed out of Dinah's by Leah this afternoon, he'd
gone back to the office in so foul a mood none of the clerks
wanted to approach him, and that suited him fine because
he hadn't wanted to be bothered. The only thing he'd
wanted was the woman who'd been sharing a meal with his
Creole brother.

Ryder stood and ran his hands through his unbraided
hair. What was wrong with him? He was mooning over her
like a lovesick cowhand. He'd never let a woman claim his
mind this way before and it had to stop. He was a mixed-
blood Cheyenne brave. He had no business running behind
a woman with his tongue dragging on the ground, especially one he was having investigated. There were other,
more agreeable women available. *But I don't want them,* the
voice in his mind echoed.

Leah's bath had been just what she'd needed. Tired after
the long, trying day, she sat in the cabin before the fire she'd
made, oiling and combing out her freshly washed hair.
When it was satisfactorily free of tangles, she divided it in
half, then put in the familiar French braids. After twisting
the trailing ends together into a coil, she pinned it low on

her neck. Dressed in a thin nightgown, she walked barefoot across the wooden floor and turned down the lamp until only the faintest of flame showed. There in the dark, Leah sat on the bed and let the grief of the day rise up and fill her heart. She was alone in the world now, no mother, father, Monty, or Cecil. Thinking about Cecil made the tears rise once more. Their trip to Colorado had been so full of promise, and now—Leah dashed her palms across her eyes. Cecil, just like her mother and Monty, wouldn't want her wallowing in grief and self-pity; they'd taught her better than that. So there in the dark, Leah sat. But in the end she gave in, put her face in her hands, and silently surrendered to the grief.

Chapter 7

By Saturday, Leah was looking forward to the idea of going out with Seth. She and Eloise had spent the past few days planting vegetables, gathering medicinal plants, and weeding the flower beds. Leah found the work exhausting but far less so than hauling kegs or scrubbing floors, even if it did seem as if she'd spent the entire time either bent over or on her knees.

Seth arrived promptly at seven Saturday evening. Leah had chosen to wear a navy, black-tipped gown cut low on her arms. To guard against the late-evening chill, she grabbed a matching silk shawl and settled it around her bare shoulders.

She told Seth, "I didn't know how formal your friends' gathering would be. Is my gown okay?"

Seth nodded approvingly. "I'll be the envy of every man there."

Leah had to glance away from the flashing interest in his

light brown eyes. Although Seth's manner was less intense than his brother's, it held its own power.

Eloise came out of the back. She scanned the elegantly dressed Leah and smiled approvingly. "My, don't you look lovely. Seth, you're going to be with the prettiest lady in the county tonight."

"That I am."

Leah felt embarrassment warm her face.

Seth made a show of politely extending his arm. "Shall we?"

Leah placed her hand lightly on the offered limb. "By all means."

"Have a good time," Eloise told them both.

Leah hoped she would. After the events of the last ten days, she needed a bit of good time in her life.

"So, where are we headed?" Leah asked once they were on the road.

"Their names are Mr. and Mrs. Wayne. He's a barber, she—well. Folks around here call her the Great Cordelia."

"The Great Cordelia," Leah echoed skeptically.

"Yes, more ambition than three men. Were she White, she'd make some politician a great wife. As it stands she isn't, so she spends her time trying to advance her husband's aspirations."

"Which are?"

"To be a barber and to be left alone."

Leah chuckled. "Sounds like an interesting marriage."

"It is. He's rich as Midas—she's as beautiful as Venus. She grew up dirt poor in Mississippi, he resembles a toad."

"Should be quite the evening."

There were dozens of buggies, buckboards and carriages parked up and down the narrow road leading to the Waynes' Victorian mansion. A bit taken aback by the sheer number of vehicles, Leah said, "I thought this was going to be small affair."

"Cordelia never does anything small, and besides, I'm sure some of these folks came just to get a look at you."

"You told her I would be attending?"

"I did."

"I'm not sure I like that."

Seth turned her way, and said kindly, "When my father left here thirty years ago, nobody knew if he'd been killed by renegades or swallowed by a whale. I think those who were around back then are hoping you can shed a little light on the mystery."

Leah thought about Reba's words. "My mother once said, 'A man's past is his own.' "

"But a son is a part of that past. Surely, he has a right to know?"

He found a place to park the carriage in the jumble of vehicles, then set the brake. In the quiet that followed she told him earnestly, "Your father deeply regretted leaving you and your brother."

Seth's jaw tightened. "Were these deathbed regrets?"

Leah felt his underlying anger, and said quietly, "You sound like your brother."

"Touché."

It didn't surprise her to learn Seth harbored bad feelings, too. Had he spent his young life hoping his father would return? "He spoke of you on his deathbed, yes, but he said the guilt had been eating at him for many years."

"Did you love my father, Leah?"

Leah knew he meant as a husband. Since she did love Monty in her own way, she didn't feel wrong in saying, "Yes, I did love him. He was very special to me, and I to him."

"That's good to know."

Leah swallowed her guilt for partially deceiving him and walked with him to the door.

As Seth escorted her inside, the one hundred or so formally dressed guests standing around Cordelia Wayne's vast, well-furnished parlor all went silent. Leah could see them see staring at her speculatively. It was a decidedly awkward moment for Leah, but Seth cleared his throat, and said. "Everyone, I want you to meet Leah Montague."

Leah said, "Hello, everyone."

There were a few false smiles and nods, but Leah felt no more welcome. Not one person ventured over to introduce themselves. She assumed that some might be here to have the mystery of Monty unraveled, but others came just to get a look at the scandalous woman who'd been purchased by Ryder Damien. She could see it in their eyes.

Only then did the tall, storklike Cordelia Wayne step up. Leah wondered if she'd been waiting to make certain she didn't scratch in public or could speak properly before deeming her suitable to approach.

"How are you, my dear?" Cordelia asked after Seth made the initial introductions. The Great Cordelia was dressed in an elaborate gray gown that outshone every other woman's in the room. She appeared to be just a few years older than Leah. Her eyes were sharp and her skin the color of chocolate. As Seth had noted, she was indeed beautiful.

"My condolences on your loss," Cordelia offered, seemingly genuinely. "Louis was quite a figure in his day, I hear. Let me take your shawl."

Leah handed over the soft silk. "Thank you."

"And how are you, Seth?"

"Fine, Cordelia. Lot of people here tonight."

"Yes, but Lewis Price couldn't join us this evening, I did so wish to hear about his latest investments."

Leah had no idea who Lewis Price might be, but from the pretty pout on Cordelia's face it was apparent that she was quite disappointed.

"Well, Leah," Cordelia said, gazing down at her from her towering height, "I must say, that accent of yours is quite—quaint."

Leah smiled falsely. "My mother was British."

"One could almost mistake you for royalty, except we all know there's no Black royalty over there in England."

Some of the guests standing nearby chuckled at Cordelia's wit.

Leah took pleasure in saying, "Ah, but you're mistaken. Many coats of arms in Great Britain have Moors on them. Have you never heard of Queen Charlotte Sophia?"

"No. Who is she?" Cordelia looked so irritated, Leah could only assume she was unaccustomed to being corrected.

"A former queen of England and consort to King George III."

"I see. Ah, there's my husband, Barksdale."

Barksdale Wayne, drink in hand, stepped forward. He was an oily little man with too much pomade on his thinning hair. His pocked skin and fat jaws did resemble a frog's. The bright glitter in his eyes told Leah he'd begun drinking long before tonight's reception began.

"Welcome to Colorado, Mrs. Montague," he said, his bulbous eyes ogling her bosom above her neckline.

"Thank you," Leah replied coolly. She wondered if he always addressed a woman's anatomy when introduced. She'd been prepared to feel sorry for him after hearing Seth's story about the Waynes' marriage, but now—

Behind Cordelia stood Helene Sejours, dressed in a blue gown that though clean, appeared as old and worn as her furniture. The ghostly white makeup on her face was punctuated by the bright red paint on her thin lips. She purred in an accent much more pronounced than usual, "Ah Seth, and Leah. How nice to see you both."

Leah simply nodded rather than lie and say it was nice to see Helene, too. She didn't want to risk being struck down by lightning.

"Are you enjoying your stay with Eloise?"

"I am."

"So, when will you be leaving us?" Helene asked.

"Soon, I hope."

"Well, we'll say a prayer."

Inwardly, Leah snarled.

The guests filling the room had seemingly come back to life now that Leah had been seen, and at first glance appeared far more interested in their conversations and drinks than in her, but upon closer inspection, Leah could see them studying her covertly. She smiled at a few who caught her eye, but they nodded impassively before turning away.

Cordelia gently took Leah by the arm. "Let's meet all these folks. Like me, they're so glad you're here."

Leah doubted that, but let herself be led away.

For the next three-quarters of an hour, Leah was shuttled from person to person. She met businessmen, cattlemen, farmers, and their skeptical-looking wives. A few of the guests offered condolences for her loss, but others gave the impression that they'd come simply to stare. Some of the women were whispering behind their hands as she passed by, and a few of the men were looking her over as if she might be the evening's dessert. By the time the introductions ended and Cordelia sent everyone to the beautifully laid-out buffet, Leah had been gawked at so much she felt like a beached albino whale. She wished Sam or Eloise were there, but doubted these were the kinds of people they rubbed shoulders with.

"How long were you and Mr. Montague married?" Barksdale Wayne asked as he stood beside Leah in the buffet line.

Leah watched a few people standing nearby immediately stop what they were doing in order to hear her reply. Did they not teach manners on this side of the Mississippi? she wondered testily. As for Barksdale Wayne's question, Leah knew he and his wife were probably very influential community leaders. In the end it probably wouldn't pay to offend either of them, but she had no intentions of feeding the gossips by telling them her business.

Leah replied politely, "Unfortunately, we weren't married long enough."

His plump face hardened; it was not the answer he'd been after. Cordelia and Helene, standing on either side of him also looked perturbed that Leah's response hadn't been more specific.

Leah turned to Seth, and asked, "Do you think we might find a place to sit?"

But he didn't reply. He seemed frozen by the sight of something on the far side of the room. Leah also noticed that the surroundings had taken on an eerie quiet. Confused, she turned to see if she could determine the cause.

Ryder.

She had to admit he was riveting. Tonight, the long black hair was pulled back and tied. The dark vested suit and the snow-white shirt fit him impeccably as always. The strength, pride, and masculine beauty of his mixed ancestry showed in the rich dark copper skin, the prominent nose, the cut of his jaw, and the fullness of his lips. His shoulders seemed wide as the mountains, and the black eyes stared around at the silent, gaping guests with a superiority usually reserved for monarchs.

His stony gaze locked with Leah's, and her chin instinctively rose. In spite of what had passed between them and who he thought her to be, she didn't much care for being scrutinized like a woman on the block. She was certain her face mirrored that, but her feelings obviously didn't matter because his gaze didn't waver.

Ryder didn't know why she looked so offended. Every rube in attendance had come to get a good long look at the woman Louis Montague had taken as his last wife and who had been purchased by Ryder for fifteen thousand dollars. Because Ryder hadn't seen her in nearly a week, he proved no exception. She was still as beautiful as the night sky. The feline eyes beneath the winged brows could stir a man's soul, and he knew from experience that her mouth could tempt a brave into giving away all he owned. A few days ago, Sam had mentioned tonight's party, then let slip, very deliberately Ryder noted, that according to Mable, Seth would be escorting Leah. Ryder initially dismissed the information as having little value; he'd sworn off Leah Montague and would continue to do so until he received the Pinkerton report. However, the closer it got to Saturday, the more intense became his need to see her again. He'd never gotten along with Cordelia and her Black elite set, and all the way down the mountain he'd fought the idea of attending her soirée just so he could see Leah again, but he'd lost. It seemed the lure of his father's widow was far more powerful than his vows to keep her at a distance.

From behind her, Leah heard a tight-lipped Seth ask Cordelia, "Did you invite him?"

"Of course not," the hostess hissed.

When he walked over and joined their small group, Cordelia said stiffly, "Good evening, Mr. Damien."

"Cordelia." The voice was low and rich, the black eyes mocking, cold.

Ryder turned to the tight-lipped Seth. "Good evening, big brother. Good evening, Mrs. Montague."

"Mr. Damien," Leah said.

Addressing each other with such formality was ludicrous

in light of their past dealings, but for Leah it set up an artificial barrier she sorely needed.

The guests were all buzzing, and Leah had no trouble imagining what they were buzzing about.

Seth asked Ryder bluntly, "Why'd you come?"

"Barksdale invited me. Didn't you?"

Barksdale sputtered hastily, "Of course, of course. Cordelia and I are honored to have you in our home."

Leah didn't believe a word of it, and judging by the crossness on Cordelia's face, the hostess didn't either.

He seemed to have saved Helene for last. "And how are you, Helene?"

"We were having a lovely time until you arrived."

Helene's sharp tongue didn't seem to pierce him at all. "We had an appointment earlier today," he told her. "Did you forget?"

Helene suddenly began to fidget with the gold bracelet on her wrist. "I had to help out here."

Leah noticed that Helene avoided looking directly into Ryder's eyes and wondered what they were supposed to have met about.

"Tomorrow morning. Ten."

Helene's chin tightened, but she nodded affirmatively.

Ryder then looked around at all the smoldering, displeased faces, and smiled. "Think I'll help myself to the buffet now."

"Be my guest," Cordelia offered frostily.

His eyes brushed Leah in parting, and he moved on.

Leah didn't know what to make of any of this. The hostility in the air around the table was thick enough to cut, but Cordelia and the others had been as deferential as if Ryder were some dangerous predator they didn't want to rile.

When Ryder was out of earshot, Helene cracked nastily, "Squaw Boy."

Leah couldn't help herself, she had to know. "So, it's true? People here really did call him Squaw Boy?"

Seth admitted drolly, "Yes."

"Everyone?" she asked, unable to keep the temper out of her voice.

Seth shrugged as if he didn't wish to answer.

Helene had no such reservations. "Yes, because that's who he is."

Barkdsale cracked drolly in response, "Now Squaw Boy owns everything and everybody around." He then added, "Excuse me, folks, but I need another drink."

The subject of Ryder was dropped. Leah and Seth made their round of the buffet table then found seats, but she noticed that all the guests seemed to be covertly watching the younger Montague son, and she proved no exception.

It seemed not all of the women were as averse to his presence as Cordelia and Helene however. More than a few gave him secret smiles as he passed by. Dorthea Ross, the pale, red-haired wife of one of the cattlemen, had been very chilly when introduced to Leah, but now she looked as warm as a hot rum toddy as she stood across the room talking and smiling up at Ryder with flirty eyes. Her elderly husband stood beside her, jaws tight, trying to appear cordial.

Seth must have noticed where her attention lay, because he said, "Dorthea's new around here, only been married to Charlie Ross six weeks or so. She wouldn't know Ryder's reputation with women."

He paused in his eating. "I'm sorry, you probably didn't want to hear that."

Leah had to know. "Is he very popular with the ladies?"

"Let's just say, he has a well notched bedpost."

And now, Leah was one of those notches. She decided to change the subject. "Tell me about this town you want to start."

So for the next ten minutes Leah listened to Seth's hopes

and dreams for his town. At least, she tried to listen. Ryder had positioned himself in a spot across the room at his brother's back. Every time she looked up his eyes were waiting. Even though she would hastily glance away, it was never quickly enough to avoid the heat of his silent touch.

"Leah—"

She quickly gave her attention back to Seth. "I'm sorry. I was woolgathering. Go on, you were saying?"

He chuckled. "I'm sorry. Let's talk about something else. Financial talk's always pretty boring for most females."

Leah hated to be judgmental but found his words mildly condescending. "I see. Why do you think that is?"

He shrugged as he forked up a fat piece of ham. "Females care about dresses and shopping mostly. And that's okay because they shouldn't have to worry their heads over business things—that's what men are for."

Leah's punch became strangled in her throat and set off a coughing fit that doubled her over. She took Seth's hastily offered handkerchief and placed it over her mouth, but she coughed and coughed and coughed. Folks were staring, possibly wondering if she were about to succumb, but she finally found her breath. And when she did, she stood, and said, "I need a bit of air."

He stood, too.

She raised a palm. "No, you stay. I'll be right back."

"Are you sure? I can go with you."

"No, I'll be fine."

Aware that every eye was now turned her way, Leah ignored them and headed for the door.

Outside on the large verandah, she drank in the night air. She wondered what the folks inside would say about her if she shanghaied a coach and drove herself away. She didn't like this place or its people. The women were cold and stiff-backed, and the men seemed content to follow their wives' leads. Right now, she didn't blame Monty and Cecil for turning their backs on this decidedly unfriendly lot. And Seth. He was charming and handsome, but did he actually believe women had no heads for business? The views he'd expressed were terribly out-of-date in light of the strides achieved by women since the end of the war. Granted there were those women content to fill their heads with nothing but shopping and fashion, but so many others, like Leah, knew firsthand that thoughts of shopping and fashion wouldn't pay one's bills, nor put food on the table.

"You know," Ryder Damien drawled from behind her, "the longer you're out here, the more the gossips inside are going to savage you."

For some reason his arrival didn't surprise her. "I don't care. The sooner I can leave here, the better I'll be."

"Not impressed by Denver's representative elite?"

"No."

It was a beautiful night—the air was warm and the sky so clear Leah could see the stars shining like diamonds against dark velvet. "Did the Cheyenne have their own names for the stars?"

"Yes."

While Leah followed the movement of his finger, he named some of them for her: Raven Carrying the Sun, Spider God, the Star That Never Moves. He showed her the Three Hunters and the Bear, and the Headdress.

He then asked, "Do you know how the Big Dipper came to be in the sky?"

Fascinated by this side of him, Leah shook her head, saying, "No."

"Coyote."

"Coyote?" she echoed skeptically.

"Yes. Coyote's a legendary trickster—a joker. Sometimes his tricks are good, sometimes bad, but he always comes out on top. Only rarely is the trick played on him."

"So, how'd he put the Big Dipper in the sky?"

Ryder explained, "According to the legend my grand-mother told me, there were five wolf brothers who saw some grizzlies in the sky one night and wanted to go up and visit, but had no way to get there. Coyote came along, heard their story, then offered his help."

"So what did he do?"

"Took out his bow and shot an arrow into the sky. When the arrow stuck, he shot another one into the end of it, then another, and another. He kept shooting arrows until they formed a long ladder down to the earth."

"And the wolf brothers used that?"

"Yep, the eldest wolf brother even took his dog."

"The wolf—had a dog?"

He sounded amused. "Sure, dogs were as much a part of tribal life as the legends."

Leah shook her head. "Okay. So, were the grizzlies in the mood for company, or did Coyote send them up there just to get eaten?"

"No, the bears were pretty hospitable. The wolves sat down with the bears—"

"The dog, too?"

"Yes, the dog, too, but Coyote didn't trust the bears so he stood a ways off and just watched."

"Then the bears ate the wolves," Leah interjected.

"No, the bears didn't eat the wolves," he told her with amused exasperation. "Do you want to hear the story or not?"

A chastised Leah apologized. "I'm sorry. Go ahead."

He shook his head. "Anyway, Coyote didn't trust the bears, but he thought the bears and the wolves made a nice picture, so he decided everybody down on earth would enjoy seeing them, too. He also wanted everyone to be able to say Coyote was the one responsible for the picture so he climbed down and took the arrows with him as he went."

"So they were stranded?"

"Yep, and they're still up there today. If you look at the Big Dipper you can see the three wolf brothers that are the handle. In the middle is the eldest one," and, he added pointedly, "with his dog."

Leah tried to hide her smile.

Ryder continued, "Right under the handle are the two youngest brothers."

"And the grizzlies?"

"Are the other side of the bowl, the side that points to the North Star. In fact, Coyote was so proud of how it looked, he turned all the other stars into pictures, too."

Leah knew she'd never look at the Big Dipper or the stars in the same way again. She glanced up at him and wondered why all of their encounters couldn't be this easygoing.

As if he'd read her mind, he said, "Maybe we should stick to talking about constellations when we're together . . ."

Leah replied softly, "Maybe we should."

Silence reigned for a few more moments before Ryder said, "You know, you didn't have to pay for the funeral yourself."

"I'm already beholden to you enough, and it was still your money after all."

"That's not the point," Ryder said.

"Yes, it is. I owe you enough."

"But not the truth."

Leah wondered why he'd intentionally sabotaged this moment. She turned to go. She didn't want to have this conversation.

He stopped her with a gentle hand on her arm. "I apologize. That was unnecessary. We both know where we stand."

"Yes, we do," she echoed. "I need to get back inside." Leah was becoming more and more vulnerable to everything about him, and she didn't want to.

Short of using force, Ryder knew of no other way to make her stay, so he let her go.

When Leah reentered the house, chairs were being set up in Cordelia's grand ballroom. Putting Ryder from her mind, she searched for Seth and found him waiting for her just inside the ballroom door.

"I saw Ryder follow you out. Did he say something that offended you?"

She shook her head. "No." She didn't need them fighting. "What's going on here?"

"Cordelia's invited the famous Hyer sisters to perform portions of their plays."

Leah'd never heard of the Hyers, but Seth explained who they were as he led her to a seat. According to Seth and the program Leah was handed, Anna Hyer had been eleven and her sister Emma nine when they made their debut as concert singers at the Metropolitan Theater in Sacramento.

Seth said, "They were child prodigies back then, but in 1875 they founded the Coloured Operatic and Dramatic Company, and began touring the country doing Black plays and musicals about the history of the race."

Leah was impressed. "I've never heard of such a thing."

"Many folks haven't, but the Hyers are the first stage troupe to perform plays that are about us and written by us. In some places, they're very well known."

And as the performance began Leah understood why. The cast's voices were superb, the characterizations full and true to life. For over an hour, Cordelia's guests were treated to scenes and songs from some of the women's most successful productions: *In and Out of Bondage*, a musical drama in three acts adapted by Sam Hayes; *Colored Aris-*

tocracy, another three-act drama, but written by the Black novelist, Pauline Hopkins; and, *The Underground Railroad*, another Hopkins piece.

The high point of the evening came when Anna Hyer, exotically dressed in beads and a bejeweled turban, came out to portray the lead role in *Urlina, or The African Princess*. She was a gifted actress and her part of the program so moving that it ended to thunderous, appreciative applause.

It was a truly enlightening and enjoyable event, and Leah was glad she'd been invited. "Does Cordelia do this sort of thing often?" Leah asked as she stood on her feet like everyone else, vigorously applauding the end of the performance.

"She's had poets, singers, and lecturers, but nothing like this."

Leah admitted to not liking Cordelia's personality, but she adored her taste in the arts.

"Are you glad you came?" Seth asked.

Her eyes glowed with happiness. "Yes, I am." After the week she'd had, this was just what she'd needed to refresh her spirits. "Thanks for inviting me, Seth."

"You're more than welcome. Now, let's go see if Cordelia's desserts can equal the treats we just witnessed."

Leah thought that a splendid idea.

The dessert buffet consisted of more choices than Leah could possibly eat in one night. There was ice cream, and trifles, fools, cakes, and puddings. She saw pies, cobblers, and finally decided on some ice cream and a small piece of chocolate cake.

She and Seth took their dessert outside on the verandah. A few of the other guests were like-minded it seemed, finding it quieter and much cooler out here than inside. Seth wove them past softly talking couples and others laughing uproariously over to a spot on the vast verandah's far edge, away from everyone else.

He motioned her to take a seat on a wrought-iron bench shining in the moonlight, so she did. The night was just as beautiful as it had been earlier. The stars brought back memories of Ryder, so she didn't look at them. She and Seth were just settling into the silence when they heard his name being called loudly by someone hidden by the dark.

A confused Seth called out, "Over here."

Out of the darkness appeared one of the liveried waiters Cordelia had hired for the evening. "Mr. Seth Montague?"

"Yes."

"I've a message for you sir."

He handed Seth a folded sheet of paper. Seth gave the man a coin for his trouble, and when the waiter faded back into the shadows, Seth lit a match so he could see what it said. "Well, I'll be—Leah, I have to meet someone back in town. He says he wants to invest in my town enterprise, but he's leaving for Sacramento first thing in the morning. He can only see me tonight."

Leah was happy for him. "Then go. I'll find someone to take me home."

"But—"

"The time you waste taking me back to Eloise's and then driving all the way back to town could be better spent detailing your plans to him. Go on."

"You sure?"

"Positive."

Their eyes held for a moment, then he said, "You're a beauty, do you know that?"

Leah grinned. "Good luck, and let me know how it turns out."

A second later he was gone, leaving Leah with the task of finding a way back to Eloise's. She knew Ryder would escort her, but she hoped to find someone else; they'd only wind up arguing the entire way, and she didn't want to end this evening engaged in a round of verbal fisticuffs.

As if cued, Ryder appeared on the verandah nearby. "Nice night."

"Yes, it is."

For a few moments, silence reigned.

"I noticed my brother leaving. Did you two have a fight?"

Leah observed him, wondering what he was about now. "No. He's gone to meet a man interested in investing in his land project."

"Ah."

Then he asked, "How are you getting back to Eloise's?"

"I'm not sure," she replied. She then asked him, "How'd you know I was staying there?"

"Sam. Few secrets with him around."

Leah understood.

"I'll take you, of course."

"I know, but I'd hoped for a less volatile escort."

Ryder shook his head at her blunt reply. "What's your middle name?"

Leah thought that an odd question. "Jane."

"Jane. It should be Frank."

She smiled in spite of herself. "Well, it isn't. It's Jane."

Ryder decided then and there that he didn't care how the Pinkerton investigation turned out; she was too tempting to ignore. All of his vows and stubborn attempts to deny his growing attraction had resulted in nothing but sleepless nights and inner turmoil. He was tired of fighting himself. "Surprised to learn you were still in town though."

She decided he might as well know about Judge Raddock's interest in her case; after all he'd made a large financial contribution to it. So she told him. She finished by saying, "He seems to think the judgment is too old to enforce."

"He may be right."

"Will the court return your money, do you think?"

He shrugged. "Depends on whether they've already distributed the assets of the estate to Louis's creditors or not. If your Judge Raddock does manage to get the judgment reversed, it might be returned, but who knows. Every state has its own set of laws, it seems."

"Well whatever the outcome, the judge wants me to stay here until he can sort it out."

"How long?"

The darkness hid her shrug. "I've no idea, and I'm not real happy about it. I'm ready to go home."

"Do you miss it?"

"I do. I have no family there anymore, but I do have a few friends. It would be wonderful to see the ocean again." Thinking of home made Leah a bit melancholy. She decided she'd had enough excitement for one night. The Hyers were grand, but she was ready to return to Eloise's cabin. "Will you take me back?"

He nodded.

Leah knew that were she to be seen leaving Cordelia's home with Ryder, the gossips would be up all night spreading the word. To counter that, she didn't want to go back inside at all, but she had to retrieve her wrap. "I have to get my shawl."

As if by magic it was in his hand. "I brought it out with me."

Leah cocked her head. "You were pretty confident, weren't you?"

"Yes."

Leah then thought of something she had to ask, "Your brother wasn't just sent on a wild-goose chase, was he? This investor does exist?"

With a perfectly straight face Ryder told her, "You'll have to ask Coyote."

Leah's eyes widened, and then she shook her head. She pulled the shawl out of his hand and said with a humor she couldn't hide, "Lightning is going to strike you one day. Mark my words."

"My carriage is this way," he said, gesturing toward the dark.

Still shaking her head, Leah led the way.

As they drove across the quiet countryside under the moonlight, Leah said, "That wasn't nice what you did to Seth."

"He's done far worse to me, believe me, but it isn't as if I sent him over a cliff. He simply went back to town, there's no harm in that."

"It was underhanded."

"It was counting coup."

Leah had never heard the expression before. "What's that mean?"

"It's a tribal expression. Scoring points on your enemy is the simplest way to explain it."

"You consider Seth an enemy?"

"He's certainly not a friend."

"He's your brother."

"*Half* brother he'd say if he were here."

Leah knew he was right; she'd heard Seth say exactly that. "The two of you need to end this feud."

"Tell him that. Besides, we've grown up this way. Be hard to stop after all these years even if we wanted to."

Leah didn't think that made a lick of sense but kept the opinion to herself.

The short conversation died after that, leaving them alone with their private thoughts, the surrounding night, and their awareness of each other's presence. It was an awareness Leah was fighting hard to ignore, but how could she ignore the man who'd been her first lover?

Ryder was wrestling with his own demons. More than anything, he wanted to stop the carriage and take her in his arms. Back there on the Waynes' verandah he'd decided he didn't care who she was as long as he could make love to her. Finish what they'd started. Would doing so finally cure him of this rising need, thus enabling him to return to his well-ordered life? Or would it make him want her more? He put his hopes on the former. His attraction to her was as unexplainable as it was illogical. She'd been married to his murderous father, there was a Pinkerton investigating her past, but now, as they rode beneath the moonlight none of that seemed to matter. Tired of beating around the bush, he took the bull firmly by the horns, and asked, "Remember the morning I asked whether you wished to be courted or seduced?"

Leah found the question so unexpected and so filled with vivid memories it took her a moment to respond. "I do," she replied a bit shakily.

"You said you wished for both, if I recall correctly."

He looked her way. Leah bravely met his gaze even though she knew her bravery to be paper-thin. "Yes, I did, but why does that matter now?"

"Because I plan to court you."

Her blood rushed. "Court me?"

"And then, seduce you . . ."

Leah struggled to keep from swooning and falling out of the carriage. "Is this so you can count coup on your brother again?"

"No, it's because I want you, and I believe you want me . . ."

Leah studied his face. He was right of course, but she hadn't planned to admit that truth aloud. The remembrances of their one night together continued to resonate strongly within her, but the aftermath had been very painful; she had no desire to be ambushed that way again.

"I have very vivid memories of that night, Ryder, and it'll be something I'll remember to the grave; but I can't set aside what came after just because I enjoyed being in your bed."

He seized upon the words that pleased him most. "Did you?"

Leah couldn't lie. "I did."

"You're a very passionate woman."

"Well-raised women aren't supposed to be passionate."

"You'd be surprised what a well-raised woman will do behind closed doors with the right man."

Heat burned Leah's cheeks. His pointed words brought back to mind their fiery interlude with the spiced peaches. "Let's talk about something else."

"Why, are you afraid your passionate nature will lead you astray?"

"Frankly, yes."

He stopped the carriage in the middle of the moonlit road.

"Why are we stopping?"

"To see if I can give your nature some help . . ."

When he leaned over and kissed her, she knew she should have protested, but his lips were so warm and knowing, his cajoling so moving, she forgot all about it. Tender, tiny flicks of his tongue against the parted corners of her mouth made her arch closer so she could gift him with the same arousing play. They teased and tantalized each other for what seemed an eternity, but neither could bear to halt. He placed kisses on her lips, her nose, the small dark shells of her ears. As their ardor flared his hands slowly joined the fray, mapping her curves, caressing her jaw, her throat. His mouth meandered down the scented column of her neck. His hands explored her breasts possessively while his lips brushed heat across the soft, tempting skin above the neckline of her gown. He slid a bold hand inside, and the nipple cried out a joyous welcome. Her dress was drawn down and under his ardent suckling the bud bloomed.

Leah had never envisioned being made love to in the middle of the road in the middle of the night, yet here she was, her head melted back against the seat, her gown rucked down, her breasts damp and hard.

Ryder thought she made quite an erotic sight bared for him under the moonlight. He wanted to slide the silk gown up her hips and see about baring a darker, more intimate portion of her, but found encouraging her passionate nature to be exciting as well. To that end he brushed his lips across her berried nipples. A pleasure-filled moan slid from her lips, sounding all the world like a musical note against the silence of the vast Colorado countryside. Enjoying her response, he repeated the gesture, this time pausing to dally with first one budded nipple and then the other before his hands began slowly to explore the warm flesh of her limbs beneath her dress.

Leah tingled in response to the strong hands moving her gown up her legs. All of the many reasons why being with him made no sense rose to the fore, but when his intimate touch found her through the thin cotton barrier of her drawers they were reduced to ash. She crooned and arched, then shamelessly widened the way so he could give her more.

Her uninhibited responses fired Ryder's desires. He was hard for her, achingly so. He wanted to touch her for a lifetime but doubted even that would be long enough to give her all the pleasure he wanted her to receive. Looking up, Ryder saw a pinpoint of light cresting the road about a mile away. A lantern. He leaned in and placed his lips softly against her own. "There's a wagon coming—about a mile off."

His fingers hadn't stopped their wicked ministrations.

"I'm going to bring you to pleasure and then we'll get you home . . . okay?"

Leah was too busy rippling and pulsing under his tender assault to care about anything, but she whispered, "Okay . . ."

He let loose one of his rare smiles. Kissing her again, he brazenly slipped a hand inside her drawers. "No screaming allowed, *Morenita* . . ."

She was hot and swollen; already prepared by his earlier play. It didn't take long for her body to begin crying for release. He teased her for a few hot moments more though, malely enjoying the sensual way she arched and rose to the play of his hands, and how enticing her dark-nippled breasts looked bathed by the soft pale light of the moon. Kissing her deeply, he eased a bold finger into the core of her pleasure and gave her what she so desperately craved. The orgasm rocketed through her with such shattering force she screamed her joy into his shoulder.

Leah came back to herself slowly. The soft echoing throb purring in her body made her want to spend the rest of eternity right where she was. Turning her head on the seat, she looked over and found him watching her with night-shrouded eyes. Feigning irritation, she said, "This is exactly why I didn't want you to see me home."

Ryder grinned. "Then fix your clothes so we can get there."

"As if that's my fault."

Ryder reached over and softly traced her cheek. He was hard as iron. If he didn't find release soon, he wouldn't be able to walk for a week, but he knew it wouldn't be here or now. He willed his body to calm down so he could pick up the reins. As she righted her gown, he looked on disappointedly.

"What's the matter?" Leah asked as she gave the gown one last adjustment.

"Nothing. Just prefer you the way you were."

Leah smiled self-consciously. "You're too bold for me, I think."

"Didn't notice you complaining a minute ago."

He had her there, and she knew it. "Aren't you supposed to be driving me home?"

He gave her a grin and slapped down the reins.

They made it back to the cabin without any further delays. He parked the carriage out in front of the main house, then walked her to her door.

Leah could see the light on in Eloise's studio. "Eloise is still up, I see."

It was an inane observation, but Leah suddenly felt awkward and unsure now that the time had come for them to part. "Where's this leading, Ryder?"

He answered truthfully, "I don't know."

Leah remembered how incoherent she'd been on the carriage seat, then dashed the memory away. "I doubt this has any future."

"But it isn't about the future, it's about now. Here."

"It's about the past too, though—at least it is for you."

Ryder stared off into the distance. He hadn't brought her home to do this.

Leah felt compelled to continue. "Deep down inside you don't trust me—haven't since we met. To you I'm some terrible woman who married the father you hate under questionable circumstances. You say you want me, but I can't help but wonder at your motives, too."

Ryder met her eyes. Her penchant for truth was humbling. "So, what do you propose we do?"

"End this—now," she replied softly, haltingly. "Otherwise, there'll always be questions, hurt feelings. I—"

"Suppose I can't."

The power in those three words silenced her. Leah searched his unreadable features. What was he admitting?

Was he telling her there was more to this relationship than lust? Had his heart somehow gotten involved along the way? Leah found that hard to believe. She didn't know what to think or to say.

Ryder decided it was time for him to be truthful as well. "No, I don't trust you, and no, I wouldn't be surprised to find out your marriage to Louis was some type of sham. However—" His voice dropped to the softness of a caress. "I want you like I've never wanted a woman before. You could be wanted in six states, and I'd still dream about kissing that mouth, or making your body beg for my touch . . ."

The words hit Leah with such sweet force, she almost fell over. "Ryder—"

"I'm not done."

Leah quieted and noted the pulse beating between her thighs.

"I've been fighting off my desire for you from the moment we met, and I've come to a decision."

"Which is?"

"I'm not going to fight it anymore."

Their eyes held.

He added then, "I want you. You want me. I'm going to remind you of those two truths each and every time we're together, so be warned. Good night."

Leah could only blink as she watched him stride off. What an arrogant and impossible man! But when she replayed his words, her traitorous nipples tightened, and the throbbing in her body began again. A portion of herself was still undone by all she'd heard, but the woman inside smiled; she couldn't wait for their next encounter.

Leah went inside, undressed, and got into bed. She wondered if she'd dream of Ryder.

She dreamt of Cecil. His dead body was lying in a coffin in a shadowy, black-draped room. The silent room was empty but for a lone chair in the corner. On it sat Helene.

The sight startled Leah awake. She was just as alarmed to find herself shaking and covered in sweat. Wiping her hands across her eyes, she tried to calm herself. Had there been more to the dream than she remembered? What had caused such a reaction? For a moment there she'd felt absolute terror.

Throwing back the covers, Leah padded barefoot over to the dresser and by the light of the approaching dawn put on a dry gown. The dream was fading as were the resonants of terror. Leah thought a bit of air might do her good, so, grabbing a cloak, she put it on over her nightgown and stepped out into the quiet.

The birds were signaling the beginning of the new day with songs that trilled against the silence and the oranges and reds stripping the still-dark sky. Leah had no destination, but her steps seemed to naturally take her through the dew-damp flowers to Alice. Just before Leah got within sight of the statue, she thought she heard a voice. She stopped to listen for a moment to make sure it hadn't been her imagination. She heard it again. It was Eloise. The trees encircling the cleared oval of land where Alice stood allowed Leah the cover she needed to approach without being seen. Leah didn't want to disturb her landlady but she did want to make sure she wasn't in distress, so she walked slowly very quietly.

Leah could see Eloise sitting on the bench talking to Alice it seemed.

Eloise was saying, "I thought the Lord had forgiven us, Alice, but looks like we got one more trial ahead." Eloise quieted for a moment, then said, "You're right, it is a shame, but we both know it has to be done."

Leah realized Eloise was acting as if she and the marble girl were having a real conversation.

For a short time there was silence again, then Eloise said, "No, I don't know when. I'm sure the time will show itself though. Maybe then the Lord will be done with us and we can rest."

Eloise then began nodding as if listening to and agreeing with whatever Alice was saying.

"You're right, precious," Eloise replied. "We can only do what's right, and pray."

Leah had never seen anything as strange as this but supposed if she were living alone with only an old mule and a statue, she would probably exhibit some eccentric behavior, too. At least she has someone to talk to, Leah thought, and decided Eloise's talks were probably as harmless as Eloise herself.

Sunday morning meant church in Eloise's house. As Leah rode with Eloise to join the thirty or so other parishioners in worship at one of the local A.M.E. churches Leah didn't mention the encounter she'd witnessed between Eloise and Alice earlier this morning. The pastor, the Reverend Garrison, was as handsome as he was young, but he was good in the pulpit.

On the drive back, Eloise asked, "How was the party at the Great Cordelia's?"

"At first, I felt like a tuna being circled by sharks."

Eloise chucked. "That bad?"

"Ryder was there, too. He said Mr. Wayne invited him, but I don't think he did."

"Probably not. Ryder and Cordelia don't get along real well."

"Why not?" Leah asked.

"Because he wouldn't share her bed."

Leah blinked.

"Ryder's very discriminating when it comes to women. He isn't a philanderer like his father was. No offense."

"None taken."

"Did you and Ryder get to talk?" Miss Eloise asked.

Leah thought back to the ride home; its passionate middle and its fiery end. She didn't think Eloise wanted that much detail. "We did, but it turned out confusing as always."

"Well, Ryder seems quite taken with you, in spite of the problems."

"I know, but I wonder about his motives though," Leah confessed.

"What do you mean?"

"Well, he didn't exactly love his father."

"Few did, Leah, and there is the death of Ryder's mother in this, too."

Leah sighed. "I know. I just keep wondering if the only reason he's interested in me is to extract some type of revenge."

Holding the reins of Ol' Tom, Eloise shrugged. "That's quite possible. Ryder's a complicated individual. Has been his whole life. However you're a very beautiful woman. His interest is only natural, I think."

"Or just another competition between him and Seth."

"There's that possibility also. They've been competing most of their lives. When they were young the game was heavily weighed in Seth's favor. He was the legitimate Montague son, and Helene always made sure he had the best. On the other hand, Ryder had his grandmother, Little Tears, and the rest of her Cheyenne people, but life on a reservation wasn't much of a life. If the hunger didn't get you, the disease did. There were no fancy Sunday suits or trips to San Francisco for Ryder like there were for Seth."

"I can't believe people around here called him Squaw Boy."

"One of the milder slurs they tarred him with. After his

mother's death, Little Tears took him back to her people. They returned here after the massacre at Sand Creek."

"What was his mother like?"

"Beautiful, exotic. She and Louis were pretty much cut from the same cloth."

"Meaning?" Leah prompted.

"Pardon my frankness but the more they had the more they wanted. He gave her carriages, stock, gold, clothes, and she took it all willingly. Rumor had it she wanted him to marry her after Louis sent her husband to his death down that shaft, but he refused. Bernice had been dead over a year, but I guess he didn't want a Black half-breed gracing his table either. In many ways, it's good this all took place while Ryder was an infant and too young to understand."

"Why?"

"Because he'll never really know just what a Jezebel his mother was."

Leah heard the tone of disapproval in Eloise's voice, and replied, "But no one deserves to die alone at the bottom of a mine shaft, Eloise. Jezebel or not."

Eloise nodded, then said, "You're right, child. You're right."

"Now, tell me about this massacre—Sand Creek, did you call it?"

Eloise asked, "You don't know about Sand Creek then?"

"No, I don't. Where or what is it?"

"It's down by the Big Sandy River over near the Colorado-Kansas border."

"And the Indians massacred some people there?"

"No, some people massacred the Indians there. Cheyenne and Arapaho to be exact."

Leah went still.

"This happened on November 29, 1864. You have to remember how bad times were back then for the tribes; government folks cheating them out of their land, hunting them down like game to put them on reservations. Here in Colorado it was no different. As soon as a treaty was signed, the men on the government's side would break it. The territorial governor at the time was a man named Evans. He wanted all the tribes gone and didn't care how. Helping him was Colonel James Chivington and his Colorado Volunteers. Now, Chivington absolutely hated Indians. Hated them. He told folks that he'd not only come to kill Indians, but he believed it right and honorable to use any means under God's heaven to kill them."

"My word," Leah exclaimed. "He sounds depraved."

"Many think he was."

"So what happened at Sand Creek?"

Eloise paused a moment as if the memory brought her pain. "Chivington and his regiments descended on the Cheyenne and Arapaho with seven hundred men, four howitzers, and enough hate to shame the devil. The Indians were asleep. This was just before dawn, and there were hundreds of Indians in the camp. Mostly old people, women, and children. The men were off hunting. The others awakened to hell. When the shooting finally stopped, Chivington's men had killed a hundred and five women and children. That was the government's estimate. The survivors said those killed really numbered in the hundreds. Many of the children were infants who died in their mothers' arms. Then the butchering began."

"They killed babies?"

"Some, unborn."

"Dear Lord," Leah whispered. "And Ryder and his grandmother were there?"

Eloise nodded sadly. "If Chivington's men hadn't spent the long ride to Sand Creek getting drunk, countless more would've died that night, but between the drunks and the troops who couldn't shoot straight, many, like Ryder and Little Tears, somehow managed to get away."

"Did anyone back East care that this had been done?"

"Oh, there were hearings held afterward. I do have to say that a few of the army officers with Chivington that day were sickened by what they saw and told the government investigators just that."

"What happened to Chivington?"

Eloise gave a bitter chuckle. "He took a bit of heat for a while, but now he's the undersheriff in Denver."

"What?"

"Yep."

Leah shook her head solemnly. "Only in America."

"My feelings, too. So, I told you all this to say Ryder has more than just the death of his mother and his feelings toward his father haunting him."

"How old was he?"

"About fourteen if I'm remembering correctly."

"Fourteen," Leah whispered. At the age of fourteen her only concerns were raising hell at Miss Caldwell's School for Young Women of Color. Her heart ached for the fourteen-year-old Ryder. He and his grandmother must have been terrified to find themselves in the middle of such carnage.

Eloise looked over and said, "So now you know about Sand Creek."

"I doubt I'll ever forget."

"Good. Always remember in honor of those children who never drew breath."

Eloise was so silent for so long afterward, Leah peered over, and asked, "Are you okay?"

Holding the reins, Eloise slowly wagged her head. "No, just facing something down the road that's going to be distasteful."

Leah thought back to the conversation between Eloise and Alice. "Are you ill?"

"Yep, I think I am," she responded matter-of-factly.

Eloise then looked over at Leah's concerned face. "Don't worry about it though. I know the cure."

Leah felt relieved. She didn't want anything untoward to happen to one of the genuinely nice people she'd met here so far. "Well, if there's anything I can do to help, let me know."

Eloise nodded, saying, "I will."

Chapter 8

Later that Sunday afternoon, Ryder's knock on Helene's door was answered by Mable France.

"How are you, Mr. Damien?" She stepped back so he could enter.

"Fine, Mrs. France. Is Helene here?"

"Yes, I'll get her."

Ryder nodded as Mable went off. While waiting he looked around. The place was as stuffed with furniture as always, making Ryder feel a bit claustrophobic. Having spent most of his early years living beneath the sky, he didn't like the sensation of being hemmed in. He supposed it was the reason he'd built Sunrise on such a grand scale. He remembered the first time he entered this house. He couldn't have been older than four or five. His grandmother had some business with Helene, who wouldn't let either of them enter; too dirty, she'd said. She'd been in her glory back then; the profits from the mine left to her by

Louis were enough to make her a queen, and she'd basked accordingly. She had the fanciest clothes, the finest horses, and an attitude concerning the tribes that mirrored the general populace: Indians were lazy lying thieves. When Miss Eloise and Little Tears enrolled him in school, Helene and a few others in her circle had protested Ryder being educated along with their own. Even though he went on to prove innumerable times that he was by far the brightest student in the small segregated classroom, Ryder spent more time in detention than he did with his books. The almost daily fights he'd had were a direct result of being teased about his parentage, taunted about his mother's death, and being made to take his lessons seated on the floor at the back of the room; he might contaminate the other children had been the claim. He supposed they'd all expected him to turn the other cheek as the missionaries kept preaching to the reservation Cheyenne, but that rarely kept the bullies out of his face or off his back. So he'd retaliate—swiftly, openly. He didn't care that they expelled him; he'd do his studies with Miss Eloise at her kitchen table, but he did care about standing up for himself, and he always had.

Helene's glory days were over now. When her mine had gone fallow back in the late seventies, so had her world. Presently she didn't have two coins to rub together. Three years ago, when she walked into his office to offer him the deed to her house in exchange for some much-needed cash, he hadn't laughed or turned her away. If she were coming to him, he knew she'd exhausted all other sources and was at the end of her rope. She'd had to come to him, Squaw Boy, and that knowledge alone made up for all the verbal abuse he'd endured under her sneering presence while growing up. He'd taken the deed, given her her asking price, then signed the note at a percentage rate so high, she'd still be paying him ten years after she died and went to hell.

Helene entered the room. He noted the anger on her pale powdered face, but he didn't care. "Your note was due on Friday, Helene."

"I can't pay it."

He surveyed her. She looked uncomfortable, and well she should be. He had the power to put her fancy Creole self out on the street for all the world to see. "Are you planning on moving out?"

"Of course not. I'll have the money for you in a week."

"It was due *last* week," he reminded her pointedly.

"Surely seven days won't much matter to you."

"If the shoe were on the other foot, would you be benevolent?"

They both knew the answer.

Her blue eyes were as frigid as a Minnesota winter. "You're enjoying this, aren't you."

"My enjoyment isn't a factor. I carried you for six months last year. I told you then that was the last time."

"You've more of your father in you than you think," she retorted nastily.

"From you, I'll take that as a compliment. It doesn't change matters though. Either pay me or prepare to move."

"But this was my sister's house."

"A house you thought me too dirty to enter when I was young, remember?"

She looked away.

"So," he told her coldly, "you have until four on Friday." He touched his hat and left.

When Ryder got back to his office he wondered how long it would be before Seth came barreling in to plead his aunt's case. He looked at his watch. He figured sometime after lunch.

He was correct. At half past two, one of the clerks came

to the door and announced that Mr. Seth Montague was in the outer office demanding to speak with him.

"Send him in."

Seth barged in. "How dare you threaten Helene."

"And good afternoon to you too, brother."

Seth glared. "You've been waiting for this, haven't you?"

"For my money. Yes, I have."

"That isn't what I mean, and you know it."

"Then what do you mean?"

Ryder hadn't risen from his chair behind his desk. He sat there, his arms folded casually across his chest.

Seth declared, "You can't just toss her into the street."

"Sure I can. The deed she signed over to me three years ago gives me that right. Are you by chance here to pay in her stead?"

Ryder knew the answer to that. Seth owed so many people so much money, he couldn't get a loan to buy penny candy. That was partly the reason why he hadn't been able to find backers for his homesteading plans. Only a fool would lend money to a man apt to lose it an hour later in a card game. "You haven't answered, Seth."

Seth shot him a malevolent look. "You have a lot of Louis in you. Do you know that?"

"Second time I heard that today. Thanks for the compliment. Anything else?"

Seth's eyes blazed angrily.

Ryder drawled, "Guess not. Close the door on your way out."

As if Seth were already gone, Ryder went back to reading the mining reports on his desk.

"You'll pay for this," Seth promised.

Ryder didn't look up. In the resulting silence Seth stormed out.

As the echoes of the slammed door faded away, Ryder

looked up with a smile that did not reach his dark eyes. Like Seth and Helene, many folks abhorred the idea of a rich Black half-breed owning so much; but like a moth in a buffalo robe, he'd wormed his way so deep into the fabric of the economics here, they couldn't separate his money from their own without bring financial ruin raining down on all their heads. He had his fingers in so many pies, no one dared call him Squaw Boy anymore, at least not to his face. In reality he didn't care what they called him behind closed doors because thanks to hard work, a quick mind, and the strengths inherent in his mixed blood, he now had more wealth than even his father had at his age.

Louis.

Thoughts of Louis made memories rise, memories of the dark lady, the *Morenita*. Ryder had been trying not to think of her, but to no avail. His manhood stirred every time he thought about last night's tryst. She'd been bewitching, passionate, his. It didn't make sense why he was still so hell-bent on pursuing her in the face of what he knew about her, or what he thought he knew about her, he reminded himself pointedly. He knew very little, thus the Pinkerton; but he seemed to be the only person disturbed by the shadows shrouding her marriage. It was quite apparent that Sam and Eloise had taken her into their hearts unconditionally. They cared about her. He, on the other hand, had angrily rebuffed her attempts to explain that night, and he continued to kick himself for being so pigheaded. He hadn't expected to be her first, let alone be bothered by the fact that he was. In hindsight, he should have listened, but because he hadn't, they were forced to dance around each other instead of with each other. Last night he'd boldy tossed down the gauntlet, and he'd meant it. The Cheyenne always like a good hunt, especially if the prize was challenging, and Leah Montague was all that and more.

A few days later, Leah and Eloise drove Ol' Tom into town to pick up the new paints Eloise had ordered and to see if there were any messages for Leah at the telegraph office.

The telegraph clerk recognized Leah right off. "Hi there, ma'am. Telegram came in for you a few days ago. I sent it around to the address your man left here."

"Oh." The news surprised her somewhat, mainly because Seth hadn't been out to Eloise's to let her know about it. She assumed he'd gotten busy with his land-development project and had let the telegraph slip his mind. "Well, I'll go over and see him. Thank you."

He nodded.

Outside, Leah and Eloise walked back up the crowded street to retrieve the wagon tied up at a post a few shops down. "Do you know where he lives?" Leah asked Miss Eloise.

"Yep. Not too far from here."

As they were walking they saw Cordelia and Barksdale approaching. "Man the harpoons," Leah cracked sarcastically.

Cordelia, wearing an expensive wine-colored ensemble and matching hat, stopped and said, "Good afternoon, Mrs. Montague. Did you enjoy the Hyers?"

"Yes, very much so."

Cordelia barely smiled. "Well, where I'm from it's very impolite to leave someone's home without saying good-bye to the hostess."

Leah winced inwardly. "My apologies. In the crush I didn't think I'd be missed."

"You were. As was Ryder. Hello, Eloise."

Eloise nodded.

Leah could see Barksdale looking her over hungrily. "Hello, Mr. Wayne."

He grinned and nodded.

Cordelia asked, "I'm wondering if you'd like to be profiled in my newspaper, Mrs. Montague. It isn't often a widow takes up with her late husband's sons. I think everyone would be very interested in your story."

"No thank you."

"Surely you don't wish me to write it without having all the facts."

"I doubt that will matter," Leah replied.

Cordelia gave her a rattler's smile. "You're right. The paper will be out in a few days. Happy reading. Come, Barksdale."

Barksdale winked boldly at Leah, then did as he was told.

Leah eyes were narrowed as she turned to Eloise, and asked, "Maybe I should've knocked her into the street and really given her something to write about?"

Eloise chuckled. "Now that, I'd've loved to see."

They continued on up the street. Leah asked, "Does she really have a newspaper?"

"More of a social rag than anything else. Folks try to stay on her good side lest they wind up skewered on her front page."

Leah could almost feel herself being poked through like a kabob. She vowed to steer clear of Cordelia in the future.

The street was so crowded with vehicles of all shapes and sizes, it took Eloise a moment to get Ol' Tom and the wagon into the flow of traffic. When they were finally under way, Eloise told Leah, "That building over there is where Ryder keeps his offices."

Leah studied the two-story place. The sign across the front read: DAMIEN MINING CO. The brick building looked new and sported quite a few windows. She wondered if he were inside and what he might be doing. Telling herself she shouldn't be thinking about him, she set her attention forward.

Eloise drove them to a section of town Leah had not seen before, and it contrasted sharply with the other areas. There, instead of windowed shops and fancy eating places, poverty reigned. There were shacks with rusted tin roofs and listing, poorly maintained boardinghouses with hard-eyed men congregated out front. Dirty children ran through the rutted streets, playing in the dust with misshapen hoops and skinny barking dogs. There were garishly dressed women standing in front of saloons and vice dens. The women eyed Leah and Eloise suspiciously as they rode by.

"Where are we?"

"Still in Denver."

Leah saw tents so dirty they'd taken on the color of the dust. In front of them tired-looking women in drab clothing cooked on open fires while their smudged-faced children ran nearby. Leah could smell bodies, burned food, and despair.

"This is where the poor live. The tourists who come here to see the mountains and the old gold areas aren't shown this part of town. Many of these folks came out here hoping to strike it rich, but those days are gone."

"So they wind up here?"

"Yep. Here and other places nearby. Some folks want to leave but don't have the money to make it back home. Most of the stories are real sad."

Leah found the conditions heartbreaking and thought the town fathers should be made to lend these folks a hand. "Are there any aid societies in town?"

"Cordelia and her cronies pretend to help out, but most of the work is done by the churches and those genuinely interested in improving things."

Eloise stopped the wagon in front of a small clapboard house that needed paint. It was in as much disrepair as the rest of the area's buildings. The houses on either side had collapsed into piles of weathered, rotting wood. "Well, we're here."

Unable to keep the surprise out of her voice, Leah asked, "Is this where Seth lives?"

"Yep. I'm going to let you out and go see one of the families a few houses down. Their eldest was sick last week, and I'd like to see how she's getting along. I'll swing back by when I'm done. Shouldn't take more than a few minutes."

Leah nodded and got out. As Eloise drove away Leah marveled that this could possibly be the place the elegant and urbane Seth called home. Making her way up the weed-choked path, she stepped up onto the dilapidated porch and heard angry voices coming from inside via the paneless window. The higher-pitched voice belonged to Helene. The deeper one sounded like Seth. Although Leah had never been one to eavesdrop, the voices drew her like a moth to a flame. She stood quietly and listened.

"I want him dead!" Helene snapped. "I don't care how or by whom."

Seth laughed cynically. "You can't kill him!"

Leah's eyes widened. Who in the world were they talking about?

"That dirty nigger half-breed! How dare he threaten to put me out of my own house!"

Leah had the answer to her question.

"You were the one who borrowed the money from him," came Seth's voice. "I told you it was a bad idea."

"I had no choice. Where else was I going to go, to you?"

"Then sell some of your furniture," Seth told her casually.

"No," she shot back. "I've a reputation to maintain."

"You won't have anything to maintain when he evicts you. The house is *his* after all. Didn't Louis leave it to him and that grandmother?"

So Cecil had been right, Leah thought. The house had been left to Ryder and Little Tears.

"I was not going to turn my sister's house over to ignorant savages. I gave the old woman some money for the deed and sent her away."

Stunned and disgusted, Leah shook her head.

Seth said, "Well, whatever happens with you, my own problems may be solved. Here, read this."

There was silence for a moment, and then Leah heard Helene ask, awestruck, "Does this mean what I think it does?"

"Yes. She's got some White judge back East trying to get the settlement overturned."

Leah realized they were talking about her now.

Helene asked sarcastically, "And how's this going to help you?"

He didn't hesitate. "Maybe the will will be reinstated. Then I'll court the widow."

"Ha! As if she'd have you. Your brother's already mined that claim."

"But that's over. He sent her packing. She told me so herself."

Helene's voice held a bitterly amused tone. "You must be blind. That night at Cordelia's, he never took his eyes off of her. Wake up, Seth. To have her you're going to have to go through that Indian. A woman like her will spread her legs for any man if the price is right, and your brother can pay."

Leah wanted to burst in and straighten Helene out once and for all, but forced herself to stay put. She needed to hear more.

"Well, I'm not going to worry about her and Squaw Boy," Seth said confidently. "He only wants to bed her, and once that's accomplished, he'll discard her like the rest."

"And she'll need a sympathetic shoulder to cry on," Helene replied knowingly.

Leah imagined them both smiling triumphantly, and her lip curled disgustedly. She'd fallen into a nest of vipers.

Seth spoke then. "I will see what I can do about keeping Cordelia under control though. She's threatening to write about Leah if I don't keep my distance. I'd no idea she'd come so unglued over a few innocent evenings."

"Jealousy does that. I told you she'd be a liability one day. She's not going to let you discard her so easily."

Leah's eyes went round. Seth and Cordelia?

Helene added, "Tend to Cordelia, but continue to pursue the widow. If Ryder wants to interfere, let him. In the end, he'll be doing us a favor."

Leah didn't know what to say or think. They were trying to weave her into a malevolently spun web that would reach her no matter where she turned.

Helene asked, "Do you really think you can gain her heart?"

"I know I can."

Leah rolled her eyes sarcastically.

"Well if you can, our financial worries will be over. It may be a lengthy court fight to get back Louis's estate for Leah, if the court entertains it at all."

"This Raddock sounds pretty influential, but I don't care about the time. Once I have the pigeon in my coop, I can wait until I'm seventy for an estate that size."

"Just so you understand it may take years."

"Oh, I've already thought about it. I'll do whatever's necessary."

"Even marry her?"

"I'd marry the devil himself if gets me close to Louis's money."

Leah let out a sigh. *Seth, Seth, Seth*, she said to herself. Granted, he'd almost taken her in with his manners and his charm, but now—now she knew the truth, and it didn't sit well. So, he'd court the devil himself, would he?

As if she'd just arrived, Leah walked over to the door and knocked soundly.

When Seth opened it and saw her, his composure slipped, exposing wide startled eyes. He immediately composed himself and his face broke into a broad smile. "Leah? How wonderful to see you, but what are you doing here?"

"The clerk at the telegraph office said he sent a telegram here for me. Eloise wanted to visit a sick child so I asked her to drop me off. She'll be back in a short while."

Seth gestured Leah inside, where the sparse furniture matched the house's overall run-down appearance.

"How are you Helene?" Leah asked.

Helene answered distantly, "Fine, and you?"

"I'm well."

Leah turned her attention back to Seth, "So, was there a message for me?"

"Ah, yes. It's right here." He went over to a small table where the note lay.

Leah took it from his hand and read:

FILING INJUNCTION TO STAY JUDGMENT. FEDERAL COL-
LEAGUES AGREE. NO PRECEDENT. WILL CONTACT AGAIN
SOON. BEST REGARDS, RADDOCK.

"Judge Raddock's been very busy it seems," Leah voiced. She then asked Helene, "Did Seth tell you about the judge's efforts on my behalf?"

Helene nodded. "Yes, he did. How long have you known him?"

"Not very."

"Men just melt in your mouth it seems."

Leah's chin rose. It was a nasty thing to say. "Did life turn you this bitter, Helene, or were you born this way?"

Helene threw back her head and laughed. "Touché. I forgot, you aren't afraid of me."

"No, I'm not."

"Well be afraid of whoever poisoned Cecil. If the pattern proves true, you'll be next."

"Aunt Helene!" Seth snapped.

It was the second time she'd repeated her theory concerning Cecil's possible poisoning. Coupled with Saturday night's eerie dream of Cecil, Leah began to wonder if maybe she should talk with someone about that possibility, but whom? Leah waved off Seth's false show of support. "It's all right. Helene's simply worried about my well-being."

Helene nodded. "Leah's right, of course, Seth. We wouldn't want another of Louis's women to come to a tragic end. There's enough death ringing his name."

Leah wondered how the two would react if they knew she'd overheard their conversation. The sound of a wagon outside distracted her thoughts and sent Seth to the leather-shaded windows. "It's Eloise, Leah."

Leah nodded. "Okay. Thanks for taking care of the message. Good afternoon, Helene."

"Good-bye, Leah. Oh," she said as if suddenly remembering something, "I've ordered new furniture for the house, so tell Eloise I'll be selling some of my old things tomorrow, and that she should let her friends from the church know, in case they'd like to stop by."

Recalling Helene's adamant refusal to put her furniture on the block earlier, Leah guessed she'd changed her mind and chosen to swallow her Creole pride and attempt to pay the piper. So Leah simply nodded, asking innocently, "Will the sale be at a certain time?"

"Yes, from ten in the morning until four in the afternoon."

"I'll tell her." With a wave, Leah left them to their plotting.

That night as Leah lay in bed, she admitted being disappointed with Seth. She had known Helene didn't care a fig about her, but Seth, too? Leah turned over and punched her pillow. Even though she hadn't seen herself getting serious about Seth, it pained her to know he'd been leading her down the garden path. She assumed Ryder knew all about this side of his brother but had left her to find out on her own.

Ryder.

So far, she hadn't heard from him. After their parting Saturday night, she wasn't sure she wanted to. He'd declared himself to her as no other man had before, and even now his blunt words made her blood rush. She didn't see him proposing marriage, nor did she expect him to, but she didn't see herself in the relationship based on lust alone; she wanted more from life than that. She also didn't see herself revealing the details of her marriage to Monty because she didn't think he'd understand why Monty believed the marriage to be such a necessity. In fact, Ryder might feel that it proved Monty cared about someone else's child more than his own flesh and blood. If she knew him better, maybe she could take the plunge, but she didn't. Even though she'd gone to his bed a virgin, that fact hadn't changed any of his other assumptions; it only added more fuel to the fire. Yes, he knew she'd scrubbed floors and where she'd attended school, but what else? He knew neither her heart nor her soul, and until he did, she thought it prudent she keep the truth to herself.

The next morning, Eloise came out to the cabin. "Leah, there's an invite here for you. It seems Sam and Mable have gotten engaged, and they're throwing a party."

"What?" A laughing Leah took the invitation—sure enough there was the announcement scrolled on the fancy paper in black and white. The party would be two Saturdays away at Sunrise, and both she and Eloise had been invited. "I knew he was seeing her, but engaged?"

"Yep. I think it's sweet."

"I do, too. Sam's a nice man. I hope he'll be happy," Leah said.

Eloise cackled, "I know Mable will. A lot of other widows around here won't be, but Mable sure will."

It was the end of May; the rhubarb in the garden was high, and the summer flowers were peeking above the earth, signaling that warm weather had finally arrived.

A few days before the engagement party Leah and Eloise went into town. While Eloise did errands, Leah went over to the telegraph office to wire Eloise's address to Judge Raddock. She also asked the clerk not to send any more of her messages to Seth. She wanted them sent to Eloise's. The less Seth and his aunt knew about her doings, the better she'd feel.

The day of the party, Leah had to pound on the closed door of Eloise's artist's room in order to draw her attention to the time. "Eloise, we're going to be late!"

"Okay," she called back. "Just give me a couple of more minutes, and I'll be right there."

Leah shook her head. Eloise was working on a new piece and had been spending every free waking moment sequestered in her sanctuary. Leah had no idea if the creation were a painting or a sculpture, but she did know if she left things to Eloise, the party would be over and done with before Eloise called it a day.

Leah went back to her cabin to dress. For the past few weeks she'd set aside the expensive attire she and Cecil had purchased in Boston in favor of simple skirts and blouses. Eloise had been trying to convince her to purchase a pair of denims, insisting they were much more comfortable for gardening and the like, but Leah hadn't the nerve so far. Tonight's event required elegance, however, so she opened the wardrobe holding her fancy gowns and tried to decide which one she would wear. As she viewed each of the four gowns in turn, it suddenly came to her that the midnight blue dress she'd worn that night with Ryder wasn't there.

She thought back. Last she'd seen it, the gown had been pooled on the floor before the fire! Surely she hadn't left it behind? The answer to that question seemed quite obvious since the dress wasn't here hanging with the rest. *Good lord, how do you ask a man for the return of your dress,* she asked herself. Sighing, Leah took down the first gown her hand found and laid it across the bed.

When Eloise pulled back on the reins to stop Ol' Tom in the paved drive leading to Sunrise, Leah was overwhelmed with mixed feelings. On one hand, she couldn't be happier for Sam and felt honored to be among the invited guests. On the other hand, there was Ryder; she didn't need to say more.

The happy couple greeted them at the door. Sam was dressed to the nines in black-and-white formal attire. His eyes shining, he gave both Leah and Eloise a big hug, and thanked them for coming.

Beside him stood a Mable France whom Leah hardly recognized. Gone was the frumpy woman dressed in the formless, white-aproned costume of the servant. In her place stood a confident, buxom woman in a beautiful blue gown that showed off her ample figure to advantage. The severe bun had been replaced by an elegant twist, and there was a smile on her face.

"Thanks so much for coming," Mable said.

"Thank you for the invite," Eloise replied, speaking for both herself and Leah.

Mable then added, "Sam why don't you take Eloise out back with the rest of the guests. I'd like to speak with Leah for a moment."

Leah was a bit surprised by the woman's request but let Sam and Eloise go on ahead. She then asked Mable, "What did you wish to speak with me about?"

"I owe you an apology," Mable said.

"For what?"

"For being so tight-mouthed with you when you first arrived. I thought you'd be like Helene, ordering me around, looking down your nose, but you're not."

Leah found the confession touching. "I appreciate that, but may I ask you something?"

"Sure."

"Were your family's men really killed in one of the Montague mines?"

Mable nodded. "Yes, they were. And although I hate to say it, I'll go to my grave cursing Louis Montague's name because of it. He refused to invest in the safety measures his men wanted."

Leah nodded understandingly, then confessed, "Cecil told me some of the stories. My late husband wasn't a very benevolent individual in those days."

Mrs. France nodded. "No he wasn't, but I changed my mind about you that morning you spilled the coffee."

"Why?"

"Because you went and got the mop. *She'd've* made *me* clean it up, but you took care of it yourself."

"It never crossed my mind to have you do it for me."

"Well, you impressed me. I knew then and there you weren't a fancy woman. You might've been married to Satan, but you're just an ordinary woman, like me."

Leah considered that a compliment. "Well, I'm glad we won't have that standing between us. I'd hate to have Sam's lady love not care for me, because I like him a lot."

Mable smiled. "He likes you a lot as well. It's one of the reasons I wanted to get all of this off my chest, so you and I could start new. I didn't want him to be distressed because you and I were at odds."

"I appreciate it," Leah said.

"Well, I feel better. Let's go and join the others."

Leah thought that a fabulous idea.

When Ryder saw Sam and Eloise appear, he politely excused himself from a group of Sam's old cavalry buddies to greet her. He had to admit he'd expected Leah to be with her and felt a twinge of disappointment that Eloise had arrived alone.

"Hello, Eloise," he said, giving her a kiss on her smooth brown cheek.

"Hello, dear. And how are you?"

"Not bad," Ryder replied.

"Hoping to see Leah, I'm betting."

Ryder covered his reaction by taking a drink of his lemonade. "How is she?"

"Doing fine. She and Mable are talking. She'll be here directly."

Ryder stared.

"Happy now?" Eloise teased.

"You're an evil old woman. Do you know that?"

Eloise smiled. "I'm going to get some punch."

Armed with the knowledge that Leah would be appearing shortly, Ryder took up a position to wait. He was looking forward to another challenging evening with her but vowed not to throw the first stone. He didn't want anything to mar Sam and Mable's event, mainly because he knew Sam would hold him responsible.

When Leah arrived, Ryder tried not to stare, but it was impossible. Her beauty outshone every other woman in attendance. The low-cut, emerald green gown showed off her neck and shoulders and had a full, airy skirt. She'd worn the locket again, and memories of placing his kisses against it as it sweetly rode between the enticing, upper swells of her breasts aroused him shamelessly. He wanted her, wanted to sweep her up into his arms, spirit her away, and find a secluded place to make long leisurely love to her.

Leah couldn't help noticing Ryder as Mable introduced

Leah to her small group of guests. He was boldly watching her, and she felt her nipples tighten in response. Trying to ignore him was impossible; even if her mind could, her body couldn't. She vowed not to fight with him this evening though. Sam and Mable would never forgive either of them should she and Ryder start battling, so she looked over his way and nodded.

Ryder sipped his lemonade and met her nod of greeting. He wondered if she knew what kind of effect she had on him. Just having her walk into his line of sight made him hard. Encouraged by the way her eyes kept sliding to his, he walked over to where she stood talking with Eloise and a few of the women from her church.

Eloise welcomed him by asking, "When are Sam and Mable going to be married?"

"About a month. Sam's taking her to Virginia City. Then they're going on to San Francisco."

He then turned to Leah. "Hello."

"Hello, Ryder. How've you been?"

"Well, and you?"

"Just fine. Just fine."

Eloise told her friends, "Ladies, how about we go and see if Mable needs any help setting out the food?"

It was a badly veiled attempt to leave Ryder and Leah alone, but the group just smiled and followed Eloise over to the white-clothed, trestle tables set up a few yards away.

"Would you like some lemonade?" Ryder asked.

"I'd love some."

Sam was laughing over a story one of his buddies had just told, and when he saw Leah and Ryder walk by, he smiled approvingly, then turned his attention back.

"Sam certainly looks happy."

"Yes, he does," Ryder agreed. "And I'm happy for him."

"Where will they live?"

"Sam has a place about ten miles from here. We've been working on it for the past few years, and it's finally finished."

"Will you miss having him around?"

"Undoubtedly. We've been through a lot, he and I."

When they reached the refreshments table, he slid the ladle into the crystal punch bowl, dipped her out a portion of lemonade, and handed her a cup.

"Thank you."

As Ryder watched her take a small sip, he couldn't help wondering if her lips would taste like the lemonade if he kissed her.

Leah thought now might be the time to ask about her navy dress. The nearness of a few other guests stopped her though. She didn't want anyone to overhear and possibly set off a whole new flurry of gossip.

Looking up at him, she asked, "Will you walk a ways with me? There's something I'd like to talk to you about."

He gestured her forward, all the while wondering how much longer he could keep from dragging her off somewhere and sampling her kisses.

They took a walk down to the small creek running at the base of the cleared acreage behind the house. A few of the other guests were there, too, but not close enough to intrude.

Ryder asked, "What did you want to talk about?"

"I—um left my dress here the night we—"

"The night I made love to you?"

His bold eyes made Leah's body tighten sensually. "Yes."

"I have it upstairs. I'll get it for you before you leave."

"Thank you," Leah said.

"Anything else?"

"Yes." She paused for a moment in an effort to pull her thoughts together. "I made a pact with myself not to fight with you. I don't want to ruin Sam's day."

"And neither do I. So how about we agree to conduct ourselves accordingly?"

Leah smiled. "I think that's a marvelous idea."

They clinked cups to seal the agreement.

Ryder held her gaze. "So that means if I drag you behind a tree and kiss you, you won't protest out of fear of wrecking Sam's day?"

She realized he was quite serious.

He then asked, "Remember what I said about the two truths?"

She did. *I want you. You want me,* he'd said. He'd then promised to remind her everytime they were together.

"Well I meant it."

Tingles broke out all over her body.

"So," he added, "let's walk back. Looks like it's time to eat."

Leah had a very hard time trying to appear nonchalant, but managed to walk calmly at his side.

There was so much food spread across the tables, Leah didn't know where to begin. She saw chicken both fried and grilled, pork ribs gleaming with sauce, steaks, smoked fish, and a splendid array of mouth-watering collards, mustards, squash, and yams. The dessert table was no less impressive. Many of the women in attendance had brought their specialties. There were coconut cakes, chocolate cakes, fools, trifles, and pies.

Eloise was one of the women helping out at the dessert table and when Leah and Ryder walked up, she said, "Leah, I make the best rhubarb pie on either side of the Mississippi. Care for a piece?"

Leah shook her head. "I'll have to pass. I'm allergic to rhubarb. Makes me swell up like a bullfrog."

Eloise looked truly disappointed.

But from behind her, Ryder boasted, "That just means more for me. Cut me a big piece, Eloise."

Some of the guests standing nearby chuckled. Eloise's face brightened, but Leah could see she was still unhappy about Leah not being able to sample her prize-winning recipe.

Leah took her small china plate of desserts to one of the benches and sat down. Ryder followed and took a seat beside her.

"This has been a very nice gathering," Leah said, casually watching the people milling about.

"That it has, and we haven't crossed swords once."

"No we haven't."

"Quite an accomplishment, wouldn't you say?"

The softened tone of voice made her turn his way. *He's so handsome*, she thought. *All that thick, rich hair, the vivid eyes, his godlike face. He can also be quite nice when he chooses to be.*

He asked, "What are you thinking?"

"Just how nice you are to be around sometimes."

"Operative word being 'sometimes'?"

"Yes."

Their eyes were saying all their words couldn't, and Leah could feel herself being drawn to him in spite of her decision to keep him at arm's length. The memories of the last time they'd been together rose unbidden, her body remembering the vivid touch of his hands and the passion of his kisses. She settled her attention back on her plate.

Ryder was proud of himself. So far, he hadn't carried her off or pulled her behind a tree. However, the lure in her was slowly breaking down his hold on his will. If he didn't find someplace for them to sneak off to soon, he was going to wind up kissing her right there, the gossips be damned.

"What are you thinking?" she asked quietly.

"About where we can go so I can kiss you without everyone being in our business."

Leah took in a deep trembling breath. It was certainly not the answer she'd been expecting. She felt singed. "You are probably the boldest man I've met."

"Good," he replied, not bothering to hide his amusement. "A man likes to be memorable."

He took her by the hand "Come on. Bring your cake."

"Where are we going?"

"Just come on."

"Ryder—"

In front of God and everybody, he led her over to where Eloise stood talking to Mable. Still holding on to Leah's hand, Ryder leaned down and whispered something into Eloise's ear. When he was done, Eloise looked at him, then over at Leah. A smile crossed Eloise's face. Then she nodded and said, "Okay."

A confused Leah had no time to ask questions because Ryder was once again leading her away. She sensed the watching eyes of everyone in attendance. If he considered this bold exit to be the way to keep the gossips at bay, she couldn't imagine what he'd do if he'd wanted their leaving to be noticed.

They wound up out in front of the house amongst the carriages and wagons owned by the guests.

Leah asked, "So, what is it?"

"It's time for truth . . ."

Leah stilled.

"I want to make love to you again . . ."

Leah told herself she wasn't affected, but every fiber of her being was shaking, trembling, remembering how it felt to be his. "We agreed not—"

"*You* agreed. I took a different position, if I recall."

She was so mesmerized by his burning eyes she had to turn her back. *Desiring him makes no sense*, an inner voice railed, *but his kisses . . .* whispered another.

He slowly came up behind her and gently placed his hands on her arms. "Let me love you the way I should have done that first night . . . Let me give you all the passion you deserve."

The voice was tempting, seductive. His body heat warmed her through the fabric of her fancy green gown. When his hands toured slowly up her arms, she trembled. He bent and brushed his lips softly against the side of her neck and her defenses began crumbling.

He husked out against her ear, "Say, yes, *Morenita* . . . say you want to be loved as much as I want to love you."

Leah couldn't explain why she was so susceptible to this one man, but she was and so she turned to face him.

The heat in his eyes was as strong as her heartbeat. He reached out and stroked the softness of her cheek. Her eyes slid closed in response. He drew a slow passionate line across her mouth.

"Say, yes," he whispered. "Come with me and let's finish what we started . . ." He placed a series of short fiery kisses on the edges of her throat, and her head slid back uselessly. His strong hand supported her arching back as he brushed his lips over the swells of her breasts. "Say yes . . ."

Leah's defenses were vanishing as fast as her logic. She had no way to counter his overwhelming effect and admittedly didn't want to. Why deny herself? Why continue to hold out against something she craved as much as he? So she gave him the reply that sealed their fate. "Yes," she whispered. His hungry lips met hers, and she whispered urgently, "Yes."

Pulling her flush against him, he kissed her so long and passionately, the cake plate in her hand slid to the paving stones and broke.

Pleased, Ryder pulled away, concentrating now on the

scents behind her ear and on her throat. He whispered, "You're going to be in big trouble with Sam. That's one of his best plates."

Leah rose up on her toes so she could taste his mouth. "I'll just tell him it was your fault."

He drew her closer. The kiss deepened. Neither cared who might see or what might be said. For weeks they'd been trying to deny their feelings, but now, under the night sky, there was no need.

"How about a midnight ride?" he asked huskily.

"On a wagon or a Cheyenne brave . . ."

The saucy retort burned his manhood, and he hardened instantaneously. To reward her for that, he brushed his lips against hers, seeking out each tender corner with the tip of his tongue. "I was talking about a wagon ride. Never expected you to say something like that . . ."

"That's your fault, too."

He ran his hands possessively over her breasts, molding them, rubbing his thumbs over the tight peaks until her head slipped back again and she moaned.

Wanting to play with her in earnest, Ryder slid the snug-fitting silk away from one breast and pleasured it boldly. "Do you want the wagon . . ." he queried hotly before he suckled in the turgid tip. "Or do you want the brave . . ."

Leah knew her body would explode into flame. There in the silence, he dallied with her exposed flesh, flicking, teasing, making her slide her hand over his thick unbound hair as if imploring him to do more. His hand roamed hotly over her hips and down her thighs.

He had her answer.

Picking her up, he carried her into the house. The musicians hired for the evening were entertaining the guests out back. As Ryder bore her through the shadow-filled darkness of Sunrise's interior and up the stairs to his room,

Leah could hear the sweet sensual strains of a seductive guitar.

He laid her down gently on his big bed, then left her for a moment to close the windows and pull the black-velvet drapes. He didn't want anyone to hear their passion. Once Sam and Mable married and Sam moved into his own place, Ryder planned to make her scream his name in every room in the house.

After lighting one lamp and turning the wick down to just a flicker, he sat on the bed beside her and slid a slow knuckle over the breast he'd freed outside. He watched her shadow-shrouded body softly purr in response. The sensuous sight made him bend and suckle one dark tip until it was damp and jewel-hard again. "I'd have taken more care last time had I known . . . this time, we'll do it right . . ."

As he boldly freed the other breast and used his fingers to prepare it for feasting, she arched in vibrant response. His play left the nipple as rigid with wanting as its twin. Only then did he lower his lips to her. She groaned in response to the dazzling lights that flared across her senses. His mouth was hot, knowing, experienced; she was yearning, sighing, and filled with a humid fever. He slid his hands up and down her legs, making the billowing silk of her gown rise and fall.

"Had I known," Ryder told her quietly. "I'd have spent more time . . . here."

He slid a hand beneath her dress and boldly explored her through her thin drawers. "I'd have touched you more . . ."

Leah's hip rose in silent invitation.

"Made sure you were ready . . ."

Sliding her dress higher, he undid the tapes of her drawers and eased them away. As he ran a lazy finger over her hair she didn't know if she should tighten her thighs to keep in the throbbing heat or spread them shamelessly so he could mine more.

He solved her dilemma by whispering softly, "Open your legs, *Morenita* . . ."

Her breath ragged, Leah complied. The touches he gave her then were more than she could bear. A blazing, few moments later, orgasm claimed her; rushing over her like a buffeting wave, and she twisted and groaned under his watching, glowing eyes.

When she quieted, he bent down and gave her a soft kiss, her reward for being so beautiful and passionate.

Leah had no idea a woman's body could react so powerfully to just a few well-placed touches. He hadn't stroked her very long at all, yet—

She looked up and met his eyes. Rising slowly to a sitting position, she ran a finger over his lips. He covered her hand with his own and kissed the tips. He turned the palm and placed a soft kiss in the center. "Let's start again . . ."

Leah's senses leapt. She ran a caressing hand down his strong jaw, then leaned in so she could kiss him as deeply as he'd kissed her. Without breaking contact with her lips, he dragged her onto his lap. His hands roamed possessively over territory just recently explored, but for both him and Leah, each touch felt thrillingly new.

Her nipples hardened all over again; her lips parted passionately. When he laid her back on the bed and lazily pushed her voluminous skirts to the tops of her thighs, she began to shudder. His magic touches circled the damp swollen part of herself, filling her with such carnal bliss her dark legs slid wider. He smiled, then bent to place a soft kiss on the inside of each wantonly spread thigh. When he straightened, his fingers renewed their sweet dawdling, and Leah groaned low in her throat.

Looking down at her, he whispered thickly, "Had I known, I'd have prepared you . . . this way . . ."

He bent again, and this time, his kisses brushed against her hair. Leah stiffened and drew back. "What are you doing?" she asked uncertainly.

The sight of her wide eyes made him smile. "What I should've done the first time we were together."

He straightened and slid a finger over her mouth. "I thought you wanted to learn to ride a Cheyenne brave . . . ?"

His voice was hot.

She was hotter.

"Then lie back and let me give you your lessons . . ." Ryder told her. He leaned in and kissed her mouth until her mind turned to pudding.

"Lie back, *Morenita* . . ."

So she did; she had no will to do anything else. His thickly spoken promise to give her "lessons," echoed through her erotically.

Ryder slid the emerald silk aside to expose a darker, more arousing silk. He first circled her with a flame-filled finger, then flicked his tongue against the citadel of her pleasure. She groaned, her hips arching and rising. He dallied brazenly, teasing, conquering, paying her the ultimate tribute while she gasped, cried out, and crooned. Her release didn't take long; it was swift, powerful, and searing.

When she came back to earth, he was beaming down like a brave very much pleased with himself. She passed a caressing hand over his cheek. "Did I pass my examination?"

He nodded. "You did an excellent job, but the second part may be harder . . ." Taking her hand he brought it against his swollen need. "See . . . ?" he whispered.

Leah had never touched a man in her life, but found the feel fascinating, stimulating. Uninhibited because of what they'd just shared, she ran her hand over him slowly, all the while wondering if her lessons would include how to give him as much pleasure as he'd been giving her. "Will you teach me how to please you?" she asked without shame. She was finding with him she hadn't any.

Ryder could feel his desire stacking up like heat lightning. Her hot little hand was well on its way to learning without his help. As she continued to explore the shape and length of him, he asked himself: who knew she'd take to passion like a fish to a stream? "You're doing fine. . . ."

But he had to pull away after another few moments. In the shadowy silence he removed his trousers. There was just enough light for Leah to see. Nude, he was magnificently made—powerful shoulders, arm, thighs. Her eyes lingered over the proof of his desire. "This night has been quite educational."

In response to his quiet chuckle she reached out and closed her hand around his bare length. She watched his eyes close and his head drop back. Pleased with herself she continued to offer him her novice caresses, and wondered how something so hard could also feel so soft and alive. It was like holding iron encased in velvet.

Ryder could feel the tremors in his legs and the straining of his manhood. In a few more moments he'd have nothing to continue her lessons with, so vowing to teach her all she needed to know about this particular portion of the examination at a later date, he backed away, pulsing and breathing harshly.

"Did I do something wrong?"

"No, *carinita* . . . not at all. You're just a bit more experienced at this than you know."

Leah dropped her head to hide her pleased eyes.

He joined her on the bed and to her surprise pulled her atop him. Still in her rucked-down dress, she held his eyes in the half dark. He slid his hands beneath the silk and slowly roamed them over her bare hips. "*Seda . . .*" he whispered softly.

She leaned up to kiss him, asking, "And that means?"

"Silk," he husked back against her lips. "You have skin like dark silk."

His passion-thickened voice, and bold, seeking hands set her aflame once again. "This dress is ruined, Ryder."

He kissed her deeply. "I'll buy you another."

"I should take it off . . ."

"After we're done. Right now, you've lessons to take, and I want them to be in this fancy gown."

His words made her smolder. Was this the way of lovers? All her thoughts dissolved as her final tutoring began.

He took her back to the heights of passion, slowly, majestically. Each pass of his hand, each kiss from his lips sent her soaring. He taught her things she would never forget, magical things, vibrant things, soul-shaking things, and when he felt her ready to receive all he had to give he brought her down onto him slowly, guiding her hips with his big hands.

Leah knew she'd die from the pleasure. In this position she could take in as much as she wanted as often as she wanted. He could tease her nipples or slide the silk of her dress lazily over her sensitive hips. It was one of their most thrilling encounters yet.

Beneath her, Ryder let her set the pace. Even though her virginal tightness threatened to send him plunging over the edge, he kept himself reined in until she felt comfortable. She was still new at this, and he wanted her to enjoy their lovemaking to the fullest.

But soon, he lost the reins. The sights and feel of her riding him so sweetly, made him grip her hips tightly and increase the pace. He rocked her, raised her, and brought her down again. Moments later she stiffened with the rictus of release. Ryder knew he should withdraw from her, but he wanted just a bit more, and by then, it was too late. His orgasm shot through him, increasing his thrusts and ripping a growl from his throat.

In the silence that followed, Leah could hear his heartbeat pounding beneath her ear. Their bodies were dewed with the moisture of their activity, and she was so sated she couldn't move.

Ryder held her atop him with an arm across her back. Having her so near felt right, natural. He couldn't move either.

"So," he asked softly, tracing a finger over the damp skin of her neck, "think you've learned enough for one night?"

Leah lifted her head so she could see into his dark eyes. She smiled. "I don't know, professor, is there homework?"

He reached down and lovingly squeezed a soft hip. "You are something."

She placed her head back on his chest, content. "As I said before, it's all your fault."

Her dress, now twisted and crushed, clung damply to her hips and limbs. "We should get you out of this dress," he offered quietly.

"Good idea."

She eased her body from his and rose on her knees so she could reach the hooks at the back. In a moment it slid from her, showing him her dark nudity. After all they'd shared, Leah knew it was too late to be modest now, but being naked with a man was not something she did every day.

"Surely you're not shy?" he questioned as he toyed with a taut nipple.

Leah lowered her eyes. "A bit."

"You have no reason to be. Your body's as beautiful as are you."

He leaned up and kissed her. "How about we get cleaned up?"

She kissed him in return. "I'd like that."

He took her by the hand, and they padded over to a door

that connected his room to the bathing room. He lit a few lamps to banish the shadows while Leah couldn't help but marvel over the ingenuity he'd employed in building such a novel space.

"I've seen a few places back East that had indoor plumbing, but none was as extensive as this."

"Well, soon, every home in the nation will be equipped this way."

He turned on the spigot for the shower. The sound of hot water pouring into the wood-and-glass stall filled the air. "Shall we?" he asked gesturing.

Leah's eyes widened around her smile. "Together?"

"Sure. Consider it another one of your lessons."

Not certain how she was supposed to handle such a man, Leah shook her head and walked over.

"Go on in," he told her. "I want to get us a couple of towels and some soap."

Inside, the water was hot and steamy. Leah basked in the feel, wondering playfully how she could slip all the pipes and spigots into a carpetbag and take them home. She'd never imagined such luxury.

When he stepped into the steamy space, she moved aside so he could enjoy the full force of the water for a moment. Leah watched the shower turn him into a sleek, gleaming god. The sight of the muscles rippling in his arms and powerful legs were enough to make arousal lick at her thighs. When he'd rinsed himself off sufficiently, he beckoned and she came willingly. Using a clean cloth he soaped her from neck to hips, then up and down and in between. The feel of his slick hands and the hot water contributed to her already burgeoning arousal, and she knew it wouldn't be much longer before she was once again in full bloom.

Ryder took a moment to wash himself, all the while watching the passion lighting her eyes. The realization that she appeared ripe for another lesson made his manhood harden. He had the strong urge to take her right there, but feeling the water begin to cool, he hurriedly finished his task. They had the rest of the night to enjoy themselves.

Once outside the stall, he dried her with the bathing sheet, caressing her, warming her, teasing those parts of her body he knew would make her croon. Leah stood there pulsing, rippling, wondering if she'd ever become accustomed to his fervent touch. Truth be told, she hoped not.

They were soon back in his room. Their reentry into the sweet storm of love commenced with humid kisses, wandering hands, and his heat-filled whispers of how he planned to have her next. Leah felt treasured and then bliss as he eased his hard, thick promise into the place they both wanted him to be. He rode her slowly, carnally. He made her arch to his thrusts, and she didn't care how scandalously she responded. He made her climb peaks and discover valleys that were previously unknown. When the dam broke, he growled; she cried out hoarsely, and together they were flung to paradise.

"You know," she told him a few moments after they'd regained calm, "everyone's going to be wondering where we are."

"Let them."

She rolled her head in the direction where he lay on his back beside her and held his eyes. "That's easy to say if you're you, but I'm not."

He asked, "I thought you've been fighting gossips all your life?"

"I have, but I never caused any."

"Just because someone names you something, doesn't mean you must wear it."

"I suppose you're right. I've never been in a situation like this before, is all."

"Never had a man court you?" he asked.

"No," came her quiet reply.

Ryder once again wondered who she truly was. "You know, I'm going to find out the truth eventually."

She didn't try and deny it. "I know."

He rolled over and kissed her swiftly. "In the meantime, are you hungry?"

Glad that they'd moved away from talk of the past, she raised a saucy eyebrow. "Hungry for what?"

He chuckled, "For food, woman. Food. That's all."

She pouted.

He kissed her again, this time longer and more passionately. "I can see now that I'm going to have to put you in a cage."

She giggled beneath his lips. "Try it, and I'll never take lessons from you again."

He sat up and grabbed her by the hand. "Let's go find something to eat."

She pulled back. "You don't have on a stitch of clothing."

"Neither do you. What's your point?"

"The point, my handsome brave, is that one, what if Sam and any lingering guests are in the kitchen, and two: Ryder I must go home. Eloise is probably worried sick."

"No, she's not."

She eyed him for a moment, then asked suspiciously, "How do you know?"

"Remember when I stopped to talk to her before we went around to the front of the house?"

She nodded.

"I told her then I'd bring you home sometime before dawn."

Leah's eyes widened. "You didn't?"

"I did."

Outdone, Leah fell back on the bed. "What must she think?"

"Come on, now," he chided her softly. "Eloise is a

grown woman. She knows we're not up here playing checkers."

She gave him a guilty smile.

He looked down into her black eyes. "So, shall we wash again and then eat?"

"Only if you go downstairs and make sure the coast is clear, and, you give me something to wear."

He bent and kissed her. "I can do that. Although I do favor your present attire."

He teased a finger over her nipple until it peaked then, grabbing a long silk robe from a nearby chair, he shrugged it on and departed.

Chapter 9

While Leah waited for Ryder's return with the food, she looked up at the shadows on the ceiling. In many ways, she was happy as a clam—who'd have ever thought she'd have a lover, and one so magnificent at that— but in other ways she knew this brief lusty respite wouldn't last. The past would rise up and smite them both, plunging them back into the throes of distrust and anger. If only she had a magician's wand, she could wave it and make time skip over the ugliness she sensed lay ahead and place the two of them on the other side, where lying across his bed would begin and end each day, where she could explore the countryside with him, take long sensual showers, and eat spiced peaches. With a start, she realized she was musing upon him being a prolonged part of her life. Surely that would never happen, would it?

She sat up and shook herself free. No, it wouldn't. Monty stood between them. Ryder would never let go of his bitterness and mistrust. She had feelings for him, but didn't expect them to be returned because of who she was and what she represented. Realizing she'd have plenty of time to be melancholy once she was back at the cabin and alone, she scooted off the bed and went to the shower to wash up before he returned.

Downstairs, Ryder walked into the kitchen, and there sat Sam and his army buddies ringing the table. The tabletop was littered with bottles of champagne, food, and partially filled flutes and whiskey glasses. They were obviously having a good time because he'd heard the raucous laughter as soon as he started down the stairs. Ryder assumed the other guests were gone.

Sam and his men greeted him loudly, and he smiled. He was just about to ask Sam where he'd put the food left over from the party when he looked up and saw an obviously angry Mable seated in a chair in the corner. She met his eyes; the tears sparkling in them moved him greatly. He cast a withering look at the cavalry, then walked over and leaned down close to Sam's ear. "Can I talk to you for a moment, privately?"

"Sure," Sam returned brightly. "Boys, keep the champagne flowing, be right back."

Ryder led Sam into his study and closed the door. He then asked, "What the hell are you doing?"

Sam, filled with a bit more spirits than he was accustomed to downing, replied, "What?"

"Dammit, Sam, when was the last time you noticed Mable?"

"Mable?"

"Yes, Mable. Remember her, the lady you're supposed to be marrying next month?"

"She's sitting in the kitchen."

"Yes, she is, but doing what?"

Sam thought a moment, then the full meaning of Ryder's

questions seemed to hit. "Not paying much attention to her, am I?"

"I don't know, Sam, are you?"

Sam dropped his gaze. "Me and my buddies haven't seen each other in a while and—" The frost in Ryder's face cut Sam off. "That's no excuse, is it?"

"No, it isn't. That woman was nice enough to say yes to an old broken-down soldier like you and you've got her sitting in the kitchen corner like one of your pots."

Sam's voice was filled with remorse. "Guess I have to tell the boys to leave."

Ryder nodded. "I guess you do, unless you're planning to stand up with them instead."

Sam was quiet for a moment, and then he chuckled. "Since when did you become so all-fired caring?"

Ryder shrugged. "Must be the company I'm presently keeping."

"Well keep it up. Six week ago you wouldn't've cared one bit about Mable's feelings."

Ryder didn't like hearing himself described so accurately. "Where'd you put the leftover food?"

"In the icebox and in the pantry. Want me to fix you and Miss Leah a plate?"

"No. You just go and take care of your business. I'll take care of mine."

Sam smiled. "See that you do, because if you let that little lady get away again, you'll regret it for the rest of your life."

Ryder didn't respond.

His hand on the door latch, Sam turned back to his best friend, and said genuinely, "Thanks for pointing out something I needed to see."

Ryder replied softly, "You're welcome, old man."

His eyes twinkling, Sam left.

Ryder returned to his room with enough food to feed a

dozen people. The tray held sliced meats, bread, desserts, and a pitcher brimming with lemonade. He set everything on the writing table.

Leah looked at the mountain of food, and, remembering his giant's appetite, asked teasingly, "You didn't bring anything for me?"

He shot her an amused look. "Very funny. Being around you, a man has to keep up his strength. Now, come eat."

She walked over to him and his eyes glowed at the sight of her lush nudity. Leah had no trouble interpreting the gleam. "You promised me clothes, remember?"

"I lied."

She snorted in amused amazement. "Can I have something to wear please?"

"No," he replied easily, and began preparing himself a sandwich.

"Ryder?" She had a hand on her hip, but a smile on her face.

He turned to her. "What? Aren't you going to eat?"

Leah looked around the room. Spying a large chest of drawers, she went over and pulled the top drawer open. Socks, drawers, and handkerchiefs. *Can't wear those.* She shut the drawer, then opened the next: bedding. Next drawer: shirts!

Leah playfully stuck out her tongue at him, then withdrew a red check flannel shirt and slipped it on. The shirt's hem fell past her knees and the long sleeves had to be rolled up, but she was covered. She walked back to him with triumph on her face. "Now, I can eat. No help from you."

"Purely selfish," he confessed.

She shook her head and made herself a small plate. "So, are all the guests gone?"

"Looked like it. I had to make Sam send his cronies home though."

"Why?" Leah asked.

"Because while they were all sitting around the table drinking and telling lies, poor Mable was sitting in the corner with tears in her eyes."

"Oh, no."

"Oh, yes."

"Did you talk to Sam?"

Ryder nodded. "I did. Asked him if he were standing up with Mable or his buddies."

Leah found his championing of Mable impressive. "Good for you. Anybody else know you have a soft spot in your heart for women's feelings?"

"No, so keep it to yourself."

She grinned and bit into her sandwich.

After their meal, they sat on the black settee positioned near the huge stone fireplace and Leah got her first good look at her surroundings. Ryder's bedroom was like all the other rooms at Sunrise—large. Decidedly a man's quarters, too. Most of the furniture was made from deep, dark wood, and as in the other rooms, trophy heads adorned the walls. There was a ram's head, complete with huge, elaborately curved ivory horns on the stone chimney of the fireplace, and another ferocious-looking bear's head above the big four-poster bed. She was glad she hadn't seen his snarling face until now. There was a writing table and chair. The hems on the black-velvet drapes were trimmed with a red, Indian-based design. The large black rugs on the floor also bore the signs and prints of Ryder's tribal roots.

There were two paintings of warriors on the wall by the door to the bathing room. Leah had seen enough of Eloise's works to guess they'd been done by her hand. A black headdress in a glass case on a table on the far side of the room drew her curiosity so much that she had to walk over and see it up close.

"What is this?" she asked. Unlike the war bonnets she'd

seen in the newspapers back East, this one had feathers that stood straight up, and the tips were scarlet red.

"Belonged to one of my uncles. It's a Dog Soldier bonnet."

"What's a Dog Soldier?"

"One of the six Cheyenne warrior clans—the fiercest and the bravest."

"I've never heard of them. What type of feathers are these?"

"Raven, and that's red down on the tips."

Leah peered at the glass. "Why's it in glass?"

"To preserve it. An archaeologist friend of mine says it's the best way, short of sending it to a museum, which I refuse to do. They've stolen enough."

Leah could sense the power and pride a brave must have felt donning such finery. It had a cold beauty that radiated majesty. Dog Soldiers. "Did you want to be a Dog Soldier?"

"I did. They always inspired such awe and respect. They'd set up their own camp within the big camp and had their own rules and ceremonies. They fought the Whites long after everyone else had surrendered."

Leah thought back to her conversation with Eloise about Sand Creek. "Were there any Dog Soldiers at Sand Creek?"

From his seat across the room, Ryder studied her for a moment. Her question caught him off guard. Few Easterners, if any, knew about Sand Creek.

As if reading his mind, she explained, "Eloise told me some of the story."

"No, there were no Dog Soldiers in camp that day," he responded in a voice void of emotion.

She saw pain and bitterness in his eyes.

He continued distantly, "When Chivington rode into camp with his seven hundred men and his cannons, there were only a handful of warriors with us. Most of the others, my uncles included, were up at Sand Hill. The soldiers found only the old chiefs, the elders, and the women and children."

"But they still fired on you all?"

"Yes. Cheyenne Chief Black Kettle was what they called a peace chief. He'd signed many treaties and was convinced the Americans stealing our land and butchering our game meant us no harm. In fact, an Indian Affairs Commissioner had given him an American flag as a symbol of Washington's word that they wanted peace. When Chivington's soldiers arrived at Sand Creek, Black Kettle grabbed up the flag and placed himself and all of us behind it. The commissioner said all he had to do was show it and any soldiers we encountered would leave us be."

"These didn't."

"No, when they saw the flag, they opened fire."

"Had Black Kettle been on the warpath?"

"No, he and the other old chiefs had been trying to find a way for both peoples to live together peacefully but, the Americans didn't want peace. They wanted our land, and for the tribes to disappear."

"Eloise said over a hundred of women and children were killed that day."

"And butchered and mutilated. Soldiers were riding around with the privates of our dead women stretched over their saddles. I saw one man dismount and drop to his knees so he could accurately shoot a child no more than three winters old."

He quieted then as if his mind were recalling that day. "The massacre went on for seven hours. From dawn until that afternoon. White Antelope, an old Cheyenne chief, seventy-five years old, yelled at the soldiers, trying to make them stop. They gunned him down too. He died singing the death song, with a medal he'd been given by President Lincoln around his neck."

A sharp sadness filled Leah. "But you and your grandmother managed to escape."

"Yes, and joined the rest of the survivors on the long walk northeast to join the warriors camped at Smoky Hill."

"This took place in November?"

"Yes, the Cheyenne call it *Hikomini,* the Month of the Freezing Moon."

"So it must've been cold."

Ryder nodded. "Cold, ice, wind. We had small children and women with us, many of them wounded, so the going was slow."

"But you made it."

"We did, and from there we headed north to join the Northern Cheyenne up by the Republican River."

Silence filled the room. Leah couldn't imagine how horrible it must have been for a fourteen-year-old male child to be suddenly called upon to defend his people. How courageous he and the others had been.

She retook her seat. "I didn't mean to bring up such sad times by asking about the bonnet."

"No harm done. At least I can talk about it; back then I couldn't. I had nightmares on and off for years."

Leah didn't find that admission surprising. "Eloise said Chivington is now a sheriff in Denver."

"Sure is. Pretty ironic. A lawless, murdering man, now in charge of enforcing the law."

"Where are your uncles now?" Leah asked.

"Dead, in various battles. The one who wore that bonnet was the oldest of my mother's three brothers. He died with the great Cheyenne Chief Roman Nose at what the Americans called the Battle of Beecher's Island."

"What did the Cheyenne call it?"

"The Fight When Roman Nose Was Killed."

Sadness held Leah. No wonder Ryder kept his true feelings hidden. He had good reason to. After Sand Creek, the conquering of his tribe, and the death of his mother, it was a wonder he had any feelings at all.

He looked her way, and asked, "How about we change the subject?"

She nodded.

He said, "Tell me something I don't know about you."

"Okay. Let's see?" She thought for a moment, then said, "I really enjoy being with the man who lives inside Ryder Damien."

He searched her eyes. "Do you?"

"Yes."

Ryder's heart filled with a satisfaction he couldn't name. He'd never talked with anyone but Sam about Sand Creek; he'd certainly never admitted he'd had nightmares. Was Sam right? Was this woman slowly changing him? "I'm enjoying you, too, both with and without your clothes."

She laughed. "I'm being serious."

"So am I."

She picked up one of the small, Indian-designed pillows resting on the settee nearby and playfully swatted him with it.

Laughing, he tore it from her hand, and while she mockingly screamed her outrage he dragged her kicking and flailing onto his lap. "In the old days, a brave would beat his woman for committing such an outrage."

"Well, these aren't the old days. Beat me, and I'll have Sam feed you arsenic with your eggs, and as much as you eat, you'll keel over before you leave the table."

He grinned, then ran an admiring finger over her smooth dark cheek. "I would never beat you."

"Never?"

"Ever."

"Good. I'll never beat you either."

"Good." He ran his eyes over her unorthodox attire. "My shirt fits you well."

They both knew that to be a lie, but Leah replied haughtily, "It's what all the fashionable women are wearing back East."

Grinning down, he pulled her into his chest and held her close. With his heartbeat sounding against her ear, Leah said, "May I ask you something?"

"Sure."

"Why don't you ever address me by my name? You've called me many things, but never Leah."

She looked up to gauge his reaction.

Ryder met her eyes and saw the seriousness reflected there. "You want the truth?"

"Yes."

"And you won't get angry and demand to be taken home?"

She shook her head.

"Leah's the name my father called you, am I correct?"

"Yes,"

"Well, I want you to be someone I name."

"Why?"

"Purely selfish," he replied, but this time there was no playfulness in his voice. "So I call you *Morenita . . .*"

"And it means?"

"Little dark lady."

She smiled. She couldn't help it. It was a name she didn't mind wearing in the least. She placed her head back on his chest. "Thank you."

He touched his lips to her forehead. "You're welcome."

After a few moments of silent contentment, she told him quietly, "I should really be getting back to Eloise's you know."

"I know. I was hoping you'd forget."

She chuckled softly.

Ryder reached down and lifted her chin so he could look

into her eyes. "Will you have dinner with me tomorrow night?"

"Where?"

"Here. Just like this."

Leah realized she was half in love with this man already. Lord help her if the other shoe dropped. "I'd like that."

"Good, I'll pick you up around, oh say, two in the afternoon."

Puzzlement claimed her face. "Did you say dinner or lunch?"

"Dinner."

"Then why so early?"

"Purely selfish."

Amused, she shook her head. "Two it is, then."

He slowly traced her lips, then kissed her so deeply, her world was still spinning when he left her for the shower.

On the ride back to Eloise's, Leah was glad it was night because no one would be able to see her rumpled dress or the other one she had balled up on the seat beside her. Both had been ruined during her lessons and she'd never be able to wear either of them again, but she didn't care. Leaning against Ryder's shoulder while he slowly drove the team through the dark countryside, she wished this day could go on forever.

He looked down, and asked, "What're you thinking?"

"How I wished the day wouldn't end."

In the dark Ryder smiled. He'd been having the same thoughts. This dark jewel of a woman had given him a lot of pleasure this evening and not all of it in his bed. She was witty and intelligent, not to mention passionate. Being with her was making him view his world in different ways. Sam had been right; before meeting his *Morenita*, he wouldn't have cared one way or the other about Mable's plight. He'd have fixed himself a plate of food and proceeded back upstairs. She was changing him somehow, and he wasn't sure if he knew how to be someone else.

When they reached Eloise's place the light in her studio was still burning. As Ryder walked Leah around to the back where Leah's cabin sat, he asked, "Any idea what Eloise is working on?"

"Haven't a clue, but she's been shut up in there for the past week or so."

"Another masterpiece probably."

Leah nodded. "Probably. Do you know that she talks to Alice?"

"Always has. Always will, I suppose. Seems harmless."

"Well, here we are," he said when they reached her door.

A twinge of sadness pricked Leah. "So we are."

"I'll see you tomorrow?"

"Two o'clock. Thank you for a wonderful evening, Ryder."

"You're welcome, and thank *you*." He lifted her chin so he could place a kiss of sweet farewell on her lips. "Good night, *Morenita*."

"Good night, Ryder."

He waited for her to go in and light a lamp. Then he was gone.

Leah awakened the next morning to rain. Lying in bed, she listened to the rhythmic sound of the drops drumming against the roof. Her thoughts drifted to Ryder. What an evening. In spite of this being Sunday morning, she didn't think it wrong to recall how wonderful he'd made her feel. The idea of being able to see him today put a smile on her face. She chided herself for being so giddy, especially at her age, but she'd never been in a situation like this before, never had a man whisper *Morenita* in her ear or tell her how beautiful she was. This was all new.

However, as much as she'd have preferred to lie there all

day thinking only of Ryder, it was Sunday morning, and that meant church. She got up, bathed, and dressed. Donning the old oilskin slicker Eloise had loaned her for such occasions, she ran pell-mell through the downpour to the main house.

Eloise was already sequestered away in her studio, so Leah knocked on the door and called through the wood, "Eloise?"

Eloise yelled back. "Mornin', Leah. How are you?"

"Fine. No church this morning?"

" 'Fraid not. I'm working. I left you some sausages and grits on the cookstove. Help yourself."

"Thank you. You coming out of there anytime soon?"

"Doesn't look like it's going to be today. Maybe tomorrow. You okay being by yourself?"

"Yes, ma'am. Ryder and I are having dinner later. He'll be by around two."

"All right, dear, I'll see you when I do. Tell Ryder I say hello."

"I will."

So, that was that. Whatever Eloise was working on seemed to be taking up all of her time. Leah had never been around an artist before, but she supposed one had to seize creativity when it called. Maybe the two of them would get a chance to sit and visit tomorrow.

Going into the tiny kitchen, Leah fixed herself a plate of sausage and grits. She poured a cup of hot, black coffee, then went back out to the crochet-covered table in the front room to sit and eat. On the table's other chair lay several newspapers. Leah picked them up to read as she ate.

Denver had four daily newspapers and fifteen weeklies; only one of the weeklies, the Denver *Argus*, was published by and for members of the race. Founded by a Black man named Isaiah Mitchell, the paper was less than a year old. The first few items Leah read pertained to events and ser-

vices at the area's two Baptist and one African Methodist
Episcopal churches. Zion Baptist was celebrating Founder's
Day at seven on Tuesday, and Shorter A.M.E. was soliciting
donations of clothing for the less fortunate.

Farther down was some news everyone in Denver had
been speculating upon. Andrew Green, a twenty-five-year-
old Black man with roots in St. Louis had been arrested on
May 24 and charged with the May 19 murder of a Denver
streetcar operator. According to the report, the authorities
had had no idea the suspect would be revealed as Black;
they'd assumed the foul deed had been done by a White. As
Leah read further, she learned that Green had been drunk in
the notorious G.A.R. Saloon on Larimer Street, when he
began boasting of his role in the shooting. Green was cur-
rently in jail awaiting trial.

Leah shook her head sadly and picked up one of the
other papers. This one, a copy of the *Rocky Mountain News*,
also carried news of the Green arrest in a large article on its
front page. It read in part that because Green had no money,
a White lawyer by the name of Edgar Caypless had agreed
to take the case free of charge. Leah chose not to read more.
The White papers rarely reported on the comings and go-
ings of Blacks in the community unless there had been a
major crime as in the Green incident, or unless some sensa-
tional racial event had occurred, so she scanned the rest of
the pages for national news.

She stopped at an item on the Knights of Labor. She remembered reading about them on the train ride to Denver. It
seemed the Knights and groups with similar goals were ex-
periencing a drop in membership due to all the violence
stemming from their continuing efforts to secure an eight-
hour day. On May 3, a confrontation between police, strik-
ers, and strikebreakers at Chicago's McCormick Harvesting
Machine Company had resulted in the death of one person
and the injury of many others. The next day, May 4, a rally

was held in Chicago's Haymarket Square to protest the brutal actions of the police. According to the *News*, the gathering stayed peaceful until the police arrived to disperse the crowd. A dynamite bomb was thrown. Seven policemen were killed, sixty others were injured. Although the authorities had no clue as to the bomber's identity, one of the rally leaders, August Spies, and seven others were charged with aiding the unknown murderer.

Leah put the papers away. Their reports were as dreary as the day.

Although it was Sunday, Ryder was in his office in town. He was also reading a paper: Cordelia Wayne's publication, the *Wayne Banner*. He'd never liked Cordelia. Under her cultured veneer she was manipulative, predatory, and if the current edition was any indication, not very smart. Under a small gossip column titled: I'D LIKE TO KNOW, she'd written:

> *I'd like to know which stepson the Widow Montague intends to keep? Does she not know polygamy is illegal? Witnesses report the brothers almost came to fisticuffs over her during a lunch last week at Dinah's. While they argued, the Black Widow looked on with a pleased smile. Let's not forget that had it not been for the timely and admittedly scandalous intervention of the younger stepson, she'd be languishing in the women's territorial prison. So which one will she choose? I'd like to know.*

Ryder tossed the paper aside, grabbed his slicker, and headed for the door. Six weeks ago, he'd have ignored this, but now he couldn't. He needed to pay Cordelia a visit.

It was still pouring rain when he drove up to the Waynes' mansion. His brother's fancy black carriage was tied up out front, but that didn't surprise him; Seth had been putting horns on Barksdale Wayne for nearly a year now. He supposed Cordelia was drawn to his brother's Creole good looks and prowess in bed because Cordelia loved money and Seth didn't have a dime.

At first, no one answered the door pull, but a few moments later, a tight-faced Cordelia snatched it open and froze at the sight of Ryder. He silently noted that she'd misbuttoned her blouse and that her hair appeared hastily fashioned.

"Barksdale isn't here," she stated dismissively.

"I came to see you."

After scanning his emotionless features, Cordelia slowly backed up and let him enter. The entrance hall, with its Victorian mirrors and paintings of landscapes, rivaled those seen in the homes of Denver's richest citizens. There was no denying Cordelia had taste, but he hadn't come here to compliment her on her decorating skills.

Carefully keeping her eye on Ryder, Cordelia called up the stairs. "Seth, your brother's here."

Ryder had no idea why she chose to involve Seth, unless she felt threatened, and Ryder hoped she did. He had no plans to harm her physically; what he had in mind would be far more painful.

When his brother appeared at the top of the stairs, Ryder greeted him. "Good morning, brother."

Seth's shirt was only partially buttoned. "What're you doing here?"

"I came to speak with Cordelia, but she seems to think you should be a party to the conversation."

The cold amusement in Ryder's eyes made Cordelia ask impatiently, "What do you want?"

"Your printing presses, and maybe, this house."

Her response was smug, "Well, you can't have them."

"I'd like to know," he began pointedly, "what you expected would happen when I read that drivel in your paper?"

She stiffened.

From the top of the steps, Seth warned, "I told you not to print that bull about Leah, Cordelia. I told you."

"Shut up!" she snapped.

She turned her icy glare on Ryder. "You can't tell me what I can or cannot print. My husband paid for those presses—"

"With money he borrowed from me."

Her eyes went wide as saucers.

Ryder smiled coldly. "So you see, I *can* tell you what to print."

He leaned close so there would be no mistake. "You will never, ever write about Leah Montague again. Even if she's seen brawling in her underwear in the middle of town. As far as you and your paper are concerned, she doesn't even live in Denver." Her sullen and hostile face made him add, "Defy me, and it won't matter that you're a woman, Cordelia. I will crush you. I'll take your presses, his barber-shop, and this house. Do you understand me?"

The anger in his face was strong enough to touch.

A disgusted Cordelia nodded.

Ryder looked up at his brother. They evaluated each other silently.

Then Seth called down cordially, "Leah's a hot little piece, isn't she?"

The words pierced Ryder like a lance in the back.

Seth showed a triumphant smile. "Taught her everything she knows."

White-hot rage blazed across Ryder's vision. Urges both primitive and deadly flared inside.

As Seth chuckled, Ryder grabbed hold of himself and turned back to Cordelia. "I'll let myself out." He ignored her smug smile as he headed back out into the rain.

Leah's a hot little piece, isn't she? The words taunted Ryder as he drove away from the Wayne mansion. *Was that the reason she'd been so uninhibited with him last night?*

She'd been a virgin the first time he'd taken her to his bed, but had she visited Seth's in between? He told himself Seth's boast had been nothing but a lie, nothing more than an attempt to get back at him, but what if Seth hadn't been lying? Had he really shared her kisses? Had she crooned for his brother the way she had for him? That the answer might be yes bothered him, no, *tormented* him. It made him want to go to her now and demand she tell him the truth about her past, her marriage, Seth—everything. In his present state, Ryder knew it made more sense to go home and cool off, but instead he turned the team toward Eloise's. He had to know.

The noon hour brought the end of the rain. It also brought Ryder to Leah's door.

"You're awfully early," she said, pleased to see him.

"Have you slept with Seth?"

Caught very off guard by the abrupt demand, Leah observed him silently. What had happened since last night's parting? He had thunderclouds in his face. His jaw was tight, his lips thinned. "No. Did you think I had?"

It was an obvious question, she knew, but she needed to hear him say it. When he didn't respond, she asked him again, pointedly, "Did you think I had?"

"It's what I was told."

"By whom?"

"Seth."

"And you believed him." It was a statement not a question.

Ryder met her pain-filled eyes and tried to deny the effect the sight had on him but couldn't. "I want you to tell me about your marriage to Louis."

"No."

As if stunned, he stared. "No?"

"No," she repeated firmly. "I realize you don't know me as well as you'd like, and I don't know you either, but for you to believe I'd do with someone else what we shared last night—?" Leah was so outraged and yes, offended, she couldn't even find the words to continue. *How dare you,* she wanted to scream at him. *How dare you!*

"A man has to be sure—"

"Sure of what, that's he's the only bull in the pen?"

He looked away.

Leah lowered her voice. "Get out, Ryder. Now."

He was angry.

She was angrier. "Now! You haven't earned the right to know about my past. You don't have enough trust inside you to handle the present."

She walked to the door and snatched it open. She waited.

Ryder sighed bitterly. Well, he'd certainly messed this up. It wasn't an admission he made easily. Obeying her request, he left. Leah slammed the door behind him.

Leah hated crying, always had, but she couldn't help herself. Tears made of rage, pain, and loss all slid from her eyes. "Damn him," she whispered emotionally. She should have known this was coming. Damn him!

She dashed away the wetness staining her cheeks. *And damn Seth for his hatefulness.* His lie had plunged her and Ryder back into the abyss. Why would Ryder suddenly take the word of a man he'd been at odds with his entire life? She had no answer. It had been obvious from the beginning that she and Ryder weren't meant to be together, and now she had the broken heart to prove it.

Back at home, Ryder stormed into the house.

"What's the matter with you?" Sam asked, looking up from the kitchen table with great concern.

Ryder told him about the article in Cordelia's paper, the confrontation with Cordelia and Seth, and the angry words he'd had with Leah.

Sam shook his head. "I told her you were slow, but you win the prize today. Since when did you start believing anything your snake of a brother has to say?"

All the way home, Ryder had asked himself the same question. He had no answer. "It was a stupid thing to do."

"Certainly was. Broke her heart, I'll bet."

Ryder paused and scanned Sam's face. Broken heart? Did she care for him in that way?

Sam seemed to read his mind. "Don't know why you're looking like that. She cares a lot about you. After today, though, she probably won't care if you get run down by a streetcar."

Ryder couldn't deny that, and he didn't really blame her. He hadn't handled their meeting well. Damn Seth! "I need to go back and talk with her."

"Why, so she can shoot you this time? You'd be better off just leaving her alone for a couple days—give you both time to simmer down."

To Ryder it sounded like good advice; however, he kept seeing the pain he'd put in her eyes. He'd hurt her, badly. He needed to try and fix that, but he had no idea how. He let out a resigned sigh. "Why did I let Seth bait me that way?"

"Because, whether you're up to admitting it yet or not, you care a whole lot about that little lady. I do, too."

Ryder didn't know what to admit. He did know he never wanted to see her look so hurt again.

Sam said sagely, "If it's meant to work out, son, it will."

Ryder was a man of action. He didn't have the patience to stand around waiting to see what the fates had in store. "I need to see her, Sam. Try and straighten this out."

"I know, son, but let her be for now. Go saddle up that nag of yours and take a ride. I'm going over to see Mable later. You'll have the place all to yourself."

Realizing there was nothing else he could do concerning

the *Morenita* just then, Ryder nodded. "I'll see you this evening, then?"

Sam's old eyes took on a mischievous light, and he waggled an eyebrow. "Maybe you will, maybe you won't. Depends on Mable."

Ryder chuckled lightly, then went upstairs to change into his riding gear.

Ryder mounted the stallion and rode toward the setting sun. For seemingly the hundredth time he asked himself: Was Sam right? Did he indeed care for the *Morenita* but was simply too pigheaded to admit it? The answer kept coming up yes, and Ryder knew no more what to do with that truth than he knew how to clear up the mess he'd made. By the Spirits he'd been stupid, stupid and prideful and arrogant, so arrogant she'd probably never speak to him again. That thought didn't sit well. Now that he'd begun making peace with his feelings for her he certainly didn't want it to be all for naught. He'd never been made this loco by a woman before; never. The idea that Seth might have made love to her had momentarily cost him his sanity. Sam would probably define that as jealousy, another emotion Ryder had no experience with, but it was exactly what he'd felt in response to Seth's vicious taunt—green-eyed, white-hot jealousy. She'd somehow gotten into his blood, and he hadn't even known she was there. How long had she been simmering below the surface of his being? When had he become so possessive that he wanted to paint himself for war and hunt down her enemies? Had his father found her that moving?

Ryder dashed that thought aside. He needed to stop thinking of her in those terms if he really wanted to be truthful about how he felt, but could he? He'd spent his entire life hating his father and everything connected with his name. That hate had driven him to succeed in the face of all odds; it made him work tirelessly and become wealthy beyond his wildest dreams. It had taken him abroad, and into the inner sanctums of well-heeled boardrooms, where he and the servants were the only men of color. Wanting to be better and mightier than Louis Montague had been his reason for living. If he gave that up, what would fill the void? In reality, he already knew.

A few days later, Leah received a letter from Judge Raddock. It read:

My dear Mrs. Montague,

I hope this letter finds you well. An appeal has been filed on your behalf through my office here in Boston. A colleague of mine, Daniel Morton, is presently traveling to Denver to represent you. This will not be an easy task, so I'll not tell you to hold high hopes, but Daniel will be an excellent advocate. I've given him your address there, expect him within the week.

Best to you,
Judge Raddock

Leah showed the letter to Eloise. They were having dinner.

When Eloise finished reading, she handed it back. "Sounds promising, if nothing else."

Leah frowned. "At this point I don't care how it comes out. I just want to go back East so I can be myself again."

"Well, if it's any consolation, I like having you around. Alice likes you, too."

Leah laughed at the idea of the statue having likes and dislikes. "Well, tell her I said thanks."

Eloise nodded. "I will."

Done with the meal, Leah followed Eloise into the kitchen to help with the cleanup. Eloise washed while Leah dried.

"So, no word from Ryder?" Eloise asked.

"No."

Eloise studied her for a moment. "He hurt you bad this time, didn't he?"

"Yes."

"Then you must care for him," Eloise remarked.

"I thought I did."

Eloise glanced at her. "You still do. For all of his Cheyenne ways, Ryder's insides are soft as pudding. Always have been, always will be. Seth, on the other hand, knows that. He's made it his life's work to wound his brother anyway he can. It's one of the things he does best, I'm afraid."

"Well, he gave a grand performance this time."

"I'm sure Ryder is somewhere kicking himself for letting Seth send him around the bend. He'll be around to see you soon, I'm betting."

Leah shook her head. "I don't think so. He and I are back to being oil and water."

"You know, if you add a little seasoning and a few herbs to oil and water and give it a good shaking, you get a passable vinaigrette."

Leah chuckled. "Well with all the shaking we've had we should be more than passable."

Eloise smiled as she handed Leah the last dish to dry, then said, "The church is having a box lunch auction this weekend. Do you want to go? We're raising money for a new building."

"Will Ryder be there?"

Eloise studied her. "Maybe, but probably not."

"How about Cordelia and her stuffy friends?"

"Nope. Just plain old folks like you and me."

"Then I'd love to tag along. I could use some cheering up."

Eloise smiled. "You have to bring a box lunch for the gentlemen to bid on though."

"No one's going to bid on mine. Folks here barely know me."

"Don't worry, by now every man of color within thirty miles has heard how pretty you are. They'll bid."

"But I'm also a widow, Eloise."

"Leah, around here men have been known to show up on a widow's doorstep less than an hour after she's put her man in the ground."

Leah smiled. "Okay, if you say so. What should go in the lunch?"

"You just leave that to me. When I make mine, I'll make one for you too."

Saturday dawned bright and beautiful. As Eloise drove, Leah took in the glorious surroundings. The sky was blue, the sunshine warm. The gorgeous weather was the best she'd experienced here so far and she hoped it would be indicative of how the day would be. She was nervous. After the hostility she'd had to endure at the Wayne's reception, she didn't know what to expect from the folks she'd meet today, but rather than worry herself into a fit, she decided to accept Eloise's word that everything would go fine.

The people were gathered in a wide, rolling meadow edged by multicolored wildflowers and towering pines. As Eloise drove them closer, Leah spotted children playing among the blankets and quilts spread over the ground. Men were setting up tables and chairs, and women were talking in groups and holding baskets covered with colorful cloths. A few of the faces were familiar from Eloise's church, but most weren't.

Eloise pulled the buckboard to a halt in an area of the meadow that held a number of other wagons and buck-boards. As they stepped down, a passel of eager children ran to Eloise as if she were the Pied Piper of legend. They swarmed her with smiles and hugs and requests for pepper-mint which she handed out gladly. Leah recognized some of the children as members of Eloise's Sunday school class. Only that class had gotten Eloise out of the studio last week.

"Children, you all remember Miss Leah?"

Leah scanned the happy faces of the ten boys and girls, and said, "How are you all?"

"Did you bring a lunch?" one of the little girls asked. She was short, with two thick plaits, and had lost both her front teeth. Leah guessed her to be six or seven years of age. The gap added charm to her small brown face.

"Yes, I did," Leah replied kindly as she indicated the bas-ket on her arm. "How about you?"

The girl, whose name was Dorcas, looked so surprised by the teasing question, the other children laughed.

"I'm only six," the girl answered. "But my sister Callie did. She's sweet on Mr. Ryder."

Leah raised an eyebrow. "I see." She wondered if sister Callie knew Dorcas was over here spreading her business.

Miss Eloise promised the children a game of hide-and-seek later. Content with her promise and her peppermints they ran off to resume their play.

"They like you a great deal," Leah noted to Eloise as they began the walk across the meadow to join the rest of the gathering.

"I like them too. Always have loved children." Leah looked around the open meadow. "Is this where the new church is going to be built?"

"Yep. Ryder owns this land, but he's offered to donate it once the building's up."

In spite of her personal problems with Ryder, Leah found his generosity impressive. "When will that be?"

"We hope very soon. The money brought in today should put us over the top."

Leah thought the meadow would be a wonderful setting for a house of worship. Churches and schools were often luxuries in small communities of color, but once erected became rallying points of pride and purpose. The small A.M.E. church she'd attended back home served not only its people's spiritual needs but fed the hungry, gave clothes to the needy, and agitated on behalf of the race. She hoped the folks here would get their new church building soon.

Leah could see people watching her curiously as she and Eloise approached. Again she worried how she'd be met. Did Monty have enemies here, too?

The pastor of the church stepped away from a group of women to greet them. The tall, light-skinned Reverend Garrison was dressed in a worn black suit and a clerical collar. "Good afternoon, Sister Eloise. Sister Leah. Glad you could come."

Pastor Garrison had performed the service for Cecil's burial, and Leah would be forever grateful for his assistance that day.

"Reverend."

"I hope that basket you're carrying has a lunch the bachelors can bid on," he told Leah.

Amused, she replied, "As a matter of fact it does."

"Good, then while Sister Eloise helps with the last of the organizing, I'll introduce you around to those folks you don't know. If that's okay?"

Leah looked to Eloise and saw approval in her eyes. "Lead the way, Reverend."

Leah found everyone just as nice as Eloise had promised. No one sneered or turned away; no one asked impertinent questions about her marriage or questioned her morals. In fact, they all seemed genuinely pleased to make her acquaintance. Leah's modestly designed, but costly green dress, with its lace-edged collar and row of tiny jet buttons down the front made her stand out like a peacock among the dull browns and calicos worn by the other women, but no one seemed to hold it against her. These were plain folks: farmers, miners, lumbermen, domestics; they looked her in the eye and offered genuine smiles. They made Leah feel right at home.

Her peace was ruffled by the sight of Seth dismounting from his expensive rig. Leah wondered if he were part of the congregation because she didn't remember seeing him in church before.

The reverend said evenly, "I didn't expect him here today."

"Is Seth a member of your congregation?"

"No, but we welcome all."

Leah was curious about the disapproval clouding the Reverend Garrison's angelic features but was distracted as Seth, still a few feet away, called out to her and waved.

Leah pasted a false smile upon her face and waved in reply.

The reverend looked down at her, and asked, "Do you know the true nature of the beast?"

Leah paused for a moment to study the reverend's now masked features; she knew without further words that he'd been talking about Seth. She nodded solemnly. "I'm beginning to."

He nodded.

"Good, then I'll go and see if anyone needs my help."

He left her, and Seth joined her a few moments later. "Leah, hello. I heard about the auction, and thought I'd see if you were here."

"Why?" she asked coldly.

He appeared taken aback. "Just wanted to maybe spend some time with you."

"Why did you tell your brother I'd slept with you?"

He visibly jumped, then tried to charm her with a smile. "He didn't believe me, did he? I was just trying to get his goat."

Had Leah a pistol she'd shoot him right between the eyes. "I'm no longer available to keep company with you, Seth."

"Aw, Leah don't be mad. It was a prank, nothing more."

"Some prank. You believe a woman's reputation is something to make light of? How about we go find Barksdale Wayne and you can joke about sleeping with Cordelia."

He paled. Leah was glad to see her harpoon had hit. She had nothing further to say, so she turned and walked back to the gathering.

On the Reverend Garrison's signal everyone gathered around. He led the assemblage in the Lord's Prayer and once it was done, the festivities began.

First up were Eloise's Sunday school children. As the adults and adolescents made themselves comfortable on the tarps, blankets, and seats of the two trestle tables, the young ones lined up. With Eloise standing before them, she raised her hands like a conductor, and the young voices broke into song. They were dangerously off-key but sang the up-tempo hymn with such boisterous enthusiasm, those watching could only smile.

Once the children finished, they sat down to rousing applause and were followed by Callie Dotson, the aforementioned older sister of little Dorcas. Leah guessed the young woman to be about eighteen years of age, far too young to be anywhere near a man like Ryder Damien. She was a beauty though: clear brown skin, short-cropped hair, and a heart-shaped face. Her dress, like the ones worn by the other women, looked to be her best, but like the dresses Leah had worn back home, the garment had seen better days. There were small, discreet patches near the waistline, and the shiny lines above the hem bore evidence that it had been let down more than once to compensate for her growth. However she had a voice gowned in gold. The high pure soprano soared majestically over the meadow as she sang, "Precious Promise." That she'd been given a gift became readily apparent; her voice gave Leah goose bumps. Listening to her made Leah forget about everything but the rising beauty of Callie Dotson's hymn.

When the last moving note faded away, thunderous applause erupted. Smiling shyly, Callie bowed and took a seat next to her proud parents.

The Reverend Garrison stood up and gave a few announcements about upcoming church meetings and the baptism scheduled for the next Sunday. He also spoke about the whirlwind swirling around Andrew Green, the man charged with the shooting death of the streetcar conductor. "The sheriff's talking about a public hanging if he's convicted."

Leah, like many others, shook her head sadly. Thousands were likely to attend the hanging, bringing box lunches and their children. No one deserved to be executed as the center act in a circus.

The reverend continued, "Now nobody's disputing this Green fellow is a bad type. He's a thief, a drunk, and even shot his own daddy when he was just a youngster, according to folks here who know him, but nobody should be hanged like that. In your prayers remember him."

While he went on with a few other announcements, Mable France appeared seemingly out of nowhere and took a seat on the blue quilt beside Leah and Eloise. Mable greeted them both with a smile.

There were now close to fifty people assembled. Many

had come after the start of the hymns and had quietly taken up positions in the back so as not to cause a disturbance. The majority of the late arrivals were men dressed up in their Sunday suits. Many of the suits looked worn, but were clean. Leah spotted Sam among them. He was gussied up, too, and when his eyes met Leah's he touched his hat politely. Glad to see him, she inclined her head in greeting.

She leaned over and whispered to Mable, "Sam's here."

"I know," she responded with a blush.

Leah grinned.

It was now time to start the main event. All of the women came forward and placed their baskets on the trestle table, then returned to their seats. The first group of lunches up for bid had been prepared by married women. Under good-natured teasing and calls from the crowd their husbands came up one by one, placed their winning bids in the crock, and purchased their wives' baskets.

The unmarried women came next.

The Reverend Garrison said, "Now, since we have a visitor in our midst, I say we put hers up for bid next. This basket comes from Sister Leah, Montague. Oh, and she's a widow by the way."

Leah saw the smiles directed her way and found all the attention a bit embarrassing.

"Now, we don't know if Sister Montague can cook, but she's so pretty, I'm sure you men won't mind if she can't. Let's have the first bid."

Laughs followed that disclaimer and a grinning Leah dropped her head, embarrassed once more.

Seth's hand shot up. "Five dollars!"

The crowd reacted with surprise. The other baskets had gone for fifty cents, a dollar at the most. Five dollars was a lot of money in this setting. In reality, Leah was shocked to find that he hadn't slunk back under his rock after the tongue-lashing she'd give him, but then remembered his boasts to Helene about courting her in hopes of gaining the keys to Monty's estate. Leah turned and hoped no one saw the glare she gave him.

Because of his exorbitant bid, she doubted any other man would be so foolish as to top his offer. For the sake of the church, she resigned herself to Seth winning her basket.

"Any other bids, men?"

A silence fell over the meadow. Then, from somewhere behind her, Leah heard a familiar voice declare loudly, "Fifty dollars, in gold!"

As the crowd gasped, Leah stiffened.

Ryder.

Chapter 10

Leah hissed at Eloise, "I thought you said he wouldn't be here!"

Eloise shrugged innocently.

When Leah turned to see where he was standing, his dark eyes were waiting for her. She looked away, irritated with him for a variety of reasons, the least being making her the center of a whisper-filled controversy once again. However, as she glanced around at the crowd she saw that these people didn't appear scandalized; instead they were smiling fondly in her direction. Some of the older women even had knowing looks on their faces and others were out and out grinning. They appeared genuinely pleased by this startling turn of events, but Leah had no explanation as to why.

She leaned over to ask Eloise, "Why is everyone smiling?"

"They like him, and they like you, dear."

Applause accompanied his walk to the front of the

crowd. He had his hair in two plaits today, and they hung in front of his shoulders. They were a cultural contrast to the suit coat thrown over his arm, the open-throated white shirt and tailored trousers. Leah assumed they were congratulating him on his large contribution to the church's building fund, or at least she hoped they were.

Under the reverend's approving visage, Ryder placed his gold pieces in the crock. He then picked up her basket, and as the auctioning continued, began a slow walk in her direction.

Nervous, Leah asked Mable, "Why's he coming this way?"

"He gets the honor of your company for lunch."

Leah shot Eloise a look. "You didn't tell me that part."

The woman simply smiled.

Leah didn't want to share the basket with him. He'd hurt her feelings, or had he forgotten again? However, with so many folks looking on, she had no recourse but to sit politely and wait for his approach.

As Ryder crossed the field to where she was sitting he had no trouble reading the frostiness in the *Morenita*'s black eyes. Even though he still hadn't figured out a way to convince her to talk to him again, he was ready to try.

When he reached the quilt, he said, "Afternoon, ladies."

Mable nodded, and Eloise said, "Thanks for the bid, Ryder."

"You're welcome."

He looked down into Leah's cool gaze. "Shall we?"

She studied him for a long moment, then slowly got to her feet. Ryder could see Seth looking on; his brother appeared furious at having been bested. Ryder mockingly dipped his head in Seth's direction, then didn't give him another thought. His dear brother once owned the mortgage on the land where the congregation's old church now stood, and if Seth hadn't foreclosed on that land and the building in order to make good on some of his gambling debts, none of this fund-raising would be necessary. Ryder supposed Leah's presence had drawn Seth to the event, because there wasn't a person there who didn't wish the fancy Creole elsewhere.

Some of the couples sharing the auctioned basket lunches were seated on blankets they'd spread out on parts of the meadow that were a short distance away from the main gathering. For courting couples it offered a measure of privacy yet kept them in plain view of their mamas and the rest of the congregation.

Basket in hand, Ryder walked Leah through the knee-high grasses and flowers to a spot near a small clearing on the meadow's edge. "This field could use some Grass Dancers," he told her.

Leah lifted her hem in hopes of making the walk easier. "What are Grass Dancers?"

Ryder was relieved that she was at least speaking to him. "In my grandfather's day, they were the men who'd dance down the high grasses so the new villages could be erected."

Leah stopped. "Wouldn't that take a long time?"

He halted, too. "Usually, but they didn't measure life in terms of time. Grass dancing had a purpose, but it was also an event, a celebration. There'd be drumming and challenges to see who danced the best." He began walking again, and added, "Besides, the women loved the Grass Dancers."

She followed his trail. "Why?"

"They were usually the fittest and handsomest men in the tribe."

Grass Dancers. Leah had never heard of such a thing.

He stopped, looked around, and asked, "How about right here?"

She saw that although they were a distance away, they weren't too far from everyone else. "This is fine."

Only they didn't have a blanket.

He spread his coat on the ground, gestured at it, and took a seat beside it.

"I can't sit on your coat."

"Why not? You planning on eating standing?"

"I didn't plan to eat at all."

Their eyes met. She had her hand on one hip.

He told her honestly, "After the last time we were together, I suppose I deserve that."

"No, you deserve much more," she countered flatly.

He winced. "You know, if you don't sit down, folks are going to think you don't want to share your lunch with me."

"And they'd be correct."

"Then I'll just go and get my fifty dollars back."

"Now you're stooping to extortion?"

"Whatever it takes to get you to smile at me again. What I did was wrong, stupid, uncalled-for, and I hurt you very badly, I know that now. Please, *carinita*, sit, and let's talk."

Don't call me that, she wailed inwardly. She didn't want to let go of her anger, she didn't want to be hurt by him again, but the whispered plea reached out to her, touched her, and *damn* if parts of herself weren't responding. Leah swore she was sitting only to ensure he didn't go and retrieve his coins; it had nothing to do with the softening of her will.

"Thank you," he said softy.

She didn't reply.

A three-piece band was playing back at the main gathering. They were as terribly off-key as Eloise's children's choir had been, but Leah and Ryder were far enough away not to have to hear it up close.

Leah waited as he removed the red-checkered cloth covering the contents in the basket. Inside were sandwiches, a jar of lemonade, and fat slices of freshly made pound cake.

Ryder looked over at her. "All of my favorites."

He peeled back the bread a bit and looked inside. "Yep, ham and mustard. How'd you know?"

Leah shot him a look. "I suppose pound cake is your favorite, too?"

"Sure is." He grinned, biting into the sandwich.

Leah smelled a rat and its name was Eloise. Leah had had no idea what the basket held because Eloise had handed it to her just before they climbed onto the wagon. Had Eloise known in advance that Ryder would be getting the lunch and therefore packed it with his favorite things? The answer seemed pretty obvious. Leah bit into her sandwich.

The ice in the lemonade had melted and the sweet drink was a bit watery, but it was still very cold. Watching Leah drink from the frosty jar, Ryder scanned her silently. He liked the dress she'd chosen to wear. Emerald green with a high neck and long sleeves, there were tiny jet buttons marching down the front that he'd have enjoyed spending an afternoon slowly opening. The well-tailored bodice fit her lines smoothly, subtly emphasizing the tempting swells of her bosom and the trimness of her waist.

As Leah ate her cake, she could see him watching her. She wanted to stare him down and show him just how angry she was still, but found it difficult because of the genuine sincerity in his apology. "Thank you for bidding on my lunch. Eloise said today's auction would go a long way toward getting the church built."

He finished his lunch and was now lying on his back in the grass, looking up at the clouds. "You're welcome. Are you talking to me again?"

"No."

He told her solemnly, "You know, if you're carrying my baby, you'll have to marry me."

"No, I don't."

He rolled his head toward her. "And I want daughters just like you."

The quiet conviction in his eyes and voice shook her to her toes.

"Daughters as fierce and prickly and beautiful as their mother."

Leah didn't know what to say. The idea that she might be carrying his child was a real possibility. Her courses were two weeks late. But could she marry a man so hobbled by the past? Her mother had raised her without benefit of a husband, and as a result Leah had suffered the slings and arrows associated with such a birth. Did Leah want her child subjected to the same treatment by the same narrow minds and views? "And when some brash young Cheyenne brave comes courting these daughters of yours?"

"They'll have to offer me thousands of ponies just to learn their names . . ."

Leah turned away.

Ryder sat up. He said it again, "I'm sorry, *Morenita*. I truly, truly am."

Leah hated crying, but she seemed to be doing it again. Why did he have to be the one able to twist her heart?

Ryder leaned forward and gently kissed one tear-filled eye, and then the other. "Forgive me," he whispered.

Leah realized that no matter where she chose to hide, the fact that she'd fallen in love with this man would always find her. "You hurt me very badly, Ryder," she replied in the same hushed tones. "Very badly."

"I know, and I'll cut out my own heart before I let it happen again . . ."

They were only a breath apart.

"If you can't forgive me right away, I understand," he told her genuinely. "What I accused you of is not something easily forgotten, or forgiven."

"No, it isn't."

Silence fell between them as they sensed each other, felt their feelings for each other rising again like dawn vanquishing the night.

"I want to kiss you . . ." he whispered.

"I know . . ."

"People will talk," she reminded him, hardly aware of the crowd.

"Let them . . ."

The bittersweet kiss was filled with regret, forgiveness, and promise. They didn't care who might see or what might be said. They were trying to find their way back.

When he slowly pulled away, Ryder fed himself on the watery light shining in her dark eyes. "Are you talking to me now?"

"No," she whispered "I'm kissing you . . ." And she lifted her lips for another, right there in front of God, the congregation, and everybody, including a seething Seth, who upon seeing them embrace, turned on his heel, stormed back to his carriage, and drove away.

Ryder pulled her in against him and held her tight as he murmured against her ear,

"I'll never hurt you like that again, I promise."

Leah clung to him; her heart believed him, but her mind knew the possibility of being hurt again would remain until the past was laid to rest.

He leaned back and stroked her cheek. "I have to go to Virginia City for about two weeks. Would you like to come with me?"

She replied disappointedly, "I can't, I'm waiting for the lawyer from Boston."

"Lawyer? What lawyer?"

"Judge Raddock's filed some sort of injunction, and he's sending out a lawyer to represent me."

"When's he coming?" Ryder asked.

"I'm not certain, but soon, I'm guessing, and if he's successful, I suppose I'll have to put up with Seth and his grand plans again."

He looked confused.

She explained what she'd overheard that day on Seth's porch.

Ryder shook his head. "He and that aunt are quite a pair."

That reminded Leah of something she hadn't wanted to think about—Cecil's death. "Helene keeps saying Cecil died the same way her sister did—that he was poisoned. Do you think that's possible?"

He shrugged. "Anything is possible I suppose, but probable—who knows?"

"Maybe she's just trying to rile me. From what Cecil told me, he and Helene didn't get along very well back then."

Ryder thought for a moment. "She doesn't get along with anybody now either, but what does she gain by wanting you to think Cecil was poisoned?"

"I've no idea."

"Has it been bothering you?"

Leah nodded. "He's been in my dreams lately, and I keep asking myself, what if she's right? What if he was murdered? His death was quite sudden, if you think about it. I don't ever remember him being ill like that before."

"We could have the body exhumed if you want to be sure. I've a friend up in Boulder who does autopsies. It may take a while for the results, but it would ease your mind."

Leah shuddered at the idea of such a gruesome task, but knew she owed it to Cecil to find out for sure. "What do I have to do?"

"You don't have to do anything. I'll take care of it."

"I want to be there when his casket is brought up though. I owe him that much."

"Whatever you wish."

She had to ask. "Do you think I'm overreacting by having him exhumed?"

He leaned over and kissed her lightly on the nose. "No. If he was poisoned, we need to know and the sheriff told."

Buoyed by his support, Leah set the matter aside for now.

Ryder looked around the meadow. "All the other couples are back over with the group. Do you want to join them?"

"I suppose we should, though I'd rather sit here with you."

Ryder liked the sound of that. "I'd rather sit here, too."

She plucked at a few blades of grass. "Why are you going to Virginia City? Business?"

He nodded. "Yep. Stockholders' meetings, and to look over some potential mine sites."

"Wish I could come with you."

"Me too, but—" He got to his feet, then holding on to her hand, pulled her up. "I'll have to settle for just thinking about you."

Leah liked the sound of that. "When are you leaving?"

"In the morning, first thing."

Leah sighed. If he kissed her now, they would be seen for sure, but she wanted another.

He correctly interpreted her desire. "You're looking like a woman who wants to be kissed."

"I am."

He grinned. "How about I see you home?"

"We can't just leave. That would be rude."

"Yes, it would be, but I'm known for that."

Amused by his honesty, she shook her head. "Well, I'm not."

"How about dinner this evening, then?"

Leah wasn't sure how she felt about where the evening might lead.

Once again, he read her mind. "Just dinner. Nothing more," he assured her sincerely. As a man he wanted her in his bed, but as a man whose feelings for her seemed to be rising and solidifying by the minute, he didn't want her to believe bedding her to be his sole concern.

"Where will we go?" she asked.

"Dinah's?"

Leah smiled. "That sounds fine."

They agreed on a time. He picked up his coat, grabbed the basket and escorted her back.

Much to Ryder's delight everyone was packing up to go home. There was church tomorrow morning and folks had chores to do before sunset.

With Eloise's blessings, Ryder drove Leah home. He set the brake and walked her around to the little cabin. He pulled her into his arms. "One last kiss and I'll go."

"Only one?" she teased back.

"You are such a naughty woman."

"That, too, is your fault."

Laughing, he kissed her long and hard.

"Um, excuse me, I'm looking for a Mrs. Leah Montague."

They both turned to the sound of the strange voice. An obviously embarrassed young White man stood there. He had blond hair and blue eyes. His gray suit bore the familiar rumples of a train passenger.

An equally embarrassed Leah backed out of Ryder's arms. She smoothed her hair. "I'm Leah Montague."

His blue eyes widened. He then stared at Ryder.

Ryder, arms crossed, stared back. He hadn't liked being interrupted. "And you are?"

"Um, Daniel Morton."

Morton then looked at Leah again. "But the judge didn't say you were—" His words faded to a stop.

Leah raised an eyebrow. "Black? Colored?"

Ryder fumed silently, then asked, "Is this the lawyer?"

She responded. "I believe so."

She saw that Morton's young face had turned an even brighter red. For some unknown reason, his youth maybe, Leah took pity on him, and asked, "Shall we start over?"

He nodded vigorously, gratefully. "Please. My name is Daniel Morton. Honored to meet you, Mrs. Montague."

"Pleased to meet you, too, Mr. Morton. This is Mr. Ryder Damien."

Morton seemed puzzled a moment, then he knelt and opened his valise. He extracted a paper tablet that had writing on it. He stood, silently scanning the words, muttering, "Ryder Damien. Ryder Damien."

His face lit up. "Ah here it is, I knew the name sounded familiar. Let's see, Ryder Damien. You're—"

He stopped then as if he couldn't believe what he was reading. When he looked up, his eyes were wide once again. "Why, you're Mr. Montague's son!"

Leah supposed he was a bit surprised to find the son kissing his stepmother, but life was sometimes complicated. She wondered if he were old enough to understand that yet.

Ryder asked distantly, "Is there a problem?"

"Uh, no sir. Not at all."

Morton turned back to the more friendly face of Leah. "I've taken a room in Denver. I'd like to sit down and talk with you sometime in the next day or so. We have the preliminary hearing on Wednesday."

"So soon?" Ryder asked.

"Yes, I believe the sooner we begin to move on this, the better."

Ryder agreed, but wondered why the judge had sent this cub to represent her interests. He didn't look old enough to *spell* law, much less practice it.

"Would you like to meet now?" Leah asked.

Ryder's eyes widened. She was supposed to be having dinner with him.

Morton smiled. "I'd hoped to, but I wouldn't want to impose."

Ryder was about to say, *good she'll see you tomorrow*, when Leah replied, "Then let's meet now."

Leah saw that Ryder looked like a little boy who'd just been told he couldn't have any ice cream.

"Mr. Morton, would you excuse us for a moment?"

Watching Ryder warily, he responded, "Certainly."

She beckoned her lover over to the porch. Ryder gave Morton a look that made the young man tug nervously at his collar before walking over to where Leah stood. It took all she had not to smile at the sullen look on his face. "Ryder, I do believe you're pouting."

"Cheyenne braves don't pout."

She smiled. "My apologies. We can have dinner when you return."

"I know." Ryder also knew he was being selfish. However, he resigned himself to not seeing her tonight and not being able to hold her again until he returned from Virginia City. He wasn't happy about it though. "I want you to have Sam telegraph me if any trouble comes up."

He looked over at Daniel Morton. "Couldn't the judge have sent you someone older?"

"He's supposed to be very good," Leah assured him.

Ryder didn't appear impressed. "Well, I'm going to head home. I'd kiss you good-bye, but I don't want to shock the children."

She grinned, then said genuinely, "Have a safe trip."

He stroked her cheek and stepped off the porch. Walking by Morton, he growled, "Represent her well, or I'll have your hide."

Hearing that, Leah's hands went to her hips and she shook her head with mute amusement. As he disappeared from sight, she missed him already.

Leah showed the young lawyer into her small residence. He looked around at the sparsely furnished space, then, at her request, sat on one of the chairs. He pulled out his papers and pen. "I already know some of the details surrounding your marriage, but I need to be clear on everything."

Leah began by explaining the relationship between Monty and her mother, Reba, then told the truth behind her own marriage.

Morton asked, "So in reality, the marriage between you and Mr. Montague was a sham."

"Essentially yes. He hoped it would ensure my future."

"A noble gesture," he voiced while he wrote on his tablet, "but let's hope our worthy opponents don't find out."

Leah asked, "Will I be called upon to testify?"

"More than likely. We're going to try and prove that the thirty-year lien on Mr. Montague's assets and the subsequent confiscation of the estate by the court to pay the lien was improper. If I were they, I'd challenge your right even to inherit the estate, so we must be prepared to counter that."

They talked well on into the evening about strategies, how he wished her to dress, and the demeanor she needed to maintain while being questioned by their opponents.

"Now, this matter with Mr. Damien." He held her eyes. "I have no idea how his presence in your life will affect our chances of regaining the estate. Honestly, it can't help, especially if everyone already knows the two of you are—involved."

Leah sighed. "Well, we can't wave a wand and make it disappear."

"I know, but they'll have trouble seeing you as the deserving young widow when you've taken up with your late husband's illegitimate son."

Leah's jaw tightened.

He smiled kindly, "I mean no offense, but I want you to be prepared to hear exactly that, and more, because they'll undoubtedly attack your character."

He gathered up his tablets and papers and placed everything back into his small black valise. "They're also going to challenge your rights to the estate because of your race."

Leah nodded. "I know."

"Just so you're prepared."

He stood and put on his rumpled coat. "We'll be waging an uphill battle and I have no idea if we'll prevail, but I will them give them a fight. I don't want to hand my hide to Mr. Damien."

Leah smiled. In spite of the awkwardness of their initial meeting, she felt confident having this young man on her side.

It was dark when she walked him to the door. "Thank you, Daniel."

He nodded. "Thank you."

He gave her the name of his hotel, then said, "We'll get together again before Wednesday but I'll be doing some investigating on my own in the meantime."

Leah nodded. "If there's anything I can help you with, please let me know."

"I will, and I'll see you in a couple of days."

After he was gone, Leah stood with her back against the door. She was admittedly nervous about Wednesday's proceedings but vowed to face it with her head held high no matter the outcome.

By the time Ryder made it home, he'd already decided to cancel his trip to Virginia City. An underling could be dispatched to the stockholders' meeting and the Nevadans who wanted his money to invest in their mine would simply have to wait. He had more important business here. The creditors who had been awarded Louis's estate would undoubtedly mount a formidable campaign to keep it. If he were they he'd have already conducted an investigation into the widow's past, so whatever dirt was unearthed could be presented to the judge. Failing that, her race would be attacked next, along with her relationship with him. With that in mind he planned to alert his own lawyers in the morning, just in case the back East cub needed reinforcements.

Ryder also needed to find out what the hell had happened to the Pinkerton he'd hired. If there was some damaging news, he wanted to know before her opponents. In reality, though, he didn't care about the Pinkerton's report or how the hearing turned out; he just wanted everything over so he and the *Morenita* could concentrate on the future. He had more than enough money for her to live comfortably by his side for the rest of her life, so the monetary value of the estate and the fifteen thousand he'd lost meant little. Leah, however, had come to mean a lot.

Leah got ready for church the next morning, then went to the house to see if Eloise were ready as well. The house was quiet, though, and no one answered Leah's knock on the studio door. Deciding to see if Eloise might be with Alice, Leah went back outside.

Moving as quietly as she had done before, Leah peeked through the tress bordering Alice's domain, and sure enough there sat Eloise.

She was saying, "I know it has to be done, but this will be the hardest one."

Leah wondered if Eloise was referring to her studio work.

Eloise quieted as if listening to Alice, then responded, "Well it's going to be finished soon. Then we'll both feel better."

When Eloise rose, Leah came out of hiding and casually revealed herself as if she'd not been eavesdropping, "Good morning, Eloise."

A startled Eloise swung sharply around. For a moment Leah saw something strange in the old woman's eyes, but it vanished so quickly, Leah thought she must have imagined it.

The eyes were now shining with the familiar kindness. "Good morning, dear. You startled us. Didn't she, Alice?"

"I'm sorry. I just came to see if you're ready for church?"

Eloise smiled. "Sure am. You go on around to the front. Let me grab my Sunday school books, and Ol' Tom and I will be there in a minute."

Leah nodded then left to go wait out front.

When they returned from church, Eloise went back into her studio, and Leah journeyed on to her cabin. A folded note had been tacked to the door. Hoping it might be a parting note from Ryder, she took it down and hastily opened it. The letters of the words had been cut from newsprint and were glued to the paper. Ice filled her veins as she read:

> *Death to all the Montague Whores. Three times is the charm. You're next!*

The words filled her with such fear, she thought she'd be sick. Her hands were shaking, and a cold sweat ran down her back inside her blue dress. Not knowing what else to do, she ran to the house yelling, "Eloise!"

Eloise met her in the kitchen. She took a look at distressed Leah's face and asked with alarm, "What's happened?"

Leah handed her the note.

Eloise read it and whispered, "Dear Lord. Where'd you find this?"

"On the cabin door."

"We have to tell the sheriff. Come on, I'll hitch up Ol' Tom."

For a moment, Leah couldn't move. The raggedly spaced words kept echoing in her head. Someone wanted her dead!

"Come on, Leah!" Eloise called urgently.

Her voice seemed to free Leah from the spell. She shook herself and followed Eloise out to the barn.

Because it was Sunday, many of the shops and businesses in Denver were closed. There were fewer people on the streets than during the week, but there were plenty of folks in front of the sheriff's office. Late last month, a mob had attempted to storm the jail with the intentions of lynching Andrew Green and his accomplice, a Black man named Withers, but had been turned back by Sheriff Cramer and the city police. As a result, a large contingent of law-enforcement officers was now guarding the facility around the clock.

Leah and Eloise were stopped by one of the guards far short of the jail. When they showed him the note, he looked between the Black women, and said, "I'll let the sheriff know. He's at home right now."

"But—" Leah began.

He cut her off. "I said, I'll let the sheriff know."

"Isn't there anyone else I can speak with?"

"No."

Realizing she'd get no satisfaction there, at least not today, she asked, "When can I see him?"

"Try back in a couple of days. This Green thing's got everybody's hands full."

"And if I'm dead before those couple of days are here?" Leah asked.

He didn't even flinch. "I'll let the sheriff know." That said, he turned away and went back to his post beside the door.

An angry Leah shared a look with the tight-lipped Eloise. They returned to the wagon.

"Maybe it's just a prank," Eloise voiced as she drove them home.

"Some prank."

Pranks brought to mind Seth. "Seth said telling Ryder we'd slept together had been a prank. You don't think he do something like this, do you?"

Eloise shrugged. "I wish I could say no."

Leah knew she could also add Cordelia and Helene to the short list of enemies she'd made since coming here, but what if the note had been penned by someone she didn't know, someone still holding a grudge against Monty? He and Cecil had left behind many enemies. Thinking about it a bit more though made her tend to believe this was a nemesis she knew, someone who'd known she and Eloise attended church on Sunday mornings and that they'd be gone long enough for the perpetrator to leave the deadly calling card without fear of being discovered.

"Eloise, how much do you know about the deaths of Bernice Montague and Ryder's mother, Songbird?"

"Not much, except Bernice died very slowly. I couldn't save her, and neither could the big fancy doctors Louis brought in."

"Do you think both women could've been murdered?"

"Now, we know Songbird was murdered, but Bernice's death wasn't so cut-and-dried. There were rumors that she was poisoned, but it was never proven."

"I'm going to have Cecil's body exhumed."

Surprise filled Eloise's face. "Really? When did you decide that?"

"At the church social. I was telling Ryder about Helene's belief that both Cecil and her sister were poisoned, and he suggested exhumation as a way to put my mind to rest."

"Do you really believe his death was unnatural?" Eloise asked.

"I don't know what I believe at this point, but having an autopsy performed will let me know one way or the other—at least I hope so."

Eloise waved at a couple passing them by on the other side of the road. "You know some folks thought Helene was responsible for her sister's death."

Leah was surprised. "Didn't they get along?"

"In public yes, but not in private."

"Why not?"

"Bernice had Louis, his money, and his grand house. Helene had nothing that Bernice didn't give her, and Bernice never missed an opportunity to point that out. Helene resented being treated like a poor relation."

"Could she really have poisoned her sister?" Leah asked.

"Louis was convinced it was her."

"And you?"

Eloise shrugged. "Helene lived in the house, so she had the opportunity, but who knows? Would she really have killed her own sister?"

"What a mess."

Eloise nodded. "It certainly is. We need to let Ryder know about that note."

"He left this morning for Virginia City. Sam can wire him though."

"Good. Do you know how to shoot a rifle?"

"No," Leah said.

"Well no sense in giving you one for protection then."

"Probably not, I'll just wind up shooting myself."

Eloise smiled. "Glad you still have your sense of humor."

"That's about all I have. It isn't often I have my life threatened."

Eloise nodded her understanding. "Well, let's go by Helene's and talk with Mable. Maybe she's seeing Sam today and can have him wire Ryder in Virginia City."

"Good idea."

But Mable wasn't there. According to Helene it was Mable's Sunday off.

A curious Helene asked, "Why do you need to speak with her?"

Leah gave her the note and carefully watched Helene's expression, but the woman only raised her usual eyebrow.

Helene handed it back. "When did you receive this?"

"It was on my door when we returned from church this morning."

"And I assume you have no idea who it's from?" Helene asked.

"None."

Helene sighed. "As I said before, by coming to Denver, you've awakened something that's been asleep for thirty years. It killed my sister, the Indian woman, Songbird, and probably Cecil Lee. You'd best be careful."

She then closed the door and left them standing on the porch. Leah tried to shake off her fear as she and Eloise returned to the wagon, but found it impossible.

Since Ryder had changed his plans about going to Virginia City he decided to pay the *Morenita* a surprise visit. It would be dark in a few hours, but he didn't care. He saddled his stallion and rode off.

He went to Eloise's door first in case Leah was there and was rewarded by her answering his knock on the screened door.

Leah's face filled with surprise. "I thought you were leaving town."

"Changed my mind."

Relieved, she sagged against the doorjamb. "Thank goodness."

A bit puzzled by her response, he opened the door and stepped inside. "What's the matter?"

"This."

Ryder took the folded paper from her hand. As he read, his eyes widened. "Where did this come from?"

She told him.

"Where's Eloise?"

"In her studio."

"You go and gather up your things. You're coming back with me."

Leah nodded. She had no intention of acting like an addle-brained heroine in a dime novel and arguing with him about being able to handle this situation alone only to wind up dead. She knew without a doubt that he'd protect her with every fiber of his being. Anyone wanting to harm her would have to come through him first. She gave him a kiss on the cheek and hurried off to pack a carpetbag.

While Leah went to the cabin, Ryder knocked on the door of Eloise's studio. "Eloise?" he called.

"Ryder, is that you?"

"Yes. Can you come out a moment?"

"Be right there." Eloise appeared in the doorway, and he caught a quick glimpse of the artistic clutter inside before she stepped out and carefully closed the door behind her. "Glad you're here," she said. "Did she show you the letter?"

"Yes. I'm taking her back to Sunrise with me."

"That's probably wise. Whoever it is will probably think twice before trying to harm her there."

"Any idea who might've put that trash on her door?"

"Not a one."

"Well, I intend to find out."

Anger rose inside Ryder. He wouldn't allow anyone to

harm her, not and live. "Will you be all right here by your-self?"

She waved him off. "Sure, you just keep Leah safe."

"Don't worry, and if that lawyer of hers comes around, send him out to my place."

"I will."

Moments later Ryder placed Leah in front of him on the horse and then galloped them off into the fading light of the day. Neither spoke. No words were necessary. She needed protection, and they both knew he would provide it or die trying.

After arriving at Sunrise, they entered the kitchen to find a worried Sam and Mable seated at the big wooden table.

Sam stood and surveyed Leah anxiously. "Helene told us what happened. Are you all right, Leah?"

"I feel better being here. Evening, Mable."

"This is so terrible," she replied. "Helene's convinced it's all tied to the past."

Ryder said, "She could be right, but for now, I'm going to take Leah upstairs so she can relax. We'll see you two later."

They nodded in response.

Once inside his room, she set down her carpetbag. He took her into his arms and whispered against her hair, "You're safe here."

Leah held him tight. She did indeed feel safe. His strength seemed to be flowing into her, easing her anxieties and fears.

He leaned back a bit. Looking down into her eyes he made a solemn pledge, "We'll find this person."

"I know."

Leah placed her head against his chest and basked in his nearness.

Ryder wanted nothing more than to stand there and hold her until dawn, but knew that to be impractical, so he led her over to the black-velvet settee in front of the fireplace.

"Come on, let's sit down."

She sat in his lap, and they were both content.

"Now," he said, "I want you tell me everything that's happened since you found the letter."

So she did. When she related the treatment she'd received at the hands of the sheriff's deputy, Ryder's jaw tightened. "I'll pay him a visit tomorrow."

She then told him about the encounter with Helene, and Helene's words.

Ryder admitted, "I hate to give that old harpy any credence, but in this instance—"

"I know, the letter implied that this person knew about the deaths of Bernice and your mother, and could be responsible for them."

Ryder agreed. All his life he'd believed Louis Montague guilty of his mother's murder, and now he found himself questioning that assumption. Had Louis really been innocent? On the surface the letter seemed to indicate he may have been. If so, that changed things; it wouldn't bring his mother back nor erase all the emotional pain he'd suffered as a child, but finding the real killer might bring him the inner peace he had been seeking. "I'd prefer you stay here until this is sorted out."

"I'd like that."

He stared down at her face. "Scared?"

"Yes."

"I'd be worried if you'd said no."

"I'm not naive. Someone in this town wants my life. Only a simpleton wouldn't be afraid."

"They'll have to go through me."

She cuddled closer. "I know."

For a long while neither of them spoke. Each seemed content just to pass the evening cozied up on the settee, but as dusk faded and night rose, the room filled with darkness. "Should we light a lamp?" he asked softly.

"If you want. Sitting in the dark like this is fine."

And it was. His heart was beating steadily beneath her ear. Being held by him this way made her feel sheltered, treasured, almost loved, even though she knew his feelings for her weren't rooted in that. He cared for her, yes, but love? To love someone involved surrendering parts of oneself, and she didn't think Ryder's past would allow him to do so. It made her no never mind though, even if she were to leave him tomorrow and never see him again, the memories of him and what they'd shared would remain with her forever.

"How'd your meeting go with lawyer Morton?" Ryder asked.

"Quite well. He asked a thousand questions, though. He's thorough if nothing else."

"That's good to hear."

"He thinks the other side will probably attack my relationship with you."

They shared a look, then he asked, "Will you be able to handle that?"

"I believe so. People keep forgetting that I don't care whether the estate comes to me or not."

"No?"

She shook her head. "No. All I want is my staid, uneventful life back. If I have to return home penniless, so be it."

Her talk of returning home didn't sit well with Ryder. "I don't want you going home."

"I'll have to eventually. If the estate falls through, I'll have to make a living."

"Not if you stay here with me."

Leah searched his face. He was so handsome and so awe-inspiring, a woman would have to be a fool to want to leave him, but she knew eventually he'd move on, and she'd be left with nothing but those aforementioned memories. "I won't have you making a commitment you'll come to regret."

"You underestimate me."

"I don't think so. When I was young, I'd always hoped to meet a man like you. One who'd teach me what it meant to be a woman, and who'd keep me safe, but one who'd be my husband. I've enjoyed this time we've spent together, but I can't live my life wondering if this is going to be the day you decide to take your kisses elsewhere."

"So you want me to marry you?"

"No, Ryder, I don't, because that isn't what you want." She cuddled back against him again. "How about we just be happy with where we are right now. The rest will take care of itself."

Above her Ryder nodded, but didn't know how he felt about what she'd just said.

The sweet slow sounds of a guitar slid through the open windows on the breeze. Leah slowly sat up. "Where's that music coming from?"

"Sam serenading Mable."

"I didn't know he could play."

"Yep. He learned from a Mexican guitarist when he was in southern Texas with the Ninth. Spanish tunes are the only ones he knows though."

The music was haunting, sensual. "It's beautiful."

"Yes, it is." *Much like the woman being held against my heart,* Ryder thought.

The two of them sat in the dark and listened to Sam's Spanish nocturne. The notes rose and fell, exuding desire and longing. Leah had never been aroused by music before but felt her body beginning to slowly blossom in response. Ryder seemed to be affected, too, because he raised her chin and began brushing his warm lips across her own. He whispered to her in a mixture of Spanish and Cheyenne; expressing his need, his fire and once again his apologies for the hurt he'd caused. "Let me love you . . ." he murmured. "Let me take you away from all this for a while . . ."

Leah accepted his kiss eagerly, hungrily. As it deepened they gathered each other closer. Heat sparkled and flared. In the passion that followed, the buttons gracing the front of her dress were undone as were the thin rawhide ties crisscrossing his shirt. Leah ran a lusty hand over the rock-hard softness of his now bared chest, then leaned up for another taste of his lips. Fueled by the magic of the music, they embarked upon a slow, erotic journey that rose and fell with the notes. He removed her clothes languidly, pausing between garments to make sure her mouth stayed kiss-swollen. Once she was undressed he treated her body to a thorough, wanton conquering that left her panting and pulsing on the big bear rug on the floor. Only then did he remove his own clothing. Nude he stood over her in the moonlight and she swore no handsomer man had ever been made. He looked sculpted, powerful. Shameless anticipation licked at her thighs.

He joined her on the rug and moments later they were both riding the storm. When they were done the only music they heard were the raw hard notes of release. He carried her back to the bed, and they slept.

Leah had never awakened in a man's bed before, but being with Ryder seemed to be a series of new experiences. She turned over slowly and found him propped up on one elbow seemingly waiting for her to open her eyes.

"Good morning," he said softly.

She smiled sleepily, "Good morning."

The room was filled with the soft light of a new dawn.

She scooted back so she could lie spoonlike against his warmth. He draped a possessive arm around her waist and held her close. "Did you sleep well?" He kissed her hair.

"Yes."

"I'm going into town later on, want to come?" he asked.

"Yes. I think I should let Daniel Morton see that letter. Maybe he can get the sheriff to do something about it."

He looked down at her. "I'm going to see the sheriff too, but investigating crimes against folks of color isn't a high priority around here."

"I sensed that." Receiving justice under the law was becoming more and more rare for members of the race as the reforms of Reconstruction continued to be eroded. "I need to wash before we go anywhere."

"How about a nice hot bath?"

Leah found the invitation intriguing. "In that fancy red tub?"

"Yes."

She smiled saucily. "It looks big enough for two."

"It is."

Leah had never shared a tub with a man. Once again he'd offered her a novel experience, and just the idea of it filled her with sensual anticipation.

Grabbing one of his shirts from the dresser drawer, she put it on and went downstairs to start the morning's coffee. She tiptoed to the stairs to listen for sounds. She didn't know if Cecil and Mable were in the house. Silence greeted her, so she dashed to the kitchen. She wanted coffee, and knew Ryder would also.

When she rejoined Ryder in the bathing room, she could see the water rushing into the tub. "Now tell me the story behind this," she asked, indicating the tub.

"Card game in San Francisco. Won it off of some French count from Mexico."

"That would account for the fleur-de-lis." The red tub was decorated with gold renditions of the stylized symbol of France.

"Probably. It was all he had left to wager. He'd been cleaned out of everything else, including his saber and his boots."

Ryder opened the drapes on the room's French doors. The sunrise filled the glass. "This is my favorite time of day. Just before the dawn. The world has a freshness to it, a newness. It's as if the Spirits are giving you yet another chance to walk the right path."

Leah had never seen this side of him. He was always so cynical, she hadn't known he could be philosophical as well.

He turned to view her.

"I like the dawn also."

The tub was full by then, and he turned off the spigot. Silence settled over the room. Under his glittering eyes, she undid the buttons on her borrowed shirt and slowly slid her body free. She felt a womanly power as she watched him taking in her dark nudity. His gaze was appreciative, admiring, lustful. In her mind he was already caressing her, teasing her.

However, reality was far more intense than fantasy. He had her stand in the heated water while he knelt beside it, then took an inordinate amount of time soaping her up and down. The soft cloth lingered over her peaks and explored her valleys. His free hand joined in to spread the slick soap and she trembled as he played wantonly. He rinsed her off with handfuls of cascading warm water. When he was done, she could hardly stand.

He joined her in the tub. Unable to contain himself, he sat and then eased her down onto his ready manhood and slid inside. Bliss filled him. He wanted to thrust himself to paradise then and there, but he also wanted to savor her for as long as he could. "Comfortable?" he murmured.

"Mmmm," she replied pleasurably, answering his strokes.

Smiling, he took that as a yes and continued to guide her in a slow, tempting rhythm. He thought this a delightful way to begin the morning and hoped it would be just the first of many more to come.

He brought her forward so he could kiss her lips, and slide a hand over her breast. The nipple was berry-hard against his palm. His hand followed the flare of her lines down to her hips and squeezed them possessively while she continued to rise and fall lustily.

Leah was hazy with desire. She admittedly liked this position; she could move at whatever pace she chose and he could touch and tease whatever and wherever he wished. Soon, all that riding and touching and teasing sent her over the top. The orgasm grabbed her with such force, she had to bury her face in his strong shoulder to keep her screams inside.

His release followed a heartbeat later, making him thrust strongly and, unlike her, yell loud enough to be heard around the world.

Two hours later they were riding into Denver. As it was Monday morning, all the shops were open and the plank walks were teeming with people, as was the street they were trying to drive down. All manner of vehicles were clogging the road as folks went about their business. Leah didn't mind the congestion, though; she'd started the day by being loved to within an inch of her life and all she could do was smile.

"You have an awfully pleased look on your face," Ryder told her as he finally found a place to park his rig.

"I wonder why?" she teased back.

He grinned and got out. Coming around to her side, he gave her a hand to help her down, saying wolfishly, "And if you're a very good girl, there'll be more of the same tonight . . ."

A spurt of flame sparked between her thighs. "Is that a promise?"

Ryder wanted to drag her off someplace private and reward her for being such a sassy temptress. He hadn't gotten nearly enough of her that morning. "I promise."

"Then I'll be . . . very good . . ."

Ryder smiled the smile of arousal. "Let's go inside before I lift your skirts right here."

She reached up and fleetingly touched her navy gloved fingers to his lips. "You can do that later too . . ."

Eyes glowing, he kissed her fingertips, then gestured her toward the door of his office building.

Chapter 11

Inside, Ryder introduced Leah to his small staff.

"Pleased to meet you all," Leah said to the two young men and lone woman. The woman appeared to be early twenties. Leah noted the barely veiled hostility in the girl's eyes and wondered if she had a crush on her employer.

Leah followed Ryder into his well-furnished office and sat down. The first order of business was to send one of the clerks over to Daniel Morton's hotel with a note asking him to visit Ryder at his earliest convenience. When that was accomplished, they sat back to wait.

Daniel Morton was shown into Ryder's office less than an hour later. He was impeccably dressed in a brown suit and there wasn't a wrinkle to be seen. "Good morning, Mrs. Montague."

The seated Leah inclined her head. "Good morning, Mr. Morton. I hope you've recovered from your long train ride."

"I have, thank you."

He then turned his attention to Ryder, who came out from behind the desk and shook Daniel's hands. Ryder gestured for the blond gentleman to take a seat.

Leah opened their meeting. "Mr. Morton, I believe you should see this."

He read the letter, and his reaction mirrored everyone else's. "Where did this come from?"

Leah explained, and when she was done, he continued to stare wide-eyed. She then told him of her frustrating encounter with the deputy.

Daniel seemed unable to speak.

Ryder added, "I'm going to visit the sheriff later. Want to come along."

Daniel nodded. "Yes, I do. This is outrageous." He then reread the threatening letter. "And you have no idea who may have left this on your door?"

Leah saw the seriousness in his blue eyes. "No."

"How much do you know about these other deaths?" Daniel asked.

She told him what she knew from the bits and pieces she'd learned about the deaths of Bernice and Songbird since her arrival in Denver.

He heard her out, then asked Ryder, "So Songbird was your mother?"

"Yes, she died when I was very young."

"And the culprit was never found?"

Leah said, "Everyone here seems to think Louis Montague was responsible."

"But you don't believe that?" Daniel asked.

"Monty didn't kill anyone," Leah said with conviction.

"Mr. Damien, what do you think?" the lawyer asked.

Ryder looked over at Leah, then replied, "I believed him guilty too, but now? I don't know."

It pleased Leah to hear Ryder admit he had doubts. When they first met he'd been so adamant about Monty's guilt, she was sure he'd never change his mind. Who'd have ever thought so much would happen since then, or that she'd be in love with him and possibly carrying his child.

She turned her attention back to the matters at hand, and said to Morton, "There's also another potential piece to this conundrum."

She told him about Cecil's death and Helene's theory that he'd been poisoned. "Ryder's making arrangements to have the body exhumed."

Morton shook his head at the enormity of what he'd just heard. "And on Wednesday, we go to court."

It was quite a full plate, Leah knew, but Wednesday's date meant nothing when compared to the threat left on her door.

Morton said, "I'm going over to the courthouse to see if we can delay the proceedings for ten days or so. This threat against your life may be tied to this case, and it may not. Either way there's a whole lot to look into before I can consider myself prepared to represent you to the best of my abilities. Judge Raddock will never make me a partner if the client winds up dead."

Leah liked his dry wit. "The client won't be pleased either."

He nodded, then began replacing his papers and pens in his valise. "Are you ready to take on the sheriff, Mr. Damien?"

"Ready whenever you are." Ryder stood, and asked Leah, "Do you wish to come along?"

She shook her head, "No, if I have to put up with the same treatment I received the last time, I'll probably be arrested and thrown into the cell with poor Andrew Green."

An amused Ryder said, "Then you should stay here. I didn't bring any bail money."

Democratic Sheriff Frederick Cramer had been elected to his post in last November's election, a decision some of the city's electorate had come to regret. Ryder didn't like the man, not because of his questionable character or record of improprieties—he was, after all, a politician—but because he'd appointed the Cheyenne murderer Chivington as undersheriff. That appointment said more about his character than all the other accusations levied against him combined.

Cramer wasn't in. The deputy at the door took their information and promised he'd let the sheriff know. Since the man didn't write down any of the details, neither Daniel nor Ryder believed a word of it.

As they stood outside the jail, a frustrated Daniel Morton remarked, "Well, looks like we're on our own."

"Yes, it does."

"I'll see about the stay and start digging."

Ryder gave him a calling card. "If you hear anything or need something, here's my address both in town and at home."

"Thank you. I'll be in touch. Keep Mrs. Montague safe."

"Don't worry."

They shook hands and parted.

Daniel Morton sent word the next day that the judge had denied the stay. Leah was instructed to report to the courthouse at ten o'clock Wednesday morning.

As Ryder drove within sight of the courthouse Wednesday morning, Leah had butterflies in her stomach. Evidently, she and her case had become news. Yesterday's papers had all carried sensationalized stories. In lurid tones they'd described her as a conniving young woman who'd married an old man for his estate. There had even been a quote from Seth, who supposedly speaking on behalf of the family had voiced his concerns about her possibly ulterior motives for marrying his late father. The reports went on to regale the scandals surrounding the deaths of Bernice Montague and the Cheyenne woman, Songbird, and Monty's possible connection to them.

Ryder parked the rig a few doors down and the reporters surrounded them, circling like a pack of barking dogs as they shouted questions. Their clamoring and efforts to get answers resulted in the jostling of the rig, and Leah looked to Ryder with concern. He grabbed up his rifle and fired a couple of shots into the air.

"Back off!" he shouted.

The barking ceased instantaneously. They were given the space they needed to get down from the buggy, but the men immediately pounced again, many of them pushing and shoving. Ryder threw a protective arm around Leah and guided her through the gauntlet toward the doors of the courthouse.

Inside proved no friendlier. The small courtroom was packed with lawyers, the press, and spectators. An area of seating in the back had been segregated from the rest with rope, and inside it sat the few Blacks in attendance. Leah was glad to see Eloise and the Reverend Garrison; she was not pleased to see Seth, Helene, or Cordelia. Sam and Mable waved, but Ryder hustled her to the front, where Daniel Morton stood waiting, so she didn't get a chance to speak to anyone.

Daniel gave Leah a smile as she approached. "Good morning, Mrs. Montague. Are you ready?"

Leah nodded. "Thank you for taking this on."

"You're welcome. This is possibly my most interesting case to date. I wouldn't miss it for the world."

He then turned to Ryder. "Mr. Damien, I'm going to ask you to sit behind us, if you would."

"Whatever you say." Ryder gave Leah's shoulder a departing squeeze of support, then took his seat.

Leah could see the lawyers at the other table silently

evaluating her, but she paid them no mind. She concentrated instead upon listening to her lawyer's last-minute instructions.

When the judge entered a few moments later, everyone quieted. It was the same man who'd presided over the case the last time. She didn't know if his presence would work in her favor or not.

The judge looked out at both sides, then said to Leah, "Mrs. Montague, you've got some pretty powerful friends to be able to get this case reviewed."

Leah had no idea what kind of response he expected her to give, so she didn't offer one.

He added, "I don't think I've ever seen anyone come to the aid of a Colored woman this way. Makes me feel good about this country. This your back East lawyer?"

"Yes, sir."

"What's your name, son?"

Daniel answered.

"You're pretty young for something like this aren't you?"

"Yes, but I'm prepared."

The judge smiled. "Glad to hear it."

"Mr. Earle?" the judge then called.

A tall, thin, impeccably dressed man seated at the other table stood. "I'm Jacob Earle."

The judge looked him up and down. "You got your ducks in a row?"

"Yes, sir, and it's our opinion—"

The judge cut him off. "You'll have plenty of time to give me your opinion in a minute. Who are you representing?"

Earle rattled off a list of about fifteen businesses and names. Leah assumed they were the creditors trying to keep their share of the estate.

The judge wrote something down. "All right, Mr. Earle, let's hear your side."

Earle stood. He primped importantly for a moment and then began. "Your Honor, not only do we see no clear reason for your first, well-rendered judgment to be overturned, but we question this woman's right even to inherit Mr. Montague's estate."

"Why's that?" the judge asked.

"We don't think the marriage is legal."

The crowd began to buzz. Leah stiffened. Were they going to make her confess to having married Monty on his deathbed? She wanted to turn and judge Ryder's reaction but kept her attention focused forward.

Earle was saying, "I'd like to call Mr. Seth Montague to the stand."

Leah could see people craning around to get a look at this first witness. Seth silently made his way to the front. He was sworn in and instructed to sit in the witness chair.

Earle opened the examination by having Seth state his name and his connections to the Montague estate. "So you're Montague's only legitimate child?" Earle asked when Seth was done.

"I am, sir."

"Tell us what you know about the woman calling herself your late father's widow."

"I know nothing. Well let me amend that, I do know she's having an illicit affair with my half brother, but other than that—" Seth shrugged.

Daniel jumped to his feet. "Objection, Your Honor!"

The judge nodded. "Mr. Montague, stick to the straight and narrow, we're not here for gossip."

Earle disagreed. "But Your Honor, this speaks to the widow's overall character. It's one of the cornerstones of our case."

The judge seemed to ignore him. "Straight and narrow, gentlemen."

Daniel sat. His face mirrored his anger.

Jacob Earle went on. He asked Seth when he'd first met Leah.

"I met her the day she arrived."

"Did she seem to be grieving over her husband's death?"

"She appeared to be, but she didn't rebuff me when I volunteered to show her around."

"So, she attended some social functions with you?"

"Yes, we had lunch also."

Earle turned to the judge. "Widows are supposed to be reclusive, not kicking up their heels all over Denver, your honor. Mr. Montague, thank you."

The judge looked to Daniel who responded by saying, "I've a question or two for Mr. Montague, Your Honor."

"Go to it."

Daniel walked over to Seth and said, "Mr. Montague, did you have any ulterior motives for squiring around your stepmother when she first came to town?"

Seth looked genuinely offended. "Of course not, I was being a gentleman. She claimed to be my father's widow, I treated her accordingly."

"So you weren't doing this in hopes of gaining her heart so you could gain access to your father's estate."

Earle jumped up. "Objection, Your Honor."

Daniel said, "Your Honor, I'm not impugning the witness, I'm simply trying determine what type of man Mr. Montague considers himself to be. If he says he was just being gentlemanly, I believe him."

The judge gave Daniel a warning look then told Earle, "Objection overruled, but son, this better be going somewhere."

"It is, Your Honor."

"Continue."

"All right, Mr. Montague we've established that you're a gentleman, or at least you consider yourself one. Am I correct?"

"You are correct."

"Then why in heaven's name are you so deep in debt?"

Earle jumped to his feet, yelling his objections, but Daniel proceeded to read the names of Seth's creditors from a handwritten list two pages long. The spectators added their decibels to the din, and the judge pounded his gavel, yelling for order.

Finally, quiet settled over the courtroom and Judge Moss looked at Daniel Morton and said, "Son—"

"Your Honor, Mr. Earle put Mr. Montague on the stand as someone capable of judging Mrs. Montague's character. I just wanted to show that character's in the eye of the beholder."

"Don't you ever disrupt my courtroom like that again. You hear me?"

"Yes, Your Honor."

Daniel looked to the visibly furious Seth and said coolly, "You may return to your seat."

Leah wanted to cheer.

For the next hour or so they heard from the various parties who'd claimed financial injury in the original case thirty years ago. There were suppliers, former employers, and business associates. On the surface the claims seemed ironclad. According to the law, the original judgment had to be brought before the Colorado court once a decade, and Mr. Earle's father, one of the original plaintiffs, had done that. When he died, five years ago, his son took up the gauntlet.

Judge Moss asked a question. "Mr. Earle did you send notice to the Massachusetts court that this judgment was on the books here?"

"I did, Your Honor, but we only learned of Mr. Montague's whereabouts a few weeks before he died."

"How?"

Earle seemed to squirm a bit. "Mr. Montague wired his sons, sir."

Leah knew that meant someone in the telegraph office had alerted Earle. She wondered if that was against the law.

Judge Moss continued, "So why didn't the court in Massachusetts enforce the judgment?"

"By the time we got all the documents in order, Mr. Montague's money had already been put into an account set up for Mrs. Montague."

"I see. Continue."

Earle then called a few more of the claimants to the stand. Daniel remained silent but had a question for the last witness, a man who claimed to have been swindled out of thousands of dollars because he'd taken Monty's investment advice. "Mr. Carson, when did you get this advice?"

"September of '56."

"Yet, Mr. Montague left Colorado in June."

"That's what he wanted everybody to believe, but he was still taking investments in the Faith Mine that September."

"This was the mine he owned, am I correct?"

Carson nodded.

"Are you sure that money went to Mr. Montague?"

"Sure, I'm sure. He sent me a receipt. I kept it all these years. Mr. Earle has it now."

Daniel looked to the judge and said, "Your Honor, I'd like to see Mr. Carson's receipt if I may?"

The judge nodded. Mr. Earle searched through his documents and handed over the small yellowed letter.

Daniel scanned the document for a long few moments, then asked Carson, "Is this your receipt?"

"Yep. It has Montague's signature on the bottom."

"Had you ever seen Mr. Montague's signature before receiving this letter?"

"No, I was a first-time investor."

"So you don't truly know if he signed this?"

Carson thought a moment, then admitted, "No, I don't, but—"

Daniel cut him off. "Thank you, Mr. Carson. Your honor, I submit that Mr. Louis Montague didn't sign any of these letters or bills. If I can get you to compare the signature on Mr. Carson's receipt with this signature on his will, you'll see that although they're very similar, they aren't the same."

All hell broke loose in the courtroom at this startling turn of events. Earle started yelling objections. The plaintiffs were on their feet protesting, and Leah was inwardly smiling. Monty's old friend, Judge Raddock had indeed sent her a worthy representative.

The judge was banging his gavel trying to restore order. Leah turned around and met Ryder's smile. Daniel Morton on the other hand was standing patiently.

Silence finally prevailed. The judge took the two documents from Daniel and peered at each one closely.

Daniel added, "If you'd concentrate on the letter *G*, Your Honor, you'll see that they're written differently. Again they're very close in nature, but Mr. Montague didn't pen the signature on Mr. Carson's letter."

The judge looked up. "Then who did?"

Daniel shrugged. "Someone who made quite a bit of profit thirty years ago by fraudulently using Mr. Montague's name."

Leah knew that both Seth and Ryder were too young at the time to be guilty, so that only left—

"I'd like to call Helene Sejours to the stand," Daniel announced.

Whispers ricocheted through the crowd. Helene stood. Her blue eyes were steel-hard as she stepped up to be sworn in. Leah wondered if Helene would lie under oath?

Daniel asked her who she was and what relationship if any she had with the deceased Louis Montague.

"He was married to my sister, so that made me his sister-in-law."

"After your sister's death, you raised Seth, am I correct?"

"Yes."

"How?"

"Explain that please?" Helene asked.

"By *how,* I mean, what was the source of your income?"

"I made my money on mine futures and investments."

"From where?"

"The Faith Mine."

"But according to the documents on file here in the courthouse, Mr. Montague left that mine and the house you're living in to his other son, Ryder. How did you get possession?"

Helene seemed calm. Leah sensed Ryder leaning forward as if he were particularly interested in her answer.

Helene stated, "I knew the mine wouldn't last long in the hands of an ignorant Indian, so I paid her off and took control, in Seth's name."

"And who was this 'ignorant' Indian you are referring to?"

"Ryder's grandmother, Little Tears."

"How much did you give her in exchange for a mine that was bringing in a profit of over ten thousand dollars a month."

Helene appeared smug.

"Fifty dollars and a promise to pay for his schooling."

The crowd reacted with gasps. Some in attendance laughed at Helene's cleverness.

The judge banged the gavel.

When it was quiet again, Daniel echoed skeptically, "Fifty dollars?"

Helene responded proudly, "Yes."

"And did you sign your brother-in-law's name to any documents in Seth name?"

"No."

She was lying. Daniel knew it; the judge knew it; everyone in the courtroom, including Mr. Earle, knew it. However Daniel didn't press her any further. "Thank you, Miss Sejours, you may step down."

The judge asked Earle, "Do you have any questions for the witness?"

The nattily dressed barrister shook his head. "No, Your Honor."

Mr. Earle, like everyone in attendance, realized the air was slowly leaking out of his case. Daniel Morton had cast enough doubt upon the validity of Monty's signature to call into question the legitimacy of all the other claims. Daniel might have been young, but he was good.

Daniel looked to the judge. "In the face of what we've just learned, I respectfully submit that the thirty-year judgment against my client's late husband has been proven to be illegitimate based upon the fraudulent signatures on the documents set before this court."

The judge told him, "I'll take it all under advisement when I make my final ruling, Mr. Morton."

He then turned to Mr. Earle. "Mr. Earle, unless you have any objections, I'd like to get some lunch."

Earle sighed. "That's fine, Your Honor."

The judge banged his gavel. "This court is in recess until one o'clock."

As the judge stood and departed, noise swept the courtroom. Leah slumped back against her seat weak with relief.

Daniel looked her way and smiled. "Almost home."

From behind them, Ryder asked, "Will they put Mrs. Montague on the stand next?"

Daniel nodded. "Probably. Earle doesn't have much else, but if I were he, I'd be filing papers against the Sejours woman. It's obvious she's at the center of this whole affair."

Ryder looked up in time to see Helene and Seth making their way to the door. Helene's white-powdered face was stiff with anger as she tried to force her way past the barking pack of newspaper reporters. The press wasn't being the least bit cooperative. They had her and Seth hemmed in and were shouting questions at her as if she were running for political office.

Leah's party slipped out of a side door and reconvened in Ryder's office, where Sam, Eloise, and Mable waited with a prepared lunch of sandwiches, coffee, and pie. As they ate, Ryder said to Daniel, "How'd you know about the signatures?"

"I didn't. I was bluffing."

Leah's eyes widened. "Bluffing?"

Daniel nodded around the pie in his mouth. "When Carson said his letter was dated in September, I knew I was on to something. One of the most valuable lessons I learned in school was that if you don't have a case, dance around until you find something to waltz with. In this case I found a grand partner."

Ryder shook his head with amazement. Had Helene really forged Louis's signature? He supposed she'd looked upon her deception as a way of keeping herself afloat, and that even if Louis had returned he'd have more than enough money to settle up. Had Ryder learned of her complicity six months ago, he'd already be filing papers to sue her for swindling him out of his share of the Faith Mine's profits; however, it didn't seem to matter anymore. All he wanted was for this to end so he could take the *Morenita* home.

Eloise then asked a question they'd all been thinking about, "So, does this mean Helene is responsible for the threatening letter Leah received also?"

No one knew.

When the court proceedings recommenced, Ryder stood at the back of the room with Sam. Word of the morning's revelations must have spread like wildfire because there wasn't a seat to spare. There were dozens more people in attendance now. Ryder and Sam wanted to be near the exit so that when the hearing ended one of them could hustle out and retrieve the rig while the other worked to spirit her out of here as quickly as possible.

Daniel had been correct. Mr. Earle called Leah to the stand as his first witness of the afternoon.

"Your name please, ma'am?"

"Leah Jane Barnett Montague."

"According to your marriage certificate you married Mr. Montague when?"

Leah gave him the date.

."And when did your husband die?"

Leah glanced back at Ryder, then replied, "The same night."

Ryder stiffened with amazement as the crowd reacted noisily. Had he been correct? Was she really nothing but a scheming adventuress? Even Sam looked distressed.

The judge's gavel sounded. "Quiet down!" he demanded. "Or I'll have you all removed!"

The room grew silent.

Mr. Earle was smiling at Leah like a patient shark. "So, tell us where you worked before you married, or allegedly married, your husband."

"I owned a tavern."

"A tavern previously owned by your mother, am I correct?"

"Yes."

"What was the nature of your mother's relationship with your late husband?"

Once again, Leah's eyes slid to Ryder's, and the ice she saw reflected there burned coldly into her soul. "They were companions."

The crowd grew restless once more.

Earle chuckled patronizingly, "Oh come now, Miss Barnett. They were more than just companions weren't they? Weren't they—lovers?"

Leah ignored the shocked reaction of the on-lookers. "Yes."

She could see how tight Ryder's jaw had become, and she wanted to run to him and explain, but she couldn't.

Earle was asking, "And they were lovers for nearly thirty years, am I correct?"

Leah's chin rose. "Yes."

Earle, playing to the crowd, next asked, "So what, your mother died and you took her place in his bed?"

Snickers were heard. Daniel rocketed to his feet. "Objection, Your Honor!"

The judge eyes were hostile. "That's enough, Mr. Earle. I've warned you once."

Earle bowed mockingly. "My apologies, Your Honor." He then continued, "So you married Louis Montague on his deathbed."

"I did."

"Miss Barnett, don't you think that a bit odd?"

"It sounds that way, yes, but—"

He cut her off. "Thank you. I'm done here, Judge."

Earle had left everyone with the impression that she was a scheming woman of loose character. Leah looked at Ryder. When their eyes met, the distance in his broke her heart. He inclined his head mockingly, then turned and exited. She watched Sam hurry after him but her attention was drawn back by Daniel's question.

"Mrs. Montague, how long had you known Louis Montague?"

"Since I was about three years old."

"Did he love your mother?"

"Very much."

"Did he love you?"

Leah didn't hesitate. "Yes, he did."

"But his love for you was different than his love for your mother, am I correct?"

"Yes, he loved me like a father loves his child."

Leah saw Sam return. Ryder wasn't with him.

"Now, Mrs. Montague, I want you to tell the court why Mr. Montague proposed marriage."

Leah looked at the judge. "He wanted to ensure my future, Your Honor, nothing more." She then spoke to Daniel. "He and Cecil considered the idea of legally adopting me as his child, but they knew that would be a long process, and Monty didn't have that much longer to live. So he asked me to marry him."

Daniel asked, "So you did?"

Leah nodded. "Yes."

Outside the courtroom, Ryder stood listening near the door. The chamber had gone so quiet during Leah's turn on the stand, he had no trouble hearing her testimony. Learning that she'd married Louis on his deathbed had turned his heart to stone. Only Sam's haranguing had made him stay and hear the rest; Ryder was glad he had. If he hadn't, he wouldn't have known that Louis had been trying to protect her by giving his name, that she was neither actress nor schemer. As Sam had predicted, she was just a decent young woman, nothing more. Ryder felt like a fool, another galling confession, but with her he seemed to be taking his feet out of his mouth with staggering regularity. He was sure she'd seen the thunderous look on his face during Earle's questioning, and he was equally certain that she thought he'd deserted her. Well he hadn't. Hoping he could convince her to forgive him one last time, and to marry him when all this dust settled, Ryder quietly stepped back inside.

Leah, still seated on the witness stand, looked to Daniel. He'd promised this would be his last question. "Now, Mrs.

Montague, many people here don't think your marriage was legal, so I'm going to apologize in advance for asking such a delicate question."

"Okay."

He smiled kindly. "Were you an innocent when you married Mr. Montague?"

"I was."

"Are you now?"

Leah assumed he was trying to prove the marriage had been consummated, but by phrasing the inquiry in the manner that he had, she could freely answer, and without perjuring herself. "No, Mr. Morton, I am not."

"Thank you. No further questions, Your Honor."

The judge turned to the very defeated-looking Mr. Earle. This hadn't turned out to be a good day for his side: first, the questionable signatures, and now, Daniel Morton's cross-examination had repainted his portrait of the defendant as a scarlet woman into a wronged saint clothed in white. "The lady can step down," Earle allowed.

The judge nodded at Leah, and she went back to her seat. He then looked out over the packed courtroom. "I will render my judgment within the next thirty days."

He sounded the gavel. "Court dismissed."

Havoc overtook the courtroom, and the press descended on Leah en masse. In the rising din, Daniel's shouts that his client had no comment fell on deaf ears. Leah was so hemmed in by reporters waving their tablets and pens, she couldn't even get up from her seat.

Next thing she knew, someone yelled, "Get the hell outta my way!" And reporters were being tossed aside like feathers flying off a plucked chicken.

Ryder.

When he reached her, she smiled, and said, "Who needs the cavalry when there's a Cheyenne brave around."

He didn't reply. He simply scooped her out of the chair

and up into his arms. The look on his face dared anyone to impede his passage. No one was loco enough to do so. A pleased-looking Daniel Morton watched Ryder depart.

Outside, Sam had the rig waiting. While seemingly half of Denver looked on, Ryder placed her on the seat, then came around to the driver's side. Sam stepped down and handed Ryder the reins. Ryder slapped the leads down on the backs of the team and drove toward the city limits.

Leah assumed his silence stemmed from his anger over finally learning the truth, but since he hadn't been in the courtroom to hear the full explanation, she had no idea how to broach the subject. Watching him leave the courtroom had twisted her heart. Once again he hadn't had enough faith. What a mess.

"So," she stated, wanting to get this over with, "now you know."

"I do."

He turned her way. "I feel like a fool."

Leah's lips tightened.

"I do. My bitterness was stronger than my faith."

Leah stared. That was not the answer she'd been expecting. Very confused, she asked, "What are you talking about?"

"Me leaving the courtroom. Sam made me stay though."

She went still. "You heard all of it?"

"I did, and like I said, I feel like a fool."

Leah collapsed back against the seat and succumbed to a case of relieved laughter.

He looked at her as if she'd gone round the bend. "What's so funny?"

"You, me—us."

She had so much happiness in her eyes, he couldn't help himself, he began to smile too. "What?"

"I thought you weren't speaking to me because you hadn't heard everything—that all you knew was that I'd married Monty on his deathbed."

"No. I heard every word, thanks to Sam."

"Remind me to give that man a big fat kiss the moment I see him."

"I will. So, go ahead and give me both barrels for not believing in you. I deserve it."

"No. I'm sure Sam's tongue-lashing was quite enough."

Ryder thought back amusedly. "That it was. He pointedly reminded me what happened the last time I went storming around on half-baked information."

Leah remembered, too, and she'd never forgive Seth for the pain he'd caused them both that day.

"And," he added, "how much I'd hurt you."

Leah's heart swelled. "So you stayed?"

"I did. Louis must have loved you a great deal."

Her personal memories rose. "He did."

Once again, Ryder called himself a fool. "And that's what you've been trying to explain to me since the first time we met, isn't it?"

"Yes."

"Why didn't you just walk away and say to hell with me?"

She shrugged. "I have a soft spot for braves, I guess."

He stopped the team and pulled back on the brake. "Come here," he invited softly.

Leah didn't have to be asked twice. She was in his arms and kissing him before she drew her next breath.

After a night spent reaffirming the undeclared love they felt for each other, Leah awakened the next morning, sated and content. Dawn was just rising, and her Black Cheyenne brave was moving quietly around in the fading darkness.

She sat up, the sheets riding across her bare waist. "What are you doing?" she asked him sleepily.

"Going up to see if there are any signs of the King. You're welcome to come along if you want."

Ryder looked over at her sitting up in his bed, her face

filled with sleep, her dark breasts teasing him from above the quilt, and knew he couldn't let her go. He wanted to see her just like this every morning for the rest of his life.

Leah responded, "The King? Oh, that's that big elk Sam told me about. The one he claims you'll never catch, because the elk's smarter than you."

He shot her a look. "I do have a remedy for that sassy mouth of yours."

She purred and stretched languidly. "Do you?"

Ryder felt his manhood rise and harden in response to her sensual movements. "Ever made love outside in the sunshine?"

Leah paused. Desire flared. "No. Is that going to be my punishment?"

Lust filled Ryder's eyes. "Wicked woman . . . get up so we can go."

Leah mimed a kiss by puckering her lips, then left the bed so she could shower.

Leah's behind was sore. She didn't have much experience riding, and they'd been on the trial climbing toward the mountains for what seemed like hours. "How much farther?" she asked.

Mounted atop the gear-packed stallion, Ryder turned to her. "Not much, another few miles or so."

They were heading to a hunting lodge he and Sam had built a few years ago.

"Well, I need to stop, my behind's killing me."

Her honesty made him chuckle quietly. "Want to ride with me the rest of the way?"

She shook her head. "No. Your horse is carrying enough weight."

"Aw, he won't mind. Like I said, it isn't much farther."

So they stopped. Leah was so stiff she could hardly move, but somehow managed to dismount. He tied the reins of her horse to his saddle and once she was seated comfortably in front they continued on their way.

She rode cuddled against his hard chest.

"Better?" he asked.

"Yes." The blankets covering the horse's back were far softer than her saddle had been. Being close like this let her feel the warmth of Ryder's body and hear the steady beating of his heart.

Ryder put both leads into one hand and with the other began to undo the buttons down the front of her shirtwaist, and then the two on her thin cotton chemise.

She looked up at him with sly eyes, asking, "And just what do you think you're doing?"

"Giving you something to think about besides your sore bottom."

As he filled his warm hand with her breast, a soft groan of pleasure slid from between her lips. They were miles from the prying eyes of society, so Leah didn't mind being fondled so possessively. Once he'd awakened her nipple to his distinctive call, all thoughts of everything but him and the way his caresses made her feel were summarily banished.

From behind her, he stated, "I should make you ride this way all the time . . ."

She raised her mouth for a kiss, and he rewarded her with a slow, fierce intensity. The reins fell from his grasp and the well-trained horse slowed to a stop. Only when Ryder seemed certain she was no longer occupied with her stiff limbs did he guide the horse back up the trail.

By the time they crested the rise where the cabin sat, Leah was still sizzling. He'd made it a point to keep her warmed and ripened for the balance of the ride, and her difficulties in dismounting this time stemmed not from aches and pains but from the hazy fog of desire she seemed encased in. He hadn't allowed her to redo her buttons, so her nipples had been his to play with while they rode. They were now hard and full, and a corresponding yearning pulsed between her thighs.

Playing with her had worked Ryder into such a high state of arousal that the sight of her standing there with her dark breasts bared to his eyes and to the sun made him want to make love to her here and now. However, he made himself wait. He'd brought her up here to savor her, seduce her, and fill her with so much desire she'd have to say yes, when he asked her to marry him. He'd keep an eye out for the King, but he hadn't come here to slay an elk, but to slay the *Morenita*'s heart.

Leah had no trouble recognizing the desire in his eyes. He'd turned that hot gaze on her many times. "You look a bit hungry . . ."

He smiled knowingly. "And you look good enough to eat . . ."

Passion pierced them like sweet tipped arrows. Walking over to her, heat soaring with every step, he stopped before her and gazed down into her eyes. He caressed her cheek with a tender hand, wondering when she'd become his life. He brought his mouth down to her lush lips, lightly at first, inviting her to part them so his tongue could delve into their sweetness. When she did, he flicked the tip across each sensitive corner, then eased it in to lustily mate with her own.

They stood out in front of the cabin, kissing for a long time, then he reluctantly pulled back. A bit short of breath, Ryder said, "We need to unpack our gear . . ."

Sparkling with the desire he'd planted inside, Leah nodded.

Although they couldn't pass each other without stealing a kiss, Leah and Ryder managed to get everything inside. Leah looked around the cabin and found the shadowy interior quite cozy. It consisted of two rooms: one large front room that had a big fireplace and a small kitchen complete with stove. Hides of all kinds covered the log walls, and on the floor in front of the fireplace lay another ferocious-looking bear skin.

"Like it?" he asked, bringing in the bedrolls.

"I do," she admitted truthfully. "But where do you wash?"

"Stream out back."

"Oh." She wasn't looking really forward to washing up in water cold enough to make her teeth chatter.

"We can heat water for the tenderfoot."

Grinning, she curtsied. "Thank you, Your Majesty."

"Anytime."

They unrolled the bedding and took the cooking utensils into the kitchen. Ryder placed them in a large wooden crate that stood beside the stove. "Sam keeps threatening to knock out a wall so he can turn this into a real kitchen, but it suits me fine just the way it is."

Knowing Ryder as she did, she imagined he did prefer the starkness. "Do you and Sam come up here often?"

"Five—six times a year. Mostly in the fall though."

Leah walked over to the now opened back door and looked out onto a view that took her breath away. The rise was surrounded by trees, mountains, and blue sky. She'd finally come to appreciate the rugged beauty of this land. Like the ocean, it had its own character and called to the soul in much the same way the waves had at home.

"Hey, you hungry?" he asked.

She turned and nodded. He was hunkered down beside one of the packs, extracting some cans. "Beans are quick."

"Sounds good."

Leah grimaced as she took a step in his direction. Now that she'd stopped moving around she'd grown stiff as a length of pine.

"Sore?" he asked, pouring the thick beans into a pot.

"And stiff."

He smiled sympathetically. "I'll heat you some water soon as I get these beans on. You look pretty tuckered out."

"I'd've made a lousy warrior wife."

"You're just new to riding. Next year this time, you'll be riding like the wind."

"Good, because now I can barely walk."

Moving like an old woman, Leah made her way outside. Maybe sitting in the sun would help. She lowered herself gingerly onto the edge of the porch and hoped she would be able to stand up again if she needed to, but for the moment, all she could think about was resting her aching limbs and savoring how happy she felt inside knowing her secrets had been revealed. Ryder finally knew the truth, and as a result there were no more barriers for them to hurdle. They could approach each other honestly and openly and not have to do it across a minefield. She wondered what Monty would have thought of her falling in love with his son. Had he known it would turn out this way? Had he somehow planned this? She wouldn't put it past him. He'd always had a wicked sense of humor.

But what about the murderer? a small voice in her mind asked. Leah buried the voice. She didn't want to think about that now. She was glad when Ryder stepped out to join her.

"Beans'll be hot in a minute. I'll start that water."

From beneath the porch he withdrew two large black cauldrons and a big old iron washtub. "This will have to do for your bath, *Morenita*," he said, indicating the tub.

"That's fine. It looks like it'll hold me."

He carried the cauldrons to the pump beside the cabin and filled them with water. He then built a fire in the twin grates in the fire pit near where Leah sat, then placed the huge pots atop them. "It'll be ready in a bit."

She smiled her thanks. He came and sat beside her. Placing an arm around her waist he pulled her closer. She rested her head on his chest. "If I'm ever able to walk again, I think I'll enjoy being up here with you like this."

He kissed the top of her head. "Me too."

"Can we stay here forever?"

"And a day if you want."

She hugged him, content.

Leah hadn't bathed outside since she was a small child. Bathing outside as a woman full grown was entirely different though; there was a man involved, and his glowing eyes stroked her as she undressed. She felt absolutely brazen being under the sky without a stitch on, but she stepped into the tub, knowing she had his full attention. The tub was only large enough for her to kneel in, but when he slowly poured the water from the cauldron down her shoulders and back she groaned pleasurably. It felt so good and soothing, the tension in her body seemed to melt away. As the last of the water in the first cauldron cascaded down, she didn't want her personal waterfall to end.

"You can rinse with the other," he told her quietly. He then handed her a bar of scented soap and a cloth and she went to work.

The soap smelled like violets. "Where'd you get this soap?" she asked as she rubbed a lather into the cloth.

"Found it in town. Thought you might like it better than the plain soap I use."

"It smells wonderful. Thank you."

"You're welcome."

While she washed, he refilled the first cauldron and set it back on the fire so its water would be hot for his turn in the tub.

Leah stood, ready to be rinsed. She was once again transformed into a nymph in a waterfall, then she stepped out gleaming and refreshed. He tossed her a towel, then took off his shirt. Leah paused in her drying to feast her eyes on his male beauty. As he tipped over the washtub to rid it of her water, she found herself fascinated by the play of his muscles. She'd never seen his rich brown skin in the full light of day nor the long faint scars traversing the skin of his lower arms. The cuts looked very old. "Did you get those tangling with a bear?"

He looked down at his arms, then back at her. "No," he responded quietly. "I gave these to myself with a knife—after Sand Creek."

Leah face reflected her confusion. "Why?"

"Grief, anger. It was how we expressed our pain. The streams were red with blood that day . . ."

Leah couldn't imagine being filled with that much heartache, but then she'd never seen children butchered or had her way of life destroyed. "I didn't mean to pry."

"You don't have to apologize. To be with me, you need to know." He then said, "Do me a favor and make sure I'm not burning up those beans."

She nodded and went inside to check.

Leah ate her beans in the afternoon sun. Dressed in nothing but a clean, knee-length chemise far too thin to be worn anywhere but beneath her clothing, she sat beside the silent Ryder. "Did I open up old wounds?"

He shook his head. "No, but sometimes I feel that wounds are all life's ever given me."

He turned to face her and she saw the raw honesty in his eyes. She reached up and gently cupped his jaw. He took her hand in his and kissed her fingertips, saying, "And then you came into my life, tossing me into the air and defending Louis at every turn, no matter what I threw your way."

The quiet awe in his voice and eyes filled her heart. Leah responded, "You're a very special man, Ryder Damien."

He smiled. "Be my heart, *carinita* . . . marry me . . ."

The love Leah had for him surged over her dikes and flowed free. Tears filled her eyes.

He grinned and traced her cheek. "Are you going to say yes, or not?"

"Yes," she whispered thickly.

He pulled her into his arms and held her tight.

"Yes," she voiced again, happily. "Yes."

That night, Ryder made love to her on a quilt placed beneath the stars.

He was up before dawn. After the rousing night they'd had she couldn't imagine why he seemed intent upon making her wake up too.

"Wake up, *Morenita*. We need to get moving."

Too sleepy to believe he was actually talking to her, she asked, "What time is it?"

"Almost five."

"Five? Ryder, where could you possibly be going at this hour?" She pulled the sheets back over her head.

"To find the King."

She groaned. "Can't we wait until later? It's still dark. He's probably asleep."

He grinned. "I'm not leaving you here alone, so come on sleepyhead, get up."

Feeling like a recalcitrant child, Leah threw back the sheets. Naked as an angel, she lay there with her eyes closed, hoping he'd change his mind. "Why couldn't I have fallen in love with a dentist? I bet they don't go chasing around in the dark looking for elk."

He laughed. "I'm giving you ten minutes, then you're coming, dressed or not."

Leah cracked with a smile. "You'd prefer the *not* part of that sentence, I'm betting."

"You'd win, now come on," he said, whining like a little boy anxious to open a gift.

Leah sat up. "I can't wait to see what you're like at Christmas time."

He grinned while she left the bed to get dressed.

They'd ridden about an hour when Ryder turned to her with a finger across his lips, signaling silence. Leah stopped her mount.

He then whispered. "There's an elk up ahead."

Still partially asleep, Leah hid a yawn behind her hand.

"I want you to dismount quietly."

Leah nodded and very slowly got out of the saddle. Standing beside her horse, she looked around. She didn't see anything moving among the trees surrounding them, but she knew better than to doubt his claim. When she turned back she saw Ryder untying a big beaded bag from his saddle she must've been too sleepy to notice earlier because she didn't remember seeing him add the thing to his gear. The bag appeared to be made out of soft pale leather and the intricate red-and-black beadwork adorning it must have taken many hours to complete. He set the large oblong bag upon the ground, and out of it came the biggest bow Leah had ever seen in life.

"What're you going to do with that?"

"Guess."

Leah stared. "You're going to shoot the elk?"

"We need meat for the coming winter."

Leah had seen elk before. They were stately, regal creatures. The idea of eating such a beautiful animal did not sit well. "Can't we eat something else?"

"I like elk," he responded easily.

Leah watched as he withdrew a handful of arrows. The ends were decorated with a single feather. "Why the feathers?"

"To tell your arrow from someone else's."

She supposed that made sense, more sense than eating elk.

"Let's go," he told her softly. "Quiet now and stay behind me."

Leah nodded, but felt no better about the event to come.

As he dropped to the ground and began to shimmy up a small rise, she did the same. Leah could feel stones and twigs digging into her knees and the palms of her hands, but forced herself to ignore both them and the pain they caused. When he stopped so did she. When he slowly raised his head to see what lay ahead, she followed his example and saw the biggest, most magnificent elk she'd ever seen.

"Is that the King?" she whispered.

He nodded.

The King stood many hands high, and the muscular development in his dark brown chest and legs spoke to his power. The rack atop his head was large and ornate. Leah knew that antlers that spectacular denoted a male in his prime.

Beside her Ryder was rising silently to his feet all the while raising the bow. Leah looked at the elk standing there so regally in the soft morning light and without thinking jumped up and began yelling and flapping her arms. "Run King! Run!"

The elk bounded away.

A frozen Ryder stared at her with wide, disbelieving eyes. "What the hell did you do that for?"

A guilty Leah looked down at the toes of her boots.

"Do you know how long I've been after that elk?" He didn't give her a chance to answer. "Eight years."

"I'm sorry."

Ryder didn't believe her for a minute. "Lightning's going to strike you down, lying like that. You aren't a bit sorry."

In reality she really wasn't. "He was too beautiful."

"Be glad you are too. Let's get back to the horses."

The ride back to the cabin was a silent one. When he

hadn't spoken a word to her by the end of the first half hour Leah asked, "Are you ever going to speak to me again?"

"No."

She smiled.

He added. "You'd make a brave a terrible mate."

"I couldn't let you shoot that magnificent animal."

"So what are you going to eat this winter, tree bark?"

She didn't reply.

"Where do you think the meat on your table comes from?" Ryder asked.

"The butcher shop, where they have everyday meat, like chickens, fish, and pigs. Back home, we didn't eat elk."

"You've never had venison of any kind?"

"No," she told him.

"Well, here we eat it a lot."

Leah raised an eyebrow.

"I'll pass."

"You can't pass."

"Sure I can."

He went silent again.

She said, "I don't think I should go with you next time."

"I don't think I'm going to ask you to."

She peered over at him. "You really are mad, aren't you?"

"So mad, I want your drawers."

Leah snorted. "My what?"

His eyes were twinkling, "You heard me."

"I'm not giving you my drawers."

"Sure you are. You rarely have them on when you're with me anyway, so that's your punishment. Hand them over."

Leah looked around at all the nature surrounding them. "Here?"

"Now."

She was so amazed and amused she didn't know what to do. She *had* cost him his elk, and she probably *did* owe restitution, but this punishment was both novel and provocative.

"I'm waiting, *carinita*."

The lust in his eyes made her nipples harden and her thighs pulse. Leah dismounted. Their gazes locked. Lifting her black skirt she undid the strings and slipped them off.

Eyes blazing, he held out his hand. She walked over and gave him his boon. He put them into his saddlebag.

"Now—" he whispered. Reaching over he caught up the reins of her horse and tied them to his saddle. "You can ride with me . . ."

The intense heat flaring between them made her body bloom with desire. He lifted her and placed her sideways on his mount's back. As he looked down into her eyes and boldly undid the buttons on her blouse she thought she might dissolve. She did dissolve when he kissed her. When he finally kicked the horse into a trot, she couldn't have recited her name.

There was more restitution to be paid, she learned. He stopped more than once on their tree-shrouded journey to reacquaint himself with how well her nipples rose and hardened in response to his touch. At one point, passion had them in such a storm they dismounted. He tossed down a bedroll, and there in the sheltered silence he showed her erotically and explicitly why he preferred her without drawers. Her release made her scream his name.

They stayed at the cabin for another two days, days filled with bliss, love, and happiness. On the ride back to Sunrise, she asked playfully, "You planning on taking all my drawers when we get back?"

He swung around to face her. "Yep. Haven't I proven to you yet that you don't need them?"

She shook her head with amusement. "So how long is this punishment going to last?"

He looked toward the sky as if thinking. "Let's see? I've

been after the King for eight years." He met her eyes again
"Eight years."

She guffawed. "You can't have my drawers for eigh
years."

"Why not, they're not promised to another man, are
they?"

She reached over and socked him in the arm. "No."

He shrugged. "Then they're mine."

She couldn't believe he hadn't as of yet cracked a smile.
The next thirty years were definitely going to be interesting.
"Will you be this bold when you're an old man?"

"If you're by my side, you can bet on it."

Dusk was settling in when they finally made it back to
Sunrise. Thanks to the lusty brave holding the reins, her
clothes were grass-stained and wrinkled, but by then she
was properly buttoned up. Because the twin French braids
knotted at her neck, her hair didn't look as if she'd been
well loved atop a bedroll on the ground. Although her lips
might appear kiss-swollen, no one would know that the future Mrs. Ryder Damien had returned wearing no drawers.

They found Sam and Mable out back grilling chickens.
Smiles met smiles. Leah went over and gave Sam a hug, and
then a big fat kiss on his cheek. "Thank you," she whispered.

Sam hugged her back. "You're welcome. Everything all
straightened out?"

"Yes." Because of Sam's loyalty and persistence, she
would be happy and loved for the rest of her days.

Leah then looked to the pleased Mable and declared,
"Mable, if you ever decide you don't want him, send him to
me. I'll take him."

Ryder looked wounded. "I thought you were going to
marry me?"

Before Leah could respond, Sam's face brightened, and
he yelled, "Hallelujah! Mable pack your bags. We're get-

ting married in the morning. This boy's finally got himself a woman!"

Mable simply shook her head. "Whatever you say, Samuel."

A short while later, they all sat down to dinner at the kitchen table. While they were eating, Sam asked, "Ryder, did you see the King up at the cabin?"

Ryder looked over at Leah. She kept her eyes on her plate, hoping he couldn't see her smile.

He could. "Yes, I saw him. Had him in my sights until Miss—I-don't-eat-elk here scared him off. Actually told him to run!"

Sam burst out laughing.

Leah offered up a chagrined smile.

Ryder said, "It still isn't funny."

A fairly howling Sam disagreed, "Oh, yes it is. You told the King to run, Leah? Oh, Lord. I think I'm going to hurt myself."

Leah had tears of mirth in her own eyes, mainly because of the thunderous look in Ryder's as he observed Sam's hysterics. She reached over and squeezed Ryder's hand sympathetically. He raised her hand to his lips and kissed her fingertips. Leaning close, he whispered in her ear. "Eight years."

Leah smiled delightedly.

Leah and Ryder were both so tired from the journey home that when they finally climbed the stairs to his room, they shared a shower, donned clean night clothes, and slid between the bed's fresh, crisp sheets. He pulled her against him, kissed the back of her neck, and, moments later, they were both asleep.

Chapter 12

The next morning, Leah hitched a ride to town with Ryder. She wanted to let Eloise know that Ryder had proposed. She also needed to vacate the little cabin and get her trunks and things gathered up so they could be moved to Sunrise.

"I'll be back to pick you up later this afternoon," Ryder told Leah, as she stood by the wagon in front of Eloise's white picket gate.

"Okay," Leah said. She leaned up for a kiss, then stepped back.

"Tell Eloise I'll visit with her when I come and get you."

"I will," Leah responded.

He drove off and she headed up the flower-choked walk. The screened front door was unlocked as always so she went on in. "Eloise?" she called out cheerily.

No answer.

Figuring she was probably sequestered in the studio, Leah headed down the hall. "Eloise?"

Silence.

The studio door appeared to be closed, but as Leah knocked, it slowly swung open. Leah hesitated. She'd been warned by Eloise not to peek in, but a natural curiosity called temptingly. She looked back over her shoulder, guilty that she might be found out, then took a few hesitant steps in. Sunlight filled the room through the two large windows, but what it illuminated amazed her, shocked her, and froze her with a cold fear. Every inch of every wall held framed, twisted images of what appeared to be Louis Montague in his youth.

One portrayed him as a red-horned Lucifer. The yellow eyes gleamed with an evil glee, and in the bloody, fang-filled mouth, lay the limp body of a lifeless child.

Another showed Monty's severed head, swimming in blood. The eyes in the decapitated head looked terrified, the mouth appeared to be uttering a scream.

Trembling, Leah turned and saw a painting of woman who bore a great resemblance to Helene; Bernice maybe? Leah wondered. The painting showed her as a gaunt corpse, her eyes, black unseeing holes, the skin of her face covered with leeches. Leah tasted bile in her throat. There were others on the walls depicting the same woman; all done with hate and skill.

Heart beating fast, Leah scanned a painting of an Indian woman copulating with three drunken men. Ryder's mother, Songbird? The scene was so raw and vile, she had to turn away, but her eyes spied something else that made her blood run cold. A partially finished painting of Cecil rested on one of the worktables. His lips were smiling, but his face, as bloated as a drowned corpse, had fat white maggots feasting upon it.

Leah knew then that she had to get out of there, but when she turned to the door, there stood Eloise. She held a long-bladed hunting knife in her hand.

"See what happens when you trespass? Now you know," Eloise said casually. "Or at least you should."

Leah swallowed in a fear-dry throat. She didn't want to believe the evidence she'd uncovered or the conclusion she'd come to, but there seemed to be no other explanation.

Eloise readily admitted, "Yes, I killed them all. Had good reason to."

Leah wondered how she could get past Eloise to freedom.

As if reading her mind, Eloise smiled and quietly pushed the door closed. She then threw the bolt on the inside. "Now, we won't be disturbed."

Shakes claimed Leah, but she forced herself to take deep breaths so she could think.

"Have a seat, dear," Eloise invited politely, "I want to tell you a story."

Leah didn't want to sit, but knew the longer Eloise talked, the longer she'd have to come up with a way to escape that knife. Leah sat on a nearby wooden bench.

Eloise smiled. "Good. Now, let's start at the beginning. Once, a very long time ago, my little Alice was a real girl."

Leah tried to hide her skepticism but failed.

Eloise paused and then remarked, "You look doubtful."

"I admit I am."

"Well, she was. I was looking forward to buying her prams and lacy dresses, and living happily with her and her father."

"What happened?"

"The father didn't want the child. Me either as it turned out. He used me for one night, then offered me money to go away." She paused again and stared unseeing off into the distance. Her eyes were sad. "He didn't want either of us," she whispered. "I took the money, but I'd given him my innocence because I thought I meant as much to him as he did to me . . ."

Eloise's eyes reflected a terrible pain.

Leah knew where this was leading, and it felt like a rock on her heart, but she had to ask. "Monty fathered your child, didn't he?"

Eloise nodded stonily. "Yes, he did, and he paid me off himself. Probably didn't want that little worm, Cecil Lee, to know he'd made sure me and Alice went to California so we wouldn't be around when that fancy, Creole bitch came to town to be his wife."

So that was why Cecil hadn't had reason to worry that Eloise was one of Monty's castoffs. He hadn't known. No one had. Eloise's quick slide from pain to hatred scared Leah back to the reality of whom and what she faced. Eloise was a murderess, one so clever her victims went back over thirty years. Leah couldn't afford to lose sight of that if she wanted to survive. "How did you kill him?"

"Monkshood."

"What's monkshood?"

"A flower. Comes in purple and blue, sometimes white and yellow. Back in the old days it was called wolfsbane. Healers used it to lower fevers. Grows fairly common in these parts."

Leah'd never heard of it. "And it's poisonous?"

"Deadly."

"When did you poison him?"

"The day Ryder first took you up to Sunrise. Cecil Lee came to my house late that next night to talk to me about how Ryder might treat you. He was very worried, it seemed." Eloise paused for a moment, and then explained, "You see, the day I heard you two had come to town, I made a cake especially for Cecil, hoping I'd have a chance to offer him a piece. Got the idea for it from reading about a doctor over in England who poisoned his brother-in-law with some cake that had monkshood in it. Satan's Butler thought it was pretty tasty. I never had a chance to kill Louis, so I killed his lackey instead. It was almost as satisfying."

Leah shook her head sadly. *Poor Cecil. The past had come back to extract a terrible toll.* "So what happened to your daughter Alice? Did she take ill and die?"

Eloise's eyes went cold. "No, when I realized she wouldn't have a father, I went to an old midwife who lived here at the time. She gave me a mixture of herbs to sweep my child from me."

Leah stared, horrified.

Eloise shrugged. "I was a churchgoing woman—had been my whole life, even during slave times. I couldn't have an out-of-wedlock child, not and see Heaven."

Leah thought about her mother, Reba. When Leah's father died at sea, she'd faced a similar dilemma, but she'd cherished the tiny life forming in her womb. Eloise seemed to have cherished hers also but felt forced to make a different choice. Had that experience hurt her so terribly that it twisted her into the murderess she'd become?

Eloise went on, "So I created that statue. Dedicated it to my unborn child, and the rest of my life to destroying everything Louis Montague loved. Bernice was easy to poison. She was a hypochondriac, complained about one mythical malaise after another, and she always came to me to give her something. Well, I did. Poisoned her over a few months and made sure she took a long time to die. Creole bitch."

Leah shivered. "What about Ryder's mother?"

Eloise cackled. "She and Louis had just had a fight. I found her crying, right near the mine where Louis had sent her husband to his death. I offered to drive her home, and when she turned her back, I clubbed her, tossed her body down the shaft, and went home."

The silence that fell over the room was as chilling as the triumph in Eloise's eyes.

"You placed that note on my door, didn't you?"

"Yes. Remember when I went back into the house for the Sunday school books and to hitch Ol' Tom?"

Leah did.

"It only took me a moment to tack up the letter and then meet you out front. I hoped it would scare you enough to make you go back East. Alice and I knew you had to die, but we didn't want to do it. Unlike Bernice and Songbird, we liked you."

Leah remembered how concerned Eloise had been when they found the threatening missive upon returning from church. She'd even driven her into town to see the sheriff. Sadly, it had all been an act, a well-performed sham. "But Monty's dead. You can't hurt him anymore."

"No, I can't, but you're the last woman he loved—you said so yourself in court. After I kill you, I can finally rest."

Leah took a discreet look around the room for some type of weapon. She was fairly sure she was carrying Ryder's child, and she had no intentions of letting that joy be snuffed out by a deranged woman from Monty's past. "I thought you cared for Ryder. We're going to be married, and I think I'm carrying his child. You'd hurt him that way?"

"I do love him, always considered him mine in a way, but he's known pain before—he'll survive."

Leah didn't think he would, but then neither would she if she didn't leave this room. "Eloise, I'm not going to my death willingly."

"I don't expect you to, dear." She smiled. "But die you will." And she pounced.

Leah scrambled off the bench just in time to miss being sliced by the wicked knife. Eloise kicked over the bench and some easels in an effort to get at Leah. Leah stayed one step ahead of her, throwing easels and paints in her path while Eloise stabbed and slashed the air. Placing herself behind a table, a heavily breathing Leah evaluated her opponent, all the while searching for a way out. Eloise lunged again, but Leah darted away. Anger in her eyes, Eloise tipped over the table, sending paints, brushes, and jars of water crashing to the floor.

Desperate now, Leah picked up a clay pot and sent it sailing through the windowpane. The shattered glass surprised Eloise just long enough for Leah to launch herself through the jagged opening. Eloise's scream of rage blended with Leah's scream of pain as the points of glass dragged across her arms and shoulders. She was free.

Leah ran for her life. Her pounding heart echoed with each step. Blood was pouring down her arms, but she didn't stop; nor did she look back. Thinking it might be best if she ran under cover of the trees and shrubs bordering the road, she tried that for a few yards, but kept being snagged by the foliage. Roots twice sent her sprawling to ground. When she righted herself she ran back to the center of the road, where the footing was more sure.

She could taste the coppery flavor of her own blood in the corner of her mouth. Wiping at her cheek, she drew back red-stained fingers. She hadn't known until then that she'd been cut on her face, but she paid it little mind. She had to get away.

From behind her on the road, she heard the ominous churn of a wagon's wheels. Turning, she saw Eloise whipping Ol' Tom up to a full gallop. Leah darted back into the trees. She could hear herself crashing through the silent surroundings. Fat roots and snagging branches slowed her pace, but she kept moving. A large, aboveground root caught her foot, and she went down with a scream of pain. She tried to scramble to her feet, but her right ankle refused to hold her weight. It was either broken or very badly sprained. Tears of hurt and frustration filled Leah's eyes. Hobbling back to the edge of the road, she braced herself against a tree in hopes that Eloise might have missed her and driven on by. She hadn't; she must have spotted Leah fleeing into the trees, because she was driving slowly, peering closely for signs of her prey.

Leah drew herself up and remained perfectly still, praying Eloise would move on, but she didn't. Breathing hard, Leah watched her climb down from the wagon and begin to search the bushes bordering the road. Eloise then wiped a finger across the tree trunk where Leah'd fled into the woods. She surveyed the red staining her fingers, and smiled.

Looking around Eloise called out, "Your blood's leaving a trail, Leah. Come on out and stop this foolishness. I'm going to find you. It'll just be a matter of time."

Leah held her breath. She didn't move.

"Okay then, dear. Let's see if we can flush you out."

Going back to the wagon, Eloise lifted out a rifle. She fed in some shells, primed it, and began firing random shots into the trees. One bullet whizzed so close by Leah's head she could smell its scent. Fear pumping her heart, and grimacing from the body-shaking pain in her ankle, Leah tried to decide what to do. She couldn't run anymore, not with her injury, but if she stayed there, Eloise would surely find her.

Eloise continued to shoot, the bullets sounding loud against the silence. It was as if she knew exactly where Leah was hiding because more and more shots kept coming her way. Leah ducked in terror.

Suddenly the shooting stopped. Leah stiffened, wondering why, until the sound of approaching wheels gave her the answer. Someone was coming down the road! Leah didn't care who it might be, but this was possibly her salvation, so she hobbled out of the trees. It was Helene!

However before Leah could flag her down, Eloise began shooting, more rapidly this time. Bullets bounced off the dirt road, trying to take Leah's life, but she desperately moved on down the road as fast as the injury would allow. "Helene!" she screamed.

Helene had stopped her wagon upon hearing all the shooting, but upon seeing the bloody Leah waving in the middle of the road, slapped the reins and came toward her at full gallop. Eloise tried to warn her off with a shot or two, but she kept coming and didn't stop until she was abreast of Leah.

"Get in!" Helene yelled. Leah scrambled into the bed. Helene let the reins fall and quickly snatched up her own rifle.

The woods were silent. Eloise's wagon and Ol' Tom were still beside the road, but Eloise had apparently hidden herself among the trees. She was nowhere in sight. Leah was flat on her back in the bed of the wagon trying to catch her breath and giving thanks for being rescued.

Helene kept a wary eye on the surroundings, asking, "What is this all about? Who's shooting?"

"Eloise. She killed your sister, and now she's after me."

Helene's wide eyes met Leah's. "Eloise?" she whispered.

Leah nodded. "I think my ankle may be broken."

"My Lord, look how you're bleeding."

"Don't worry about that now, just get me to town. The sheriff should be told."

"Eloise killed my sister?"

"Yes. She poisoned her just like she did Cecil."

"Well, well, well," Helene murmured. "And now she's after you?"

"Yes. Let's get out of here before she kills us both."

But to Leah's dismay, Helene shouted, "Eloise, come and get her. She's all yours."

Leah's eyes widened, and she struggled to sit up only to

have Helene turn the rifle on her. "Don't move," she commanded.

Unable to believe what was happening, Leah looked into Helene's cold but smiling blue eyes. Helene said reassuringly, "This shouldn't take long."

She called out again, "Eloise! I've got her all wrapped up. You just need to add the bow."

There was movement in the trees to their right. Eloise stepped out. She had a smile on her face. Helene smiled; too, then shot her right between the eyes.

Helene drove them silently back to town and braked her wagon in front of Ryder's building. "I'll get him, you stay here."

As Helene went inside, Leah was so shattered by the day's events she could do nothing else. Moments later, Ryder came running out. He grabbed Leah up and held her so tight she thought her ribs might break, but she didn't care. She was alive!

Later that evening, as Leah lay resting in Ryder's big brass bed, thoughts of Eloise sent a chill across her soul. So much evil had been hidden behind that mask of kindness and concern, an evil that went back more than thirty years. Thanks to Helene there would be no more sacrifices. Yet the memory of what her eyes recorded when Helene pulled the trigger and fired would be with Leah a long time.

Sam had bandaged her arms. Some of the cuts were fairly deep, and before he could stitch them up he'd had to use a magnifying glass in order to remove some of the slivers embedded in the skin The pain in them and in her now wrapped-up ankle was still sharp, but she bore it. She could be dead.

A soft knock sounded on the door. "Come in," she called.

Ryder. And with him entered a very concerned-looking Daniel Morton. "Are you all right, Mrs. Montague?" he asked walking in farther.

The interior of the room with its drums, feathers, and mounted growling bears made him stare around a bit. Dressed in his crisp, blue, back East suit, Leah thought he looked very much of out place inside Ryder's brave domain, but she liked him. "I've been better, and please, call me Leah."

He nodded. "Thanks to your story, Miss Sejours won't be charged. The sheriff says it was a matter of self-defense."

"Good." Leah doubted she'd ever come to like Helene, but the woman had saved her life.

Ryder sat on the edge of the bed. Her love for him shone in her eyes. He bent down and kissed her brow softly. "You sure you don't need anything?"

She could use his arms around her while she slept but she didn't want to tell him that with Daniel looking on. So she lied. "No, I'm fine."

She then turned her attention back to Daniel who'd taken the free moment to go over and peer at the beautiful black Dog Soldier bonnet encased in the glass. "What is this, Mr. Damien?"

"It's a Dog Soldier bonnet."

Daniel stared back puzzled. "A dog soldier?"

"Yep."

When Ryder didn't offer up more of an explanation, Daniel said, "Oh, well, I'm heading back East tomorrow. My wife's having our first baby, and her time's soon."

"Congratulations," Ryder and Leah said in unison.

"Thanks, we're both pretty excited."

The news warmed Leah. It brought to mind her own growing child. She still hadn't had a chance to tell Ryder yet, but would later tonight. "So, where does our case stand?"

"In the judge's chambers right now. If he rules in their favor, do you want to appeal?"

She didn't even have to think about it. "No."

She looked up at Ryder and saw loving approval in his eyes. As she'd mused before, the estate had brought her nothing but pain and sorrow. She wanted it to end. Besides, with Ryder by her side, she didn't need anything else.

Daniel asked, "Are you sure? They'll definitely appeal if they lose."

"I don't care. I want this to be the end of it."

Daniel didn't seem to agree, but shrugged. "Whatever you say then."

"Thanks."

They spent a few more moments talking about his baby and his plans for the future.

Finally, Ryder said, "You should rest. I'm going to take Daniel back to town."

"Okay." She then told Daniel sincerely, "Thank you so much for everything."

"You're more than welcome. Like I said, it was my most interesting case to date."

"Please send Judge Raddock my thanks also, and tell him I believe you deserve a promotion."

He smiled. "I'll be sure he gets your message. Take care of yourself now."

"I will."

Ryder gave Leah's shoulder a soft squeeze. "I'll be back soon as I can."

She nodded, then using a finger, beckoned him down. When he complied she gave him a soft kiss. "Hurry home," she whispered.

He nodded. The departure of the two men left her alone. A minute later, she was asleep.

She was awakened a short time later however by Sam.

"Seth's here. Do you want to see him?"

A sleepy Leah didn't really, but she rubbed her eyes, and asked, "What's he want?"

"To see how you're faring, he says."

Leah sat up and pulled up the covers. "I'll see him, but just for a few minutes."

"Want me to stay with you while he's in here?"

"Please."

Sam left with a smile.

Moments later, a very concerned Seth entered the quiet room. "My God, Leah. Aunt Helene told me what happened. Are you okay?"

"As well as can be expected I guess." She waited.

He read the mistrust in her eyes and turned away as if he were uncomfortable. "I just came to say, I owe you more apologies than I can give and that I'm leaving Denver as soon as I can make the arrangements."

"Where are you going?"

He shrugged. "Somewhere no one knows me. I want to start over. I'm thirty-eight years old and all I have to show for it is a mountain of debt and a mistress who'll never leave her husband."

He held her eyes.

Leah said, "I wish you luck then, Seth."

"Thanks."

Silence fell over the room again, then he said, "Tell Ryder good-bye for me, will you?"

She nodded.

"I guess, he won you, huh?"

She nodded yet again. "We'll be married once I'm up and around."

"Maybe, one day before we die, he and I'll be able to put the past behind us."

"If it's what you both truly want."

He seemed to be far away and didn't respond.

Leah asked, "How's Helene?"

"Doing well, considering. Will you and Ryder keep an eye on her after I'm gone? I know she's hard to be around, but she doesn't have anyone else."

"We will, whether she wants us to or not. She saved my life. I owe her that much."

"Thanks," he replied genuinely.

Seth looked over at Sam standing just inside the bedroom door. "I promised Sam I wouldn't stay long, so, I guess I should be going."

He held her eyes. "Take care of yourself, Leah."

"I will. You do the same."

He nodded, then left.

Leah burrowed back beneath the quilt and slept.

After Ryder dropped off Daniel, he went by his office to pick up a few things, one of which was the unread Pinkerton's report delivered a few days ago. Then he drove to Eloise's house. Getting out, he looked at the place standing so innocently in the dark. Who knew a murderess had hidden there all these years? The sheriff would be out tomorrow sometime, but there was something Ryder needed to do before then. He hopped down from the wagon, and went inside.

His familiarity with the place made a light unnecessary but he lit one anyway because he wanted to be able to see. Using the lamp to show him the way, Ryder went down the hall to the studio. Leah had described the macabre interior, but he wanted to view it for himself. The door was unlocked of course, and as he entered he saw the signs of struggle everywhere. Paints of all colors were splattered over the tables and floor, and broken glass made him step carefully. His eyes searched for the paints he needed: yellow for his forehead; black for his chin; blood red for his nose. Only after he'd painted himself for war did he turn to view the monstrous portraitures. And they were monstrous. He could only imagine how Leah must have felt stumbling upon them. Some made even his skin crawl. Using the lamp as a lantern he scanned the walls until he came across the paintings of his mother. Eloise's great talent made the horrid characterizations even more perverted. Ryder turned away. Hate filled him, as did anger and most of all grief. Songbird's only crime had been her love for Louis, yet for that Eloise had taken her life.

Ryder took down the three paintings of his mother and placed them on the floor. He extracted some matches from his pocket and set fires in all four corners of the room. Because his mother's body had lain at the bottom of the Faith Mine for days before she was discovered, he was certain no one had sung the Death Song for her. He did now. *Nothing lives long. Only the earth and the mountains.*

As the flames rose around him, Ryder's song came to an end. He took one last look around, then left the house to burn. Outside he watched the eerie glow. He felt no remorse. Although Eloise had shown him many kindnesses in his life, she'd killed his mother and tried to take the life of the woman sent by the Spirits to heal him and to love. With her death and the death of her work, maybe now he would know peace.

It was very late when Ryder returned to Sunrise. The house was dark, and he thought everyone asleep until he noticed Sam standing by the windows. In the half-light provided by the moon, Ryder knew the paint on his face could be seen, so he asked quietly, "You waiting up for me, old man?"

"Yes," Sam responded simply. "Wanted to make sure you got back all right."

There was silence then.

Sam finally asked, "Is it done?"

"Yes."

"Good. Leah's asleep.

"Do me a favor?"

"What is it?"

"The Pinkerton's report was waiting at the office. Toss it into the fireplace."

Sam took the package from his hand. "But it doesn't even look like it's been opened."

"I know. I'll see you in the morning. Good night, Sam."

Sam smiled in the dark, "G'night, Ryder."

Ryder climbed the dark stairs and went first to shower. He wanted to remove the paint from his face and the smell of smoke from his body and hair before going to bed. When he finished, he padded nude into the bedroom and silently slid between the sheets. Leah stirred and he pulled her back against him.

"That you?" she whispered.

"No, it's a strange brave come to steal you."

Leah smiled sleepily. "Did Daniel get back to his hotel?"

"Yep."

Ryder savored her smells and warm skin. His eyes settled on her bandaged arms. "Are the cuts still burning?"

"Not as much. Sam said to give the salve a couple of days."

He kissed her ear. "Are you sure you're okay?"

"Yes, especially now that you're here. I'm afraid I'll have nightmares of her stalking me and how she died for quite some time though."

"The fear will fade."

"I know."

She then said, "Your brother stopped in."

Ryder stiffened. "Why?"

"To say good-bye. He's leaving Denver."

"When?"

"Very soon. He wants to start life someplace else. He said to tell you good-bye, and that maybe one day in the future the two of you can set aside the past. He left us Helene."

"Oh, wonderful."

Leah smiled. "Be nice, now. She did save my life."

He kissed her hair. "Yes she did, so I guess I should be grateful."

Silence slipped between them for a moment, then Leah said, "Guess what?"

"What?"

"We're having a baby."

He sat straight up. She turned over and smiled up at him in the dark.

"A baby?!"

"A baby," she responded. "Late winter, if my counting's right."

"Damn!" he declared happily.

"Maybe it'll be that daughter you wanted," Leah whispered in response to his obvious joy.

"I could teach her to hunt and ride—"

"Yes, you could," Leah admitted. She could see father and daughter now, still trying to bring down the King.

He eased himself back down to her, and said, "Thank you for coming into my life, Leah."

She noticed he'd addressed her by her name for the very first time, and her heart swelled with happiness. "And thank you for coming into mine."

"Will you love me forever?"

"And a day . . ."

He kissed her soundly, and when they slept there were no nightmares, only dreams of love.

Author's Note

I do hope you enjoyed the story of Leah and Ryder. Thought I'd throw you a curve and treat you to a book with a cast of all new characters. I've let my fans pick a few of the last stories, so this time it was my turn. (Smile.) I'd like to thank Anne Sulton for her help with the legal case. She advised me, but the words are mine, so if there are any mistakes, they rest solely with me.

Unfortunately, the tragic events at Sand Creek did occur, and for the Cheyenne it was the beginning of the end of all they held dear. A year after the massacre, Congress condemned Chivington's heinous attack. Reparations were promised, but never came. On November 7, 2000, President Bill Clinton signed a bill creating the Sand Creek Historic Site. This is the first national historic site created to commemorate Native American massacre victims. Please honor those who lost their lives that day by taking the time to not only visit the site but to do some reading on the history of

America's Native Peoples. Their stories continue to be a valuable though often neglected part of the American History Quilt.

Andrew Green was a real historical figure, and his public execution was a circus. Thousands came to watch, but as with most hangings, the apparatus used was not weighted properly. The horror some in the crowd felt watching him being slowly strangled to death, moved the legislature to finally outlaw the practice of public hangings. Their decision made Andrew Green the last publicly executed man in the state of Colorado.

The prayer Ryder recites is part of a prayer titled *An Indian Prayer*. So far, I've been unable to find the name of the author. If anyone out there can help me give credit where credit is due, please write me at my PO Box. A special thanks to Ana Kinnison for helping me with Ryder's Spanish endearments and for introducing me to the word *"Morenita."* Leah's prayer is a verse taken from Psalm 67.

Here's a partial list of the books and articles I consulted while writing *Before the Dawn*.

Abbot, Carl. *Colorado: A History of the Centennial State, Revised Edition*. Boulder: Colorado Associated University Press, 1982.

Brown, Dee. *Bury My Heart at Wounded Knee: An Indian History of the American West*. New York: Henry Holt and Co., 1970.

Hine, Darlene Clark, and Thompson, Kathleen. *A Shining Thread of Hope: The History of Black Women in America*. New York: Broadway Books. 1998.

King, William M. *Going to Meet A Man: Denver's Last Legal Public Execution, 27 July 1886*. Niwot Colorado: University Press of Colorado, 1990.

Schultz, Duane P. *Month of the Freezing Moon: the Sand Creek Massacre, November 1864*. New York: St. Martin's Press, 1990.

Armitage, S., Banfield, T. "Black Women and Their Communities in Colorado." *Frontiers*. V. 2, No. 2, 1977.

Riley, Glenda. "American Daughters: Black Women in the West." Montana: *The Magazine of Western History*. Spring 1988.

While on tour last fall I met fans of all races, creeds, and ages. I heard stories about my books that made me laugh, and felt such love I was reduced to tears everywhere I went. Although everyone touched my heart, a few folks deserve special recognition. In Baltimore: Anna Curry and her sister Clara, joint owners of Sepia, Sand, and Sable Books. In Dallas: Emma Rodgers and her staff at Black Images Books; and also Cindi Louis and the Romance Noir Book Club of Dallas. In Atlanta: Nia and the staff at Medu Books; Sylvia's of Harlem Restaurant for hosting the fan dinner; Hazel Clark and TLC Book Club; Charmaine Françoise and the Savy Sisters Book Club; Linda Gaddis; Carla Fredd; and Monica and Paul King. Thanks also to Shirley Covington and her husband Fred for driving all the way from Greensboro North Carolina to see me in Atlanta.

In Austin: Joyce Hunt and the great fans and folks at Mitchie's Fine Black Art and Gifts. Thanks for flying me in, Joyce. The alligator was great!! Thanks also to Yvonne Williams for gifting me with a pair of Worf and Guinan Star Trek action figures. She will be pleased to know they're fearlessly guarding my computer from all intruders, 24/7.

My biggest hug however goes out to Ms. Lois Ann Clark of Atlanta for coordinating the fan dinner at Sylvia's. Lois, you did a fantastic job. Stand up and take a bow!

Last but not least, a special thanks to my publisher HarperCollins and to Heather Garvin in Publicity for their support at the Miami Bookfair. Without them my appearance wouldn't have been possible so, thanks again, Heather.

Thanks also to the fans who were in Miami, especially Ms. Jackye and the members of Miami's Onyx Book Club.

In closing, I give thanks to you my fans for your continued support. I still get letters *every* day, and I still open them like a little girl at Christmas. I'm also as behind in responding as ever, but please keep those letters coming. Your continued faith, prayers, and love fuel me more than you'll ever know. Until next time. Peace.